THE SUMMER THE WORLD ENDED

MATTHEW S. COX

DIVISION ZERO PRESS

The Summer the World Ended
A novel by Matthew S. Cox
© 2015 All Rights Reserved
Revised edition © 2018

ISBN (ebook): 978-1-949174-66-3

ISBN (print): 978-1-949174-67-0

CONTENTS

NAGGING DOUBT

O blivious to the rambling voices in the living room, Riley McCullough stared at the shapeless white lump on her plate. They didn't look like much, but her mother had found the sweet spot of garlic in the mashed potatoes. The salmon smelled fine and the asparagus looked perfect, but she couldn't bring herself to eat. She caught only one in ten words from the TV, something about stock markets, too boring to tolerate. A steady thrum from the central air unit was more interesting.

She slid her sock-covered feet back and forth over the linoleum. Sitting in a sideways lean, face propped up in her palm and eyes closed, Mom seemed as interested in food as Riley felt. Something wasn't right. She wasn't ever this quiet. Today had been the last day of eighth grade, and Mom should've been an explosion of questions about her day, what she wanted to do with her summer, and all sorts of the usual parental chatter that occurred every single night.

Riley pouted at her lap. The repeating series of dancing teddy bears on her red pajama pants mocked her with their vapid smiles.

"Your food okay, hon?"

Riley straightened in her seat, taking the weight of her face off her left fist. She let her arm fall flat on the table. "Yeah, it's fine."

"What's bothering you?" Mom attempted to sound comforting, but came off tired.

Oh, yeah, that too. In addition to Mom being strange, her plans for the most awesome summer ever had gone up in smoke. She'd get to spend the first fourteen days alone and bored.

"Amber's parents are dragging her off to Puerto Vallarta for two weeks."

Her mother made a weak attempt at a chuckle. "I'd hardly call that being *dragged* off."

"They sprung it on her as a graduation present… we had plans. I can't believe she's gonna be gone for two whole weeks. It's not fair. This is like the *big* summer before high school."

"Riley… you've got the whole break ahead of you. Two weeks isn't a big deal. Besides, what plans did you have? Hanging out at the mall?"

"Ugh, Mom…" Riley rolled her eyes. "We're not mallrats. We were gonna try and start a guild."

Mom set her fork down and worked her fingers over the bridge of her nose. "You'll be a freshman in a couple of months, Rile. You can't spend your whole life shuttered in your bedroom with video games. Have you given any thought to a summer job?"

"No." Riley stabbed a fork into the lump of potatoes. "I can't work; I'm only fourteen."

"Fourteen? Wow, I had no idea." Mom smirked, though she seemed distracted or exhausted. "I checked groceries when I was your age for a couple hours a day. I'd like you to consider it this year, but I won't force you. Next year, young lady, is another story."

Riley poked at her salmon. "I guess I could apply at GameStop or something."

"Wow, no argument?" Mom pushed herself upright with visible effort. "What's really bothering you?"

"You're too quiet." Riley stared at her plate for a moment. "You're never this quiet."

"Oh, I've just had a horrible day at the bank. Pritchett's been riding me about the second quarter customer satisfaction figures, the Fed is coming in for a 'routine audit,' and I've got a city inspector giving me grief about the building. He can't seem to understand I'm just the branch manager… I don't own the damn place." Mom deflated. "Oh, and Mr. Hensley thinks I'm going to Hell."

"Pritchett's the pudgy, bald guy that wears his tie so tight it looks like his head's gonna pop like a grape?"

Mom laughed once, her expression bleeding to a wince. "Yes, but don't repeat that at the Christmas party... you'll get me fired. He's the district manager, and a complete control freak."

"Are you okay?" Riley stared into her mother's eyes. "You look like shit."

"Just a headache." Mom closed her eyes and massaged the bridge of her nose. "Oh, and I heard that. Mind your language, Rile."

Riley grumbled inside, wondering what Mom would think of the way the kids at school talked. She looked up, ready to argue, but the exhausted expression on her mother's face stalled the argument before it started. "'Kay."

"Mmm. Hey, would you mind loading the dishwasher when you're done? I think I'm going to pop some ibuprofen and close my eyes. Damn stress is getting to me."

"Sure, Mom." *It's my turn anyway.* Riley glanced at her mother's glass. "Is that water?"

"I already feel sick. Not up for the Manhattan tonight."

"Oh, damn. I'll call Guinness."

"Hush, you." Mom scoffed with a hint of a smile. "I don't drink *that* much."

For ten-ish minutes, only the clank and scratch of forks and knives on dinnerware broke the silence.

"Looking forward to your first day of summer?" Mom again tried to smile.

"Amber can't even come over tonight... they're leaving in the morning. I get to be alone for two weeks."

"You can get started on your summer reading then. You haven't even taken them out of the bag yet."

Riley rolled her eyes. "Yeah, I'll jump on that right away."

Mother stood, smiled, and wandered down the hall to the bathroom. Riley glanced at the open archway, the din of financial news from the living room a dull murmur in the back of her consciousness. Mom hadn't questioned the attitude in her voice. Worry danced in her belly, but maybe the simple truth was she'd been too worn out to start a meaningless argument. They both knew Riley would wind up at least skimming the books... probably in the last three days before school started.

September felt like an eternity away, too far ahead to worry about now. She picked at her food until the squeak of the bathroom faucet cutting off made her look up. Mom shuffled down the hallway with her eyes closed, swaying as if dizzy. After a moment, she made her way to the living room, bracing a hand along the wall for support. After eating the rest of the fish, half the potatoes, and two sprigs of asparagus, Riley shoved the rest in a small plastic container and fridged it. Mother hated throwing food out, even if it was green vegetables. Riley's insistence on going vegetarian 'for the animals' lasted about six months. Still, pork or beef rarely saw the inside of their kitchen. Chicken and fish provided a routine break from quinoa and various all-veggie things she found online.

Why did Mom ask me to pack the dishwasher? She knows it's my turn since she cooked.

She gathered utensils, plates, pans, and cups in no particular hurry. Amber would be waiting for her online; at least they could stay up late tonight, mothers-be-damned. Maybe they could get two weeks' worth of hanging out accomplished in a few hours. A squirt of detergent in the reservoir preceded her lifting the door with one foot and kicking it closed while stretching to shove the bottle back in an overhead cabinet.

Once the dishwasher started up, she crept up to the archway and peered into the living room. Mom sat askew in the recliner facing the fifty-inch flat screen, a hand on her face as if deep in thought. She had refused to let Riley connect the Xbox to the 'main TV,' declaring that one for 'TV purposes.' Three middle-aged men in suits sat behind a desk covered in strips of neon, debating stuff about Wall Street.

"You okay, Mom?"

"Fine, fine. Just waiting for the Advil to kick in." Mother rubbed her temples. "Haven't had a headache like this since"—she waved her hand around—"since I got promoted."

Riley tiptoed closer. "You sure you're okay?"

Mom took her hand, offering a weak smile. "It's just a headache, Rile. Really, I'm fine. Don't get yourself so worked up."

"'Kay. Yell if you need something."

Mother shielded her eyes with her hand as soon as Riley let go to walk away.

"Another migraine?"

"Probably," whispered Mother.

"Want me to call Dr. Gest?"

"If it doesn't go away in a few hours, sure."

Riley lingered at the door watching her mother for a few minutes. No alcohol, no nagging, not even the usual supportive talk about her lack of friends, and how she should try to make more. *She's gotta be exhausted. That job is killing her.*

"Mom, take the day off work tomorrow. Let's have a movie day... we haven't done that in like months."

"I'll think about it." Mother paused to take a few quiet breaths. "There's a bunch of new Pixar ones you haven't seen."

"We're out of popcorn."

Mother looked up, forcing a smile. "Easy enough to fix that."

Riley's worry lasted another few seconds before she grinned and drifted away from the arch, dragging her feet on the way down the hall to her bedroom. Aside from one Captain Jack Sparrow poster above her headboard, she had decorated her room with video-game couture. Amber had accused her of murdering an older brother and stealing his digs. The theoretical location of the body had been a two-year running joke.

That girl likes pink way too much.

Three pillows covered in navy-blue linen formed a pad upon which she sprawled, propped up on her elbows before a thirty-six inch flat screen hooked to an Xbox sitting on top of two milk crates full of DVD cases. The spot in her computer desk where the PC should go contained a graveyard of old controllers, some smashed in anger, others worn to the point of death.

After putting on her chat headset, she kicked her feet back and forth while waiting for the console to power up. A moment later, she popped into the e-lobby for *Call of Duty.*

"Hey, where the hell have you been?" Amber's yelling flooded her skull from both ears, making Riley cringe. "I've been bored off my ass for like an hour. Come on, Rile, the noobs won't shoot themselves in the head."

A few button taps put her in the same virtual space as her friend. DoomBear14 appeared on the line below her friend's username: IH8Toobers.

"You need to de-cute your tag, Rile. You look like a squeaker."

Riley grinned. "I like makin' the old men rage quit when they get killed by someone with a silly name."

"You're such a bitch, Rile."

"I know." Riley examined her fingernails. "Piss them off, and they can't play for shit."

A flurry of other names filled in both sides of the roster, and soon the lobby screen switched to a level-loading image.

"Ugh, I hate Panama. Nothing but goddamn campers," grumbled Amber.

"Crap, we got squeakers," said a man.

Riley forced her voice up into a preteen range. "Hi everyone! This is my first time. I just got this game for my birthday; can someone tell me how do I shoot?"

Voice chat erupted with the expected laughs, taunts, and 'aww, leave her/him alone' requests.

Fifteen minutes later, the opposing team realized Riley was the Irish word for 'Troll.' After twenty-two kills and four deaths, the entire other team called her a cheater. She giggled every time she got the drop on 'DeltaForce187,' and after the seventh un-answered kill, an incoherent roar came over the voice chat and he logged out.

"Victory for team Bear," squeaked Riley.

Another two rounds came and went; despite it being more of the same, it never got old. The simple tactic of sticking with Amber and working as a team protected them from the lone wolves, but every now and then, they'd land in a match with a competition squad and get soundly smashed—though twice she held her own enough to be extended an invite.

Until they heard she was fourteen.

A patina of camo-clad bodies, Eastern European backdrops, and bullets faded to an automatic routine.

"I still can't believe you're going to Puerto Vallarta for two weeks."

"Yeah, it sucks," said Amber.

"Wait, what?" asked a boy that sounded about their age. "In what world does that suck?"

Amber sighed. "There's nothing to do there."

"You could work on your summer reading," said Riley.

"Go to hell." Amber cracked up laughing.

"Jesus Christ, is this friggin' high school? Come on, play the goddamn game."

"Aww, someone's got their old man diapers on too tight," said Amber in a sing-song tone before lowering her voice to mock a man. "This is the virtual military, hut hut. Serious faces, please."

Riley laughed, biting her lower lip as she snuck up on a sniper hiding in a stack of sewer piping. The player, a deep-voiced man, launched into a diatribe of obscenities after she knife killed him. She was pretty sure his anger stemmed mostly from the girlish squeal he let off as she scared the crap out of him.

"I found the knife button." The cursing got worse when Riley giggled like a five-year-old.

She made her way down off the elevated position to the next best sniper roost on the map, the roof of a big warehouse. The spot was empty, but she hid behind a stack of what looked like concrete bags.

Four death announcements flashed by.

"I found the grenade launcher," said Amber.

An expected series of complaints about the 'noob-tube' followed.

"Hah," said a boy. "'I hate toobers' just killed people with a tube."

"It's called irony," said Amber.

A minute later, Riley twitched when a digital soldier went by. The same sniper she knifed minutes before ran to the edge of the roof and flopped down in a prone position. She crept out, planted a C4 charge between his boots, and backed away to her hiding place.

"How does the semtex work?" asked Riley, again making her voice sound like a little kid's.

Boom.

The sniper's virtual body went flying like Superman to the middle of the map.

"Oh, I get it." She giggled.

For another twenty minutes, the girls tormented that particular sniper until the round ended and the game dumped them back to the e-lobby.

Amber's voice came over a private chat. "Hey Rile, it's been like two whole hours, and your mom hasn't bothered you once. It's a miracle."

"Yeah, it's nice." Riley dropped the controller and moved around to sit up, stretching and rubbing her sore elbows. "I think she's getting sick."

"Oh, that sucks. She drunk again?"

"She doesn't get *drunk* drunk, just has enough to turn into the nag-o-tron 3000." Riley glanced past the door, at the dark hallway. The murmur from the TV now sounded like some late-night show. According to the clock, it was 12:11 a.m. and Mom was still up. "Amb, I got a bad feeling. I'll be right back."

"Your mom is like the terminator, 'cept without like the killing and stuff. She'll kick it." Amber yawned. "So what are you gonna do for two weeks?"

"I dunno." Riley couldn't look away from the hall. Something felt *wrong.* "Wanna bail on the trip and stay here?"

"I would ask but… the vacation is supposed to be like a surprise present for me. Be kinda crappy to do that, even if they are my parents."

"Yeah… Uh, one sec. I wanna check on her."

She peeled the headset off, stood, and walked out into the hall. More canned laughter broke the silence in intermittent bursts between jokes only an old person would understand. With her fingers tracing the wall, she snuck up to where the corridor opened to the living room. Half hidden behind the corner, she peeked at her mother who remained seated in the recliner in the same pose she'd left her in.

"Mom?" whispered Riley. "It's late. You should go to bed."

The curtains on the TV behind the host's chair saturated the room in an unearthly dark blue light. With the volume way down, she couldn't make out why the guest was laughing so much. She couldn't even tell who it was aside from he was someone famous—but not so popular she could place where she'd seen him.

"Mom? You look pale." Riley stopped at the arm of the chair and put her hand on her mother's shoulder. "Mom? Wake up, it's like midnight."

"Hmm?" Mom let off a disoriented moan. "Midnight?"

Riley shivered at the sound. "Yeah. Come on. Go to bed. You need to call out tomorrow. Are you sure you don't want to go to the doctor?"

"I'm not going to work tomorrow."

Mother leaned forward in the chair and reached for the coffee table. Her fingers grasped at the wood four inches to the right of the TV remote. She tried again to grab it, missing. Mother tilted her head up at Riley with a confused look, as if she couldn't understand why the remote wasn't in her hand.

"Mom?" Riley clutched her mother's shoulder after she looked down and tried unsuccessfully for a third time to pick up the device. "Mom, you're scaring me. I don't care if it's midnight, I'm gonna call Dr. Gest."

"Wha…?" Mother looked up again.

The whites of her eyes had gone blood red.

Riley stepped back, covering her mouth. Mom gazed into space, with no trace whatsoever of recognition or awareness. After a few seconds of silence, she slumped back in the chair, mouth agape.

Riley screamed and stumbled away.

She stood for a few seconds after her lungs emptied. Mom's chest rose and fell in slow, shallow breaths. The room spun. The voices from the TV sounded like they were inside her head.

"Mom!" Riley shrieked again. "Mommy!"

Mom didn't react.

What just happened? No. No, this isn't real. Mom's not sick. She ran two circles around in front of the TV, looked at Mom again, and sprinted to her room. Six seconds passed as she stared dumbstruck at the Xbox lobby.

Why am I in my room?

She turned on her heel, glancing at the weak moonlight coming in the kitchen windows. *Mom? Oh, shit, Mom!*

Riley ran to the kitchen and grabbed the cordless phone with enough force to knock the base off the counter. She punched 911, not breathing until she heard a ring tone.

"911. What's your emergency?"

She gazed at nothing.

"Hello? This is 911. Do you have an emergency?" The woman on the other side muffled the mic. "No, it's not dead, I can hear someone breathing."

"Uh…"

"911 Emergency. Do you have an emergency?"

"Yes."

"Okay, you sound like a kid. Are you okay?"

"Yes… no."

"Take a few breaths, and tell me what the problem is."

Riley burst into tears. "Mom. My mom…"

"Easy, sweetie. Take a breath and tell me what happened?"

"She's sick." She babbled past a few sobs. "Her eyes are red. She's not moving."

"Try to stay calm, sweetie. Your mother needs you to stay calm. I'm sending people to help."

"Okay." Riley sank to her knees in the middle of the kitchen, bawling.

"Don't hang up, okay, sweetie? Stay with me until they get there."

She sniffled. "'Kay."

"How old is your Mom?"

"Forty."

"Tell me what she's doing right now."

"I'm in the kitchen." Riley coughed and sputtered, unable to stop crying. "Hang on."

She crawled to the three-step stairway from the tiled kitchen to the carpeted living room. Mom hadn't moved.

Riley looked away, not wanting to see her like that. "She's slumped in a chair staring at the ceiling."

The voice on the phone blurred, becoming an indistinct series of comforting lines, likely read from a flash card. Riley offered the occasional 'mmm-hmm' or 'huh' as bits and pieces of words snagged on her consciousness. She scooted closer, inch by inch, until she could reach up and hold her mother's limp hand. Though her skin was warm, her contact got no response. Riley curled up against the side of the recliner.

Three minutes later, red and blue lights flooded the front door window. The same meaningless word repeated from the phone; Riley looked up at the silhouettes of a pair of cops in the frosted glass of the front door. Answering the bell would require letting go of Mom.

"Can you get the door, sweetie?" asked the woman on the phone.

"Um."

Riley stood on autopilot, trudging to the foyer as a distant siren gained in volume. A blast of thick June wind pushed the air conditioning away as she opened the door. A police car had parked out front, half nosed into their driveway; an ambulance rounded the corner at the end of the block and gunned the engine. Riley stared up at the cops as if they were aliens. One grasped her by the shoulders and eased her out of the way while his partner hurried inside.

"Is there anyone else here with you?"

Riley blinked.

"It was only a headache," she muttered.

"Are you alone?"

"My mom..." She looked to her left over the front lawn as the ambulance doors banged open and a gurney clattered out. "Just my mom."

2

UNREAL

Headlights washed over the plain white room from a car outside navigating the lot. Gusts from an overhead vent teased at her hair, making Riley thankful she'd kept her sweatshirt. The cloying, medicinal smell pervading everything here added to her worry and made it difficult to keep from throwing up. No matter how hard she tried to think about anything other than the sight of her mother limp in the living room chair, she couldn't stop trembling. It wasn't the cold, though the over-cranked A/C didn't help. Her gaze settled for a moment on the empty seat at her left.

She didn't remember the cop taking her to her bedroom to grab her sneakers, or the ride to JFK Medical Center. Somewhere within the past twenty minutes, he'd gone for coffee and left her under the watch of an older, thick-bodied nurse who didn't seem at all happy to get stuck watching a kid. Her initial glower melted after one look at Riley's face. The woman settled for glaring at a mini TV out of sight below the counter, abusing a contestant on Jeopardy instead… calling him a moron over and over when he got stuff wrong. Whenever she looked up to check on Riley, she transformed from *Throw Momma From the Train* to 'Friendly Grandma.'

Riley draped her hands in her lap, hating the grinning teddy bears up and down her pajama leggings even more. How dare they smile at a time like this.

Please, Mom. Be okay. I swear I'll get a job this summer if you're okay.

A large, round, analog wall clock read 2:11 in the morning. It didn't feel like she'd been sitting there that long, and she wondered if Amber was still trying to get her on the Xbox. They'd planned to stay awake all night before her friend's parents hauled her off to Mexico; the tiniest sliver of resentment at being denied even that time with her friend made her cringe with guilt.

"Over there," muttered the nurse.

Rustling plastic drew her attention to a dark-skinned man with thick eyebrows, approaching with an uneasy smile. His teal scrubs and white doctor's coat filled her with dread, as did the greenish booties over his shoes.

A weary-looking heavyset woman with cherry red hair in a bob followed a half step behind him. Her rounded face gave her the look of a wingless cherub who hadn't slept in four days trying her best to look reassuring. She wore a bland, grey skirt-suit with a frill-fronted pink dress shirt. The whole outfit looked disheveled and a little too large, as though someone else had dressed her.

"Miss McCullough?" asked the man.

"Yes," said Riley, into her lap.

"I'm Doctor Farhi. This is Mina Lewis; she's here to help you."

"Hi." The woman offered a weak wave.

"Can I see my mother?"

Doctor Farhi kept silent for a moment. As soon as Mina sat next to her and took her hand, Riley's throat tightened. She looked up at them, face frozen in panic. Tears streamed down her cheeks, and her heart pounded.

"I'm sorry, Riley. Your mother has passed away." The doctor looked at his shoes, as if debating how much to say.

"No…" She shook her head hard enough to fling tears. "No… She can't have a heart attack; she's not old. Mommy…" Riley pulled away from Mina and buried her face in her hands. "No, you're lying!"

Mina put a sympathetic arm around her.

"She didn't feel any pain." The doctor shifted. "Your mother didn't have a heart attack."

"What?" None of the hundred things she wanted to say could fit past the lump in her throat.

"It's important for you to understand you couldn't have done anything different." Mina sat up, trading an arm around the back for holding her hand. "Nothing you could have done would have changed anything."

Riley stared at the wall, feeling like she floated off to another world. "What"—she swallowed—"w-what happened?"

"She did not suffer." The doctor offered a comforting smile.

"I wanna know." She took in a deep breath, fighting back the urge to cry. "Please."

Doctor Farhi hesitated. The look in his dark brown eyes betrayed his pain at having to dump something like that on a child; he kept glancing at the hallway as if hoping some older family member might walk in. Riley cringed, cradling Mina's arm to her chest like a stuffed bear. After a few quiet seconds, the doctor sat on the bench next to her and took her other hand.

"Your mother had a cerebral aneurysm, which suffered an acute rupture." He paused, giving her a moment to process. "For all intents and purposes, the woman she was died immediately. Aside from the headache leading up to the event, it's doubtful she suffered."

"She didn't die. She was still breathing." Riley sniffled.

"Basic brain functions operate below the level of the damage, and continued for a short while after. The injury was... not survivable." He bit his lip. "You had no way to know. Most patients don't even realize they have this condition until a rupture."

"She was only forty." Riley repeated the phrase three times in decreasing volume, the last a whisper.

Mina squeezed her hand.

"Certain things exacerbate the risk factors, chiefly stress, alcohol, some recreational drugs, genetic factors—"

"Stress and alcohol." Riley wiped at her face. "Yeah. That sounds like Mom."

"I'm sorry... there was nothing we could do for her. The damage was too extensive. I'm sorry." Doctor Farhi looked at her like someone had shot his dog.

"Can I see my Mom?"

The doctor glanced at Mina. "I'm not sure if—"

"Please... If you can clean Mrs. McCullough up, it will help her cope," said Mina. "She needs to see her mother to say goodbye, to understand this is real."

"Alright. It'll be a few minutes." Dr. Farhi stood and walked off.

Riley felt like a rubber statue of a person, jostled about by Mina's attempts at comfort. She locked her gaze on a small cross-stitch of a flower vase on the wall, trying to force herself to wake up in her room with her mother nagging at her about oversleeping.

Please be a nightmare.

Mina squeezed her hand. "Is there anyone I can contact for you?"

"I dunno." Riley tried to bore a hole through the floor with her stare.

"No relatives?"

She lurched forward as an overenthusiastic hand rubbed her back. All the times she'd felt angry for not having a 'whole' family rushed back like a river of lame. When she was eight and nine, she'd been furious at the world for not having a father. Mom had never told her why he left—only that he was still alive. That had been the one subject capable of getting the woman to stop talking. Eventually, Riley had stopped asking.

"I guess I have a dad somewhere. I haven't seen him since I was little."

"Any grandparents? Did you mother have any siblings?"

Grief and exhaustion drained her to a monotone. "Mom was a broken condom… I think I was four when my grandfather died. Never saw Dad's parents. They never even mentioned them. Mom's got an older sister somewhere, but she's like… old now, and a bitch. Hates everyone. It's just me and Mom."

She let her head droop, feeling the water building up at the corners of her eyes again.

"I'm so sorry, hon. It's okay, let it out. There's no shame in crying."

Silent minutes passed; the sound of Riley's grief seemed to have a muting effect on the angry nurse's belittlement of Jeopardy contestants. Mina rested a sympathetic arm around her back and let her sob without trying to talk over her.

June 16th had been the last day of school. Tomorrow—well today, technically—Friday, was supposed to have been the start of the 'big summer' between eighth grade and freshman year. Her last summer as a 'kid.'

Now, it was a giant pile of fear and suck.

Mina squeezed her hand around 2:37 a.m. Riley looked up, and followed the woman's gaze to Doctor Farhi who stood at the opening of a hallway leading deeper into the hospital. The sight of him got her shaking again; she pulled her hair out of her eyes, but couldn't bring herself to say anything.

"She's ready," said the doctor.

Riley stood, still trembling, and clutched Mina's hand as they walked behind him to the fifth room on the left. She hesitated at the door; the overwhelming silence felt like a physical presence in the air, warning her away from what awaited her inside. She swallowed. Until she went in, Mom might still be alive. Until she laid eyes on her, this could still be an awful, awful dream.

"It's okay. Take a breath." Again, Mina patted her back. "It's okay if you can't do this."

I'll never forgive myself if I don't.

The doctor's neutral expression could have said, 'we prepped her, you better not change your mind' as likely as it offered consolation. She let go of Mina's hand and forced herself to enter the room. Her mother lay on a bed, pale and lifeless, head slumped to the right as if asleep. A blanket covered her to the waist, a basic patient's gown the rest of the way. Bandages wrapped the top of her head, though a little dried blood lingered in her ear. No equipment was connected to her, though they had taped gauze over several spots on her arms.

Mom's so... white.

One look left no doubt her mother was no longer there.

She ran to the side of the bed, put a hand on her mother's arm, and stifled a gasp at how cold the skin felt. Ignoring the unnatural temperature, she cradled the limb to her chest.

"Mom…" she whispered. "I should've called the doctor. I should've made you go to the hospital." Sniffles grew to tears. "You can't die."

Minutes of uncontrolled crying eventually evened out to quiet breathing. Riley looked to her right where a different nurse stood watch at the foot of the bed. This woman looked younger than the one at the desk, slim, with dark skin, and had water at the corner of her eyes too.

"If you want to ask about anything…"

"They shaved her hair," muttered Riley.

"Yes." The nurse pointed at the bandages. "They operated on her brain, trying everything they could to save her."

"What's an aneurysm?"

The young nurse moved up alongside her. "A blood vessel in her brain swelled up like a balloon."

Riley sniffled. "If I dragged her kicking and screaming to the hospital at seven, would she be alive?"

The nurse cast a sorrowful look at Mom… at Mom's body. "It's hard to say. It depends on how she presented to the doctor. She might've been sent home with headache meds if she didn't display any other symptoms."

Riley glanced at her mother again; Mom would have appeared

downcast if her eyes had been open. "I'm sorry I felt happy you didn't bug me"—her calm faded as whining sobs overtook her—"tonight when I was online." She rocked back and forth, trying to squeeze life back into her mother's arm. "Mom had a headache; I thought she was sleeping."

Mina walked up behind her. A hand touched her back. Riley jerked away, not wanting this stranger to touch her. Mina stiffened; a worried expression flickered over her face. Riley took one more look at her mother's pallid face and whirled to cling to the woman she'd only just met, wailing. Mina ran a hand up and down her back, patting and swaying side to side. The nurse sniffled.

A few minutes later, Riley calmed enough to peek at the body. "Make her get up."

"I'm sorry, honey, that's not something we can do," said the nurse.

Riley squeezed Mina's arm, shaking it. "I need my mom. I don't have anyone else. I don't wanna be an orphan. Please, make them fix her."

Mina pulled her close. "It's no one's fault. There was nothing they could have done for her."

"Your mother didn't suffer," said the nurse. "I'm so sorry for your loss."

"She was gonna stay home from work tomorrow... We were gonna have a 'movie day.'"

Mina swayed side to side, patting her on the back, murmuring platitudes like 'it'll be okay,' 'she's in a better place now,' and 'let it out.' Riley tolerated her clinginess, resting her head against the woman's side while studying the peaceful calm on her mother's face. She refused to blink, trying to dislodge her last memory of her mother: that horrible, red-eyed, gaping 'nobody home' expression.

She had to know something was wrong. She looked so confused.

Never again would Pritchett torment her to the point of working until 10 p.m. on weeknights. Never again would her mother have one too many Manhattans and nag her every fifteen minutes about some trivial chore she'd already finished. Never again would they spend all day in their pajamas watching movies together. Mom wouldn't be there for her first boyfriend, or her wedding; her kid (if she ever had one) wouldn't have a grandmother. No, she wasn't ready to stand on her own two feet. She needed her mother.

Riley shook the limp arm. "Mom, come on. You gotta get up."

The young nurse stifled a sniffle.

She's really gone... I-I'm never going to see her again.

She draped herself over her mother, giving her a final hug.

Mina patted her on the shoulder. "I'm so sorry. Take as much time with her as you want, then I'll bring you to a place you can stay for the time being."

Riley clutched her mother's arm to her chest like a beloved doll. Mina Lewis looked sympathetic, but also about to fall asleep on her feet. The nurse hovered close, with a comforting smile. After a few minutes, and countless useless wishes, Riley stood.

"Bye, Mom." Riley laced her fingers through her mother's for the last time. She held on for a moment before lowering the arm to rest at her mother's side. "I love you."

Riley backed away, unwilling to turn her back on Mom. Maybe, if she waited just one more second, she'd stir and open her eyes. At the doorway, Riley's legs gave out, but Mina caught her. The nurse rushed over and helped Mina carry her back to the waiting room bench. Riley curled up, hands clutched to her chest, too sad to cry.

3

SHELTERED

Leaf-shadows bounced on the peach-colored wall six feet away, paint on cinderblocks. Dark brown metal framed an immobile window with a small, rectangular bit at the bottom that could open inward. Too small for even a child to squeeze through. The sweet scent of blueberry pancake syrup wafted in from the not-quite-closed door, followed by the echoes of a handful of much younger kids. If not for the lack of bars on the door, it might as well have been juvie.

Riley lay on her side, semi-fetal, still wearing the same sweatshirt, pajama pants, and sneakers she had on when her mother died. She didn't remember sleep; at some point, staring at patches of moonlight had become staring at patches of sunlight. Aside from a supervised visit back home to collect a few belongings hours ago, she hadn't moved from that spot. None of this felt real, this *shelter,* this place that wasn't home. Again and again, she went over the layout of the house, walking back and forth across her home in her mind.

Every piece of furniture called back memories, as did all the little figurines and random crap her mother had decorated the place with. Mina didn't let her take anything like her Xbox or TV, just some clothes and toiletries. She glared at the shifting patches of sunlight; that was still *her* house. Being 'escorted' as if she no longer belonged there made her angry. She wanted her mother to show up and tell her it was all a bad dream. Even if Riley accepted she was gone, why couldn't they let her sleep in her own room, in a house that still smelled like Mom?

How can I steal my own stuff?

Frantic, high-pitched shrieks in the outside hallway rose over more distant murmuring.

"He's gonna find me. He's gonna kick in the door, and find me, and he's gonna kill me. He's gonna kill me, and you, and Sadie, and everyone."

A child's wailing followed.

Riley shivered. *This isn't happening. I'm not in this crazy place. Mom... please get me out of here. Please don't let them keep me here.*

"Calm down, ma'am," said a husky voice, also female. "He ain't going to find you."

"You don't know Boyd. You don't know what he's capable of. You fu—"

"Ma'am. Please calm down. You're not being detained. You're free to leave at any time, but you're as safe as you can get here. He can't get to you if you stay with us."

Figures moved by the door: a big woman, a skinny woman, and a sniveling three-year-old girl. The door to the next room opened and closed, muted voices murmured through the cinder blocks behind her. Riley debated the odds of a psycho ex rampaging around the shelter and picking her room by accident. The place went from feeling like a prison to feeling like a death trap. *Am I ever gonna see my home again? They can't just take all Mom's things away, can they?*

The conversation next door stopped. A few seconds later, a soft triple-knock invaded her cocoon of spaced-out silence.

"Hey there," said the deeper feminine voice. "You're new here, aren't ya? Name's LaToya. You let me know if you need anything, 'kay? You hungry?"

"No," muttered Riley.

"Did you sleep?"

"No."

"Would you like to get cleaned up? Have a shower or something?"

"No."

The door creaked. Riley shifted enough to look at a more-than-six-foot tall woman in medical scrubs; the pants were teal, but an explosion of color spread over the smock with little regard for the lines of a scene of palm trees and tall birds. Short dreads sprouted from a fist-sized polished wooden ring at the back of her head, making it resemble a humanized pineapple sitting atop massive shoulders. Riley stifled a gulp, a measure less afraid of any and all enraged exes.

She'd kill him.

"What's wrong, dear? Can I get you anything?"

Riley slid back on the bed. "I wanna go home."

"Child, you know we can't leave you alone in a house all by yourself."

As opposed to being alone with someone else? Riley made a face. "I'm fourteen. I can handle it. Mom trusted me alone. I've been home alone after school since, like, forever."

A loud metal crash outside preceded the sound of a different screaming child, and several sets of running footsteps.

"You ain't ready to handle a job yet. Rent payments, taxes, driving…"

Her mother's voice floated out from her memory. Next summer she'd have to get a job. She flung herself over and stuffed her face in the pillow to hide tears.

After a few sniffles, she yelled, "I hate it here."

"You're one of the lucky ones, child."

Riley pushed herself over on her side and glared. "How the hell am I lucky?"

LaToya's placid smile showed no dents from the angry scowl directed her way. "It's horrible what happened to your momma, but you stills got a dad to take care of you. Most of the little ones who come through here ain't got even that."

"My dad?" She sat up. "He doesn't want me. He left us. I wanna go home."

"You want things to be like they were before. Going back to that house might let you think everything's the same, but it won't be."

Riley wiped her face.

"You need to eat and get cleaned up. Imma give you a pass on lunch, but if I hear you skipped dinner, I'm gonna drag you to the cafeteria and feed you like a baby."

The threat would've been terrifying if not for the huge grin on the woman's face.

"'Kay."

"You need anything, you find me and ask, okay?"

Riley nodded.

LaToya walked to the door. "Remember… you eatin' dinner later."

"'Kay."

She collapsed onto the mattress on her side, daydreaming about her mother's last meal. *How long before I forget what her voice sounded like?* For at least an hour, she lay there drifting in and out of periods of crying and staring off into space. An attack of sniffles stopped at a chirp from the bag on the floor. A little rummaging unearthed her iPhone, showing a series of texts from Amber:

BRB = few mins.

Rile? Wtf. Where are you?

Guess you got reamed for being up too late. Txt me.

Rile? Hello? Text me, k?

Going offline, on plane.

Back. WTF x 3.

Riley McCullough... Mexico calling Riley.

She stared past her reflection at the blue bubbles of text. Her best (only) friend was probably sitting on a beach in Puerto Vallarta, possibly enjoying her 'graduation present.' She teased at the keypad with a thumb, battling between her need to let everything out and not wanting to ruin Amber's trip. Better to drop a bomb like that in person.

She typed: *I'm okay. Mom went to hospital. Sry for leavin you hang. Talk when u back.*

No sooner had she put the phone on the little nightstand than a reply came in.

Hospital wtfomg. Ur mom ok?

Teardrops splattered on the screen, magnifying the text into red, blue, and green spots. Her hands shook as she forced herself to reply.

Will talk when ur back in Jerz. Have fun in Mex.

The phone beeped a few seconds later. *BS. U like don't go to Mex now u say have fun.*

Don't waste ur trip worrying 4 me. I'll explain all when you come back. How is the food?

Riley couldn't stop crying as the texts bounced back and forth for at least twenty minutes, as though nothing at all had happened.

G2G, dad raging @ me for texting since I do it @ home. Txt if u wana talk.

"Later," Riley spoke and typed at the same time.

She curled up around the phone for a while, watching the waving shadows of trees fade with the onset of evening. A touch past 5:30 p.m., Mina poked her head in.

"Oh, Riley…" She walked in, clucking her tongue. "You're still in the same clothes."

"Oh, hey, your eyes work."

"Come on, get up. You're taking a shower and going straight to the café. Toya told me you skipped lunch."

"You're not my mother."

Mina folded her arms. "You're right, young lady, I'm not. You're skin and bones. Would your mother want you starving yourself?"

Riley cringed. "How long do I have to stay here? Can I shower at home?"

"Maybe when your Dad gets here… I assume he'll want to take you there instead of a hotel."

No way! She shot upright. "You found him? W-what did he say? Wait, 'gets here?' He's coming?"

"It will take him a while; he's driving." Mina sat on the end of the bed. "He's worried about you. I… told him you weren't coping too well."

"How am I supposed to 'cope' with my mother dropping dead in front of me?" Riley felt her face scrunching in preparation for another bout of sobbing, and tried to resist it.

Mina threw an arm around her. "I'd be worried if a kid your age coped 'well' with news like that. Anyone, really. Your reactions are perfectly natural given the situation. Don't bottle things up."

This woman is obsessed with rubbing my back. She frowned at the white iPhone 4 on the nightstand. "I wanted to tell Amber, but I didn't."

"Who's that?"

"Friend."

"I see. Why didn't you tell her?"

Riley shrugged. "She's in Mexico. Parents took her on vacation for graduation. I didn't wanna ruin it. Besides, it didn't feel right to text that my mother—" She swallowed the word 'died,' unable to spit it out without bursting into tears.

Mina patted her on the back again. "That was very mature of you to think of her like that."

"I don't have a lot of friends… at least not ones I've met for real."

"Sometimes I worry about our society. Everyone's online all the time these days. No human contact. What about at school?"

"Everyone there thinks I'm anorexic or bulimic 'cause I'm so thin." Riley fidgeted. "I'm not. I got tired of being picked on, so I ignore everyone. Not my fault."

Mina failed to conceal a pained expression. "I got teased in school too."

Not gonna say it. "Sorry."

"I'd always been a little heavy." Her knuckles whitened around her knees. "Diets never worked, exercise never helped. This is just who I am. It took me a very long time to come to terms with that." Mina bit her lip. "My own father used to call me Miss Piggy."

Riley gasped.

"Oh"—Mina waved dismissively—"he wasn't trying to be mean about it… he thought I looked like the puppet. He didn't know how it felt, and I never told him."

"I'm sorry. People at school call me Anna."

Mina looked puzzled.

"Rexia. Anna Rexia." Riley scowled at the floor. "I'm not. Really. I swear."

"I believe you." Mina patted her back again. "I stopped giving them power over me. Took me too long to convince myself that the only opinion that mattered was mine."

"Yeah… screw what they think."

"You'll be okay, kid… I got a feeling you're tough inside."

Riley looked up. "So… You really found my dad? He wants me?"

"Yep." Mina grinned. "I got in touch with your mother's attorney, he had the contact information."

"What?" Riley blinked. "Mom knew where he was this whole time? She said she had no idea."

"Well, that could be true. His 'contact information' was an email address… that doesn't mean she knew where he was."

"Why did he leave?" Riley bit her lip.

Mina's eyes widened and rolled as she pursed her lips. "That's something for you to ask him. I honestly don't know. However, I *do* know that he is *very* keen on having you back. He asked me to make sure you understood he never stopped loving you. The man got himself so worked up to get out here, he hung up on me before I could ask him if he wanted to talk to you. You know, I think the man ran right out his door."

"I was eight. He didn't come home from work one day. Mom was all normal and stuff until I asked why Dad wasn't home yet, and then she cried. She said was I was too little to understand; the best answer I ever got was they decided it was in everyone's best interest to separate."

"Not every marriage works out. You'll have plenty of time to talk to him about that. It's really not my place to speculate what happened."

He wants me? She bit her knuckle and sniffled.

"What's wrong?"

"I didn't know... I thought he hated us."

"Okay, enough negativity." Mina tucked a finger under Riley's chin and lifted her gaze off the floor. "Grab clean clothes and I'll show you where you can take a shower. After that, you are eating dinner. Toya isn't kidding. She will strap you to a chair and spoon-feed you if she has to."

Riley slid to the edge of the bed, kicked off her sneakers, peeled off her socks, and stood. *Dad's coming for me.* Dark orange light shimmered through the tiny, prison-like window. *I'm getting out of here.* She shrugged off the sweatshirt and threw it in a ball to the ground next to the bag. After pulling a clean set of clothes out of the small suitcase she'd brought from home, she managed an almost-smile at Mina.

"Thanks for finding him."

"You're welcome." Mina draped a metal bead chain over Riley's head like a necklace, with a key on it. "This is for your room. Lock your door on the way out."

She crept out after Mina. The smell of turkey and mashed potatoes flooded the corridor. The dormitory area seemed quiet at this hour, most likely because everyone was already eating. After stooping to lock the door without taking the key off, she followed Mina to the bathroom at the end of the row. She'd been terrified the showers were public, but breathed a sigh of relief at finding private rooms.

"Need anything?"

"Uhm, towels?"

"Inside on the shelf." Mina gestured at the door. "Put them in the bin in the corner when you're done."

Riley slipped inside and locked the door. The plain bathroom area looked like something you'd find in a hotel, complete with a stack of tiny one-use soap bars and shampoo bottles. She felt vulnerable enough being in a strange environment without her mother; the idea of taking a shower here felt wrong... as if to do so would accept that the house she grew up in was no longer her home.

After a few minutes of staring at her toes, she pushed her pajama pants off. The soft, red fabric gathered atop her feet. She scowled at the grinning bears, and kicked them across the room. Her PJ pants hit the wall and snagged on a hook. The sight of them dangling and the thought of how angry she must look brought an unexpected chuckle, though her mirth was short-lived. With a sigh, she shed the rest of her clothes and stepped into the tub, trying not to pay attention to the sobbing woman on the other side of the wall.

One thought kept her going.

I'm not an orphan.

4

LONELY REQUIEM

Dresses had never been high on Riley's list. It's not that she disliked them; in the summer, she was more of a shorts and flip-flops girl. Special occasions, and Mom, had sometimes demanded them. Since this unwelcome *special* occasion was all about Mom, she decided to wear one without protest because it's what her mother would have asked her to do. Another trip to the house, again 'under guard,' led to the realization she had no dresses suitable for a funeral. The blue one she'd worn for graduation was too cheerful, and it made her think of her mother's smile too much.

In Mom's closet, she had found a plain black dress that fit, albeit the way a sleeping bag fits a broom. Mom probably wore it to some boring office party at the bank the last time it saw the light of day. Mina helped with a couple of safety pins in spots she couldn't reach and got the dress to a point where it looked reasonable.

Riley occupied the center of the front row of folding chairs in a dim, burgundy room at Samuels Funeral Home, the only person present aside from Mina. Two floral arrangements flanked a white casket; one bore a card signed by the people who worked at the bank branch Mom managed. The other one was from Mina, who lurked by the door out of respect for the family.

What family? Riley frowned at her kitten heels. *It's just me and Mom.*

Aunt Bea won't show up. Guess I know what the B stands for. Mother's old joke sent a lone tear sliding down her cheek.

For over an hour and a half, she sat alone, clutching a tiny purse in her lap and staring at her mother's body. The mortician had brought the color of life to her face, but Mom looked as though she were made of wax. *She seemed more alive at the hospital.* The wig wasn't too awful, though the body lying in the casket didn't look like Mom anymore. Long, straight sand-brown hair gave her the appearance of a forty-year-old, taller, thicker version of Riley. A dark-brown pixie cut had been the norm for at least four years, but she couldn't find a decent photo to give them.

When she was in sixth grade, one of the tellers had passed away and Mom brought her along to the wake. She couldn't wait to get out of there. Now, she didn't want to leave this room.

Bustle by the door preceded an older couple walking over to the casket. They paid their respects and paused by her chair on their way past.

"We're so sorry about your Mother, dear," said the woman. "We worked together for ten years. So tragic."

"So young." Her apparent husband bobbed his head, looking much like she must've looked at the teller's wake... eager to skip out as fast as possible.

"Thank you," said Riley.

A few minutes later, a disheveled man about twenty stumbled over to the casket in a t-shirt, shorts, sneakers, and a jacket that belonged to a dress suit. He blinked at the body and wiped his face with one hand, sniffling.

"Whoa... Damn, missus M. That sucks." He fumbled around as if not sure what to do, knelt on the padded bench and bumbled his way through a few minutes of prayer. He made eye contact with Riley as he stood to leave. "Oh, hi. I'm Scott." He sniffled again and wiped his nose on his sleeve. "I work at the bank. You're the kid, right? She's got your pic on her desk." He fidgeted and hurried away, as if expecting her dead mother to lunge up and grab him. "Uh, sorry."

She watched him walk to the front door, hesitate, and circle back to a seat in the last row.

Another old man stopped by, wan and rickety. He flashed a dour, disapproving expression at Riley before aiming it at Mom. He grumbled as he ambled over to the casket and took a knee, making the sign of the cross as he continued to mumble too low to hear. The longer he muttered, the less Riley cared for him. By the time he'd finished whatever he'd wanted to say and braced a shaking arm on the coffin to stand, her glance had become a glare. He whirled about and toddled right up to her; it appeared to take great effort on his part to present a neutral mood.

"Here you go, child." He held out a small, rectangular object, which she accepted out of reflex. "I pray you don't make the same mistakes your mother did."

Once he walked around to the bank of chairs behind her, she glanced down and discovered the gift was a pocket Bible. She put it on the seat to her right, not too worried if she forgot it there.

A slender woman with deep wrinkles on her face and hair too black to be natural walked by as if Riley didn't exist. Her outfit and makeup seemed more suited to a college co-ed than someone old enough to be a grandmother. She spent ten minutes talking at Mom as if she were alive; trivial questions flowed from one to the next without a pause to slip in an answer. Riley wondered if she always did that to people. All Riley got was a two-second wave as the mourner teetered past on extreme heels that made her calves look like dead guinea pigs stuffed into socks.

Eleven more visitors, three married couples, three men, and two women, arrived over the next fifteen minutes. Riley remembered a few of them from bank parties Mom had brought her to. Mrs. Harris was the head teller. Mr. Eaves was the district manager for the security company that handled the bank's account. The rest all worked at the bank or in the building across the way. Her mother's former coworkers trickled past one by one, spending a moment to talk to Riley and offer the usual condolences, as if they'd all rehearsed the same lines ahead of time.

I swear I'm going to scream if one more person says she 'looks natural.'

The dull murmurs of her mother's former employees and a few regular customers lent a heavy presence to the room behind her. Conversations about work, relatives, pets, and the weather went on for-seeming-ever. *That bald guy didn't bother to show up.* Riley shifted in her seat, peering over the crowd behind her. No one from the big corporate Christmas party was there, and none of Aunt Bea's people could be bothered. *Good. She never liked me anyway.*

Riley faced forward again, gazing at her mother in hopes of finding a sign of life. Maybe they'd all made a mistake and Mom wasn't really dead yet. Despite the crowd, she still felt like the only person there.

Metal clanked to her right as a gaunt man in a maroon flannel shirt over a white tee, plain blue jeans, and brown work boots bumped the front row of chairs. A store tag still dangled from his left sleeve. Dark rings lined his eyes, and a few days of beard shaded the lower parts of his face. He didn't approach the casket, or even look at it, keeping his gaze down as he drifted closer. When he made eye contact with Riley, it lasted all of two seconds, and he seemed almost afraid of her. She squeezed the little purse in her lap as he lowered himself into the seat beside her. An instinctual urge to lean away from him gripped her. Something about him seemed... not quite right. Riley peered over her shoulder, searching for Mina with a 'help me' stare.

The man looked at Mother with an expression more tired than grieving. Riley gave up hunting for Mina in the crowd and faced forward.

Who is this dude? Oh, this must be that homeless guy Mom bought lunch for.

She sat stiff as a board, trying to ignore him and force life back into Mother with her eyes.

"You sure got big, Squirrel."

No one's called me that since... Her head popped up, mouth agape. "D-Dad?"

He looked nervous as anything, and fidgeted while studying his boots. "I'm sorry it took something like this to... for me to..."

"You look like hell."

A weak smile flickered across his lips, dying to a flat line after three seconds. "Been driving three days... didn't sleep a whole lot."

"Oh." *He's so different.* She picked at her purse. "Thanks for coming for me."

He reached out to hold her hand; she leaned back without conscious thought. Dad looked down. "Sorry. Suppose you're pretty mad at me."

"I guess. When I was like nine. I..." She forced herself to ignore the uneasy feeling she got from him and grasped his hand, finding his skin calloused and dry. "Sorry. I'm—"

"Upset." He squeezed her fingers. "That Lewis woman told me to expect you'll need some adjustment time. I'm not supposed to take anything personally."

"Feels like I don't know you anymore."

"I work a lot; sometimes, I forget to eat." Dad glanced at the coffin. "She looks so natural."

Riley clenched her jaw, grumbling. "No, she doesn't. She looks like they stole her from a wax museum. They got the hair all wrong."

"Lily used to wear it down like that when you were small, before she got that job with the bank. Didn't have the time to take care of it after that."

"Are you really here?" She stared at him, lip quivering and eyes full of water. "Y-you really want me?"

"Yes, Riley." He squeezed her hand. "Not a day went by I didn't think of you."

"Why'd you leave?"

"Mr. McCullough?" A dark-skinned man in a black suit with a red satin shirt walked over with one eyebrow lifted.

"Yes," said Dad. "I am."

They shook hands.

"I'm Victor Samuels, with Samuels Funeral Home. I'm so sorry for your loss."

"Thanks," said Dad.

"Miss." Victor bowed to Riley and shifted his attention back to Dad. "I am to understand that in accordance with your wife's wishes, there will be no mass?"

"That sounds like Lily. I just got here... I... haven't had time to review any documents."

"That's fine, sir. With your permission, I'll say a few short words and we can be on our way to her final resting place."

Riley broke down at the word 'final,' sobbing into her hands. The purse slid out of her lap and plopped to the floor, but she didn't care. Dad's arm settled around her shoulders and pulled her close. She hadn't seen him in six years. He cradled her to his chest; his scent filled her breath, bringing back old memories. As different as he looked, he still smelled like Dad.

Victor Samuels became a blurry smear in the corner of her vision. He drifted to the front of the room and cleared his throat. "Excuse me everyone."

Within the hour, her *mother* would be left in a hole in the ground, never to be seen again. She didn't care about what the man said, what the people behind her whispered, or even what any of them thought of her carrying on like a little girl.

"First, I'd like to convey the family's thanks to everyone in attendance today. It is Mrs. McCullough's wish to have a secular service. As such, we will be proceeding directly to Hillside Cemetery. Directions are available at the front podium."

"She's no atheist anymore." A creaking elderly voice silenced the room. "God has shown her the error of her ways."

Riley's tears ceased. She leaned up from her father to peer over his arm at the people seated behind them. The man who'd handed her the bible was on his feet, imperious finger aimed at the coffin. She stared at him in utter disbelief.

"He is watching. Behold the fate that awaits all who deny Him. She'd still be alive if she had not turned her back on God."

A few mourners gasped.

Riley wanted to scream and curse at him, but all she managed to do was start crying again.

"Have some respect, dammit... her daughter's right there," muttered some guy.

"The poor girl's just lost her mother, how dare you," yelled Mrs. Harris.

Dad jumped up and spun with one foot on the seat of his chair and his fist drawn back. He seemed about ready to pounce on the old man and beat him senseless, but a brief glance back at Riley took the fire from his eyes. He exhaled and lowered his arm.

"Sorry... if we weren't in a funeral home." He glared at the geezer. "Don't they teach you in that church of yours not to speak ill of the dead? Have some respect."

"I warned her, but she refused to hear the word," said the man.

"Mr. Hensley, that's quite enough," snapped a full-figured brunette. Riley had seen her at the bank before, in the back glass-walled office, but wasn't sure what she did there. "You should leave."

"She got what she deserved. You all will," muttered Mr. Hensley.

Dad started around the row of chairs, headed right at him with murder in his eyes. Riley shivered in her seat while some people from the funeral home ran over to separate her father from the old man. Victor Samuels and a man that could've been his brother escorted the bible beater to the door.

Mina scowled at him. "With her daughter here? You should be ashamed of yourself."

Whispers wafted around about the old man. He owned a bookstore next to the bank, and Mother's unrepentant atheism had fuelled a years-long rivalry between the two. Not that Mom ever went out of her way to discuss it with anyone. That wasn't her way; she spent more time dodging him than anything, but he kept trying.

Dad backed away from the crowd toward her, staring at Mr. Hensley while opening and closing his right fist. Victor offered apologies to everyone for the disruption and rushed into a murmured conversation with Dad. It took her father a few seconds to peel his eyes away from the door.

Others stood, getting ready to join the procession of cars to the graveyard. She rushed to the back of the room and grabbed Mother's hand.

As stiff as a wooden statue.

Riley recoiled and clutched the edge of the casket. *Could God really have struck her down for not believing in him?* She never talked to her about religion, or her lack of it. The only thing she'd ever said was it would be her decision to make whenever she felt like making it. Riley stared at the not-right face propped up on a small violet pillow. The sound of people shuffling out through the foyer lit a sense of urgency in her heart. She wanted as much time as possible with her mother before they took her away forever.

I'm sorry, Mom. A dozen minor arguments over the past school year replayed themselves in her head. Bedtime, curfew, cell phone bill, getting a C in math... so trivial, but how much stress did they pile on? The guilt was worse. Whenever Mom said she was too tired to spend time with her, Riley would sulk and walk away without a fight. That had to have made mother feel awful. She slumped to her knees on the cushioned pad, forehead atop her fingers, and wept.

Dad moved up alongside her. He didn't say anything until the room behind them fell silent.

"It's time to go."

"I don't wanna." She lifted her head. "I wanna stay with her. I..."

"It's all right," said Victor. "We just need a little room."

Riley backed up two steps, clinging to her father's arm instead of the coffin. Two men folded in the padding around the edges while Victor turned a crank, lowering her mother flat inside. She stared until one of them reached to close the lid.

"Wait!" she yelled, surging forward.

The man froze with a startled look as if he'd been about to step on a puppy. She hovered over her mother's body, sniffling.

"I love you, Mom." Riley kissed her on the cheek.

Five minutes later, Dad threaded his arms around her from behind, peeling her away from the casket so the men could lower the lid. It shut with a dull *thunk* that felt as if it hit her in the heart. An attendant gathered up the pleated curtain concealing a wheeled, metal frame beneath the coffin.

Riley hung limp in her father's embrace as the men pushed her mother around the bank of seats and out the door.

SLUMPED ON A PLASTIC FOLDING CHAIR IN THE SHADE OF A GREEN CANOPY the cemetery staff had erected to protect attendees from the relentless sun, Riley alternated between sniffling into a tissue and staring into space. With no clergy invited—at her mother's request—her coworkers took turns droning on about how great a person Lily McCullough was. No one dared touch on anything approaching religion or spirituality, though several commented on Mr. Hensley chasing away the homeless while Mom sometimes bought them lunch. Riley didn't have any tears left. She gazed at the white coffin perched above a hole, surrounded by mats of fake grass, ignoring eleven people in a row all saying more or less the same thing: pretty, smart, went before her time, oh her poor daughter, on and on.

Eventually, the nattering faded away, replaced by the rustle of formal clothes and the rattle of cheap chairs. Metal doors slammed in the distance, engines started, and cars drove off. A few workers congregated around the coffin, one tactless enough to give Riley a 'come on, get going' look.

"Mina's going to take you back to the shelter for a little while to collect your things."

"What?" Riley snapped out of her daze, looking up at him. "I'm not going with you?"

He sighed as if annoyed. "I've gotta sign some stuff, show some papers... prove I'm who I say I am. It shouldn't take more than an hour or ten."

"I hate that place. It feels like jail." She stood, wandered as close as she dared to her mother, and sat on the grass. "Can I wait here for you?"

Frustrated, the worker pushed a button. Electric motors whined as the coffin started its sluggish journey downward.

"No, Squirrel, we can't leave you out here."

"Don't call me that." Riley squinted as the sun glimmered off the sinking casket. "I'm not six."

"Do you really want to sit here while they fill in the grave?"

"Yeah. I wanna sit here forever."

He took a knee at her side. "Don't talk like that. Lily wouldn't have wanted you to give up just because something bad happened to her."

Riley frowned.

"You're all that's left of her in this world, kiddo. I swear you two could be clones."

"Great, my brain's gonna explode too?"

Dad kept quiet for a moment as the casket slipped out of sight behind a line of grass. "Guess you'd better not work for a bank then."

It took a second to register the meaning of her father's words. He'd said it in such a matter-of-fact tone, with a straight face. *Did he just crack a joke at Mom's funeral?* She blinked at him. As horrible as it was, she giggled —and couldn't stop laughing.

He lowered himself to sit next to her, put an arm around her, and waved at the workers. "Don't mind us."

For an hour after the last shovelful of dirt fell, Riley sprawled in the grass, unable to find the strength to stand. Mina waited a few steps back, saintly in her patience. Her father and the woman exchanged a look.

"Come on, Riley."

She didn't move.

"Wouldn't you rather sleep in your own room than out here?"

Riley crawled to the edge where grass gave way to dirt. "I don't want to leave her here."

Dad stooped next to her. "Your mother's at peace now."

She collected a few tears in her hands and poured them over the grave. "I love you, Mom."

5

UPROOTED

The sun forced its way through the heavy curtains over Mom's bedroom window. Riley lay at the center of the queen-sized bed, curled up like a cat who lost her human. Blue flannel pajamas—selected because they lacked smiling bears—stopped an inch above her ankles, leaving her feet cold. She had hated spending three nights at the shelter, the whole time wanting to be in her own room again. After only an hour of staring at a square of moonlight on her bedroom ceiling, she migrated here. Mom's presence lingered in the air; the bedspread still smelled of perfume and shampoo. Mother always showered at night; there was never enough time in the morning.

She looked from the limp hand a few inches in front of her face to the flaking blue glitter-infused polish on her toenails. *Mom was still alive when I painted them.* The door creaked open as her father walked in, trailed by the fragrance of coffee—coffee Mom bought.

He scuffed up to the edge of the mattress. "Are you hungry?"

"Mmm."

"We could hit Denny's or something."

Mom has food downstairs. "Mmf."

"I'm sorry… we need to figure out what we're keeping and what we can't take with us."

"Mmm." She hugged her knees to her chest, curling her toes.

"About a week. Maybe two. There's a lawyer coming by soon to help with everything."

Riley grunted.

"I know you want to stay here, but it's just not possible."

She sniffled.

Dad sat on the edge of the mattress. "I miss her too."

No, you don't. You're just saying that. She stared at her feet, daydreaming about the trip to the mall with her Mom and Amber. Some little Chinese woman sold the nail polish from a fake pushcart. Mom had a cheeseburger at Friday's afterward, and gave the waiter a hard time over not getting sweet potato fries like she'd asked for.

"Mmm."

"I was going to sell this bed since I don't have room for it, but I suppose we can keep it in storage so you can go visit it."

We're going to New Mexico. I won't be able to visit Mom. She sniffled again and wiped her nose.

He sipped his coffee. "You know the Sentra is paid off. You can get a permit at fifteen. We could keep it."

Riley sat up, twisting to face him. "Really? I thought you wanted to sell everything and forget her."

"I couldn't forget her if I wanted to." He offered a weak smile, as if discussing something as blasé as his favorite sandwich. "It's just a matter of practicality. I've only got so much room and... keeping the car, I'm going to have to pay someone to ship it."

"I wanna keep it 'cause it was hers." She scooted to the edge and let her legs hang. "I could get a summer job or something to help. Mom wanted me to get a job this year anyway."

"I think you should take the summer to come to terms with things. I know I haven't been part of your life for a long time, but this is a lot for a kid your age to handle."

"Why did you leave?" She frowned at the carpet. *Mom liked powder blue.*

Dad sucked in a breath and stiffened. "Sometimes things just happen and... I had a job that was taking up all my time and we got to arguing and—"

"I don't remember you guys fighting."

He stood. "Well, we didn't want you to see it. I, uh... Look, Riley, it's complicated. It wasn't about you."

She slid her feet back and forth on the rug to warm them. "You're full of shit."

"I didn't want you to get hurt. My job..." He spun in place. On the second rotation, he waved his arm at the bureau. "Whenever you feel up to it, go through the room here and pack up Mom's jewelry and whatever of her clothes you want to keep."

Riley folded her arms and scowled as he rushed out. He was taking her away from everything she knew, and he couldn't even tell her the truth about why he left. *What's he hiding? Doesn't he trust me?*

Soft thuds from downstairs disturbed the quiet, Dad fussing around. It sounded like he paced back and forth across the entire house. Riley didn't feel like moving. She didn't want to pack, didn't want to play Xbox, didn't want to go outside, watch TV, eat, or do much of anything except be with Mom.

Silence was nice.

The phone rang, startling a shriek out of her. She stared at the cordless handset on the nightstand, unable to remember the last time anyone bothered calling the landline. On ring three, she got to her feet and crept over. Dad evidently wasn't planning to answer it. *Why would he? He doesn't live here anymore.*

Riley plucked the little Motorola out of the charging cradle and stared at the screen. *Unavailable* showed in the caller ID box. A robotic arm raised the device to her ear by ring six, and she flicked the talk button.

"Hello?" she rasped.

"Lily?" barked a male voice at the edge of shouting.

"I–it's Riley."

"Oh." The condescending hostility faded—a little. "Put your mother on the phone, please. I haven't heard from her in days. Her report on the auto loan section is late."

Pritchett. Mom's boss. Now she recognized the voice.

"She's dead, you fat, bald cocksucker!" Tears poured out of her eyes, though her face burned red with rage. "You worked her to death. Are you happy now? Screw your stupid loan reports and screw your stupid bank!"

"Young lady, that's not funny."

"Tighten your tie a little more. Maybe your head will explode too!"

Dad ran in as she reared her arm back to hurl the phone at the window. He caught her hand, pulling her into a hug as he pried the phone out of her white-knuckled grip. She wasn't done being angry with him for lying to her, but found herself bawling onto his shoulder anyway.

"Hello? Whoever you are, you better have one damn good reason for making my daughter upset," said Dad.

A murmur emanated from the phone.

"Yes, that's right. Christopher McCullough. No, we never officially divorced. I'm afraid Riley is correct. Lily passed away a few days ago."

More angry rumbling came from the phone.

"I don't give a sewer rat's swollen scrotum about your report. No, I don't have her password. Ask one of her assistants."

Dad let off a heavy sigh and set the phone in the cradle. "Asshole. Uh… you didn't hear me say that."

"He killed her." Riley sniveled. "This… it really happened."

He wrapped both arms around her. "I'm sorry, sweetie. It did, but I won't leave you again. It was a mistake I can never take back."

"Tell me why." She lifted her face from his shirt and stared into his eyes.

"I was a coward."

She glared at him. "Why don't you trust me?"

"I do." He pulled her closer with a hand on the back of her head. "I don't want to hurt you."

Four days later, stacks of boxes gathered in the living room. The gradual disassembly of Riley's life took place before her eyes, and she could do nothing to stop it. One day spent refusing to leave Mom's bed had made Dad do all the work. He didn't complain, but he didn't stop. One day spent crying, pleading, and promising this, that, and the other thing also hadn't changed his mind. Today, she'd begrudgingly accepted that the place in which she'd grown up would be home no longer.

Packing happened in fits and starts. As soon as she'd get into a groove, she'd find something special and wind up crying for an hour instead of filling boxes. She'd already put on two of Mom's wooden bracelets and her huge, knit sweater over the camouflage tee shirt and shorts she'd plucked off her floor. While going through the kitchen shelves, she stumbled on Mom's recipe book and its hundred post-it notes of modifications. She lifted it as carefully as if it were a handwritten Bible from the Middle Ages, clutched it to her chest, and sank into a ball on the floor under the table. A few seconds after she burst out in sobs, Dad came running in.

He skidded to a halt by the fridge, raising an eyebrow at her hugging the overstuffed tome as if he couldn't comprehend how she'd gotten so worked up over a wad of paper. Riley didn't look at him, lost in a swimming mess of memories. Mom teaching nine-year-old Riley how to make the filling for stuffed mushrooms. Baking cookies for Christmas, even though there was no family but the two of them. The first gingerbread house she tried to make looked like the Big Bad Wolf had his way with it, but Mom thought it was perfect.

"You okay, Squirrel?" Dad crouched at the edge of the table, one hand grasping the edge over his head.

Riley shook her head. "No. Mom's dead."

He offered a hand, but she ignored him. Where was he when Mom needed help? She wouldn't have had to work that awful job if he'd stayed. Who was this stranger in her house, taking her world and turning it upside down?

"C'mere, Squirrel."

"Don't call me that. I'm not six anymore."

Dad let his arm fall and offered an apologetic look. "I'm sorry. I know this is hard, it's not easy for me either."

She huddled over the book as if he wanted to snatch it away too. "You don't look upset."

"Not everyone wears their heart on their sleeve." A wistful smile crossed his face for a few seconds. "Lily always gave me a hard time about that. She could never tell what I was thinking."

"Why do we have to move?" Riley sniffled. "Can't you move in here? Why do *I* have to be the one to move? I wanna stay close so I can visit Mom's grave on her birthday and Christmas and such." *Every so often on a random Wednesday.*

He grunted and stood, moving to sit in one of the nearby chairs. "If it was even remotely possible, I would. I don't know what it is about this damn state. The property taxes on this place are more than my mortgage. I couldn't afford to keep it even if I didn't have a house payment of my own."

Riley got control of her tears and crawled out from under the table. She kept the book in her lap as she sat across from him. "I can get a summer job."

He smiled. "If only."

"What... I can." She glared.

"No, I believe you. You wouldn't make enough money. They pay kids only enough to go to the movies... or whatever it is kids do these days. You can't live here alone, and I can't afford to stay. I'm sorry we have to sell the place." He paced to the sink, peering out the window into the backyard. "I still remember when your mother and I first walked through the open house here."

Riley sniffled.

"Old couple owned it, the Stantons. Nice people. They were moving to Florida and priced it to go quick. Lily fell in love with it right away. I can't believe she already paid it off. She really was a whiz with money."

"If it's paid off, why can't you afford it?" Riley's gaze settled on the recipes; the book had more life in it than her voice.

"Taxes, hon. The state charges people money to have land."

"That's stupid."

Dad shrugged. "Well, the politicians need their limos and filet mignons. I'll make sure every dollar we get for the place goes into an account for you. I won't take a dime. I know I left and I don't deserve any of it. Mom would want you to have it."

"I don't want money; I want my home back. I want Mom back."

"I know, Riley... I do too."

What? She looked up, lip quivering. "D-does that mean you don't really want me?"

"I meant I wish your mother was still alive."

"So you didn't get stuck with me?"

He reached across the table and grabbed her wrist. "You have every right to be angry with me for leaving, but if you believe anything, please believe I have never stopped loving you. I would do anything to protect you."

She put her free hand over his. "Anything except let me stay here."

"I'd have to rob a bank. If that's what you want."

Wow... is he joking? That sounded so serious. "Uhm... Dad?"

"Of course, then I'll be in jail and you'll be in social services." He winked. "Doesn't seem like a great plan."

Whew. "For a sec there I thought you were serious."

"I am." He smiled. "If I thought it would work."

She wobbled to her feet, refusing to unwrap her arms from the book. "Stop messing with me."

"They don't keep that much money in cash in bank branches anymore." He rubbed his chin. "Mom might have some access codes I could get into the system with, transfer a dozen accounts to one offshore."

"Stop it, Dad."

She moved to the counter and set the recipes in an unused cardboard box, grabbed a nearby Sharpie, and wrote "KEEP" on the longer face. Dad edged up behind her and put his hand on her right shoulder. He planted a light kiss on the side of her head.

"I love you, Riley Dawn."

He drifted off into the dining room, where he'd set up a mountain of paperwork, leaving her to the soul-crushing task of packing away Mom's kitchen. A few hours later, she'd gone through everything she could, leaving out enough 'kitchen stuff' to cook simple meals.

She headed to the living room, passing Dad absorbed in a phone call at the dining room table.

"My God, sir. Yushchenko's dead too? Two days ago? I was hoping the intel was suspect. At least they're keeping it off the news."

Riley skidded to a halt.

"Yes, sir. I understand. They did it just like the Nemtsov assassination. The man's unhinged." Dad nodded. "Sir. Right. Understood. No, sir. Couple more days."

The conversation had animated him more than she'd yet seen, though he looked worried. Her gait slowed to a veritable crawl as she passed him, confused by the dramatic change. She stopped at the archway leading to the living room and watched him 'yes' his way past a barrage of questions. When he finally put the cordless handset down, he seemed drained.

"Dad? What was that?"

"Oh." He jumped as if he hadn't noticed her. "Colonel Bering, my… uh… other boss."

"You're in the Army?" Riley blinked.

"Not anymore, though I work for them as a civilian contractor. There's a problem with one of my guidance routines… I do software."

"You look like he told you men are on their way to shoot you." Riley crept closer. "You sure you're okay?"

He crumbled his fingers together in a fist supporting his cheek, elbow on the table. "Yeah. Yep. I'll be fine."

"I'm scared."

Calm washed over him, as if the call had never happened. He held his arms apart. "Come here."

She walked into a firm hug and a pat on the back. A weak memory of jumping on him as a seven-year-old came back. He had the same grip. When he let go, she tucked her hair behind her ear and smiled.

"It's not gonna be easy, kid, but we'll survive."

"'Kay." She looked up. "What do you mean 'other' boss?"

"Oh." He chuckled. "I get jobs from this guy Ted out of Albuquerque. Freelance programming work. Not too regular, but pay is big most times." Dad paused a moment, trying to read the look on her face. "I'm sorry."

"Yeah..."

Riley looked down and shambled into the living room. Mom's fifty-inch flat panel TV dominated a space predominantly made up in powder blue, except for the off-white carpet. The nagging urge to cry shadowed her for the next hour as she wrapped and packed all of Mom's little glass and porcelain figures. The woman sure had a thing for faeries. She wanted to keep them, but they'd probably stay in boxes until she had her own place. Something told her that taking them out at Dad's would only get them smashed. Dad didn't seem big on 'delicate.'

Plastic crinkled under her fingers the next time she reached up without looking for the next wide-eyed figurine. A translucent blue plastic bag sat tucked at the back of the shelf out of sight. Riley could tell it held DVDs as soon as she laid a hand on the package. She pulled it out and opened it, finding three movies... *Up, Brave, and Frozen.* Mom had obviously been planning to surprise her with a 'movie day' sometime soon. None of them were unsealed yet, meaning Mom hadn't even thought to watch them without her.

The dam broke again.

Riley fell over sideways, bawling. Once again, Dad came running at the outburst. His arms slipped under her, lifting her up off the floor. He backed up to the sofa and sat with her across his lap, holding on until the sobs wracking her body faded to erratic sniffled breaths.

"Ratatouille," he said.

"What?" She looked up, mouth agape. "What the hell does that mean?"

"That was the last cartoon we watched together... all three of us."

Oh, that... Her sorrowful face hardened to a scowl. She remembered hating that movie—because it reminded her of her broken family. "Yeah."

"How bout I take care of dinner tonight?" He raised an eyebrow.

"You'd burn water if you tried to boil it." Amid a clatter of wooden bracelets, Riley wiped at her face with the grey sweater sleeves.

"You're probably right, but I know how to work a phone. Pizza?"

"Mom has enough crap in the freezer to last through nuclear winter. We shouldn't waste it."

"Okay, okay..." He laughed.

Riley smirked. "How about Friday?"

"It is Friday."

"I mean next Friday." She fidgeted with the sweater.

"That's a clever attempt to stay here longer, isn't it?"

She stared straight ahead, trying not to let herself cry.

"Okay, fine. Next Friday."

Five days passed in the blink of an eye, each fading into the next. Riley didn't feel much of anything by Wednesday night. So many things made her want to cry that she tuned everything out. Her entire life, apart from a few articles of clothing, now sat in 'boxhenge' downstairs. She stood in the center of the small bathroom at the end of the upstairs hall, staring at herself in the mirror for a half hour before undressing and stepping into the tub.

She pulled the cloth and plastic barrier closed, dimming the light, and swallowed hard. This was the tub where she'd played with rubber ducks. *Another couple days, and I'll never set foot in this room again.* Riley sniffled. *I'm so messed up. I'm getting weepy over a damned shower curtain.* The process of showering went by in slow motion. How many times had she whined about being forced to take a bath before bed as a kid? She half-smiled at the memory of countless days where everything had been so boring; now each one of them seemed like a precious moment. Riley closed her eyes and ducked under the spray to rinse her hair, and wound up staying there, letting the water roll over her head and down her back until her Dad knocked on the door.

"You okay, hon? You've been in there a long time."

Wow, he sounds worried. He must think I've slit my wrists or something. "I'm okay." *Sorta.*

Riley shut off the water, dried off, and pulled on a fresh set of bright red pajamas. All the while she brushed her teeth, she stared at every line and contour of the room, committing it to memory. The thought of climbing a little plastic stool to examine her missing front teeth in the mirror brought another round of sniffles. She had grown up in this bathroom, and three days from now, she'd never see it again.

How could it feel alien already? Why did she feel like an intruder in her own home?

She spat out the toothpaste foam, rinsed, and walked down the hall to her bedroom. Mom's was almost bare now, the door shut tight. On Monday, they had packed the bed into a U-Haul trailer attached to the back of Dad's beat-up tan Silverado. He called it a '98 as if that was something to be proud of, at least until she pointed out it was older than she was. The rest of the big furniture would go with the house.

Riley hated whoever was going to buy it. Money or not, they were stealing her home.

Darkness engulfed her room except where green light glowed from the lone Xbox controller on the charging stand next to her TV. The other one sat on the floor in the same place it fell out of her hand when she went to check on Mom. She hadn't the least bit of interest in touching the game since.

So far, the devouring whirlwind destroying her life hadn't had a visible effect on her bedroom. All the packing of *her* stuff had been limited to eviscerating closets and ransacking drawers. Dad probably let her save it for last to keep things feeling as sane as possible. Tomorrow, her dresser, bookcase, and desk would go to the trailer. Her bed would be last, as she needed to sleep. She took two steps toward it, but paused as her foot brushed the abandoned controller.

It's dead too, now. Riley squatted over it, confirming her diagnosis by poking a button and getting no response. She picked it up and knee-walked to the charging stand. The clear plastic clip lit up red as she put the device in its socket. *I wish I could plug Mom in and she'd wake up.* After a few minutes of staring at the controller tree, she dragged herself to bed.

She tried to stay awake as long as she could, to 'experience' being in her bedroom. She thought of Christmas Eves past, staring at this very ceiling, trying to make herself sleep faster so morning would show up. Random images of Mom came and went, as fleeting as the glow of the occasional passing set of headlights on the wall. Despite her strongest wanting, dark became light, and the sound of voices downstairs murmured up through the floor. Eventually, the discomfort of needing a bathroom overpowered her lack of desire to do anything but lay there. After dealing with it, she made her way downstairs.

Riley stumbled into the kitchen, t-shirt pulled up enough to scratch her stomach, ignoring the suited white-haired man talking to Dad. Most of their conversation sailed over her head, but she caught enough to assume they were discussing the sale of the house. She hoped her sullen glower would be enough to keep her out of the conversation, and went for a box of Special K. Riley hovered at the counter with her back to the men, picking the cereal out of the bowl with her fingers and eating it dry.

"One moment." Dad walked up alongside her. "Morning, kiddo. If I didn't know better, I'd say you were hung over."

Crunch. Crunch. Crunch.

"At some point today, we need to load whatever of your furniture you want to keep, except the bed."

"'Kay."

"I'm sorry, Riley. I am... I just."

"Can't afford New Jersey. I know." *Crunch.* She let out a long breath. "No choice, right?"

"Something like that."

She tried to give him an 'it's okay, I understand' face, but wasn't sure if the message made it—or if she believed that. Dad returned to his discussion about setting up a 'trust' account for her and directed the house be sold at a reasonable price. There was no rush; Riley deserved a fair price for the place.

Riley walked out with her cereal bowl, leaving the box open on the counter, not wanting to hear them talk. It felt as traitorous as if she eavesdropped on people plotting Mom's death. Soon, she found herself in her room, disassembling her electronics and tossing things into boxes between flakes of cereal.

Dad knocked on the doorjamb about an hour later. "Riley?"

"What?"

"There's someone at the door for you."

Who'd come to see me? She chucked a game DVD at a box half filled with old ones she hadn't played in a year and looked up at him. "Is it Mina?"

"No... it's some little black girl. Okay, maybe not little... your age."

"Amber?" Riley's hand flew to her chest, at the base of her throat. *Oh, shit.*

She jumped up, ran past him, and raced down the stairs. Her best (only) friend, Amber Nelson, waited on the porch in a purple string tee, shorts, and flip-flops. A giant smile faded to a look of worry as Riley pulled the door to behind her, and sat on the top step. Amber's toenails were the same shade of hot pink as her shorts, and a plastic clip kept her thick, straight hair back.

"Damn, Rile... Dubya-tee-eff. You look like the walking dead." Amber looked over her at the door, sat next to her, and whispered. "We landed late last night. I couldn't wait to get over here. Who's that creepy dude?"

"My dad."

"Oh, damn. Didn't know you had one. How's your mom doing?"

"She's—" Tears rolled out of her eyes. Riley swallowed the lump in her throat.

"Real sick?"

Riley shook her head. "She died."

"No... no..." Amber grabbed her shoulders. "Fuck, Riley... I'm so sorry."

They clung to each other, crying for a few minutes.

Amber spoke first. "How'd it happen?"

Riley sniffled. "Aneurysm."

"Oh... Those are usually sudden. People don't last—"

"No." Riley stared guilt into the step between her feet. "She died that night. They said she didn't feel anything."

"You bitch!" Amber shoved her shoulder. "When I texted you... you knew! That's messed up! I've known you since fourth grade, and you didn't trust me enough to tell me? Holy shit, Rile... I'm on the beach livin' it up, and your mama's dead?"

"It's not like that!" Riley yelled. "I... you were on vacation. I couldn't tell you something like that with a stupid text." Her voice fell to a faint, leaky whisper. "I'm still not sure I even believe it happened."

"I didn't even wanna be there." Amber fell seated again with a huff. "I could've handled it. We could've talked it out. Don't look like you handlin' it."

"I'm not. I gotta go live with Dad in New Mexico."

Amber squeezed her hand. "Tell him you can't go. You can sleep over at my place."

"That didn't work so hot when I invited you over."

"Yeah..."

"I should've told you."

Amber slapped her across the back of the head, a little too hard to be playful. "Yeah, you shoulda."

"How was Puerto Vallarta?"

"How can you talk about...?" Amber gasped, stared for a moment, and got an 'ohh' look in her eyes. "It was okay. Hot. Sandy. Full of tourists. The hotel had a nice pool, but the beach was better. I'm so sick of bottled water. Mom let me wear a bikini. Purple. Dad almost passed out. They're probably *still* yelling at each other over that whenever I'm out of range."

Riley grinned for a moment, before getting somber again. "We're leaving tomorrow. They're gonna sell the house."

"Sorry. I can't believe your Mom died."

So much for the greatest summer of all. "And I'm getting dragged across the country, and I won't be able to hang with you at all."

"We can still blast noobs. We hang out online as much as in person anyway… and you can come back for like holidays and shit if your Dad's okay with it. It's not the end of the world."

"Yeah, it is." Water leaked out of Riley's eyes, though she worked on, at least, *looking* stoic.

"We got today, right? We can hang out… scrape as much time as we can."

That's what I said the night Mom died. "'Kay, I gotta pack my room first."

"Lemme help?"

"Dad's gonna order pizza tonight, can you eat over?"

"Yeah."

"You didn't call your parents to ask."

Amber shook her head while raising a defiant, waving finger. "I don't care what they say. This is your last night home. I'm sleepin' over."

6

SQUIRREL

Miles of highway passed in awkward silence. Riley aimed her eyes out the window but didn't really look at anything. The road, guardrails, grass, and trees all blurred into a meaningless haze. It didn't help that she'd stayed up until something like three in the morning. For a few glorious hours with her best friend, she'd forgotten all about everything. Amber's parents showed up at 7:30 a.m., and insisted on taking them all out for breakfast. She wondered what everyone at Perkins must've thought when she and Amber sobbed all over each other in the parking lot.

Riley's head wobbled; she caught herself fading.

"Go ahead and sleep if you want. We got a long ride," said Dad.

She drifted in and out, losing an hour here and there. A bump knocked her awake as Dad pulled in to a Motel 6 parking lot. Riley sat up and stretched out a yawn, frowning at the dark sky.

"Where are we? What time is it?"

Dad opened his door. "About fifteen miles over the Illinois border. Twenty hundred ten local time, but twenty one hundred ten eastern."

"What?"

"Uh… we crossed a time zone." Dad climbed out. "Be right back."

He walked past the nose at a brisk stride and headed for the office. Riley pulled the iPhone out of her pocket, which said 9:11 p.m. *Illinois.* A lump tightened in her throat. Already so far from home, so far from Mom's grave, her friend, her life.

She sulked at the dashboard, spacing out for about ten minutes. Dad returned, climbing back in without a word. He drove around to the back of the building and parked by a row of doors. She didn't feel like moving, sitting listless as he retrieved a backpack from the rear bench seat and went into one of the rooms. It felt like they'd betrayed Mom by selling the house she'd loved; that's where Riley wanted to be, not some lame motel. She let her forehead rest on her knees, and shut her eyes.

Dad opened her door, letting a wash of chilly air in. "Hey."

"Hey."

"I can't let you sleep in the truck. You're gonna be in it all day tomorrow too."

She spun a quarter turn to her right, slid off the seat, and jumped down. Her flip-flops hit the pavement with a loud echoing slap.

"Do you own any real shoes, or just those foam things?" Dad pushed the door closed. The truck chirped and locked.

"They're packed." Riley trudged to the room.

"You should bring something to sleep in, and a change of clothes."

"Packed." She shoved the door out of her way, halting in the space between a pair of twin beds.

"Toothbrush?" Dad pulled the door shut behind him and locked the deadbolt and chain.

"Packed."

Riley sat on the bed farther from the window, staring at her frayed jean shorts and Garfield t-shirt. The last time she'd worn them, Mom was still alive. Dad sifted through the vertical blinds on the window, looking at the sill. He pulled the chain to close them and turned. The beginnings of a smile fell away to a momentary look of concern.

"What?" She blinked.

"Oh. I was… I usually don't like to sleep near windows. Drafts."

"Whatevs." Riley stood.

Dad cupped a hand over his chin, rubbing. "No, it's okay. Pick whichever one you want. This trip isn't fun for you."

"It's fine." She flopped onto the other bed.

Dad shuffled around some papers on the table by the window. "Wanna order Chinese? Pizza? I think I saw a fried chicken place across the street."

"Not hungry."

"You need to eat something, Riley. There's nothing to you."

Riley rolled over to face him. "You should talk. I don't have an eating disorder. I get enough crap at school; I don't need it from you."

He sat on the edge of the bed. "I wasn't trying to pick on you, hon. Half a sandwich for lunch, and you barely touched your omelet this morning. You need to eat. I'm worried."

"Sorry." She shifted flat on her back, staring at the ceiling. "Why does everyone care so much what I look like?"

"It's not about body image; it's about not starving to death. I know you're upset about Mom, but rushing into the grave next to her isn't a good idea."

"Oh, my God, Dad. You are such a drama queen." Riley rolled her eyes. "Can't you just let me be sad? Fine. Chicken Lo Mein… small."

"Coke?"

"Mom said there's too much sugar in soda. Get me a water."

Dad put a hand on her forehead. "Hmm. Doesn't feel hot."

She shifted her gaze to his face, flashing an unamused smirk.

"That's fever talk for a fourteen year old. Don't like soda?"

"Mom said it's all poison and chemicals."

He held his hands up in surrender. "Alright then. Water it is."

Riley sat up as he walked away, headed for the phone. "What do you drink?"

Dad swiveled to smile at her. "Water."

THE CEILING WASN'T ANY MORE INTERESTING AT TWO IN THE MORNING than it was for the hour and change Dad watched some ancient movie after their feast of Chinese food. She had zero interest in it and tried to text Amber, but kept getting 'network error' on the top of the screen. At ten thirty on the dot, Dad killed the light and went right to sleep.

Riley grumbled and shifted onto her left side. The pillows were lumpy and dense, the mattress hard as a board. The sheet-blanket was so tight to the foot end of the bed, she had to twist herself into an Egyptian hieroglyph not to hurt her toes. Under the covers, she sweat buckets; without them, she was too cold to sleep. She thought about ditching her tee and shorts, but sharing a room with Dad in her underwear would be *way* too awkward. Granted, her long-legged pajamas would've been even warmer.

Do they have, like, focus groups searching for the most uncomfortable crap to make motel beds out of?

She rolled on her right side. An irritatingly well-placed outside light found a gap in the blinds near the top of the window to leak through. Riley pushed the blankets down to her waist, leaving her legs covered, and fanned her chest. *I wonder what Amber's doing now? Probably just going to bed.* She rolled away from the window and the annoying light, curling into a fetal position. *Amber's in her own bed.* Hers was in the trailer outside; would it still feel like *hers* in an alien room?

Mom's final look filled her thoughts, the red hemorrhagic eyes staring at Riley without a trace of awareness. *How much of Mom was left inside her at that moment?*

She curled up tighter, crying without making a sound.

The next thing she knew, the sun blared in past open blinds. The uncomfortable bed tricked her mind into thinking she was still at the women's shelter until Dad's gentle hand prodded her on the shoulder.

"Morning, Riley. It's nine hundred hours. I wanted to get going earlier, but… you looked like you needed the sleep."

"Dad…" She sat up, grabbing his arm.

"What's wrong?" He clasped a hand over hers. "I mean, aside from the obvious."

"Thanks. For getting me out of that shelter."

"There was no choice involved. You are my daughter. I'd do anything for you."

She smiled. "Like beat up a guy at a wake?"

"Jackass," he muttered. "He had no right to upset you like that."

"He's just an idiot." Riley staggered to her feet. The over-warm bed left her feeling stiff and sticky, and wanting a shower. She wandered to the bathroom. "Gonna shower, you need to use the room?"

"Go ahead."

She locked the door, stripped, and found herself staring at a confusing disc on the white tile wall. Miscalculating the meaning of the large, round fixture resulted in a blast of freezing water. Fully awake in an instant, she screamed, leapt away from the stream, and shut it off with a few feeble kicks. She shivered in place for a few seconds, water dripping from her chin.

"You okay?" Dad's voice came through the door.

"C-cold…"

He chuckled. "Yeah, it got me too."

After figuring out how to get hot water, drying off, and putting the same clothes back on, she wrapped her hair in a towel and sat on the foot of the torturous bed. Dad huddled over the little table, muttering on the phone.

"Bit less than halfway back. Almost there. Yes, I'll be able to fix it by Thursday." He nodded twice, and went pale. "The Russians did *what?*" Fingers drummed on the table. "That's not good. Especially not with the Korea situation."

"What's not good?" asked Riley.

"Yes, it is." Dad covered the mouthpiece with his hand and looked over his shoulder at her. "Colonel Bering says hello. He's sorry about Mom."

Riley forced a lackluster smile. "Thanks."

Crescents of clean, new toenail peeked above the polish, an inexorable marker of time. She scooted her feet back and forth over the thin carpet while Dad muttered a series of 'yes sirs' at the phone.

He hung up and fished her flip-flops out from under the table. "Ready?"

"No, but… Yeah." She stepped into her flops, tapped the tips on the floor to seat the thongs between her toes, and meandered outside. It wasn't even eleven yet, and the air felt hot and muggy. "Blech."

She leaned against the passenger-side door while Dad paced around the motel room in a circle, three times. He walked outside, patted down his pockets, and re-entered the room to do another circuit. The second time he approached the exit, he backed out and pulled the door closed. He hit the button on the key fob to unlock the truck and jogged over.

"What the hell was that?" Riley pulled herself up into the seat and closed the door.

"I wanted to make sure we didn't forget anything. Never know what you can leave behind that seems inconsequential, but someone can use to, uh… steal your identity."

"Right…" She let her head thud against the seat back, and closed her eyes.

The engine started; motion and bumps jostled her for a few minutes. Riley looked when the truck went over a stiff bump. *What can I say to make him turn around?*

He pulled into the drive-through of a Dunkin Donuts. "Breakfast time."

"Coffee," said Riley, earning a raised eyebrow. "And one of those croissant things with the egg on it."

The scent of coffee and eggs lingered in the cab for an hour and change after the last trace of either was long gone. Riley couldn't manage to say a word and Dad focused on the road, tapping a finger on the wheel as if worried about something. She tried to think about anything other than Mom, but everything she called to mind eventually traced back to her old life. She didn't feel like crying any more, and sank into an implosion of blah.

A few minutes past noon, Dad chuckled out of the blue.

She glanced sideways at him.

"You remember why we nicknamed you Squirrel?"

Her face reddened. "Dad. I'm not a little kid anymore. Don't call me that."

"When you were three, you got a hold of a muffin and held it in both hands like a—"

"Squirrel with an acorn," droned Riley.

"You didn't forget." He took his eyes off the road for two seconds to grin at her.

It seemed different from the last time he smiled, somehow more genuine.

She made a sour face at the door. "I didn't forget."

You used to call me that, and then you left. Her hands clenched to fists. *I hated everyone that still had a dad.* The corners of her eyes burned as overworked tear-makers struggled to find moisture. Riley gritted her teeth. *Why does he have to keep calling me that?* It made her angry with Dad all over again for leaving. It made her angry with herself for lashing out at her mother for using it.

"Sorry," said Dad.

"What"—she started to snap, but relaxed and sighed the rest—"for?"

"For whatever put that mug on your face."

"Look, Dad, just... don't call me that."

"Okay, okay... fine." He sighed, seeming sad. "I guess I'll have to learn you're not my little girl anymore."

Why did you leave if it bothers you? She squirmed in her seat. "Don't hit me with guilt. I got enough already. You left. You still haven't trusted me with why."

He squinted at the road. His mouth opened and closed a few times, words dead at the tip of his tongue.

"Is it something Mom did, and you don't wanna 'speak ill of the dead?'"

"No." He pursed his lips for a moment. "I was getting involved with some stuff at work that I was afraid would wind up putting the two of you in danger. We got a whisper that some foreign nationals were attempting to threaten immediate family to turn someone."

She furrowed her brows. "Turn someone?"

Dad wrung his hands on the wheel, causing the truck to wobble in the lane. "Pass sensitive information to hostile governments in exchange for… not hurting the people you love."

"Oh, damn." She looked straight ahead. "Seriously? That's…"

"Like something out of a movie?" He reached over and squeezed her hand. "I didn't believe it either until Dan's wife died in a crash two blocks from their house. Only her car and a garbage truck were on the street. That was no accident."

"Who's Dan?"

"He sat across the aisle from me at the office in Edison. The company we worked for at the time was a frontend for DoD software development. It let them bring in civilians to work on classified projects, each person getting a small piece of the puzzle without having access to the whole pie. The code was modularized down to a level that no one really knew what they were working on."

"Oh." She swallowed. "Are they, like, still trying to kill you?"

"Nah. I've covered my tracks pretty good." He eased to the right lane and took an exit ramp. "If it were possible, I would've quit. I'd already been approached by the Russians. I had no choice."

Riley twirled an extra-long piece of frayed denim on her shorts around her finger.

"I can't believe Lily let you wear those. You're not old enough to show that much leg. Does your ass hang out of that thing?"

"*Dad.*" Riley blushed. "Jesus… No it does not."

The truck stopped next to a row of gas pumps. Dad killed the engine and opened the door; a rapid pinging came from the dash since he'd left the keys in. "I'll run inside and grab some road snacks." He handed her a credit card. "Go ahead and fill it with regular."

Riley looked around. "Where's the guy?"

Dad paused halfway out the door. "What guy?"

"The gas dude. The one you give the card to."

"Riley..." Dad cracked up for a moment. "Wow, you don't get out much do you?"

She glared.

"New Jersey has this strange fear of people pumping their own gas. You have to pump it yourself."

She stuck the card into her chin and bit her lip. "Really?"

"Yeah, come on." He slid off the seat. "I'll show you."

Riley undid her seat belt and climbed down out of the truck, scuffing flip-flops around the nose to the gas cap behind the driver side door. She turned the credit card over in her hands, standing on tiptoe to look around. One semi truck and a few normal cars dotted the massive filling station. No one paid much attention to her standing there.

Dad pointed at the pump. "Put the card in that slot and push the button for regular."

"We're not gonna get in trouble?"

"Nope." He walked her through the steps of running a gas pump.

Riley wrestled the hose into place and squeezed the trigger with both hands, continuing to hold it.

Dad waited a minute before he couldn't stop from laughing again. "Flick the little kickstand thing down, you don't have to stand there with it."

Riley did so, and stepped back with her arms folded. "Oh."

"Be right back." Dad jogged across six lanes of filling stations, and ducked into the convenience store.

She folded her arms and stared at the numbers racing upward until the unexpected growl of a semi roaring to life startled a yelp out of her, not that anyone heard it. The truck pulled away, leaving her a clear view of Dad in the store windows. With him in sight, she felt a little safer. He collected a few items and went to the register. Around the time he gathered two bags and walked out, the pump stopped with a loud *click*. Riley pulled the hose out of the tank and hung it on the pump, still feeling a bit like she did something she'd get in trouble for. Dad slipped past her and set the bags behind his seat.

"Might wanna use the bathroom while we're here. I'd like to make some progress before we have to stop again."

"Okay." She looked around at the wide-open tarmac, wondering if there was really anyone out there who'd want to hurt her to make Dad be a spy. *No way. That's got BS all over it. When will he tell me he got caught cheating?* She glanced up at him. "Dad? You really left so no one hurt me an' Mom?"

He looked her straight in the eye. "Yes."

If he was lying, he was damn good at it. Riley found herself jogging to get behind the safety of a closed bathroom door.

7

FORLORN

Afull day of driving and another awful motel room later, they took a break at a rest stop somewhere near the western edge of the Texas Panhandle. The dashboard clock read 11:12 a.m., but it seemed wrong. Riley figured out his truck's clock must've been set to New Mexico time, which meant Texas was at noon. Her emotions had taken a beating over the past week, and offered little more than a crash-test-dummy's personality as she fell out of the truck and followed him to a place with the name Bernadette's over the door in sputtering neon. A middle-aged woman in a green apron led them to a table, gave her a strange, intense stare, and backed away.

"This is like a knock-off of Denny's," Riley muttered after they'd been seated in a window booth.

The hostess and three waitresses clustered at a counter lined with padded stools, near a cake minder full of brownies. All four of them looked at her and whispered.

Riley looked down at the menu, her appetite gone.

"Hon?" Dad slid his hand across the table. "What's bothering you?"

She let him hold her arm. "They're all watching me. Probably calling me bulimic or something."

"One, you're a beautiful girl. Two, don't let what anyone thinks affect what you think of yourself. It's your body. You're the one who has to live with it." He waited two beats. "You're not, are you?"

"No." She'd leaned on the word so hard it came out sounding more like 'Noah.'

"Sooner or later you will laugh at a joke."

"I know… It's just old." She sighed. "I eat normal, I just don't gain weight. Actually, I kinda eat a lot."

"Oh, you'll probably hit thirty-five or so, then turn into a blimp." He chuckled. "One day, your metabolism will fall on its ass."

She smirked. Her almost-laugh died as she remembered Mom battling the scale. Her mother wasn't fat by anyone's imagination, but she worried constantly about it.

"What can I get you folks?" asked a nervous woman with dark skin and straight hair. She looked a bit like Amber might after growing up and having kids. "Coffee? Juice?"

Riley shot a forlorn look at Dad, then at her abandoned menu.

"Two eggs over easy with hash, please. She'll have an omelet with Swiss cheese and mushrooms."

The waitress jotted down the order. "Drinks?"

"Two coffees, please."

"Be right back with the coffee." She collected the menus and rejoined the gossip hounds.

Riley stared out the window, watching traffic whistle past on I-40 in the distance. Dad rambled on through a story about how he and Lily met in college. He punctuated it with self-flagellating comments about how it had been a mistake to leave and he'd regretted it every minute of every day.

Her most elaborate response was "mmm."

Their food arrived, and Riley went about the motions of eating. The eggs tasted like foam rubber, the home fries oozed grease. She assaulted it with black pepper, though the seasoning had been sitting out so long it added little more than color.

Look at them staring at me. They don't think I'm gonna eat this whole thing. Or, they think I'm gonna puke it up as soon as I finish. She stared defiance at them while shoveling eggs and potatoes into her mouth. They only whispered more feverishly.

She sulked.

"Be right back. Gotta hit the head." Dad slid out of the bench and made his way to the bathroom.

Riley got two more bites of egg down before a tall waitress with strawberry blonde hair and *way* too much perfume walked over.

"Are you okay, sweetie?"

"Huh?"

The woman looked in the direction of the bathrooms and crouched, whispering, "Have you been kidnapped? We'll stall him and get a cop here right away. You don't have to be afraid. He can't hurt you."

She blinked. *That's* why they were staring at her. Rumpled clothes she'd worn three days in a row, the expression that must be on her face, how quiet she'd been. "I'm okay."

"What did he threaten you with?" The woman looked at the bathroom again, as if terrified he'd catch her here.

"Nothing. He's my dad. Chill out." She pushed potato around the plate. "My mother died two weeks ago, an' I gotta move across the country."

The waitress hesitated, looking back and forth between her and the other servers. "Okay... Sorry, we just assumed. He didn't look quite right."

Riley scowled at the woman. "He's not creepy, he's my dad. We've been driving from New Jersey. Not sleeping much."

"Sorry, sorry." The waitress stood. "You looked so... forlorn."

"S'okay. Guess it's better to ask in case you were right."

The woman hesitated, as if not quite believing her.

"Would he have left me alone if he kidnapped me?"

"Depends on what he threatened you with, honey."

"I'm fine, really."

Riley stabbed the half-omelet on the plate, and stared through her reflection at the highway. *This feels like a horrible dream. This is someone else's life. When do I get to wake up and go back to being me?*

She startled when Dad plopped himself down.

"What's got you so jumpy?"

"They didn't think I was too skinny. They thought you kidnapped me."

"Well, I suppose I did. Not like you wanted to leave home." He offered a wistful smile.

"I didn't want Mom to die." Riley pushed her plate away. Her father gave her a scolding look until she got up and moved around to sit next to him. "You're still my dad."

He put an arm around her and kissed the side of her head. She leaned against him and finished her lunch, wondering if her future might not totally suck.

8

HOMESICK

The view outside the truck seemed like something from another planet. Aside from small tufts of brush, Riley hadn't seen anything green for what felt like an eternity. Last night's motel stop hadn't left much of an imprint upon her memory. Exhaustion finally caught up to her and sent her tumbling into sleep. Per a short guy with massive eyebrows and a tweed blazer behind the front desk—who had been *way* too chipper for 7 a.m.—the place had offered complimentary breakfast: cold eggs and rock-hard bacon.

Dad kept quiet for most of the morning, though he did smile more in the past four hours than he'd done in two weeks. She craned her neck to look at the horizon, glancing right, straight ahead, and out his window. Everything was the same—flat open nothing with a single line of road. Riley spent a moment admiring her father's profile and six-day beard. He didn't seem as creepy as when she'd first seen him. Enough of his little habits rang true in her memory to tamp down her weak sense of unease. The way he held his mug, the way he hunched ever so slightly forward in his seat, and his aversion to loud noise all seemed 'right.'

Riley pulled her right foot up onto the seat and let her cheek rest against her knee. Her flip-flop fell off. She brushed her fingers over her toenails; the glittery blue paint reminded her Mom hadn't been gone that long. Heaviness settled in her chest, though she didn't cry.

Everything outside looked the same, save for the distant haze of a couple of mountains along the horizon. Miles and miles of rolling pale sand covered with a haze of short green scrub brush stretched into the distance. She closed her eyes and tried to remember the sound of her mother's voice. Somewhere on her phone or laptop, she had a couple of videos she'd taken of Mom. At least two were from birthday parties, and one had been her attempt to prove to Mom she drank too much. For a moment, Riley thought about deleting that one when she could, but changed her mind. Any memory of Mom was a memory she wanted to keep—even an unflattering one.

A little past noon, they passed a brown sign bearing the words, 'Elephant Butte Lake State Park.' Riley couldn't help herself and giggled. Less than twenty minutes later, Dad took an off ramp labeled 'Truth or Consequences' soon after an overpass.

"Gee, that doesn't sound ominous at all." Riley stretched.

The truck shuddered as they slowed and went around a giant rightward turning circle that let them out on a smaller two-lane road. Off to the right, traces of civilization poked up out of the desert. Closest was a large building she assumed to be a hotel, rectangular with large square windows and bands of brown. When they passed in front of it, she smirked at the Holiday Inn logo.

"I wonder if their beds are any more comfortable than the boards we've been sleeping on."

"You'll be in your own bed tonight." Dad smiled. "Won't be much longer now. Just gotta cut out onto 51 East through Las Cerezas."

"Geez, they have Walmarts here?" Riley pointed at a sign passing on the right.

He laughed. "Yes, Riley… Civilization *has* penetrated the desert."

They stopped at a Chevron to top off the tank and feed it some antifreeze and wiper fluid. As grungy as she felt in the same clothes she'd worn the whole trip, her surroundings were a far cry from Menlo Park Mall or anywhere anyone she knew would see her. No one here seemed to notice or care she felt frumpy.

Riley kept quiet as they headed south along a relatively large main road and hooked a left onto 51. Everything seemed so wide open; the mountains in the background still felt *weird*. Home had so many trees and so many people packed in tight, seeing this much space between buildings kept her staring around like a tourist. Most of the buildings were only one story and wide. Shops had strange names, chains that didn't exist in the east. A square house covered in multicolored stone passed on the right, a picnic table in front and a large blue plastic playground to the right. Riley made a face; it looked like people randomly built structures here and there. To her Jersey eyes, most of them looked ramshackle, as if a stiff storm would knock them down. A moment later, a tiny white house passed on the left, shingles peeling from the roof, windows broken and boarded.

Why did Dad take me here? Everything's falling apart.

Homesickness hit hard again, and she wondered what was going on inside Mom's house. Were people looking at it now? Was someone walking around in *her* bedroom at that very minute? The idea of *other people* being in *her* house brought sorrow and anger in equal parts. Riley narrowed her eyes. Dad said he'd give her any money the sale produced. She'd let it sit in the bank until she could use it to buy Mom's house back. Another four years, and she'd be eighteen, and no one could tell her where she could live.

Yeah, right. She let her head fall back against the seat. *I'd need a job good enough to pay taxes. I'm never gonna be able to go home again.* Quiet tears slipped out of her eyes.

"Riley?" asked Dad. "You okay?"

"Homesick," she muttered.

"A house is just a pile of wood. A home is everything inside, all the memories. Memories you can take with you wherever you go."

"Okay, fortune cookie." She chuckled and wiped her eyes.

"You know, it might be better for you to be away from there anyway. Everything would remind you of Mom."

"What about stability of a familiar environment?" She crossed her arms over her chest. "I gotta deal with Mom"—she still couldn't say dying —"and, um, now I'm out in the middle of nowhere." She sighed and let her arms fall to her sides. "Sorry. You didn't have to take me in. I shouldn't be ungrateful."

"You're wrong, Riley. I had to. I... You would've been happier with your mother, but we are still family."

"Is it true what you said? You never divorced Mom?"

"Yep. We didn't have *issues*. I just wanted to protect you two."

"KGB assassins coming after us?" She suppressed the urge to roll her eyes.

"Doubtful." Before Riley could smile, he continued in a scary-serious tone. "They're too busy right now with the situation in the Ukraine. I'm a mid-level programmer working on missile guidance routines and some encryption stuff for communication satellites deemed 'nonsecure.' I'm not a high value target to them. The threat is really from extremist cells from the Middle East and unstable regimes like Korea, and that whole Middle East mess, and I don't think God even knows what the hell Putin will do next."

She stared at him for a long minute in silence. *Holy shit.*

"Sorry, hon. I've been trying not to scare you, but you keep asking."

Route 51 snaked out of Truth or Consequences heading east. Large hills passed on either side, feeling a bit like they drove through a canyon. About thirty-five minutes out of the city, a tiny town sprang up around the road. One hand-painted sign read, 'Welcome to Las Cerezas.' Aside from a scattered number of private homes, she spotted a hardware store, a mechanic's garage named Lonnie's with a couple of Harley Davidson bikes clustered by the door, two churches, a couple of empty-looking warehouses, a Hernandez Grocery, and a place that looked like a restaurant with a fading sign over the door calling it Tommy's. A slim one-lane dirt road curved around behind the hills to the south toward the hint of a trailer park in the desert.

"Are you sure this is considered civilization? I think there were more kids in my class last year than people live in this town."

Dad smiled, though he didn't say a word. A handful of pedestrians paused to stare at them as they passed. Most gave off a 'what are they doing here' vibe that left her feeling uncomfortable. One guy slapped his friend on the arm and pointed. As soon as the other man spun around, he too shot them a suspicious glower.

"What's up with them?" Riley made eye contact with a tall, fat man in a cowboy hat, who shook his head.

"The place is a bit insular, hon. Don't take it personally. They don't like outsiders. I've lived here for almost five years now, and they still treat me like a foreigner."

As if inspired by a sudden muse, Dad took a hard right. The truck lurched over a bump as it entered the parking lot of Tommy's.

"It's almost one; we haven't eaten. Hungry?"

"Is this the only restaurant here?" She looked around again. "What kind of food do they even serve? The place looks like a roach factory."

"Mexican stuff or burgers, mostly." He got out. "None of that su-chee stuff you like."

She exaggerated a sigh, and shoved her door open. "You seriously want to eat here?"

Tommy's Restaurant was bigger inside than it looked from the outside. One long, rectangular room held a bar on the left and a number of battered tables covered in wood-patterned Formica on the right. The place smelled of beer and refried beans, but the spice in the air was not at all what she expected—it smelled appetizing.

"Geez," she whispered. "These chairs look like they stole them from a pizza joint."

Dad didn't wait for anyone to seat them; he wandered to a random table and fell into a chair. Riley followed. The occasional whiff of wet wood broke through the scent of food. Dad absentmindedly picked at a metal bucket of peanuts in the middle of the table, flicking his gaze back and forth from a short, stocky dark-skinned man behind the bar to the front door. Tiny red dots spotted the bartender's puffy cheeks. He smiled at Riley from across the room, but gave her father a wary squint.

She slumped her weight onto her elbows, staring at an unlit candle embedded in a red glass shaped like an avocado.

"Afternoon."

Riley jumped at the deep voice coming from her left. A boy who couldn't have been eighteen yet set a menu on the table and smiled at them. He looked as tall as Dad, with high cheekbones and straight, black hair down to his waist. A stained towel hung over the front of his blue jeans, and assorted kitchen stains marked an otherwise plain white tee shirt.

"Uh, hi," she said.

Dad pushed the menu to her. "Inferno burger for me."

The boy grinned at Riley. "He thinks we only make one thing."

Riley gripped the seat on either side, overcome with sudden concern for how she probably looked... and smelled.

The waiter turned the menu to face her and opened it. "Need a sec? You don't look like you've been here before."

She stared at him for a full minute. "No. First time."

Two men at a table in the back muttered at each other between looks at her father.

"Welcome to Tommy's." He smiled. "I'm Kieran."

"Riley." She scanned the menu. "Uh, whatever Dad got."

"You sure you want that?" Dad raised an eyebrow. "It's very spicy, and I didn't think you ate beef."

"Oh." She smirked at the menu. "I like everything, except tako."

"Since you're living here, hon, you'd better get used to the concept." Dad poked a finger at the menu. "Half the menu is tacos."

"No, Dad. Tako. T-a-k-o. It's sushi for octopus."

Kieran grimaced.

Riley stuck her tongue out. "Yeah, it's nasty. Chicken tacos, I guess."

"Okay. Drinks?"

"Is the water safe here?" asked Riley.

"Corona for me. Yes, the water's safe. We're still in the United States."

Kieran grinned at her, lingering for a moment before walking off to the kitchen.

"And you thought you'd have a problem making friends here." Dad leaned back in his chair.

Riley's face got warm. "Dad…"

"You're blushing. Maybe more than friends."

If she had a sweatshirt on, she'd have pulled it up over her head. She shrank over the table. "Not funny."

"Beware of anyone too friendly too fast." Dad leaned in close. "Anyone might be trying to get to you to get to my work."

"Seriously?" She looked up from her folded arms. "He's what, seventeen? You think he's a spy?"

"I don't know. Better to be careful until you do." Serious Dad relaxed to Smiling Dad. "So, you like him?"

"Dad!" Riley lowered her voice to a whisper. "I like, *just* saw him. Geez." *He did smile at me. Hasn't called me stick-girl yet.*

Kieran returned with a huge plastic cup of ice water and a Corona in the bottle for Dad. Blood rushed to her cheeks when he got close, and she refused to look up at him. She traced her finger along the pattern of fake wood grain in the tabletop.

"Food'll be out in a few minutes," said Kieran.

"Thanks." Dad leaned closer to her, lowering his voice… a little. "Looks like I skip right to the hard part of having a daughter."

Riley waited for the waiter to walk away. "Huh?"

"Fighting off the boys lining up at the door."

He did not just say that. "Dad!"

No boys had yet paid much attention to the gamer geek with zero shape, and the ones who did only wanted to tease her because they thought she starved herself.

Minutes later, she looked up when a plate slid in front of her. It smelled so much better than anything she'd touched in days. Her mouth watered despite the fumes from Dad's burger burning her eyes.

"Let me know if you need anything else."

She forgot all about feeling weird in his presence and grabbed one of the tacos from her plate. The chicken bits inside looked hand-cut.

"Wow, this smells so good." She took a huge bite.

"My mother and aunt do most of the cooking," said Kieran.

Riley didn't want to rush herself, and made him wait until she finished chewing. "Your parents work here?"

"They own the place."

He's still here. "Oh, uh, that's cool, I guess."

"Gonna be here long?" He seemed immune to Dad's piercing glare.

"Kinda, yeah."

"Hey, Kieran," yelled one of the men in the back, waving an empty beer bottle. "Need another one."

The boy smiled. "Nice meeting you." He pulled his hair off his face and jogged over to the bar.

"I want you to be comfortable talking to me, Riley. I'd prefer you wait until you were eighteen; but if you decide to have sex, I'd rather you do it safely rather than sneaking around behind my back."

Riley discovered that chicken tacos weren't too easy to breathe. When she stopped coughing, she hid her face in her arms, wanting to crawl under the table and disappear. She couldn't look at Dad. She couldn't look at the room.

"Riley?"

"You did *not* just say that."

"I didn't mean to sound like I don't trust you; I just wanted you to know that you can tell me anything."

She huddled there for a few minutes listening to Dad eat. When the smell of her food got to her, she sat up, still bright red. He continued munching on his burger as though he hadn't said the single most awkward, embarrassing thing she'd ever heard. After a few more bites of the chicken taco, she lost herself in it. Salsa with a hint of lime juice and garlic made her forget his lack of tact as she devoured *real* food. At least, until Kieran walked back over with another glass of water. She went rigid, staring at the mess of uneaten lettuce upon which the tacos had perched.

"Wow, those tacos never had a chance." He winked at her, and looked at Dad. "Another Corona?"

"No, thanks. Gotta drive. I'll have a water too."

She kept her gaze down as Dad finished eating, sucked down his water, and handed Kieran some cash. Riley got up and followed him to the door, feeling Kieran's eyes on her. She peeked up through a curtain of light brown hair, catching sight of his smile as he collected the dirty dishes. The look on his face seemed welcoming and curious, and made Dad's earlier comment all the more embarrassing.

Fearing he may have heard it, she scurried out to the truck and got in.

"I can't believe you said that." She glared at him. "I've never even had a boyfriend."

"It's okay if you like girls."

"Dad!" she screamed. "What is your fixation with sex?"

He started the truck. "I'm not fixating. I'm being realistic. You're almost to that age where you're going to get curious about certain things and—"

"Oh, my God, will you *stop!*"

"Okay, okay." He pulled back out onto the road. "I won't say another word about it, but if you ever want to talk about anything—"

"Dad!"

He chuckled.

Riley fumed in silence as he drove past the last of the buildings in Las Cerezas. About a half-mile east of the little town, he turned left. The truck bounced along a dirt path closer to tire ruts in the desert than an actual roadway. Metal clanking coming from the back made her worry the trailer would pop off. A few utility poles ran along the side, carrying a single wire out across the desert. He slowed to about fifteen mph. Six minutes before 2 p.m., a lone one-story house slipped into view past a hill on the left, clad in chestnut-brown siding brushed with dust. Dark rectangular panels covered almost every usable inch of roof, except for where a pair of small satellite dishes perched. A rusted wind chime made of brass pipes and a wooden disc dangled from a metal strut to the left of the only visible door. The area around the place was flat sand, except for a covered well to the left.

"Dad..."

"Welcome home, Riley."

"Seriously?" She leaned forward in the seat, gawking. "You live out in the middle of nowhere. I can't even *see* neighbors."

"You don't have to worry about making noise after 10 p.m. at least." He winked. "I like the quiet out here."

Great. I managed to make one friend in a state where two hundred people live for every hundred square feet. This is going to suck.

"This place has a real toilet at least, right? Not like an outhouse with ass-biting spiders?"

Dad pulled up out front and cut the engine. "Nope. Just pee on the ground anywhere outside. I keep the TP under the big bush there."

Her jaw dropped.

"There's a shovel on the back wall for number two. Better to bury that in shallow holes. In five years, I've only had one person drive by at an awkward moment."

She gaped at him, horrified. *H-he's not serious.* Her lip quivered as warmth spread over her cheeks.

For the first time since she'd re-met him, Dad burst out laughing. She scrunched her look of shock into a playful-angry glower and slapped at him. He caught her in a partial headlock and held her arms against her chest, trapping her. She squirmed in a half-hearted attempt to escape. After she gave up, they grinned at each other.

"I'm kidding."

She slid out of the truck and made her way to the front door, waiting for Dad to catch up and unlock it. Beyond a small foyer, the living room lay in bachelor-pad shambles. A sand-brown sofa sat facing a tiny flat panel TV, barely thirty inches, tuned to CNN with a picture-in-picture on Fox news. Text scrolling along the bottom appeared to be closed-captioning for Fox, while the CNN anchor had the audio. To the left, the room opened to a modest kitchen without much of a separation. At the end of the kitchen counter, a doorway led to what looked like a bedroom. Sand-brown paint covered the walls, white on the ceiling. The overwhelming smell of paper hung in the air.

The right side of the main space appeared as though the builder intended it to be a dining room, though Dad had set up a folding table, covered in strange tools and bottles of what appeared to be oil. Small two-inch square cloth pads were everywhere. Beyond the 'dining room,' another hallway led to the right side of the house, with three doors and two closets. The last door at the end was open, revealing a bathroom decorated in desert browns and brick red.

"Pick whatever room you want from those three." Dad headed right for the little TV. "Since we brought Mom's big ol' set, I'll move this one to my room."

She paced through the house, looking around at a mess that would've sent Mom into involuntary convulsions. At least it was all inorganic clutter: fiction novels, historical books about military intelligence operations, a scattering of DVDs with handwritten labels, stacks of papers and cardboard boxes, obsolete tech—and nothing molding or stinking. Her flip-flops popped against her soles as she walked to the first hallway door. The room beyond had the dimensions of a bedroom, painted beige, but it was crammed full of more cardboard boxes. She pulled the door closed and checked the next one. The front-corner room was a little larger, but Dad had piled a mountain of old computer parts, and yet more boxes of paper in it.

"Pack rat much, Dad?" *Geez, he should be on Hoarders.*

She spun on her heel and checked the lone door on the inside wall. The last bedroom was mercifully free of a mountain of junk. The only furniture consisted of a steel folding chair upon which sat a spiral-bound notebook. Papers hung all over the coffee-colored walls, covered in scrawled writing around pictures of men in military uniforms. Some of the photos showed buildings, aircraft, or locations in other countries. Curiosity took her, and she approached the nearest wall. The writing looked like notes of dates, times, and troop movements as well as comments about possible threats to US personnel, and locations of 'asset sightings.' A few pictures had lines traced to them from frightening remarks such as 'compromised,' 'neutralized,' or 'lost contact.'

"Riley!" yelled Dad. He rushed in and grabbed her shoulder, a look of wild fury in his eyes. "What are you doing in here?"

"Uh." She held her hands up. "You said pick a room... I was looking."

"Oh. Right." The urgency in his expression lessened. "I'm, uh..." He took a few breaths and loosened his grip. "Sorry I scared you. This is top-secret stuff. Colonel Bering would not be happy if he found out you saw it. One of my software projects is something to help the NSA track certain individuals across the globe, with the eventual goal of predicting their movements."

She looked down, shivering. "Dad, I didn't know."

"It's okay... I should've said something. You had no way to know. Look, just don't tell anyone about this stuff, okay? It could get people killed."

"There's so much crap in the other rooms." She fidgeted.

"Damn. Good point. Okay, I'll move this. Go on and start unloading the truck with the critical stuff. Leave anything you want me to carry." He spun around, appraising the charts. "I'll get this crap out of your room."

She hugged him. Losing Mom, losing her friend, losing her whole life crashed into the strange feeling of getting her father back, even if he did live in the middle of nowhere and had scary super-secret stuff all over his walls. Riley held on to him for a few minutes before she plodded back outside, keys in hand, and opened the padlock from the U-Haul trailer. The air that came out smelled like Mom's house and got her tears flowing. For a long time, she stared at the bits and pieces of her former world, until the desert air washed away the familiar scent.

She carried box after box into the house, dropping her stuff in her new room and the ones from everywhere else in the corner bedroom where all the computer crap was, since it had more space; Mom's stuff could stay packed for now. Dad's house didn't have anywhere good to unbox it, and she would never forgive herself if anything broke.

Hours later, all the sensitive information was gone, leaving only a few pushpins stuck in the drywall as well as some scraps of Scotch tape. She frowned at the black marker writing on the cardboard around her: Xbox games, books, clothes, Xbox stuff, more clothes, Anime, Movies, and one box labeled in all caps, 'Dad, do not open!'

My underwear.

It occurred to her she'd been wearing the same undies for four days. She closed her eyes and imagined the bathroom back home, the last shower she'd ever taken at the house in which she'd grown up. She sat on a box of books, rested her head on her knees, and cried. Riley hated it here. She hated the desert, the strange, angry people that stared at her, and how far away she was from everything comfortable and safe.

Why did Mom have to die?

A presence at the door signaled Dad's approach, but he backed away without saying a word.

"What?" She sniffled.

"You okay? I was going to suggest we get your bed out of the trailer first. There's a storage place in T or C where we can put your mother's. Figure I'd run over there tomorrow on the way to drop the trailer off."

It's better than foster care. "Yeah. Just thought of Mom again."

"C'mere." He held his arms out.

She walked into an embrace, sniffling. "Why'd you have to live at the ass end of nowhere?"

"You hate it here." He patted her on the back.

"Yeah, maybe I do a little"—she closed her eyes—"but I don't hate you."

A WHOLE LOT OF NOTHING

A shower and clean clothes made Riley feel human again. Despite the clutter, Dad's house felt newer than home, as if built within the past ten years. The bathroom was clean and far neater than she'd thought possible for a man living alone. The bathtub had sliding glass partition instead of a curtain, and one of those pulsating water jet heads with the long extension hose. Her new bedroom sat catty-corner to the shower, requiring only one step in the hallway to dart between them.

With her game posters on the walls, her bed beneath her, and the familiar glow of Xbox controllers charging up, she could almost imagine herself in her own bedroom again. It surprised her how cool it got at night; she'd expected to roast since Dad didn't have air conditioning in the place. *Is he stingy, or are we poor?* Despite it being late June, it got rather chilly: 48-degrees according to the thermometer in the hallway. Wrapped in flannel pajamas, she snuggled under the covers and tried to believe nothing had happened. In a few hours, Mom would come wake her up for breakfast.

A LOUD NOISE BROKE THE VEIL OF SLEEP, AS IF SOMEONE DRAGGED something heavy across the roof, scraping it. She sat up, squinting at the window. Morning was well underway, judging by the amount of light.

The noise grew louder, morphing into the recognizable sound of jet engines as her brain edged closer to being awake.

She crept to the window and peered up. Eight large airplanes with military silhouettes left cottony contrails across an otherwise cloudless blue sky in a straight, boring line. At a guess, they were green or black with swept wings that looked like they could swivel.

As far as she could see behind the house, the same flat open nothingness ran to the edge of the world. Off to the right a bit, a shallow ravine and some faint hills broke up the barrenness, but otherwise she might as well be the last person on Earth.

Riley crawled back onto her bed, after fishing her iPhone out of the jean shorts she handled with fingertips. "Ugh, forget washing these... I should burn them." She clicked the power button, but the stone dead phone didn't even display a red battery. "Dammit. Where did I put the cord?"

A short search of her room came to an unsuccessful end. She slipped on a clean pair of shorts before daring to open the door, and scurried down the hall to the bathroom. Afterwards, she wandered the house, finding no trace of Dad. She leaned against the doorjamb of the master bedroom, peering at the darkness inside. Heavy blackout curtains covered the windows; the only light came from a weak, flickering computer monitor next to three stacked PCs, and the dial of an old radio tuned to an AM news station currently dissecting some judicial confirmation hearing. A small bookshelf had been pulled from the wall, likely when he crawled in to find the line for the TV. Riley stared at an upside down book with a picture of two 'greys'—aliens with black, almond-shaped eyes. She twisted to get a look at the title. *The Conspiracy of Control.* A line along the bottom claimed the book proved the government created 'UFO hysteria' as a tool.

She whistled and edged to the computer, nudging the mouse. The screen lit up with a picture of Riley younger, grinning like an idiot in a royal blue one-piece swimsuit. She remembered the day Mom took the photo. She'd been eleven and on her way to Amber's for a pool party. Tears gathered in the corners of her eyes. Seconds later, the image changed to another shot of her at nine outside in the snow. Her legs gave out and she fell into his chair. Image after image flipped by. The oldest had to have been only weeks after he left. The most recent showed her dressed up as Hermione Granger from Halloween 2015, shoulder to shoulder with Amber's Catwoman. *Months ago. Mom took these pictures.*

After some time, the screen went black again, offering the feeble grey light of a blank screen.

"Dad?" She crept across the kitchen to the back door. Hot, dry air blasted her when she slid the glass aside and stepped out onto dusty patio stones that cooked her bare feet. She looked left and right at lots of not-Dad. A peak in the rumble made her squint at the sky toward the still-audible sound of jets. "Dad?"

Riley made her way to the front door, finding the truck gone. *He must've gone to town to rent that storage space. Why'd he leave me here alone? I'd have gone with him.* She backed inside, and caught her blurry reflection in Mom's TV. *When did he bring that in?* It had looked a little small at *home*, but here it seemed massive. She debated bringing the Xbox out to the living room. Mom never let her hook it up because she did not want to have to argue a teenaged daughter off the TV when she wanted to watch her shows.

Not like that was a problem now.

Having it in her room also let her stay up late online with Amber without getting yelled at.

Dad probably wouldn't care.

She paced in a circle around the sofa, arguing with herself if it would be disrespectful to Mom to defy her and use the big screen for games. Riley stopped and fell seated on the cushions. She didn't really even feel like looking at the Xbox, much less playing it. If she hadn't been so focused on getting online as fast as possible to hang out with Amber, maybe her Mom would've lived. If she had been more insistent about calling Dr. Gest… Riley slipped over on her side and curled up. If nothing else, at least she would have had a few more minutes with her before…

She hugged a small throw pillow to her chest and cried.

———

DAD STOMPING IN THE FRONT DOOR WOKE HER UP. HE KICKED DIRT OFF HIS boots and smiled at her when she popped up to peer at him over the sofa back.

"Hey, Sweetie."

"Hey," she muttered. "Um, Dad?"

He paused in his beeline for the kitchen to look at her. "Yeah?"

"You left me here alone."

He pressed fists into his hips, pondering. "Well, you are fourteen, right? I trust you for a few hours."

"What if I don't wanna be alone?"

"Oh." Dad let his arms hang slack. "That didn't even occur to me. Uh, sorry. You looked like you needed the sleep, so I didn't want to bug you."

Her eyebrows drifted together. "What time did you leave?"

"About zero-six-hundred," said Dad, heading for the kitchen.

She twisted on one knee, facing him as he passed. "Is that six a.m.?"

"Yep."

"We were up till stupid o'clock unpacking. How the hell did you wake up so damn early?"

He grabbed two cans from a cabinet in the kitchen and opened them, speaking with his back to her. "Practice. Lunch?"

"I didn't have breakfast."

"It's almost noon, hon."

She wandered to the kitchen table and sat on one of the hard wooden chairs. Elbow up, head against her bicep, she traced one finger over the possibly fake wood grain pattern in the basic Ikea table until the microwave beeped. A few seconds later, Dad set a bowl of SpaghettiOs in front of her and put another one in for himself.

Riley pushed the glop around with a spoon. "Again? We had this for dinner last night."

Two minutes later, Dad joined her at the table and dug right in. "I know."

"Guess you're not much for cooking?"

He pointed at a small cabinet freezer in the back corner of the kitchen. "Got some deer, jackrabbit, and... whatever that other critter was in there. Figured you wouldn't want it."

Riley shivered.

"My cooking is pretty much meat, salt, heat, done." He smiled. "Sometimes, smoke is involved."

She ate one spoonful, thinking back to the last meal Mom had cooked for them. Salmon, asparagus, potatoes... real food. Her throat constricted and the corners of her eyes got warm. Riley held in the urge to cry as a dozen different recipes danced around in her mind. Somehow, in flagrant disregard of her horrible, stressful job, Mom adored cooking. She never just 'nuked something,' no matter how worn out she was. Well, not since Riley hit about twelve. When she was little, the occasional micro-meal happened during bouts of the flu or extreme circumstance. Lately, Riley had taken over cooking if Mother had been too drained.

"Dad?"

He looked up.

"I saw your screensaver." *Do not cry.*

Guilt melted out of his face. "I… Sorry. You know I never stopped loving you."

"Messed up way to show it… running to New Mexico and never even calling." She sucked in a shuddering rush of air, fighting the urge to sob. "Mom sent you pics from every birthday."

"Riley—"

She frowned. "Top secret, yeah, I know."

Her spoon scraped at the bowl as she transferred the canned pasta from one side to the other. "I thought you hated us."

"No, Riley. I…" He stared at her, jaw trembling as if some great secret hammered at a stone wall inside his mind, threatening to crack it. "I was afraid."

"Afraid of what?" The dam broke. She looked away, sniveling. "Me?"

Dad glanced at his bedroom door. "Not now…"

"What." Riley wiped her tears and glared. "I don't hear anything."

"Shit." He jumped up, ran a splash of water around in his dish, and dropped it in the sink before rushing to his desk. She forced another spoonful of lameness down. Seconds later, his room brightened and the din of TV news muttered in the background.

Riley braced her head on one hand and stared into the orange miasma as if divining tea leaves. *Why does he keep running away from me?*

A few minutes of silence later, Dad spoke. "Yes, I'm here. Copy. Go ahead, sir."

Is that why he picked the middle of nothing to put his house? Riley traipsed over to his door. Dad sat on his computer chair in the corner with his back to her, a pair of military-style headphones on. He poked at buttons on a confusing green box covered in dials, markings, and funny protrusions, with what looked like a calculator in the middle of the front face. An odd-shaped cascade of text occupied the PC screen. *Programs look weird.*

"Assets Bravo-three-nine and Bravo-four-six confirmed in place. Last contact zero-five-fifteen this morning. Reports situation tenuous. Petulant Dragon unstable."

Riley put a hand over her heart, eyes widening. Some white-haired guy on CNN spoke about military demonstrations planned by the leader of North Korea. An older-sounding man's voice emanated from the AM radio, in the midst of a debate with a woman and two other men about the effects of another Korean war, and if the US should get involved. Whatever Dad was talking about sounded scary. She backed away and headed to the fridge, hunting for something other than SpaghettiOs. Outside, the tan appliance looked in decent shape. Inside, it broke her heart. Its only contents were a pair of Corona bottles and half a lime that looked like an experiment in home freeze-drying.

She shut the door with a sigh. *That's what I was expecting.* On tiptoe, she reached up to the cabinets above the coffee machine, grabbing a tiny doorknob in each hand and pulling.

Every inch of usable space had been packed full of SpaghettiOs cans. The next pair of cabinet doors to the left revealed the same sight.

"Whoa." She blinked. "Unreal."

"Dad?" she half-yelled.

"I understand, sir, but the Russians have rolled in some kind of ELF jammer near Odessa, and there's some unusual activity going on near Belgorod. One moment, Colonel." His chair creaked. "Yes, hon?"

"Your cabinet is full of Spag-Os. Do you have any real food?"

"Look under the sink." A loud *creak* came from his chair. "No word back from Charlie-Ten. Last contact was four days ago from Seoul. He may have been compromised."

Riley squatted and swung open the lower cabinet doors, finding them stuffed with packets of Ramen instant noodles in shrink-wrapped wholesale boxes. "Oh, hell no."

She closed the doors without saying another word, trying not to listen too closely to Dad talking about 'assets' and 'deteriorating situations.' It might've been bland, but the tepid bowl of SpaghettiOs had been her father's attempt to take care of her. She picked at it until he got quiet.

Ten minutes later, when he hadn't emerged from his room, Riley got up and clung to the doorjamb again, peering inside. He'd taken off the headset, holding it in his lap like a pet cat. Most of the color had drained from his face, and he stared at the blank computer screen. Something about his presence made her worry the tiniest sound would scare the hell out of him.

Seeing her formerly stoic Dad terrified got her heart pumping by proxy. He'd gone through the entire funeral and estate paperwork without much of any visible emotion. She could sense the hurt inside him when he held her; as he said, some men didn't show their heart to the world, which made this all the more frightening.

"Dad?" she whispered.

He turned his head toward her, eyes vacant and unfocused, as if he didn't know who she was. His hand slipped under some papers on his desk, grasping something.

"Daddy?"

The look in his eyes—no recognition—scared her mouth dry. She stared at him for a moment afraid to move or even blink.

"Riley." Some color flowed back into his cheeks. His eyes fluttered in a series of rapid blinks, and he let his arm drop to his lap. "The last status report wasn't good. Probably sounded worse than it is."

"What was that?" She placed a tentative foot out the doorway. "Are you okay?"

Dad waved her over. "It's okay. Bad news from my boss is all. We have men in place keeping tabs on erratic regimes, and a few of them have fallen off the face of the Earth. Usually, that means they've been compromised and are either dead or running."

She crept up to him as if the carpet had been seeded with land mines. By the time she got close enough for him to put an arm around her, she trembled.

"Don't be scared. It's thousands of miles away from here. I'm not sure POTUS will commit to anything military even if the Russians overstep. The Ukraine isn't our fight."

"What's a poetus?"

He chuckled. "It's an acronym for 'president of the United States.'"

Who talks like that? Riley bit her lip. "Dad, you've got a kitchen full of canned pasta and ramen noodles. No wonder you're a skeleton. You need to buy some real food. I'll cook."

"There's probably about twenty pounds of meat in the deep freezer."

Riley squirmed. "Eww, Dad. I'm not eating rabbit. They're cute."

He exhaled, seeming like his old, stoic self again. "I'm not fond of going to town. Once or twice a week for a burger at Tommy's is my limit. You saw how they looked at us. If you weren't born in the area, they don't want to associate with you."

"You can't call what you have out there food."

Dad made a noncommittal face. "It's what I have."

"I'll go. I sorta know how to drive. Mom let me practice in the bank lot a few times."

"A Sentra's a bit different than a truck; besides, I need to stay close to the radio for a day or two."

She tapped her toe on the carpet. "We need real food. If you don't wanna go to town, let me. Come on, it's all flat. Not like there's anything to hit."

"You're too young."

"I can reach the pedals just fine if I scoot the seat forward."

He leaned back, drawing a creak from the chair spring. "You don't know your way around."

"It's an L. Down the road from the house, turn right, and there's that little grocery shop thing. There aren't even any cops out here."

"Let me think about it. I don't want you getting hurt."

"Come on." She pulled on his arm, trying to get him out of the chair. "I'll drive a bit in circles around the house so you see I can do it."

He grabbed her in a tight hug, sniffling into the crook of her neck. Riley went stiff from shock at the sudden reaction.

"Uh, Dad?"

The upwelling of emotion lasted less than a minute. He let go of her, got up, and grabbed his keys from behind the old keyboard. "You remind me so much of Lily... when she got an idea in her head."

Riley stood in place, stunned as he walked outside. She wasn't sure if she should feel happy for talking him into letting her drive, or give in to the overwhelming need to mope about Mom.

"You coming?" he yelled.

"Yeah." She looked down at her flip-flops, considering the sneakers in her room. *Screw it; it's hot.*

SMALL TOWN DOUBTS

R iley scratched the sole of her right foot on the corner of the brake, waiting for Dad to make up his mind. After seven loops around the house, she'd gotten the jerkiness out of her braking. If she was going to ding a fender, better Dad's 98 Silverado than Mom's 2014 Sentra… if it ever showed up. She hooked all ten toes over the brake pedal and smirked at the dust-covered console. It wasn't *too* high, but a cop would probably pull her over for being suspiciously short.

"This is a bad idea," said Dad.

"So is eating SpaghettiOs for breakfast, lunch, and dinner."

"Why'd you take your flops off?" He raised an eyebrow. "Sometimes I'll bag a jackrabbit or a deer if they wander far enough. There's food."

Riley shrugged, pushing them around the floor with her big toe. "Mom said something about cops can give you a ticket for driving in them… get snagged on the pedals or something."

"Probably not a great idea to drive barefoot either."

"Or without a license." She grinned. "It's not too late to take over."

"If things were normal, I would, but…" Dad looked out the passenger window at the desert. "Any minute now, Colonel Bering might comm in and I have to be here. Bad things are on the horizon. If I miss a message, people could die."

Riley sighed. "If I eat another bowl of SpaghettiOs, people could die."

"I'm serious, Squirrel."

Her lips curled as if to growl at that damn name, but she held it back. Real food hinged on her winning this debate, and hurting his feelings wouldn't help that cause. She looked over at him, her throat tightening at the unusual pallor in his cheeks. His eyes had glazed over, as if the Grim Reaper himself stood in front of the truck.

"Okay. I'll go."

"Straight to Las Cerezas and back. Don't stop anywhere else. Don't talk to anyone, especially cops, and go put on real shoes before you leave."

"Okay." She reached for the door handle. "Can I talk to the store clerk or do I have to mime?"

He blinked and looked at her as if she'd just spoken French. For all she knew, maybe Dad did speak French... since he seemed to work for Military Intelligence.

"Dad?" She waved past his eyes. "You okay?"

"Yep." Color returned to his cheeks as he smiled. "I really meant cops. If you get stopped, tell them you're fifteen and forgot your permit at home."

She reached down between her legs and picked up her flip-flops. "Lying to cops is a bad idea, Dad. Especially when they can catch me."

"The cops are the first ones they'd target. All that risk and stress for low pay. The people I work for operate at a different level than the rest of the citizens. We're not beholden to them, so don't give them any advantage over you. Any information you give a cop *could* wind up getting to the wrong people."

"Uh, right. Okay."

"I mean it, Squirrel." He grabbed her forearm, a little too tight. "We can't trust cops. Their job is to keep everyone compliant and docile. If the world was aware of just how close it was to destroying itself—that would be that. Everyone would lose their minds to anarchy."

"Dad... Ow, that hurts." She glanced at her arm.

"Mass chaos." He flinched as though he'd walked face-first into a spider web. His grip loosened. "Sorry. I'm... I'm just worried about you."

"What do you mean close to destruction?" She rubbed a red spot out of her forearm.

"We're one maniac away from a new stone age. That's what we're all working to prevent." He ducked forward to peer up at the sky. "You better go soon. Permit drivers have to be off the road before sundown."

They got out at the same time; Dad headed for his room while Riley went right. After a brief stop to get sneakers, she ran back to the truck.

Five minutes later, she psyched herself up enough to turn the key. Drive engaged, she spun the wheel—and froze when Dad came running over waving his arms. Riley jammed both feet on the brake and whirled left and right, looking for what she was about to run over.

"Hey!" Dad jogged up to the driver's side window. "Might help to have some money with you."

"Oh." She exhaled through fluttering lips. "Duh, that would've sucked to figure out at the store."

Dad handed her $60, shot a guilty glance at the road, and patted the door. "Be safe, okay?"

"You sure this is cool?" She wrung her hands on the wheel, yelping when the truck moved. *Put it in park!* "I feel like I'm doing something wrong."

"Yeah. It's a straight line, nice weather, and you're fighting a one-teenager crusade against canned pasta."

Riley sat motionless, watching Dad head back into the house. He paused at the door, glancing back as if debating with himself. After a weak smile, he slipped out of sight.

"Okay, Mom. If you're watching over me… I could use a copilot about now."

She dropped the truck in gear and pulled out, bouncing along the faint dirt road back toward NM 51, which she reached about twenty minutes later. At least the directions were simple. A single right turn would take her to her destination. One could see the entire town at once, so getting lost couldn't happen.

On the way west, she got up to eighty before realizing it and hit the brakes hard enough to jerk forward in the seat. Shaking, she let the truck creep back from forty up to sixty. Going too slow would attract suspicion, going too fast would attract the police—if there even were any here.

About fifteen minutes later, she rolled into Las Cerezas. The place didn't even have a traffic light. Figuring people would recognize Dad's truck, and wanting to avoid awkward questions of the incriminating type, she pulled off onto a little side alley about a block from Hernandez Grocery, got out, and walked. She clutched her small purse to her side, clinging to it to stop from shaking. *Rile, what the hell are you doing driving without a license? You don't even jaywalk.*

Despite the rough exterior, the inside of the shop surprised her with its modernity as well as cleanliness. It reminded her a bit of a Wawa, way too small to be a supermarket, but too big to be a convenience store. She snagged a hand basket from a stack at the door and meandered around the shelves of six aisles, studying brands and tags, a lot of which she'd never seen before in Jersey. Fortunately, they had a respectable selection of fresh produce. One handwritten sign announced it arrived daily from T or C.

Riley trailed a hand along the produce cooler and walked the length, cornering at the back of the store where the meat and dairy items were. Two tall men in denim vests startled her to a halt. Both bore a dinner-plate sized picture of a 'biker dude' riding a wheeled scorpion. The one on the left looked at least six and a half feet tall, bald with a dense, curly beard. Above the picture on his vest, the word *Freebird* spread across a scroll. Between his thick arms and beer gut, he looked like a barrel on posts. Tattoos sleeved both arms. The other man had long hair under a red headband, mirrored sunglasses, and a massive knife on his belt. Both wore jeans and boots, and had wallets with dangling chains.

"Damn, this stuff's no good," said Freebird. "Gonna have to run inta town."

The shaggy one dropped a Styrofoam pack into the cooler with a meaty smack. "Yeah, li'l pricey too."

Riley backed away before they saw her, not wanting to know what a pair of big, scary bikers would do to her. As soon she had an aisle between her and them, she felt foolish; in all likelihood, they were only out looking for lunch. Dangerous badass bikers wouldn't go grocery shopping. Besides, Mom was the one who had a problem with tattooed men on motorcycles, especially the ones who loitered at the front of the bank. Riley sucked in a breath and walked back out into the open, passing them as if they were no different from a pair of schoolteachers. Neither paid her much attention.

Duh! I should get the chicken last. It needs to be in the fridge.

She ran back to the produce area and grabbed a sack of small potatoes and a couple onions. Based on what she'd seen on the shelves, most of the fancier things Mom's recipe book contained would be hard to pull off without a trip to the bigger city.

No way I'm gonna risk that. This was really stupid of me. She headed to the seasonings section looking for some kind of chicken or beef bouillon. Soup, stew, or chili she could make a big batch of and coast for a few days. *Hurry up. Faster I get home, the faster I won't get arrested.*

A pack of flour tortillas, a couple tomatoes, onions, and some chicken would be lunch later that week. She looked over the unfamiliar Mexican seasonings. *One way to figure it out, I guess. No way I'm driving to T or C for the fancy stuff. That place has cops.*

In her haste, she rounded the end of the aisle to the next, going for a loaf of wheat bread. At the unexpected sight of a Hispanic man in a dark blue police uniform, she skidded to a halt. *He knows.* She froze, staring at him as he surveyed the store's selection of jelly. He seemed a little younger and shorter than Dad, and a lot more muscular. In a sombrero and poncho, his face would seem friendly and whimsical; as it was, the sight of him almost stopped her heart cold.

A dense moustache wiggled on his upper lip as he picked up a jar of strawberry in one hand and grape in the other. For a moment, his eyes flicked back and forth between the two. As if sensing her guilt, he glanced at her, casually at first, then with a deliberate inquiring expression.

"Uh, hi," she mumbled, grabbing blind at the bread and stuffing a random loaf into her basket.

She backed out of the aisle the way she'd come in rather than walk past him, and went to the far wall by the cooler where cold air raised goose bumps on her bare thighs. Riley leaned over as if appraising the selection, but her brain had shut off. All the packets of various meats blurred into a smear of color. *He's going to come up and arrest me any second. I wonder how many years I'll get for driving without a license.* Her gaze fell to the basket. *Crap. White bread.*

Mom's voice rambled in her mind about how awful white bread was, how they bleach all the nutrition out of it. The memory reddened her eyes and set loose an exploratory tear. All she had to do was wait for the cop to leave and she could trade it for wheat. *Act casual.*

She moved along the case, walking through a waterfall of frozen air. She didn't recognize any of the brand names, but they did have chicken breasts. Riley selected the least expensive pack and added it to her basket.

"Is everything okay?"

Riley jumped and whirled to face the source of the voice—the cop. Her gaze darted to the nametag: Rodriguez, his badge, his gun, and settled on the handcuffs on his belt. Her arms trembled, rustling her collection of groceries. Her brain teased the sensation of cold steel sliding around her wrists.

Dad doesn't want me talking to the cops. She swallowed hard. *Crap. I can't just stare at him.* "Yes, sir."

Officer Rodriguez looked her up and down. "You sure? You look upset."

I'm fine, Officer. No big deal. I'm crying over my dead mother and about to piss myself because I'm afraid you'll arrest me for driving illegally. "Yes, sir."

"I don't think I've seen you before…"

"Riley." *Nooo. Dad said not to give them any information.*

"Hello, Riley. I'm Sergeant Rodriguez."

"Hi." She clenched her jaw as the frigid meat cooler touched the back of her legs.

His moustache widened with a genuine smile. "You're Christopher's daughter, right?"

Oh, damn. He's not after me. Her trembles deepened as she gazed into his brown eyes, expecting suspicion and displeasure. "Yeah." *He almost looks like a person.*

"What's got you so jumpy? Someone giving you a hard time?"

"Uh…" Riley looked down, noticing her left sneaker laces had come undone. "No. I'm okay. I um…"

Sergeant Rodriguez picked at his moustache, narrowing his eyes. "There's something eating at you. You're not a runaway, are you? Is everything okay at home?"

He's gonna keep on me until I give him something. Dammit, Dad, why didn't you wanna take me to town! Hope you got bail money. "Uh… No. Things are shi—crappy."

"I tell you that man's no good," yelled a thirty-something woman in a red apron from the soup aisle. She transferred cans from a pushcart to the shelf. "What's he doin' to you, sweetie?"

Fear took a step back to give Anger some room. "He's not *doing* anything to me. He's my Dad." She seethed for a few seconds until the presence of a police officer pinning her to the meat cooler dragged fear forward by its shirt collar. "I used to live in New Jersey, but Mom died a few weeks ago, and now I'm here."

"She had good sense to get the hell away from him," said the clerk.

Riley glanced around looking for something to throw at the woman, but settled for making fists.

"Easy, Cora," said Sergeant Rodriguez. "The man might be a loner, but it doesn't necessarily make him bad. Some people like their privacy." He softened his demeanor and smiled at her. "Are you concerned about your situation?"

"Look at her." Cora gestured with a can. "He's barely feeding her."

Riley flinched at the mention of her weight. "I'm homesick. I still don't believe she's gone."

"I'm sorry." A sincere look of sympathy lingered for a moment before Sergeant Rodriguez inhaled a deep breath. "Well, Las Cerezas isn't much to look at it, but it's friendly."

She glared at Cora. "Really?"

"Oh, don't mind her." The cop shook his head. "She's got nothing better to do than assume the worst of people. I understand the upheaval of losing a parent and having to move across the country. There's the occasional bad element around here that'll probably tempt you eventually... You know, drugs never solve anything."

Oh, he's back to sounding like a cop. "Yeah. I know."

He fumbled around in his pocket for a few seconds before handing her a business card. "I want you to always feel like you can call me if you ever need anything. There's a lot of things kids can't talk to their parents about. If you ever need an ear, please call. Welcome to New Mexico."

She eyed the plain card; the words *Sergeant Martin Rodriguez* hovered over a grey silhouette of a police badge. Email on the lower left, a phone number on the lower right. Riley picked at the corner with her thumbnail. It seemed so unreal that the man looking at her could fake the concern in his eyes. *He doesn't seem that bad, but what if it's a lie?* Riley trembled.

"Are you sure nothing is bothering you, girl? You look terrified."

She slipped the card into the pocket of her shorts. "This was supposed to be like, a special summer... I wanted to hang out with Amber and stay up late and stuff before the big change."

"Big change?" Sergeant Rodriguez raised both eyebrows.

"You know... first year of high school." She pouted, wondering what her friend was doing at that moment.

"Start high school? So you're what, fourteen?"

"Yeah." *Oh, shit. Why did I say that? Now I can't tell him I forgot my permit. Pleeease, don't ask me how I got here.*

"Marty, you shouldn't let that child stay with that man. He ain't right."

"Hush, Cora. She's going through enough already and doesn't need the town's gossip factory adding its two cents." He let off an exasperated sigh and faced Riley again. "Just to satisfy the local busybody committee... are you at all concerned for your welfare?"

A half-smile played on her lip. "Yeah, a little."

Cora shot the cop a 'see, I'm right' stare.

"What exactly is going on?" Sergeant Rodriguez warm expression shifted to concern.

"The cabinet is full of SpaghettiOs and ramen noodles. There's no real food in the place."

Sergeant Rodriguez's laughter wasn't quite what she expected, but it worked. He shadowed her around the store, making idle chitchat about the town as well as the area outside it. A permanent twist knotted in her gut; the fear of having to lie to a cop reared its head every time it was her turn to contribute to the conversation.

"Your father doesn't come to town much. That's why Cora and her snoop brigade don't trust him. They think he's hiding something."

He is. Top secret somethings. Nothing bad. "Oh, he writes"—*shut* up *Riley, geez. Keep a secret*—"software and he's worried about leaks. He could get fired."

"Aww, the people in this town wouldn't know what software is." He looked around. "Can't say I remember the last time I saw your old man."

Oh, no. He's gonna ask why Dad's not with me. "Mom had an aneurysm… right in front of me." She didn't need to act upset or fake tears. "One minute she said she had a headache, and then she just fell… I couldn't do anything to stop it."

He took the weight of the basket from her arm and patted her on the shoulder. "Oh, you poor girl. I'm sorry."

She took a moment to recover, and wiped her eyes. "Thanks."

"My father died unexpectedly too. Heart attack at the dinner table. He fell face-first in his mashed potatoes." Sergeant Rodriguez sighed. "If it had been a movie, I would've thought the look on his face funny."

"Mom looked at me like she didn't know where she was. Like she was begging me for help and then she was just… gone." Diversion or no, closing the faucet was harder than she expected.

He looked like he wanted to reach out and offer a consoling arm, but kept a professional distance. "I hope she didn't suffer."

"They told me she didn't." Riley took a few breaths and accepted the basket back. "It could be worse, I suppose. Dad left when I was little. I always thought he didn't want us anymore, but that wasn't true." *Will he ever trust me with why?*

Sergeant Rodriguez followed her to the only checkout lane, where a pudgy, grandmotherly woman waited, engrossed in a tabloid. Despite having one jar of jelly, and her a full basket, he let her go first. She set the basket down and set to unpacking it. The woman grabbed the items as they came down the belt and scanned them.

"Sounds like there's a story there." He put the jelly on the end of the lane.

Beep.

"His work pulled him out here. Mom didn't wanna leave Jersey. They like, still loved each other and stuff but… I dunno."

Beep. Beep.

The cashier clucked her tongue, muttering in Spanish.

He mumbled something back that sounded chiding. "She says you've got some bad luck."

"Yeah. Well, it could be worse. I could be stuck in that shelter, or in one of those foster places you keep seeing on the news where they lock the kids in their rooms and beat them." Riley shivered. There was a thought that had caused at least one sleepless night.

Beep.

He grumbled in Spanish. The cashier made a remark at him with a raised eyebrow; he chuckled. She pointed at the girl and raised the other eyebrow.

"I told her it was rude to speak Spanish around someone who doesn't understand it."

The cashier nodded. *Beep.*

She bit her lip at the register screen, the total approached $60 faster than she expected. "And then you did the same thing."

"I was just cursing." He smiled. "People who do that to kids they are supposed to be helping… there's a reserved level of Hell for them."

Beep.

"Sixty four thirty nine," said the sales clerk.

Riley looked over the groceries. "I gotta put something back; I've only got $60."

"Add the $4.39 to mine," said Sergeant Rodriguez.

"That's so nice of you, but I can't take your money." She picked among her items, looking for something unnecessary. Bad enough he might get her for illegal driving, taking money from him seemed like a whole other level of wrong. Her fingers paused on one item after another; she hadn't grabbed a single item of 'fluff', and couldn't make up her mind what to ditch.

"I insist. It's only four bucks. Sounds like you've had it rough lately, about time you caught a break."

She stared up at him. No way in hell would anyone in New Jersey be that nice. Heck, people would just as soon run her over if she took four seconds too long crossing the street. Unable to process what was happening, she leaned on to the chrome ridge of the checkout lane and cried. *I'm crying over $4. What the hell is wrong with me?*

Thinking of Mom earlier had been an attempt to distract him from the 'why is a fourteen year old here without her father' question that would lead to a chain reaction of bad things. Her initial fear of being arrested had waned; this man seemed too nice. The more she looked at him, the more she figured he'd probably drive her home and give Dad a ticket. Her encounter with a cop had gone as far in the opposite direction of expectation as possible. His token gesture left her flummoxed.

"Thank you." She sniffled and blushed, almost blurting 'guess Dad was wrong about cops,' but bit her tongue.

Sergeant Rodriguez gave her a pat on the back.

"Are you alright, child?" asked the cashier.

"Yeah. I'll be okay. It's weird having people I've just met be so nice to me."

Riley gathered her bags from the end of the checkout counter and headed for the door before anyone thought to ask about Dad.

LA CERVEZA

Cora's approach and additional prodding comment that Rodriguez should go out to Dad's house to do a 'wellness check' set off a three-way argument in Spanish between the cop, the cashier, and the busybody. Riley couldn't follow it, and didn't wait to see how it ended. She turned to butt-bump the door open and slipped outside amid the jangle of small bells. A thermometer sign in the store's window called the temperature ninety-two degrees, but in the dry air, it didn't feel as bad as it sounded. After so long by a meat cooler, the warmth felt rather nice.

She squinted at the little town, momentarily captivated by the journey of a tumbleweed in the distance. Three men walking by gave her the 'hmm, that's an outsider' stare, though they seemed markedly less hostile than the looks the locals gave them when she rode with Dad. Just in case, Riley flashed an 'I'm not really about to break the law again' smile.

The police car parked ten steps from the door made her pause. Rodriguez would see her drive away from here. She decided to stand there and act as if she waited on a ride, hoping he'd leave and not think anything was up. Once he was out of sight, she'd make a break for the truck. A glance back at the store confirmed the argument in full swing; Cora looked upset.

Guess they're ganging up on her. She swayed side to side. *Crap, what if he wants to wait with me.*

She took a step in the direction of where she parked, but froze at a voice behind her.

"Hey, Riley. Whatcha doing?"

Kieran. "Uh, hi." She spun around, blinking at a full-sized shopping cart full of lettuce. "Waiting for my Dad. Whoa, that's a lot of greens. What kind of crazy diet are you on?"

"Funny. It's for the restaurant." He glanced at the cop inside and lowered his voice. "That man don't come to town. 'Sides, I saw you drive past Tommy's. Didn't know you had a license."

"I don't." She widened her eyes at him. "Please don't tell anyone. All he had in the house is SpaghettiOs. Both cabinets full of them. Hundreds of cans."

"No wonder you made those faces while eating Mom's cooking." He winked. "You're welcome to come back any time you want."

"Uh." She looked away in a hurry. "Yeah... Dad's not a big fan of town, and I'm not sure I'm going to have the balls to drive again until I'm old enough. I'm like the 'never does anything wrong' girl."

"You do look like you're about to pass out." He gestured at the bag. "Need a hand with them?"

"I got it. Thanks... besides you've got like, a caravan of lettuce there." *Oh, can you sound more like an idiot?* Riley's already cop-terrified stomach collapsed with the gravity of a black hole, crushing the enormous butterfly inside.

"Officer Rod's a bit sneaky, isn't he? Bet you never saw him coming."

She gulped. "I, uh, didn't think this place had cops."

Kieran gazed up at the clouds and Riley snuck a peek at his waist-length hair drifting in the breeze. He still had on the same plain white tee he'd been wearing at the restaurant. She recognized the stain pattern. Jingling announced the door behind them opening. Sergeant Rodriguez ambled out and wandered over to them.

"Good afternoon, Mr. Trujillo."

"Sergeant." Kieran nodded at him.

"Folks doin' okay?"

"Yes, sir," said Kieran. "Oh, Dad thinks he's come up with some salsa too hot for you."

"We'll see about that." Sergeant Rodriguez winked. "Tell him we'll be by Friday night."

Kieran grinned. "Sure thing, sir."

Sergeant Rodriguez gave Riley a shoulder squeeze and walked around them to his patrol car.

The cop seems to like him... guess he's not part of 'that element.'

"Yep. We've got cops. Three of 'em. Rodriguez is like the chief. Then you got Officer Lawson, white boy from Albuquerque, and Officer Roma. I think they're officially part of the T or C police, but they got stuck out here."

Riley giggled. "A cop named Lawson?"

Kieran smiled. "You've got a cute laugh."

She thought Dad talking about sex in the restaurant had been embarrassing. His remark made her blush harder. "Uh…"

"Sorry. I didn't mean to make you uncomfortable."

"Um." She looked at the bags. "I've got chicken; I shouldn't stand out in the heat."

The police car backed up and drove off.

"It's okay, I understand."

"It's not you." She snapped her head around to look up at him. "I really have chicken."

Kieran smiled. "You wanna hang out sometime? I could give you the five minute tour of the town." He pointed at a '78 Trans Am in electric blue, complete with an airbrushed phoenix on the hood.

Aside from the car, the scenery was far from impressive. Dusty buildings, houses that looked like trailers without wheels ready to fall over in a stiff breeze, tumbleweeds, and a bunch of squinty-eyed suspicious people who didn't seem to like her. "So, what's in Las Cerezas to see?"

"Honest? Not much. It's pretty boring. Most everyone here calls this place La Cerveza."

"Doesn't that mean beer?" She tilted her head, squinting at the sun behind his head.

"Yeah. The only thing to do here is drink… or restore old cars."

"You did that?"

"Yep." He grinned. "Been working on it since I was twelve. Course, I had the engine done by pros, but everything else was me."

"Nice."

"Okay, I had the paint done by a shop too." He glanced back and forth between her and the car three times. "You're not that impressed by cars, are you?"

"Not really."

"I'm not a gearhead, really... it's just something to do, ya know? Not like I've got my heart set on growing up to be a waiter."

Her laugh trailed off to a somber stare. "Yeah, I didn't exactly want to get stuck in the middle of the desert either. What do you wanna do?"

"I'm gonna go to school, probably UNM. Electrical or aerospace engineering."

"Wow. So you're like a senior or something?"

He chuckled. "No, I just sound like one. Gonna be a junior next year, I'm sixteen."

"Aren't your friends gonna tease you for hitting on a freshman?"

"Nah, two year difference is no big. So, you wanna hang out? Tomorrow?"

Cold, clammy plastic brushed her thigh. "Uh, yeah, sure, fine. I gotta go before Dad sends the CIA after me."

"Okay. See you later."

Riley watched him go to his car, catching herself admiring him a little too much. *He thinks I'm joking about the CIA.*

BOILING OVER

U nease gathered in Riley's gut, twisting it up like a wad of rubber bands. From the moment she started the truck, fear she'd look up and see flashing lights in her mirror whitened her knuckles on the wheel and sucked all the moisture out of her mouth. She barely drove forty-five miles per hour and kept her gaze on the ground to the left, worried to death she'd miss the little dirt road back to Dad's house.

A horn blared, startling a shriek out of her. She kept screaming as she shied away from the headlights in her rearview mirror. Some guy in an unmarked white van crept right up on her back bumper, flicking his high beams so fast she thought him a cop for a few seconds. She froze, unsure what to do, letting her foot off the gas and clutching the wheel to stay in the lane.

The van weaved side to side, beeping and flashing.

He's gonna hit me. She looked at the dashboard. The needle hovered at thirty-five now, sinking toward thirty. Indistinct warbles of a man's shouting came from behind. *Why doesn't he go around me? There's no one else on the road.*

She swallowed hard. *Two cars in the desert, and he has to be on my ass. Go around me.*

Terror he was going to hit her added a little weight to her foot and she got the truck up to forty again. *Okay, I don't care if I get pulled over. Now would be a great time for a cop to show up.*

"Stupid bitch," and something about beating some sense into her made it through the diatribe. He seemed to be repetitively air-drawing the number fifty.

Bile crept up in her mouth as she tried to keep it together. Past a small hill up ahead, the ever-so-welcome sight of the dirt path appeared. She let the breath out of her lungs in a slow exhale. *Blinker.* She signaled for a left turn way early, just so the asshole behind her didn't pick *that* moment to get pissed off enough to try to pass her.

I'll turn and he'll keep going, don't panic.

She took the left, but the van followed. He ceased flicking his high beams and no longer leaned on his horn, but he still rode her bumper.

"Oh, shit."

There was nothing up that road but desert, and Dad's house. He was following *her.* Attempting to steer while half-blind from tears, shaking like a leaf in the wind, and trying not to throw up caused her to drift out of the wheel ruts and bounce over some bushes. The man backed off a little, but revved his engine and charged.

She stomped on the gas, flinging dirt into his grill and her body against the seat. A trip that took twenty minutes before passed in ten as she rambled up the unpaved path at close to seventy miles per hour. As soon as she saw the house, she ignored the pitiful 'road' and steered straight at it, slamming on the brakes in hopes Dad would hear and come running. Her groceries shot off the passenger seat and hit the floor.

The van skidded to a halt right behind her; a red-faced, potbellied guy in a flannel shirt, cowboy hat, and jeans almost stumbled and fell in his haste to get out, tangled in his seatbelt. She jabbed her finger at the door locks and cowered down in her seat.

He came stomping up along the side of the truck, and pounded on the door. "What the fuck is wrong with you, stupid bitch! Can't you read a damned speed limit sign? Who the hell taught you how to drive! Five-fucking-five means fifty five miles per hour!"

She reached up and pushed on the horn.

The man grabbed the door handle, tugging on it hard enough to rock the Silverado. "You did that on purpose just to piss me off, didn't you? Stupid little bitch! Who the hell do you think you are? The speed limit society? Open up."

He pounded again on the window; the sharp *click* of a heavy ring striking the glass made her cringe with each blow as he bellowed on about her awful driving. Her father stepped out of the house. Riley sat up, about to grin with relief until she noticed the assault rifle in his hands. All the blood drained out of her face.

Dad fired a shot into the air, bringing an immediate end to the screaming two inches from her window.

"That's a nice van," said Dad. "Be a shame if anything happened to it… like a bunch of holes."

"Shit." The man whirled on Dad, glaring.

"Nothing out here but weeds." Dad aimed at the guy's head. "No one will find you. You have three seconds to get the hell away from my daughter."

Riley shivered, whispering, "D-Dad, what the fuck?"

The man backed up, hands held out to the side. Dad lifted his finger off the trigger, but kept the rifle aimed. Riley looked back and forth from her father to the retreating cowboy as he slinked to the van. He got in without another word, backed through a K turn and thundered off to the south. Riley rattled the handle for a few seconds before she remembered how to work the unlock button, and ran to her father.

"Dad!"

He clamped one arm around her, holding the weapon in the other. "What happened?"

"I was driving a little slow 'cause I was afraid of the cops, and that asshole was all over me." She blinked. "That's a gun."

"Yes. AR15."

"You have a gun?" She swallowed again.

"About fourteen of them. There's one in the glove box."

"What?" She shivered, twisting to peer at the truck. *I had a gun with me in there? I sat in front of a gun for three days?* "Y-you have a gun in the glove box?"

"Yeah, but it's only a revolver. Open carry is legal in New Mexico." He walked over to the passenger door.

"Dad! If the Jersey cops found that, you would've gotten arrested, and I'd be in a home now." What began as a yell ended with a whimper.

He pulled the door open and stared an apology into the ground at her feet. "Uh, sorry. I wasn't thinking. They said Lily was dead and you needed me. I ran out the door in the clothes I was wearing. Had to buy a new shirt the morning of the funeral."

She crept over to him, eyeing the rifle warily, and hugged him. Her harrowing ride got the better of her, and she lost a few minutes crying and shaking. Having Dad's arms around her felt awesome.

He slung the rifle over his shoulder on a strap and grabbed the plastic bags, repacking the contents. "It's a damn miracle the eggs survived. That son of a bitch didn't bumper tap you, did he?"

"No." She looked at the dust cloud fading in the distance. "Is he gonna call the cops on you?"

"Let him. This is my property, and he was assaulting my kid." Dad nudged the door closed with his hip. "He won't. Not like he was driving courteously. A well-balanced mind doesn't chase someone ten miles out of their way just to bitch about going too slow."

She laughed and followed him inside. Dad left the rifle by the arch between kitchen and living room and carried the plastic bags to the kitchen counter while Riley diverted to his room and dropped the keys on the desk by his computer, where a notepad file displayed on the screen.

Ukraine unstable. Forces massing at the border. POTUS may authorize military intervention. Moving assets from Prague to assist. Russia saber rattling, threatening to respond 3x over. Delta-Two-Two confirm N. Korea courting Russian alliance.

She regretted reading it and fast-walked to her room, ditched her sneakers, and padded back to the kitchen with her hands on her face, trying to rub some calm into her sinuses.

"Dad, is that guy gonna come back?"

He put the chicken in the fridge. "He'll be one sorry bastard if he does, but I doubt it."

"What's that supposed to mean?" She pulled open the bags, and made some room among the SpaghettiOs for the dry goods.

"If he comes back, he's up to no good. I'm not going to bother asking him questions."

"You'd shoot him?"

"Yep." He looked over the items she bought. "I'm impressed. No cookies or junk."

Wow. She stared at him for a moment. "Uhm, you only gave me sixty bucks."

"Receipt says sixty four."

"Sergeant Rodriguez covered me."

"What?" Dad looked at her, alarmed. "Damn."

Uneasy tightness gripped her throat. "D-Dad? Why are you afraid of the cops? He seemed nice. You're not like a serial killer or something?"

His worry evaporated. "No. Oh, God. I... yeah I can see where that came from. C'mere." He held out his arm.

She hesitated for three seconds, but decided to trust him.

"The people who want to compromise my mission would target LEOs first. Get them to ingratiate themselves so they can get information. You're a kid; you'd say things to be friendly and nice, trusting a figure of authority without knowing you're giving away valuable information."

"I don't think he was compromised. He seemed like a sweet man."

"Maybe. Be careful what you say. They're always looking for something to get you on. Don't give them any more than you have to. In fact, you can just tell them you don't want to answer any questions. Invoke your fifth amendment."

"Oh, yeah, sure. Do that and they'll *know* I did something wrong."

Dad shook his head. "That's the way they control everyone. They erode the rights of the common citizen my making them feel guilty... anyway, want some SpaghettiOs?" He grinned.

"Um. No." She searched the cabinets under the sink for a decent-sized pot. "I'm going to make a stew."

"Okay." He kissed her on top of the head and wandered back to his bedroom.

Riley arranged the potatoes, onions, carrots, and a box of fresh mushrooms on the counter, and ran water into the pot. Dad's voice mumbled in the distance.

The occasional "Yes, sir" or, "That's not good, sir," was all she could make out whenever his voice got louder.

She peeled and cut the carrots, peeled and cut the potatoes, and diced the onion. The stew beef went in a pan next to the large pot, helped along with a little salt and garlic powder. Cooking made her think of Mom, but she didn't feel like bursting into tears again. *Guess I'm making progress.* She glanced at Dad's silhouette lit by his monitors. *He basically needs a mom. Barely taking care of himself.*

Every so often, she'd look up at the window over the sink, fearful there'd be a white van outside. About half an hour later, Dad wandered in and came up behind her with a hand on her shoulder.

"Hey Squirrel, that smells pretty good."

She clenched her jaw. *I hate that name. He saved me from a raging jackass, so I'll let it go.* "Thanks."

Dad looked at the ceiling as the sound of jets going overhead seeped out of the sky.

"Again?" she asked.

"Hmm. Eight B1s." He leaned over the sink to the window, staring up at a sharp angle. "What do you mean again?"

"They were flying around this morning too. Big green suckers with adjustable wings?"

He got nervous and quiet.

"What? This is the middle of the country, they're probably training."

"Not with eight planes. Things are getting tense. I bet they're getting ready to send them to Europe. Probably drilling a specific mission."

"It's that bad?" She lifted the lid to check on the stew. Thick, brown liquid bubbled like something out of Yosemite Park.

"Not yet, but it's getting close. It could tip either way."

"You think it will?"

Dad leaned over and kissed the side of her head. "I don't think even the Koreans are that foolish. They know what they're doing."

"Oh." She pointed a wooden spoon at one of the cabinets. "Grab the bread, this is almost ready."

Ten minutes later, they sat at the kitchen table having dinner like a family—at least, two thirds of one. Riley glanced at the empty seat to her right, daydreaming Mom sitting in it. Memories of having a meal with two parents at the table lurked too far back in her mind to grasp.

"This is really good, Squirrel."

She tensed.

He hurried to swallow. "Sorry. I keep forgetting you're not a little girl anymore."

Riley lifted a piece of carrot out of her bowl on a spoon, and smirked at it. "That's not really why I get mad when you call me that."

"Oh?" Dad put his spoon down. "Do enlighten me."

She glanced at him and back at the carrot. "That was your nickname for me before you left. When I was eight, Mom called me Squirrel and it was like reminding me I wasn't ever going to see you again. That was *your* name for me, and hearing it reminded me I wasn't ever gonna see you again. I yelled at her, went all super-micro-bitch on her. Threw a screaming tantrum. I might've even blamed her for you leaving." The spoon (and carrot) plopped into the bowl. "I went downstairs later and found her crying. I never saw Mom cry before, and it was my fault. Now, when you call me that name, it reminds me of making Mom cry. How could I know how much it would hurt her? I was only a little kid."

"What did she say when you walked in on her?"

"I didn't. I was a chicken. I ran upstairs. I was so mad at you. I went through this phase where I was jealous of anyone who had a father. Mom actually took me to a shrink because they thought I had emotional problems. Apparently I was 'too friendly' to grown men. I don't really remember it."

Dad reached across the table and put a hand on hers.

"I think I was eleven when I finally apologized to Mom for making her cry. She was shocked I remembered. We got real close after that. It was just us against the world." Riley felt the tears coming, but held them back with a deep breath.

Her father remained quiet for a few minutes before heaving a weak sigh. "I'd give anything to send a message back in time and tell myself not to run."

She grasped his hand, holding it for a moment. "Or at least call us on birthdays and holidays."

He looked guilty until she ventured a weak smile. "Sorry. I didn't want to run the risk someone would trace my calls and find you."

They ate in quiet for a few minutes.

"So you really hate SpaghettiOs?" asked Dad.

"If I had them three times a day for a month, I'd throw up at the sight of the can. They're okay... just not all the time."

"I never got sick of them. Sometimes I'd cut up hot dogs or jackrabbit and drop them in. You know, for a little variety."

She laughed. "Did you really eat nothing but canned pasta and ramen for six years?"

"Perhaps more than I should have, but not entirely." He winked and tilted the stew bowl to his lips to drink the last of it. "Time for seconds."

Riley fished the 'carrot of staring' out of her bowl and ate it while he ambled around past her to the stove. "Can I go to town again tomorrow?"

"Hah. I didn't think you'd be so ready to risk driving again after today."

She squirmed in her seat. "I don't wanna drive again till I have a permit. Would you take me?"

"There's no way you used up all those groceries already." He ladled out another helping of stew, replaced the lid, and returned to the table. "Did you?"

"No. Kieran asked me to hang out."

"You're fourteen; you don't need a boyfriend yet. You're better off avoiding him."

"He's not my boyfriend. You barely know me anymore. You live like a hermit in a mountain of SpaghettiOs, and you hate a boy you never met? If I'm gonna live here, I might as well try to make *some* friends." *Kieran hasn't teased me about being skinny once.*

He fished a slice of bread from the plastic sleeve and folded it in half. "I'm not sure that's a great idea. The people in that town aren't quite right."

"They said the same thing about us."

"Hmm." He dipped his bread in the stew and took a bite. "I'll need to think about it."

You took me away from my friend. She pouted at her stew. *I shouldn't say that. He didn't do it to be mean.*

Dad swabbed the last of his second bowl away with another piece of bread. The house hung in eerie silence for three minutes, broken only by the scratching of Riley's spoon. His head popped up; he dropped the bowl and bread with a clatter and ran to the radio in his room.

"Yes, sir. Copy. Go ahead."

She sat for a moment swirling her spoon around the empty bowl. *Dad should load the dishwasher since I cooked. That's how it was with Mom.* She thought about Amber, Kieran, and Mom. When it became clear Dad was engrossed, she got up and loaded the dishwasher with a lump in her throat and water in her eyes. He still muttered at his radio unit when she finished packing the extra stew into plastic bins and fridging them. Riley plodded along in a slouch to her room and fell face-first on the bed, hugging the pillow.

This sucks. Why do we have to live so far away from everything?

A little while later, a thought struck her, and she slid off the bed to sit on the floor. She grabbed one of the Xbox controllers and turned it on. The screen lit up, bearing a "No Connection" message. Riley fought with it for a moment, running the Wi-Fi scan three times, but the system detected no active networks. The controller almost went flying across the room, but she figured she'd have to drive at least two states away to buy another one in the 'land that technology forgot.' Grumbling, she set it back in the cradle before flopping face down on her bed again to sulk.

Unbelievable... he doesn't have Wi-Fi. How am I going to hang with Amber?

She sniffled on and off for a while, until a light knock came from her open door.

"Hon?"

"Yeah?" She answered without moving.

"I suppose you won't believe me about the town unless you see for yourself. If you still want to go tomorrow, I'll take you."

She rolled over onto her back and sat up. "Really?"

"Sorry if I am being overprotective. You're all I got left."

"Dad…" She scrambled off the bed and ran into a hug.

"Promise me you'll be careful."

She looked up at him, almost smiling. "I'll be okay."

13

LIVING PRIMITIVE

Riley's eyes opened a little after 9:30 a.m. the next morning. It mystified her how the desert could get so damn cold at night, even in the middle of summer. She lay still after a long stretch, staring at the ceiling and thinking about Kieran. Sixteen wasn't too bad. He was only two years older, and plenty of Mom's friends had husbands farther away in age than that. Not that she was waiting for him to propose. Or even interested in him that way. Or... well, whatever.

She got out of bed and dragged herself to the dresser, grabbing clean undies, a beige, pleated babydoll top, and a pair of black cargo shorts. A scrap of camouflage on the rug caught her eye when she closed the drawer, and she traced it to a large backpack tucked against the wall between the dresser and the bed.

"Where the heck did that come from?"

While that could wait, a shower couldn't. When she emerged from the steamy, soapy bathroom, a cloud of coffee smell greeted her in the hallway.

"Morning, Dad."

He moaned. Metal clanked.

She walked barefoot to the kitchen, finding her father in a pair of ill-fitting tightey whities, wrestling with an aluminum can. As thin as he was, if he bounced too hard, they'd be on the floor.

"Dad!" She whirled about, looking anywhere but at him. "Go put something on. You are also *not* making SpaghettiOs for breakfast. I'll deal with it for lunch, but ack... not for breakfast."

He murmured something and gestured at the coffee pot, rumbling and burbling. She kept her eyes averted and went to gather a frying pan, bread, and eggs.

"Dad. Clothes. Now."

"Okay, okay." He took his time covering the ten feet from the kitchen to his bedroom.

The static-laced crackle of his AM radio warbled on about something news-y sounding, dueling with some talking head on his TV. Riley tuned it out, searching back and forth along the counter, in hopes of finding a toaster. She had no luck in the cabinets either. "Dad, where's the toaster... and the Internet?"

"I don't have one." His voice drifted in from the other room. "I haven't had toast in years, and there's no Internet here. In case you hadn't noticed, we're a bit far out for a cable run."

"They have these things called satellites, you know." She shook her head, hands on her hips. "How the hell do you work out here? What kind of programmer doesn't have the damn Internet?"

"Security risk. I take contract jobs and bring the code to T or C on a USB stick. Besides, if I had 'net, I'd never finish a project... I'd spend all day on Facebook." He paused. "Maybe I should have... to keep in touch with you."

Yeah, you shoulda. S'pose you didn't want to. "God... you're living primitive." She smirked at the frying pan. *How hard could it be to make toast? They had to do something before electronics.* "Facebook's for old people. Did they eat toast before they had toasters?"

"I have no idea." Dad emerged in yesterday's jeans and unbuttoned, flannel shirt.

She rolled her eyes. "I guess I'm doing laundry too."

"Hey... I wash my clothes." He collected a mug and stood by the coffee maker like a dog waiting for the food bowl to go down. "Once a month."

"Eww," she droned. "That is changing."

Dad poured himself coffee and took a heavy gulp. "Ahh. Nectaris deorum."

She furrowed her eyebrows at him. "Whatever. So, about this Internet thing..."

"I'll think about it."

"You haven't left the house since I've been here." She dropped a piece of bread in a dry frying pan. "You write software, right?"

"The SINCGARS handles data transmission as well as radio. I do everything I need for the military on a secure channel."

"Oh." She frowned. Her first attempt to flip the toast threw it on the floor. "Dammit. Hey what about that… uh, Ted guy?"

"Three second rule." Dad scooped it up and ate it. "Things have been slow there lately. Plus, I don't really have time for that now."

"Dad!" She cringed. "That was on the floor! It's not even toast yet."

"You were going to throw it out though." He wandered to the table and sat, munching.

"Toast experiment take two." She dropped another piece of bread in the pan. "Well, can we maybe get 'net so I can talk to Amber?"

"Depends on what it costs out here. I'll think about it."

She started on scrambled eggs. "You say that a lot."

"I'm a careful person as a general rule. Two times in my life, I've rushed into things with no planning. I regretted one of them, more than anything. The other time was the best thing I've ever done."

Her whisk stopped beating. *First one's obvious.* "What's the other time? When you married Mom?"

"When I came back to get you." He slurped coffee. "You still want to go to town today?"

"Yeah…" She stirred the eggs more than beat them. "So, um… how'd you go from writing bank software to going all double-oh-seven?"

"The NSA and the CIA monitor just about everything that passes through electronic media. I'm not sure what made me light up on their radar. Couple years after I got out here, I get this recruitment email and—"

"You don't have Internet." Riley stared at him.

Dad chuckled. "I had an office job in T or C right after I mov—"

"Left us." Riley slammed a pan on the stove.

Neither spoke while she finished making breakfast. She set plates of food down and joined him at the table. Her attempt at home fries horrified her, but Dad seemed to enjoy them. At least he had pepper that tasted like pepper. An odd audio synchronicity developed between the crackly voice on the little radio in his room and the news commentator on the TV. Whenever the Fox guy shut up, the radio started. Both rambled about 'Chechens' and the impact of some border standoff on global markets. *They don't care people are getting hurt, it's all about the money.*

"I'd rather you didn't spend time among those people."

Why did you leave? Why won't he tell me? Riley sulked. "It's still kinda messed up you get picked to be a spy. Sounds like I'm in a shitty movie."

"I didn't believe it either. I guess it was the way I went about commenting and structuring my code. You can't recruit someone with experience for this job. They train that. What they wanted was someone with a certain meticulousness."

"You mean OCD?" Riley pushed eggs around her plate.

Dad shrugged. "Not the worst condition for someone in my line of work."

She dropped her fork with a *clank.* "Dad, I can't do what you do. I can't just sit here alone in the middle of nowhere, cut off from everyone. Why can't I go make some friends? Mom always yelled about me only having one friend, and spending more time with her online than in person… and now I can't even do that."

After a moment of him contemplating his toast without answering, Riley jammed her fork into her eggs and packed her mouth.

"I wasn't expecting it to happen this fast, but I suppose the world works by learning. I expect you will at least make him use a condom."

Eggs exploded out of her mouth, all over the table. When she stopped coughing, she gaped at him, unable to decide between screaming or crawling under her bed and not coming out for a week.

"I suppose living in New Jersey has eroded your sense of humor." He picked a bit of her egg from his cheek.

"That wasn't funny." She glared. "You think I'm like, easy or something?"

"No… no… Just trying to make a joke." He sighed. "I'm sorry. I wouldn't offer to take you to town if I didn't trust you. You're a lot like your Mom."

"It's not a 'date,' it's just hanging out with the *only* other kids within like, a hundred miles."

"T or C is a big city, there's kids there. Albuquerque is less than a hundred miles away."

"It might as well be a thousand when I can't drive."

Dad got up and put his plate in the dishwasher. "Go on, get ready then."

THE TAN '98 SILVERADO PULLED OVER AT THE CORNER CLOSEST TO THE Hernandez Grocery. A few people wandering by gave Dad suspicious looks. Riley smirked at them. When they spotted her, wariness became worry. *What's their problem?* She thought about the waitresses mistaking her for an abductee. *No wonder Dad doesn't like the people here. Dicks.*

"Meet me be back here at 6 p.m., unless you want me here earlier."

"Oh, dammit, I left my phone at the house." She sighed. "Probably don't have reception out here anyway."

"You sure you want to do this?" Dad gripped the wheel as if preparing for a breakneck car chase away from a flock of KGB assassins. He turned his head toward her, squinting. "We can still go back."

"Dad… you're a drama queen. It's not like you're about to send me behind German lines or something. I'm just gonna hang out."

He fumbled his wallet out and handed her a ten-dollar bill. "For lunch."

"Why are you freaking out?" She stuffed the cash into a pocket on the side of her right leg.

"I guess I am a little paranoid. It feels like having you back in my life is some kind of second chance to make up for the biggest mistake I ever made, and I'm so worried something is going to happen."

"Love you too, Dad." She hugged him for a moment, and opened the door. "Oh, what's with the backpack in my room?"

"It's a 'go' bag. In case they find us and we have to bug out in a hurry. It's got clothes, couple MREs, and some survival stuff."

She looked left and right at the all but deserted street, imagining a black car full of spies screeching out from behind a scrub-covered hill. How easy would it be to grab her from behind and drag her into the back seat?

Get a grip. The Russians aren't coming for you or Dad.

"Six p.m. Got it. I'll be okay, Dad." She leaned in, kissed him on the cheek, and jumped out.

He hesitated for a few minutes before pulling away, driving slow enough to give her a chance to wave him back. Riley looked around at a town that could've been an abandoned film set. The people had vanished. Nothing moved except for her and Dad's truck.

Unless I get bored to death.

14

OUTSIDERS

Riley wasn't quite sure what she was supposed to do. Even if she hadn't forgotten her iPhone at the house, it's not like she even knew Kieran's number. Her toenails had less polish than the last time she'd thought to look, a visual reminder of Mom slipping farther away. She wiggled her foot, tapping the flip-flop against her heel. Another few days, and she could no longer say, 'Mom was alive this month.' Eventually, she wouldn't be able to think, 'Mom had been alive *this year.*'

She looked up, squinting past sun glare on some cars parked by Tommy's Restaurant a little more than a football field's distance away. At Perkins, Amber had suggested Riley move in with them. She'd still be in familiar surroundings, with familiar people, going to the school she'd been alternately looking forward to and dreading. A fair number of her classmates who teased her for being 'too thin' would have stayed with her. The extra pressure of having them hound her in high school on top of losing Mom would have sucked.

On the other hand, with ninth grade came more freedom. She was supposed to be looking forward to staying up late, getting a job, and having money of her own, but all she wanted to do was crawl *home* and cling to her mother. Amber's offer, unrealistic as it was, had been tempting. It would've been a huge thing to ask of her parents, something they probably would've declined as gently as possible. Of course, with

Dad already back in the picture, she couldn't have accepted anyway. Quirky as he was, he *did* love her, and she couldn't turn her back on him.

Well I suppose I can just walk in.

Riley looked both ways before stepping onto the road and hurrying across. She caught a glimpse of the skinny biker in front of the mechanic shop, unpacking a number of small metal cases from the trunk of a battered car that looked like it cost less than the equipment it carried. Riley looked away and scurried across the parking lot in a shuffling drag-step intended to move fast without losing her flops.

The smell of cooking meat and Mexican seasonings surrounded Tommy's bar, stirring a growl in her belly even though she'd had breakfast a little over an hour ago. Old license plates clattered against the door when she pushed it open. A twinge of worry caught her when the man behind the bar cocked his eyebrow at her. Would he throw her out for being too young to enter a place that sold booze?

"Hey, Riley." Kieran waved her over from a backwards chair by a round table in the corner opposite the bar.

Four other teens—a girl and three boys—looked up to check out the new arrival. The girl had a soft, rounded face, skin a bit lighter than Kieran, and long, dark hair. Riley figured her for seventeen at least. She leaned out of her chair to the left. Her posture teetered on the verge of giving the room a peek under her short camouflage skirt, and thrust her breasts through a tight grey tank top. She afforded Riley only a brief glance before returning her attention to a boy who looked like a senior, or perhaps a year graduated, kissing him as if they were the only two in the room.

Of the group, he seemed to be another outsider, white as a sheet with freckles and unruly brown curls. He adhered to the local uniform code, a plain white tee and jeans with work boots, and paid little attention to her.

Next to the pair sucking face, another older boy with bright green hair and a goatee busied himself with a small sheet of paper and green flakes of chopped leaves. His ribs poked out of the bottom of a black half-shirt covered by a mesh top. Metal studs glinted from his earlobes, and two small chrome cones stuck to his chin a quarter inch below the corners of his mouth. He looked up at Riley, flashed a dazed smile, and resumed rolling his joint.

Riley stared at it. *That's not oregano. Holy shit!*

The youngest of the lot clutched a beat-up video game and had wide cheeks and a short, dense mop of hair that made his head look spherical.

She took him for twelve if that. He too wore a white t-shirt and jeans, though no shoes.

She walked over to Kieran, staring at the boy with drugs out in plain sight.

"Hey guys, this is Riley." Kieran gestured at her. "She's the new girl I was talking about."

The lovebirds broke lip lock long enough to say, "Hey" and "'Sup."

"Riley, this is Jesse." Kieran indicated the small boy. "You can call him El Bicho if you want."

"Pendejo." Jesse seemed to like that about as much as she liked Squirrel. "I ain't no little kid. I'm gonna be in high school next year."

"You're fourteen?" Riley blurted. "Uh…"

The other girl laughed.

"Thirteen." Jesse puffed out his chest.

"He looks like he's nine, doesn't he?" cooed the girl. "He's adorable."

"Adorable gonna get his ass kicked next year," said the kid with the metal on his lip.

The older girl squirmed about to keep talking through her boyfriend's attempt to jam his tongue in her mouth. "Oh, I won't call him that at school."

Kieran looked at the bar as the man behind it yelled for him. "Uh, sec. That's Lyle"—he gestured at the white boy—"that's Luis"—he pointed at the one with green hair—"and Camila. Be right back."

She stood in awkward silence. Her only link to these people jogged across the room leaving Lyle and Camila exploring each other's tonsils and Luis finishing his engineering project. At last, he held up a homemade cigarette.

"Is that…" Riley fidgeted.

"Weed?" asked Jesse. "Yeah, he smokes so much his hair turned green."

"But isn't it? Like, um…" Riley blinked.

"It's legal in Colorado," mumbled Luis.

"Yeah, man, but this ain't Colorado." Lyle yawned, and flashed a weary smile at Riley. "Luis here thinks he's some kinda celebrity since he's played two live shows in T or C."

"Three." Luis held up four fingers.

"Your cousin's garage don't count," said Camila. She crawled into Lyle's lap and nodded at her chair. "Go on, sit. Don't stand there like a post."

Post? Is she calling me too thin?

"Probably weird like her old man," said Luis.

Riley accepted the seat, even though she didn't much want to. "Dad's not weird, he's just... private."

"He's one of them doomsday prepper dudes," said Luis. "Ready for the end of the world."

"I heard 'em sayin' he's got a nuke bunker." Pure adoration lit Jesse's eyes. "That's so cool! I wanna see it. Probably packed it full of guns and missiles and food and water and stuff."

"It's always the antisocial ones." Lyle shifted Camila in his lap so she had her back against his chest, threaded his arms around her waist and clasped his wrist. "Heard some people say he's got bodies in his basement."

"The house doesn't have a basement." Riley felt her cheeks getting hot. "He just lives alone. Why does everyone think he's strange?"

"Because there's nothing else to do in this town but drink beer, have sex, and get high." Camila shrugged. "Your old man doesn't do any of that, so he stands out. Dude barely goes outside."

Riley slumped in her chair. "I guess I'm gonna stand out too then."

"Whadda you do for fun?" asked Jesse.

"I used to play Xbox a lot." *I should've spent more time with Mom.* Riley glanced over her shoulder at the bar; seeing no trace of Kieran in the room filled her with a mild panic. "Not so much now."

"I like to play with an X-box too," said Lyle, sliding his hand between Camila's legs.

"Hey!" She grabbed his arm and elbowed him in the gut. "Behave. Not here."

Jesse stuck his tongue out in a gagging gesture. Luis didn't react at all, still gazing upon his unsmoked joint as if he'd freed Excalibur from the stone.

"Never heard of no ex-box before," said Luis. "That like one of them used-to-be-a-girls?"

"It's a video game, dumbass," said Jesse.

A squeak made Riley look back. Kieran entered through a battered wooden door that flapped back and forth like something from an old saloon. He balanced a large tray half on his shoulder and carried a mass of plates to a table crowded by a family of eight. She watched him hand out food, somehow managing to keep his hair out of the way and not drop anything at the same time.

Jersey'd have fined the hell out of this place for letting him have his hair loose.

Her slow rotation to sit forward paused as her gaze swept past the bar. A TV mounted on the wall showed a news broadcast, muted but with closed-caption text flashing on the bottom.

"...since talks with the North Koreans have ultimately proved unsuccessful. Our Washington correspondent reports diplomatic entreaties are disintegrating as the insular nation has promised to stand with Russia should the United States involve itself in the Ukraine situation."

She clutched the seatback, hoping Dad's 'assets' would find a way to cool things off. The screen switched to an image of a Korean man in a military uniform standing behind a podium.

"So, is your Dad as weird as everyone says?" asked Camila.

Riley squirmed around to face the table and shrugged one shoulder. "He's a Dad. Of course he's weird. I dunno. No weirder than normal."

Kieran returned, dragging a stray chair over to sit. "So, what'd I miss?"

"This is perfection," said Luis. "Best one I've ever rolled. You guys gonna come to the thing Friday? Black Chakra's playin' at a thing."

"Can you vague that up a little more?" Lyle smirked.

"What's that?" asked Riley.

Kieran leaned closer. "He's in a band. They play death metal with Buddhist overtones."

Riley tried to make a face like she knew what he meant. "Uh... Okay."

She couldn't imagine what something like that would sound like. Tension grabbed her limbs. Bad enough she'd gone out in public; that in and of itself proved she was not in her right mind and desperate for... something. Even in the comfort of her previous normal life, leaving the safety of her bedroom didn't happen often. Now, there was a boy leaning close to her. A boy with silky black hair, high cheekbones, and deep brown eyes.

Her fingers kneaded at the pleats of her babydoll shirt, her spine taut like an iron rod.

Jesse looked up from his handheld. "Kieran, we still goin' to the Invaders game?"

"Yeah." Kieran grinned, ruffling the boy's hair.

"Stop." Jesse tried to punch him in the leg, but Kieran evaded. "I ain't no damn kid."

His three older friends got into a debate about music, discussing bands Riley had never heard of. Kieran drifted back and forth from his work duties, hanging out at the table with his friends as much as he could without being too rude to the customers. She felt like a fifth wheel, remaining quiet, teetering between regret at bothering and curiosity about Kieran. The lure of her bedroom called, a safe place where no one could make fun of her.

Is this the group I'm going to spend the next four years with? She stole a glance at Lyle and Camila, who made little effort to hide their roaming hands. Watching them was almost as embarrassing as Dad bringing up condoms. *No, they're gonna be seniors. They'll be outta here. Anyone with a brain would get outta here.* She exhaled too quiet to be noticed. *Luis... he's graduated already or dropped out.* She shot an uneasy look at the marijuana twirling between his fingers. Rather than revulsion, curiosity, or temptation, it made her think of the paunchy cop who'd come to speak to her class in seventh grade about drugs. That, in turn, made her remember her old life. She never really liked school, but at that moment, she'd have given anything to go back to it.

Kieran came by with a chicken burrito. "Hungry?"

She looked at it and grasped the front of her throat, choked up from her last mental wandering. Unable to speak, she nodded. He left it in front of her and jogged off. She pulled the ten out and held it up when he returned with silverware and a cup of ice water.

He closed her fingers into a fist clutching the bill. "Not necessary."

Riley stared at the hand around hers, the color of saddle leather. *He's touching me.* "Uhm."

"Really, it's okay. Mom always gives the extra to my friends."

"Means nobody wanted it," said Lyle.

Luis chuckled. "Smells good to me."

"It's not a sendback." Kieran let go of her hand. "She makes the insides in a huge batch, there's a lot."

"Thanks." Riley put the money in her pocket.

Jesse shot a longing stare at the food. She hesitated at the sight of his frayed jeans, wondering if going barefoot had been by choice or poverty. The way all the buildings here looked, she figured on poverty.

Riley nudged the plate toward the small boy. "Want half?"

"How are you not sick of this stuff?" asked Camila. "You eat the same damn thing every day."

Jesse shrugged.

Kieran nudged Riley's arm with an elbow. "Mom's putting his together now. She can't resist that face he makes either."

Eating proved to be a welcome distraction from the kids she wasn't yet sure about. Jesse seemed harmless and 'normal' enough, though the idea he was a freshman like her didn't sit right in her head. He looked like a sixth or seventh grader. Camila's initial sense of territorial challenge faded once she'd gotten a good look at Riley. It didn't hurt that Lyle had barely given her a second glance.

She speared a bit of the burrito and swabbed sauce off the plate with it. Ambivalence fit. Riley didn't much care if she became friends with them or not. Luis lived on another planet. The others didn't even seem to really *hang out* with him as much as occupy the same table. Maybe they tolerated him on the off chance his band got somewhere and they could claim to know a famous person.

An hour passed of feeble attempts at becoming part of the crew by throwing out a reference to *Call of Duty* here or *World of Warcraft* there. Riley gave up, convinced these people didn't know much about any of the things she liked. She considered bringing up *Lord of the Rings* or a handful of other fantasy books she'd read, but what was the point of being in a one-sided conversation?

I could talk to myself at home. These people don't even know what Hogwarts is.

Having lost any expectation of being welcomed by this group, she shifted in her chair and cast a forlorn stare over the barroom. A five or six year old boy at the party of eight table stuck his tongue out at her. Two cowboys that looked like retired Marlboro men ignored her. Kieran was off tending to three tables full of men in tool belts and hard hats bearing PNM logos. Three seconds before she decided to ask for a phone to call Dad, a minor miracle came in the form of an old *Roadblasters* arcade machine in the opposite corner by the front wall. She scooted away from the group and trudged over to it. A demo routine ran in a loop. She almost laughed at the primitive graphics, but it was better than nothing. Her momentary enthusiasm faded when a pat-down found no change. She jabbed a finger at the start button as a gesture of annoyance before walking away, and squeaked in shock when the game started up despite the lack of payment.

A blocky car with a huge gun on the roof... okay.

She got used to the controls pretty quick, a steering wheel with buttons and a metal gas pedal in the front of the cabinet. The fire button had seen a lot of abuse and worked only half the time. Her fourth attempt lasted a decent while before the dreaded 'Game Over' flashed. As soon as it did, Kieran nudged her.

"Hey."

She teased the start button with one finger, not pushing it. "Hey."

"I know what you mean," he whispered.

"Huh?"

He leaned his back against the machine. *He's so close.* Riley's gaze shifted from the console to where their left arms touched. "We moved here five years ago from Albuquerque. Dad was the manager of a bar there, and Mom worked in the kitchen of this little family restaurant. I was more a computer game type, like my older brother." He chuckled. "Course, moving out here... Wound up getting that car and it ate all my time."

Standing that close to him felt half like she was doing something she'd get in trouble for and half like this town might not be the most horrible place on Earth. Riley forced herself not to look up at his face, and poked the start button. The chintzy graphics reset, and her little car zoomed onward. "Why'd you move to this place?"

"Dad won a little Powerball, maybe forty grand. He decided his dream was to run his own tap house, and found this building cheap. As a bar, it did okay, but once Mom and Aunt Dakota came on board, it got better."

"Cool." She swerved around a land mine and shot down a flyer. "This game is older than I am."

"You're pretty good at it." He put an arm up on top of the cabinet as he faced her.

She pressed herself into the machine, not sure how she felt about being squeezed between him and an arcade game. He *was* exotic looking, tall, probably strong, and nothing like anyone she'd ever met. However, Riley was Riley. Four foot ten, maybe eighty-five pounds, flat as a plank. *Yeah, a boy would look at me twice.* She drove more aggressively, taking a few risks that paid off. *This is Robbie Zimmer all over again. He's setting me up as a joke for his friends.*

Another risky move didn't work out: Game Over.

"Not that good." She glanced at the clock on the wall. A few minutes past four. *Two hours.* "I gotta go. Dad wants me home before dark."

The bartender, the man she knew now as Kieran's father, made an annoying clicking sound. The PNM workers were all looking at them. *Oh, great.* She wanted to climb inside the arcade machine and disappear.

"Hang on." He flashed a mischievous smile and hurried over to the workers.

Riley frowned at the ancient technology and trudged back to the table where Camila tried to convince Lyle to take her somewhere 'less lame.' He did not seem too interested in going to T or C, and the prospect of a drive to Albuquerque elicited an even stronger frown.

Riley took the open seat, and slouched. "Where's Jesse?"

"His mom called him home. He lives next door," said Camila. "Come on, Lyle. Let's hit a club or something."

"I ain't drivin' two hours to drink. You can get beer here."

Camila thrust out her lower lip and fluttered her eyelashes.

Lyle sighed. "Fine."

The lovebirds walked away, lingering for a brief conversation with Kieran in the middle of the room before heading out the door. Alone with Luis. Riley didn't like the way he looked at her, as if trying to imagine her shirt gone. She found a little comfort in the stoned look on his face; it seemed like decent odds he lacked the coordination to pose a real threat.

After a long, awkward stare, he lifted his gaze from her chest to her face. "Hey."

"Hey." *Or maybe he was drifting through space.*

"Wanna help me spark this piece of perfection?" He held up the joint.

She scrunched her face. *Eww.* "Uh, I thought that one was like awesome or something. You wanna burn it?"

Luis flashed a dopey grin, appraising his work. "Yeah, it is like, proportional to the ratio. You're right." He set it on the table and pulled out a flip phone. "I should take a picture of it first."

So they do *have cell service here.*

Riley stood and wandered away, headed for the door. Kieran bumped into her from behind.

"You okay?"

She spun around to face him. Her response died at the tip of her brain, her body paralyzed by a momentary odd tingle in the bottom of her gut. Looking at a picture of a guy wasn't anywhere near the same as having one close enough to touch. He didn't stare at her the same way Lyle did— bored indifference, or the way Luis did—something between 'is that a girl?' and 'where am I?' His eyes held a mixture of curiosity, pity, and something else she couldn't place.

"Sorry, the guys are a little odd sometimes. Lyle has a lot on his mind; he's trying to get into the Air Force. One more year of school first though."

"Oh." She looked down at her flip-flops. "I should go."

"Never played on an Xbox. I don't know how anyone could get used to aiming a FPS with those little joysticks. Havana is such a nightmare even with a mouse."

Her head snapped up. "A mouse? All the top players have controllers, even the PC users. Havana's got nothing on Refinery for suck. So small... it's like 'use a shotgun or don't bother.'"

"Small maps can be fun, just use a fast runner with knives or akimbo Glock 18s."

Riley let off an exasperated sigh. "I hate those maps so much I don't even play serious. I just act like a squeaker and piss people off." She raised her voice to sound like a six-year-old. "Which button makes the knife work?"—she made a squishing noise, and giggled—"oh, found it."

He fixed her with a narrow-eyed squint. "That was you?"

"No effing way." She gasped. His voice was deep enough to sound like a grown man over the headset. One hand clamped loose over her mouth as uncontainable laughter got her. "What are the odds..." *that I'd be virtually knifing a guy that lives near my dad while my Mom dies in the next room.* Giggling became crying.

"Kidding. Hey." He grabbed her hand. "Sorry, I... Uh..." Kieran scratched his head. "Have no idea what about that was worth making you cry."

"I'm..." She closed her eyes and let the breath out of her lungs before wiping her face on her... lack of sleeves. *Crap.* "Sorry. That was me. Not your fault."

"Are you sure you're okay?" He tilted his head, seeming unsure if he should smile.

"Yeah." She glanced at the bar pool table behind her. "Your voice reminded me of someone I killed."

His jaw dropped.

"Xbox." She winked.

Kieran chuckled and gestured at the table. "Ever play?"

She shook her head, folded her arms, and offered a doubtful look as he ran to grab a pair of sticks. He racked and wandered over, holding up the white ball and a stick.

"You break." He pointed. "Put the white ball there and try to hit it into the pack as hard as you can."

She grabbed the cue. "I've played on Mom's computer, I know how the rules work... just never for real."

Her confidence evaporated when her stroke glanced off the cue ball, sending it curving with a limp spin. He caught it before it disrupted the rack and waved for her to try again. She whacked it dead center on the second try, not bothering to use any of the fanciness she'd gotten used to in the virtual version. Nothing went in.

She half sat on the edge of the table, waiting with one hand on the stick and the end between her feet while Kieran tended to customers. He took a shot when he returned, leaning in and hitting the ball seemingly at random. When a solid dropped, he almost grimaced as if he'd wanted to miss on purpose. He noticed her eye roll and sank two more before the cue ball wound up in a place he had no decent shot.

He chatted about a couple games, mostly about various editions of *Call of Duty,* which had occupied most of her gaming life as of late. It made her long for Amber, but also brought something familiar back into her life. Talking to him got easier as time went on, and she found herself growing more and more annoyed whenever he needed to take a break to run around the dining room. He hadn't thrown the kind of time at the game she had. At one point when he left her alone to escort a group of three obvious tourists to a table, she sulked at the fading green felt. Talking about the game left her simultaneously homesick and hopeful.

He hurried to the kitchen, and returned to her a minute later. "Did you take your shot?"

"No." She glanced at the clock. "I should go. Dad's gonna be waiting for me in like ten minutes." *Don't wanna know what he does if I don't show up. He already hates this town.* She handed him back the stick. "Thanks."

"Okay." He set them on the table, hurrying around the end. "Gimme a minute?"

"'Kay."

He jogged through the swinging door again. She slipped one foot free of its flip-flop and tapped her toes on the spongy foam. Her 'epic' summer was sure turning out weird.

"Let me walk you out?" Kieran approached, smiling. "Mom's got the floor for a few minutes."

She almost declined, but thought back to the maniac in the white van. "Sure."

Before she changed her mind, she grabbed his hand. Kieran didn't object.

They walked out the door, across the tiny parking lot to the street, and down a block and a half to where the Hernandez Grocery sat on the corner between NM 51 and a road not much bigger than a dirt path.

She looked around, finding no trace of Dad yet. "He's supposed to pick me up here."

"I'll stay with you."

Riley related the story of the idiot in the white van.

"Doesn't sound familiar, which means he's probably not local. I wouldn't worry about it. Road rage burns out fast. He probably wouldn't have hit you once he got a good look at you."

"Why?" She smirked. "Because I look like a kid?"

He put a hand on her shoulder. "You look so sad and lonely."

Thank you Captain Obvious. "Yeah well. You don't have to feel sorry for me."

"I'm not talking to you out of pity." He let his arm fall. "No one else around here has dreams. No imagination. They're all happy in this dust. I want to climb the ladder, do something with my life. Not spend it in a hole in the ground. I see that in you."

"Yeah well, I'm not from around here." She clenched and released her toes. "Dad's sure the whole town hates him for being an outsider."

"You have to admit coming to town once every three months and buying a hundred cans of pasta is a bit odd."

She covered her mouth with both hands to mute the sudden laugh. "Yeah."

He squinted at a few people watching them from the next block. "People around here don't like 'odd.'"

"Am I odd?" She raised an eyebrow.

"No." He grinned. "You're perfect."

Oh, my God. Her face flushed. "Uh..." *Wow. Awkward.*

"I like talking to you." He glanced to the right at an approaching dust cloud. "Looks like your old man's right on time. It's about thirty seconds from being six."

She forced her way out from under embarrassment enough to look up. The sight of the tan Silverado at the head of a rolling beige cloud chased away her worry.

"We're going to the movie theater on Thursday, you wanna come along?"

I didn't think they knew what movies were out here. "Uh, sure... if Dad's okay with it."

Dad drove by and pulled a U-turn in the parking lot of the Hernandez Grocery. Brakes squeaked as he came to a gentle stop in front of them.

"Great," said Kieran. "See you then?"

"Sure." She looked at the truck. "If, well... Yeah."

Riley climbed in, pulled the seatbelt on, and offered a halfhearted wave as they drove away. She bit her lip and stared down at her legs. After a moment, she pulled open the glove box and examined a jumble of papers and envelopes. A black, rubberized pistol grip lay at the bottom, a bit of a silver barrel visible on the other side.

Holy crap, he wasn't kidding.

She slammed the hatch closed.

"Who was that?" asked Dad. "Same boy from the restaurant?"

"Yeah. His name is Kieran. His parents own Tommy's."

"Did he ask you anything about me or what I do?"

I tried to resist the waterboarding and jumper cables, but I caved in and told him you were overprotective. "Nothing unusual."

"Define 'nothing unusual.'"

"They asked why you avoid town and said you act 'odd.' I told them you worked a lot and didn't have time."

"Not bad. Did you get the feeling that anyone followed or observed you suspiciously?"

"No. That place is so boring, I think the dust has dust." She rambled through a brief description of her afternoon, leaving out the bit about the joint. Not that she had any great temptation to try pot, but she had no temptation at all to endure the lecture she figured it would start.

"I feel a little guilty having you cook." Serious Dad went out the window. He loosened his grip on the wheel and relaxed his posture, even smiled. "I can heat up some SpaghettiOs if you want to be lazy."

"We still have stew left, and that's just a microwave away. Should eat it before it goes bad."

"You are my daughter. So practical."

Yeah. She leaned her head back and closed her eyes. For once, she looked forward to going back to her new bedroom, even if it was in the middle of absolute nowhere.

GROWING UP

D ad jostled her shoulder, waking her out of the first decent
night's rest she'd had in weeks. Desert cold made it so nice to
sleep. The little clock on her nightstand read 07:59 a.m. She
whined and rolled back under the covers. Dad chuckled on the way out.

"Okay, sleep in, hon. I'll warm up some breakfast."

"Wait." She stretched. "Why are you waking me up at eight in the
morning in the summer? I thought we got to sleep in."

"I need to be operational in case things escalate. I'm technically
working."

"Oh. Right." She drifted in and out of consciousness. A momentary
recollection of last night's waterboarding joke returned in the form of a
fleeting dream of being strapped down on a wooden locker room bench
while four copies of Dad poured warm SpaghettiOs over a cloth on her
face. "Gah!"

Riley leapt out of bed and darted through the house, skidding to a halt
in the kitchen where Dad fixed himself a cup of coffee. Out of breath, she
put a hand on the wall and gasped. He smiled at her, looked her up and
down, and chuckled.

"Those pajamas are adorable."

Teal flannel with a white collar, and little smiley faces for buttons on
the top. *The last time I wore these, Mom was still alive.* She swallowed hard
and closed her eyes. *Mom bought them for me when she had to replace the*

skirt that asshat Hensley spilled coffee on. Riley looked away and down, folding her arms across her chest. *Don't cry.* The sound of a mug settling down on the counter came a few seconds before Dad's arms circled her and pulled her tight. She clawed her fingers into his shirt, holding on. *Smells like Dad.*

She waited a moment before she risked using her voice. "Wanna watch a movie later? I brought some blu-rays."

"What do sea creatures have to do with movies?"

"Dad, you're such a dork." She let go and gathered stuff to make breakfast, eyed the pot, and helped herself to a cup of coffee.

The sugar in the cabinet was yellow, not to mention a solid brick. No milk in the fridge.

"I'm serious…" He looked it.

"While you were hiding in a cave, they replaced DVDs." She nudged the fridge closed. "Dad, you got any powdered creamer?"

"Nawp. Drink it black. That way you'll never be disappointed if you don't have the fluff. Besides, if you really like *coffee*, you can taste it without all that crap in it."

Riley took a sip, grimaced, and forced another. "Ugh, how long did it take you to get used to drinking it black?"

He attacked the scrambled eggs she placed in front of him before the plate was out of her hand. "Don't remember having it any other way."

She slipped into the seat across from him, crossed her ankles, and let her legs swish back and forth while dumping black pepper on everything. "How old were you when you had coffee the first time?"

"Eleven. We stopped at this little pancake shack at random one day. I ordered coffee out of curiosity. The waitress seemed more shocked than my mother. When no objection came from the parental unit, I got coffee." He looked up with a mischievous grin. "I had no idea what the little white buckets were for until months later."

"I never met your parents." She made a toast-scrambled egg sandwich.

"My father wasn't around much. Never did get a straight story outta Mom. Ran off, got killed, got arrested. It always changed. After a while, I stopped asking. Mom was a strange duck. Always thought God would watch out for her. I didn't have a lot of use for the invisible man in the sky, so she got cold and distant. As soon as I was eighteen, I was out, and that was probably the last time I saw her."

"Wow…" Riley let her sandwich drop to the plate. "I'm sorry."

"Long past now, Squirrel." He made a sheepish smile at her visible wince. "Sorry. Her loss though. Mom chose her superstition over her son."

She studied the pattern of browns on the side of the bread, searching in vain for an answer to the question nagging at the back of her mind. Mom had been a staunch atheist. Riley grinned. *She so would've given me crap about asking her to watch over me yesterday.* The old man at the funeral certainly didn't make much of a case for faith. Was everyone religious as mean as him and the paternal grandmother she never met?

Probably not. Guess it's just my bad luck again.

Dad rushed off to the radio as soon as he finished eating. Riley picked at her breakfast, sitting at an angle on the chair, taking black coffee in small sips while Dad leaned over his electronics like a buzzard. When her plate held only crumbs, and she couldn't slurp any more coffee out of her mug, she put the dishes in the machine and trudged to her room, grabbed a towel, and headed for the bathroom at the end of the little interior hallway.

She made a quick pass in the mirror on 'zit patrol,' happy to find none, and shirked out of her pajamas. A shower passed in no great hurry, after which she wrapped herself armpit to knee in the towel and darted to her bedroom.

As soon as she pulled the towel off, the doorbell rang. Riley jumped but rolled her eyes, reaching for her underwear drawer. *Dad'll get it.*

"Riley? See who it is…?" he yelled.

"In a minute, I'm…" *not going to yell 'naked.'*

She hurried into her panties, skipped a bra, and grabbed the first pair of jean shorts she saw. The top item in the shirt drawer turned out to be a pink spaghetti-strap shirt. Without thinking, she rushed out of her room to the front door.

A skinny man in a grey jumpsuit and baseball cap leaned right and left, peering in. He had a few days' worth of beard on his face, shaggy black hair, and an Adam's apple sharp enough to cut with. The low diesel rumble of a truck engine rattled outside. Riley pulled open the door; the blast of warm air hit her shower-dampened body, making her aware of quite a bit of exposed skin. Bare shoulders, only a layer of thin cloth over her chest, and shorts small enough to make Dad faint if he saw her. Mom allowed that particular pair only because she had sworn to always wear them over leggings.

Oops.

The delivery man's hurry evaporated to a leering grin. Already bulging frog-eyes got bigger as he ogled her legs. "Hey, cutie."

She clung to the door, ready to slam it in his face and scream if he twitched. "Who are you?"

"Got a delivery for a..." It took him a few seconds to peel his gaze off her thighs and check his clipboard. "Christopher McCullough."

"That's my dad."

He flicked his eyebrows up twice. "Is he here?"

Yes, fifteen yards away and surrounded by enormous guns. "Yeah, he's on the phone."

"You look old enough to sign. C'mon and show me where I can put it."

She blushed. "W-what?"

"The car?" He pointed with the clipboard behind him, where Mom's Nissan Sentra sat on top of a flatbed truck.

For a moment, she forgot about the way this man stared at her and crept out onto the porch. When she caught him trying to stare down her top, she jumped back with a yelp and clamped her hands over her chest.

"Perv!" She backed into the house. "Dad!"

The man's face reddened, and he coughed.

"One moment, sir." The sound of headphones hit the desk. "What is it, Riley?"

The driver waved his hands at her, pleading.

She narrowed her eyes. "Mom's car is here. Where do you want it?"

"Next to the truck is fine," yelled Dad.

The guy bowed at her like a gracious monk.

"I didn't want him to kill you." She crept up to the door, half-hiding behind it. "Leave it by the Silverado."

"Sorry," he whispered and ran to the truck.

Beeping rose up outside as he backed the truck up, jockeying it around to line the car up with the drop off point. Riley raced to her room before Dad could see how she had dressed, and changed into shorts a hands' width longer as well as a bra and full tee shirt. By the time she got back to the porch, Mom's car was on its wheels and the driver wound a winch cable back up the inclined ramp.

She took a step outside the door, not daring to venture too far from the house. Even in her more modest clothes, the driver looked at her every few seconds or so, smiling. She couldn't tell if it was apologetic or he'd gone back to fantasizing about her. After he'd leveled the flatbed and rolled it forward to lock, he trotted over with the clipboard held out.

He kept his gaze locked on her eyes. "Need you to inspect the car and sign off that there's no damage."

Oh, no friggin' way am I going out there with you. "Dad?" she yelled. "He says you gotta check the car for damage and sign. I can't 'cause I'm only fourteen."

Riley felt somewhat vindicated at the look he made when he learned her age. She didn't want to imagine what thoughts had been bouncing through his head. Fortunately, he didn't seem disappointed; a wave of panic flashed over his face. Dad jogged up and offered a handshake. She edged into the house, feeling guilty.

"Hon, keep an ear on the headset please?"

"Sure… how do I work it?"

"No need to 'work' anything, just put it on and yell like crazy if anyone calls for me."

"Okay."

With Dad going outside, she wandered to his bedroom. She hesitated at the door, as if she were about to invade some kind of inner sanctum. Dark blue carpeting and the blackout curtains left the room cave-like and cool. She sat on the edge of the still-warm wheeled office chair and put the uncomfortable military-style headphones on. A faint hiss filled her ears, like a stereo on a dead frequency with the volume all the way up. With each passing minute, her guilt grew.

Soon after the rumble of a departing truck rattled the walls, Dad walked in. Riley relinquished the seat and headphones without an inkling of protest.

"Nothing. No one said a word."

"Good news." He smiled, sat, and clamped the headset over his ears.

"Dad?" She stared at her toes.

"Hmm?" He pulled one earphone off.

Head down, cheeks on fire, she muttered, explaining what happened. He grew angry, but she couldn't tell if he'd become mad at her, at the driver, or in general.

Dad leaned forward and held her hand. "I trust you'll not wear those again without something else on your legs."

"It's not all *my* fault." She gave him a wounded look.

"No, I'm not saying that. Thank you for being honest. He didn't touch you?"

She shook her head. "Just tried to peek down my shirt."

"You're probably right; I would've at least hit him."

Dad let the headphone snap back in place, squeezed her hand with a smile, and swung the mic boom in front of his mouth. "Baker-four-four, SITREP, copy?"

Riley wandered the house for a while, thinking about Mom's system of awarding her tokens for doing chores. Tokens she could redeem for things like shopping trips or 'get out of grounding' free cards, though that one was expensive: 50. She'd probably had 32 in the jar when Mom...

She sighed.

For a moment, she stood at the sliding glass door in the dining room, gazing at a small spread of uneven red patio tiles and desert beyond. A patch of sun warmed her toes, and lofted the scent of wood in the air. *I wanna go home. I miss trees.* She went to the couch, sat, laid sideways, draped herself over the arm, rolled to face the back, rolled flat, and eventually slithered onto the floor. After lying there for about a half hour bored out of her mind, she got up and trudged to her room.

She flopped on the floor, back against her bed with her legs crossed, elbows on knees and chin in her palms. *This sucks.* She frowned at the shelf of books by the closet. Somehow, the school's summer reading list's titles had wound up right where her eyes landed on *The Good Earth.* She smirked. *If school wants me to read it, I bet it's boring.* She looked up and over to the top shelf at *Lord of the Rings.* Despite finishing it twice, it was more tempting than something she was *required* to read.

Riley blinked. "Duh. I'm not going to that school anymore... and technically, the one in this hellhole hasn't given me any summer work."

She laced her fingers behind her head and leaned back, proud to have won an argument with no one. Her good mood faded as she remembered the day Mom had taken her shopping. A stop to buy books she wasn't really interested in reading had been softened by Starbucks hot cocoa. Two thousand and change miles away, the bookstore at Menlo Park Mall went on as though she'd never existed. Someone may be in her house at that very moment, thinking of buying it.

Instead of crying, she sank into a sullen pout and wrapped her arms around her knees. *Maybe I'm coping.* Her throat ached from the pain of stalled sobs, but it didn't feel like it would do much good. She glanced to her right at the green glow where her Xbox controllers charged, all but useless without Internet. She looked at the game console, debating bot-matching and shooting AIs. She hadn't touched *Call of Duty* in three weeks. It used to be a nightly ritual. As much as they horsed around, she and Amber had been pretty good in retrospect. They probably could've ranked in a tournament, though in no way did she expect to win.

She got up and moped to the kitchen, stopping with her hand on the wall phone. *What the crap is Amber's number?* Riley had always tapped her face in the contact list. The only time she had ever typed the number out was the day Mom got her the iPhone two years ago. *The iPhone! I might not have cell reception, but I can look up the number.* Riley ran to her room and rummaged the nightstand drawer. She hugged the white iPhone 4 to her chest as if it were a beloved kitten and clicked the power button.

Dead.

"Shit."

Riley tore her room apart, hunting for the charging cable. When she didn't find it a half-hour later, she darted across the hall to the junk room and attacked the unopened boxes of 'stuff from the house'. The sight of Mom's things broke her resolve not to cry more, but she kept on searching. The precious white cable turned up perched atop mom's recipe book in the ninth box she checked.

Still sniffling, but wearing a broad grin, she rushed back to her room and plugged the phone in. The screen remained black. She bounced up and down on the bed, chanting, "Comeon comeon comeon."

Ten agonizing minutes later, a white Apple logo appeared. She shook the slab of technology, as if that would convey the message it needed to boot faster. As soon as it came up, she pushed the contact icon, and Amber's entry. The number hid behind a pop up warning her she had 10% battery power.

"Argh! Go away!" She mashed the dismiss button.

She read Amber's phone number four times, speaking it aloud. After repeating it twice more without looking at the screen, she put the phone down and marched back to the kitchen chanting it. When she picked up the handset and reached for the buttons, dead silence in the earpiece knocked the number right out of her short-term memory. Riley slouched, and let the receiver fall against the wall, bouncing on its cord.

"Dad?" she whispered, trudging to his room. "Dad?"

"Yes, hon?" He looked up from his radio. He seemed simultaneously happy to see her as well as scared.

"Your phones don't work."

"I know. You see any wires outside?"

"Actually, yeah. There's one off the pole."

"That's main power. The phones came with the house. Telco wanted to charge me twelve hundred bucks to run cable out this far."

Why do you live in the ass end of nowhere! Her mental voice shrieked. Outside, she remained despondent and silent. "Oh."

Head down, she plodded back to her room and collapsed on her knees, leaning against the bed with her head atop her crossed arms. Sobbing lasted a shade less than fifteen minutes, after which she slid like a murder victim to the rug. She didn't like these people. She wanted her *friend* back. All Lyle and Camila wanted to do was have sex with each other. Jesse was just a little kid, even if he was supposedly thirteen, and Luis… *Luis smoked himself retarded.*

Riley cringed at the imagined voice of her mother chiding her for using that word. 'Sorry it just slipped out' didn't make Amber any less pissed when Stacy dropped an 'N-bomb' in casual conversation. She felt guilty, not to mention hypocritical—she'd felt as angry as Amber. Overwhelming boredom seeped in. She lost track of time for a while, but eventually sat up and turned on the Xbox and her TV, leery of breaking Mom's decree by hooking it up to the big screen. She went into the game, growing more and more forlorn at the separation from her best friend as the familiar screens popped up. The game nagged at her about not being able to connect, but she managed to get it to start a single-player match against an army of computer-controlled opponents.

It had long ago become boring as it offered zero challenge compared to thinking enemies… not to mention she couldn't squeaker-troll the computer. At first, she played lazily, not caring how well she did. Playing at all felt like some kind of betrayal of Amber. Had she sworn off the game since they could no longer play it together? Had she been lurking in the lobby every night wondering why Riley hadn't shown up? Guilt grew to anger, and the digital automatons paid a heavy price in pixilated blood.

Riley went on a rampage.

"That's a lot different than the movies you used to like." Dad leaned on her doorjamb. "Looks like you're pretty good at it, Squirrel."

"Do you *have* to call me that?" She mowed down a dozen unthinking soldiers with a heavy machine gun.

"You used to laugh at that name." He sighed with a wistful stare into space. "Sometimes when I'd use it, you'd go grab a cookie and nibble on it."

"I'm not a little kid anymore." Out of ammo. Pistol time.

"No... I suppose you're not." Dad crossed the room behind her to sit on the bed.

Despite her mood, she leaned back until she rested against his knee. Soldier after fake soldier came at her in the same way, always a few seconds too slow to get a shot off before she killed them. Head shot, groin shot, head shot, head shot, body shot. When they started spawning with heavy armor and riot shields, she whipped out the claymore mines and chokepoint tactics.

"You're rather good at that."

"Mmm." She wasn't having fun, this was venting... and even that wasn't helping much. She couldn't make the AI rage-quit a match.

"Guess you played this a lot back home?"

"Can we get Internet? I'll probably need it for school... you know, to do research."

"I already called. I was going to surprise you when they showed up."

She paused the game. "Really?"

He smiled. "Yep. I hope the wireless net has enough bandwidth for your game."

"I..." She jumped up and hugged him. "I wanted it more to talk to Amber."

He squeezed her.

"Thanks, Dad." She sat on the bed next to him, shooting a guilty stare at the rug for sniping at him over a childhood nickname.

The resigned expression that spread over his face at her declaration of non-kid-dom remained. He glanced at the TV screen frozen in the image of an over-the-pistol view of muzzle flare and a man taking a slug in the cheek.

"You played that game a lot?"

Riley crossed her legs on the mattress, grabbed the controller, and un-paused it. "Yeah. Every night... usually with Amber. After we got good at it, we'd get in matches just to piss people off. A lot of old people play too, and they get all kinds of foamy at the mouth when they think little kids beat them. Some of the stuff they say is hilarious."

She took out another ten opponents, and ducked into an alley for a breather between waves.

"Do you think you could kill a man to protect yourself?"

Pause.

"What?" She whirled around.

Dad, his expression still blasé, got up and walked out. She stared at the doorway for a moment. *Freaky.* After two breaths, she resumed playing and planted a couple of claymore mines on her way up a staircase. Sniper rifles sucked for botmatching, but this was getting boring. She wanted a challenge.

Plop.

Something heavy enough to feel landed on the mattress behind her. Riley paused the game again and twisted around to find a black handgun lying there. The sight of it filled her with the fear that the police would batter down her door any second and arrest her for laying eyes on a weapon.

"Dad… is that a—?"

"Beretta 92FS, Military Police model with a 15-round magazine."

"I-is it loaded?"

"Always treat an unknown weapon like it's loaded."

She gawked at it, afraid to move, as if the Grim Reaper himself was a foot away from her ass.

"If someone was going to hurt you… could you protect yourself?"

"That's real, isn't it?" Riley lifted her gaze from the weapon to her father's unfazed, calm, blank face. "Dad… you're like, seriously freaking me the hell out."

"S'pose we'll have to fix that." He slurped coffee.

PROTECTION

R iley leaned on the counter listening to the soft, rhythmic *thrush-thrush* of the dishwasher operating, trying to decide how she felt. Too much happening at once had left her numb. *Mom... Yeah... Mom.* Dad had gotten a little spooky last night, and she was still a bit ticked off that he'd left the gun on her bed. She didn't want to touch it, afraid of hurting herself. After staring at it for heck knows how long, she risked a two-fingered pinch of the handle and set it on the floor so she could sleep.

Then, there was Kieran—and the embarrassed, eager, lonely, happy, skeptical morass that churned in her gut. The last time a boy had shown her any interest, he'd been bait in a cruel prank. The 'dark room' they'd gone to make out in turned out to be the middle of the football field, and the entire crowd saw her standing there, blindfolded, kissing empty air.

Getting stuffed in a locker was better. At least no one could see me.

A snarl escaped her at the memory of Robbie Zimmer's smug grin. *As if one of the football jocks would have really liked me.* For an instant, she was back under the floodlights, wanting to burrow a hole into the ground and hide. She shrank in on herself, hair tickling her bare right shoulder. Her oversized white shirt hung lower than the hem of her shorts, but had a huge neck opening. This time, she hadn't made the same mistake and had a tube top on under it.

I hate Robbie Zimmer. She daydreamed about Kieran fighting him.

Robbie was thicker, but Kieran probably had an inch or so height advantage.

"Come on, Riley." Dad's voice came through the kitchen wall from the back.

She pushed away from the counter and scuffed her flip-flops to the sliding glass door. Dad waited about twenty yards from the 'patio' by a folding cafeteria-style table. To her left, a large grey-white box sat on wood blocks thick enough to be railroad ties. It was almost as big as a Prius, and had four one-inch metal pipes running up to the roof. A cap at the right corner bore the label: Diesel Only. Lettering along the side read 'New Mexico Solar.' Naturally, the 'o' in solar was a smiling cartoon sun.

After pulling the door closed, she walked over to him, waving her foot every so often to get sand out from between her sole and the foam rubber. The table had a few boxes of bullets, three handguns, and that rifle Dad waved at the idiot plus two others and a pump shotgun. Riley froze in place, as if one wrong breath would cause a horrible accident.

"Holy crap, Dad. Where'd you get all these guns?" Riley blinked. "You planning on taking over a small South American country?"

He shrugged. "Picked them up over the years. Most came from this guy who runs a shop in T or C. Army Navy surplus place. I get a lot of stuff from him. 'Course you also have the occasional gun show."

"Those are assault rifles..." She shivered. "Aren't they illegal?"

Dad smiled. "Oh, you poor brainwashed child. Second amendment. That federal assault weapons ban died in 2004, and New Mexico didn't enact any replacement... not that I'd give two craps if they did. The government's afraid of a population that can defend themselves."

Riley tucked her hands under her armpits and took a step back. "Mom would drop dead if she saw these. I don't think this is a good idea."

"Go put on some real shoes," said Dad, without turning. Evidently, he'd heard them snap on her approach.

"Why? It's hot. What does it matter what kind of shoes I wear to... uh, shoot. Not like sneakers would stop a bullet."

The *click, click, click* she'd been hearing turned out to be him putting rounds into a pistol magazine. "No, and I'm hoping you're not so uncoordinated that you shoot yourself in the foot. I'm thinking about hot brass."

"Hot brass?" She blinked.

Dad held up a bullet. "I'm not sure what you see in those games, hon, but only the tip goes flying. The ass end is a casing, and after you shoot one, it's hot enough to burn. If that falls on your foot, it'll hurt and likely leave a mark." He glanced down at her feet. "Go put your sneakers on."

"Okay, okay… fine." She took three steps.

"And a top with a more closed neck. Brass loves to get under your shirt. At least you don't have any cleavage for it to get stuck in yet."

"Dad!" Crimson. *What the hell is wrong with him?*

Riley grumbled. Bad enough she had to touch guns; did she have to be uncomfortable while doing it? She ran inside, changed to a snug white tee with dark blue quarter sleeves and a Nike swoosh on it, and traded the flops for her black Keds, skipping socks. She wondered on the way back out if it was some kind of conflict of interest to wear competing products.

When she got back outside, Dad was a distance from the table setting up a couple targets. Two paper cutouts with a silhouette of a man on them as well as about forty empty SpaghettiOs cans.

Okay, those I might be able to shoot.

She didn't dare touch anything on the table.

Dad walked back over and picked up the gun he'd left in her room. "Okay. This is a Beretta 92. It's got the least amount of kick of everything I own. It's stable, reliable, and if you load hollow points, has a decent enough punch." He pointed at another gun with simpler lines. "I prefer the .45 myself, but I don't want to rush you in over your head."

"Guns, Dad? You already are."

He set the Beretta down and grasped her by the shoulders. "If something were to happen out here… or with the world, how long do you think it would take the cops to get here? They'd be coming to investigate a murder scene, not save your life."

She gulped, thinking about the creepy guy who delivered Mom's car. What might've happened if she told him Dad wasn't home? "O-okay."

"First." He picked up the Beretta, popped a magazine out of the handle and locked the slide back. "Unless you see a gun like this, with the slide back, always assume it's loaded and can kill." He glanced at it. "On second thought, amend that. Even if it looks like this, respect it like it can kill."

"Okay."

He handed it to her. She held up her hands and he laid it across her palms. It felt heavy and warm, and smelled like the table in the dining room. Oil. *Oh, crap... that table's full of gun stuff.*

"That's the magazine release." He pointed at a little button on the handle. "If you push that, the mag falls out." He held up an empty magazine. "This is the slide lock button. Hold that down and pull back the slide, and it will stay open. This here"—he pointed at a small lever at the rear end of the slide—"that's the safety. If you see the red dot, the gun can go off."

She stared at it for a moment before finding the nerve to grasp the handle and look it over. "What's this other lever?"

"Push the button on the other side, swing that little lever down, and the whole slide will come off the front end so you can disassemble it for cleaning."

"Oh."

"Here." He handed her an empty magazine. "Load it."

It didn't take a rocket scientist to figure that one out. She slid the magazine into the handle and slapped the bottom like they do in all the cop shows. It felt nothing like the game, but looked sort of similar when she sighted over it.

"Line up the three posts, right?"

Dad grinned. "Yep."

"How do I let the slide go?"

"Thumb switch." He pointed.

She fumbled at it for a few seconds and found the thing to squeeze. The slide racked forward with a click. Dad moved behind her, wrapping his arms around and tweaking her stance before adjusting her grip on the pistol.

"Be careful of your thumb here, hon. Use your left hand to support your right. When you shoot, the slide will come back hard; you don't want it to bite you."

"Okay." She aimed at some of the cans, dry firing.

"Trigger." He pulled her index finger out of the guard, and held his own hand up with his finger curled back against itself. "Put the very tip on the trigger so when you pull back, it's a linear motion without side-side jerkiness. Aim and squeeze; don't anticipate the shot. Let the gun surprise you when it goes off. If you anticipate the shot, you'll get into the habit of pushing."

He held the gun and pushed it forward, causing the barrel to droop.

"How hard does it kick?"

"Well, it's only 9mm Parabellum, but you're a little thing."

She gave him a raspberry.

"Pull the slide back and lock it."

She did.

"Remember. Never point a gun at something you are not prepared to destroy. Never put your finger on the trigger unless you want to kill something."

She left her index finger flat along the side.

"Good." Dad held up a single bullet to show her, and dropped it in the chamber. "Let's start off slow."

As soon as the bullet hit the gun in her hand, Riley's arms went stiff. Having the power to kill someone in her hands for *real* was infinitely more terrifying than any horror movie. Sure, shooting guys by the hundred in the game was visually similar, but she knew they were just pixels.

Dad said something but his words hit her brain with no more meaning than had he hummed the Star Spangled Banner. He ran his hand over her head, smoothing her hair. She stood like a life-sized plastic statue of a child soldier, barely even breathing.

"Riley."

Her head turned toward him. "I'm gonna get arrested."

Dad laughed. "This isn't New Jersey."

She gulped. "Huh?"

He grumbled. "You need a permit from the state for permission to even look at a picture of a gun there. Fascists… what are they afraid of? You know the more a government tries to disarm the people, the more they've got to hide."

"Uh, Dad? Hello? Fourteen year old with a loaded gun about to freak out here…"

His tirade skidded to a halt. His tone went from accusatory to soothing. "A gun is a tool, Riley. Nothing more. It's only as dangerous as the person holding it."

"I don't like guns." She fought to keep from trembling; was it fear or fatigue from holding it up so long?

"What if I wasn't home when that guy dropped off the car? If he attacked you, would you have rather had that or been helpless?"

"Uh…" She stared at it.

"Not saying you should've killed him. Seeing the gun would probably have made him run away. You seemed pretty comfortable with it on that PlayStation."

"Xbox," she said, in a detached tone. "It's not the same. That's just a video game. No one really gets hurt."

"You're far away from the police here. It's on us to protect ourselves."

"Easy fix for that, Dad. We could move back to civilization."

"I want you to be safe." He massaged her shoulders. "Please give it a try."

With a solid grip on the handle, her right thumb couldn't quite reach the slide release. She tilted the gun to the side and pushed it with her left. The gun jumped forward as the slide crashed home. *Finger off the trigger.* She swallowed.

"Calm down. Breathe easy. In and out. In and out. Pick a can and sight."

Aiming was easier than calming down. The distant can swiveled in a figure eight around the gun sight.

"No pressure. I'm not going to be upset if you miss. Focus on being safe before anything else. Keep the barrel pointed away from yourself, away from me, and away from the house. Always, always, always, be mindful of what goes on behind your target."

"Okay." She set her jaw in a determined clench and shut her left eye.

After a few seconds, she moved her finger onto the trigger, squeezed.

Bang.

A puff of dust rose in the distance, but none of the cans reacted. She yelped, but held on to the gun. The recoil hadn't been as bad as she'd feared, but the sound was loud. Dad wiggled his pinky finger in his ear.

"Shit. That was my fault." He grabbed a green plastic box from the table and pulled out foam earplugs. "Forgot about these."

Riley put the earplugs in. Dad motioned at the full 15-round magazine and nodded at her.

Loading that made the gun heavier, to the point of being uncomfortable. Nervousness kept her squeezing at the grip. With Dad's encouraging hand at her back, she sighted in on the same can and let all the air out of her lungs. The game had a button to hold breath as a sniper. Maybe that was why she missed—she kept breathing.

Over the course of the first fifteen shots, abject terror at holding a killing device faded to stiff apprehension. Dad nudged her feet farther apart and yelled something she couldn't fully make out past the earplugs about stability. Three bullets into her second mag, she clipped the top edge of a can and sent it spinning. Riley took her time with each successive shot; the last seven in the mag all hit a can.

She glared. *I should be sitting on the beach with Amber right now, or farming up crafting mats.*

Boom. Another can went flying.

Riley aimed at the next can. *This was the big summer break before high school.*

Boom. The can danced around the stick, shot clean through.

Her eyebrows drew together. *Now I'm in the Land that Time Forgot holding a real goddamned gun.*

Boom. The can went flying in a shower of splinters.

She tried to fire again, but the trigger didn't do much. Empty.

"Riley?"

She relaxed and set the pistol down on the table to give her arms a break, and popped out her earplugs.

"Want to take a few shots with the AR15? The Garand would probably bruise your shoulder."

"Sure." She grabbed it without hesitating and looked the weapon over. "Wow this looks just like the one in the game. That's the safety, that's the magazine release, not sure what that thing is…" She pointed at a round spur jutting out at an angle on the right side.

"Forward assist. Tap it to force the bolt in."

She peered into the ejection port. "That part moves right, like the slide on the Beretta."

"Right." He pointed out the charging handle at the back end, above the butt.

Riley hooked her fingers on it and struggled to pull it back. It slipped her grip and rammed forward. Dad pointed at a paddle shaped button above the trigger guard on the left side. "Push that down and pull the handle back."

With the rifle tucked between her legs, she strained to get the handle back and push on the button at the same time. After a grueling battle of strength, she locked it open and gasped. "Guess I'm weak."

"Maybe a little." He winked. "I've got heavy duty springs in this one."

She sighted over the empty rifle, adjusting her grip for a while before lowering it. *Maybe this could get fun.* When she eyed the loaded magazine, Dad nodded. Riley put her earplugs back in.

With the rifle in one hand pointed straight up, she grasped the magazine, wandered to the left around the table, and went down on one knee. It took her a moment to line it up and load the rifle, though Dad remained quiet and close. She slapped the underside of the mag to seat it, and lowered herself onto her belly without prompting. Dad crouched at her side.

The paddle thing locked it back; it would probably let it go too. She pushed it and the sound of the bolt slapping forward rewarded her assumption. Dad smiled. She aimed at the next can, held her breath, and squeezed the trigger.

Nothing.

"Duh. Safety." Riley sighed.

Dad grinned.

She found it in short order, noting it had only two positions. "No full auto?"

"I haven't modified it yet. It's a new one, haven't run more than a hundred rounds through it."

"Oh." She aimed again, cheek pressed to the warm metal. "This looks just like the game when you push the button to zoom."

How did I go from gamer geek/beach bum to a gun freak?

Anger washed over her as Doctor Farhi's voice echoed in her mind.

For all intents and purposes, the woman she was died immediately.

Riley growled.

Blam. Blam. Blam.

Canmageddon. Once there were no more victims, she went for the paper targets.

"Riley?" yelled Dad when the bolt locked open.

"Huh?" She pulled out one earplug.

"What's on your mind? You look pissed."

Careful to keep the empty rifle pointed in the direction of the targets, she rolled around, sat up, and stood. She looked from him down to a few stray pieces of brass in the dirt. "Mom wasn't supposed to die. She was only forty. Do you really think there's a God that got mad at her?" She glanced at the table full of weapons.

Overcome by the sudden need to feel safe, she tried to grab on to him, but he shot a purposeful look into the clouds and ran inside. Riley's arms closed, hugging nothing, leaving her staring with tears streaming down her cheeks at the man sprinting inside as if his bowels were about to explode.

I hate that radio. How did he hear it from out here?

She sat/leaned on the table of firearms and bullets, uneasy at being alone with them. All around her the wind whistled, though she felt no breeze. Emptiness everywhere. *No one will touch the guns.* She quick-walked to the patio door and ducked inside, creeping across the kitchen to Dad's bedroom door.

"I understand, sir. What I'm asking is if any of the information

Simmons and Lawry collected indicate FSB involvement in Lily's death. My daughter just brought up a good point. The woman was only forty; she shouldn't have had an aneurysm... With everything else going on here, it seems... too convenient."

Riley's intention to walk in died. She stopped, clinging to the doorjamb out of sight.

"I know it doesn't make sense, sir. They're Russian. When does anything they do make sense?"

Dad nodded at no one.

"How should I know what they'd gain from it? Lily wasn't involved in my work. Maybe they're trying to get to me." He paused. "No, sir. If they wanted Riley as leverage, they would've grabbed her in Jersey before I got there. I think someone pulled a Litvinenko on my wife, sir." He paused again, this time mumbling. "I'm well aware that was polonium-210, but they hit him in 2006. This is 2016. Who knows what they have now."

Riley backed away, shaking. Was Mom *murdered*? She silenced angry sobs with her arm as she stormed outside and back to the table. No fear remained as she grabbed the empty Beretta mag and stuffed it full of bullets. After replacing her earplugs, she slapped it into the gun, racked the slide, and aimed at the second paper target.

The sound of her opening up on it got Dad sprinting outside. He raced over, but at her apparent safe handling of the weapon, remained motionless until she'd run the mag dry.

"Riley."

She looked at him.

"I don't want you shooting unless I'm with you. Understand?"

"Yes, sir." She put the gun down. "This is serious, isn't it?"

He wrapped her in a hug and kissed her on the temple. "Yes."

"Did they kill her?" She sniffled. "A-are they going to try to kill me?"

His embrace grew tight to the point of painful for a moment. "I don't know, Riley. I don't think so."

"The doctor said stress and drinking could cause aneurysms." She pulled her face out of his flannel shirt. "Mom had a lot of stress and she drank."

"Assassinations work best when the circumstances seem likely to be natural." He glanced at the Beretta. "It's not much of a gift, I know, but I want you to consider it yours from now on."

"'Kay." She swallowed. "Dad? How come I never hear the radio go off?"

"It didn't 'go off.' I called him. I had to ask the Colonel about your mother. I never thought they'd go after her."

Riley shivered at the cold, analytical tone in his voice. The only emotion he showed came out in the tightness of his fingers pressed against her back. Mom hadn't been much of a 'hugger,' but her voice could smile.

She held on to her father and bawled like a girl young enough to be called Squirrel.

THE CRUNCH OF TIRES ON GRAVEL ABOUT FIFTEEN MINUTES LATER MADE Riley hide against him. Her first thought was the guy with the white van had decided to come back for revenge. Dad pivoted to look, forcing her to adjust her grip on him to stay out of sight.

"You know anyone with a... blue Trans Am?"

Kieran. Oh, shit. "Y-yeah."

She kept her head down to conceal her face between her hair and Dad. The car stopped, the engine cut out, and the sound of footsteps on dirt approached.

"Hi, Mr. McCullough," said Kieran. "Sorry for just showing up here, but I couldn't find a phone number."

"Hello, Kieran." Dad sounded like Mr. Business again. "We don't have a phone. No lines. Working on the Internet thing. What can I do for you?"

"I wanted to ask if Riley could have dinner at the house tonight. My mother would like to welcome her to town."

Don't let him see me like this. The idea Mom might've been murdered settled like a giant weight on her tear reserves, pushing them out. She fought to collect herself. How could she leave her dad here alone after that? Maybe he was right. Maybe they weren't interested in her at all. She'd spent three days in that horrible shelter; someone who wanted to kidnap her had ample opportunity. That place was meant to keep angry, abusive drunks away—not foreign spies. She looked up at her father. *Maybe he's overdoing the worry a bit. Colonel Bering didn't seem to think the Russians were involved with Mom's death.*

"Uh, it's up to my dad."

Tense silence lingered for a moment. Dad clasped her shoulders and held her out to arm's length. Her face got warmer.

"Are you sure, Riley? If it's what you really want..."

What's the big deal? It's just dinner with the parents, not like I'm marrying him tonight. "Uh, yeah."

Disappointment drooped his face, but he nodded. "Alright."

Riley looked down at her clothes, covered in dirt, and her hands reeking of gun. "I need to clean up."

Kieran smiled. "Great."

Riley ran to the house before he could get a good look at her red eyes. She did not want to send the wrong signal to Dad—or Kieran—and picked a Metallica tee shirt and black, skinny (full-length) jeans. She rushed the process of cleaning herself, showing up in the living room not quite twelve minutes after turning the water on. Dad and Kieran stood in the kitchen, both with a glass of iced tea. From the looks on their faces, their conversation had been civil, almost pleasant. Between her outfit and her sneakers, the only part of her not covered by black cloth were her head, neck, and arms below the bicep.

Dad smiled at her, holding up the puffy raspberry jacket Mom got her for her thirteenth birthday. "I assume you'll be coming home after sundown. It gets cold."

She took the jacket, surprising herself at not breaking down in tears at the memories of the party. *Mom, me, and Amber... some party.*

"I'll make sure she's back by ten, sir." Kieran set the glass in the sink.

"I trust you. I know where you live." He winked. "Have a good time, Riley. I've missed my SpaghettiOs."

She smirked at him.

"I'm serious. That's not attempted guilt." He shooed her at the door. "Go on."

Kieran laughed and walked toward her. The look Dad gave the back of the boy's head was scary as well as reassuring. She had no doubt he would come looking for her, likely with a gun, if she was late.

She jogged around the front of the shining car and pulled the door open, making startled noises at the unexpected weight.

"You okay?"

"It's heavy." She dropped into a black leather seat and pulled the door closed with a loud *whump.*

"Heh. It's a '78. They made stuff out of metal back then."

Riley rolled her eyes. "That sounds like something my dad would say."

Kieran grinned. "My dad said it."

The engine roared to life, far louder when experienced from inside. She held on to the seats, expecting a wild ride, but he drove down the dirt road at a conservative thirty miles per hour. However, once they hit NM 51, he opened it up a bit.

"How fast are you going?"

"A little under ninety."

She closed her eyes and swallowed. "I'm going to be sick."

Her weight shifted forward as he slowed. "Sorry. Straight roads, sports car... it happens."

Being a passenger in a car driven by someone more or less her age was scarier than trying to drive without a permit. Even if she wasn't legal, being in control felt reassuring. After a mercifully brief trip, he pulled around behind Tommy's, slipped between a battered Taurus wagon and a pair of Neons, and parked in a one-car garage.

"Your parents let you have the garage?"

"It was actually my dad's idea. Says this car looks too nice to sit out in the weather."

A door in the far end opened to a short staircase that pulled a ninety-degree right turn after three steps, and a left after another four, leading to the second-story apartment above the restaurant. The fragrance of cooking permeated the little hallway, even with a closed door in the way. Walking inside made the scent many times stronger and more appealing. The place felt dark and cramped compared to Dad's house, composed of narrow hallways and small rooms decorated in earthy colors.

Patches of cloth with intricate patterned weaves and a stylized bird symbol hung here and there, along with quite a number of wolf figurines and artwork. *His mom likes wolves... mine liked faeries. Am I going to collect little statues too when I'm old?*

Two middle-aged women bustled around the kitchen. Riley watched them, intrigued by the smells of spices she couldn't place. Perhaps if ever she got comfortable around these people, she'd ask if they'd teach her some new recipes. If the food they served in the restaurant was any indication, they knew what they were doing.

She draped her still-unworn coat over the back of one of the chairs and sat at the dining room table. *Kieran's table isn't covered with gun cleaning stuff.* His father got up from a collapsing brown recliner in front of a TV showing a football game and wobbled over, favoring his left leg.

"So this is the girl I've heard so much about?" He landed in the seat at the end with a heavy thud. "Nice to meet you."

"Hi." She shot Kieran a *'what did you tell them'* glare.

The women walked in with pots, which they placed in the center. Rice and beans, pasteles, and a bowl of small sausages. One of the women sat opposite her, the other at the end facing Kieran's dad.

"Everyone, this is Riley McCullough. Riley, that's my Dad, my mom, and my Aunt Dakota."

"Hello."

"Welcome to Las Cerezas, Riley," said the woman she assumed to be the aunt. "So sorry to hear about your mother."

Oh, kill me now. "Thanks."

"Oh, 'Kota, I'm sure she doesn't want to dwell on that," said Kieran's mother. She had the same high cheekbones as her son, and wise eyes. Something about her presence made Riley feel at ease. "The spirits work in strange ways. As awful as the reason, I think she was meant to be here."

She made no move to touch any food until Kieran's dad handed her the bowl with the beans and rice. Soon, everyone had a full plate and started in on their meal.

"So, you'll be in the ninth grade this September?" asked Kieran's dad.

"Mm hmm." Riley swallowed. "I guess the school's in T or C?"

"Yeah," said Kieran. "Hot Springs High."

"The town used to be called Hot Springs," said Aunt Dakota. "They changed the name over some silly game show years ago."

His mother offered a slight bow. "Well, I'm sure you'll fit right in."

Riley felt conspicuously white in her present company, and dreaded saying something they'd take the wrong way. "Uh, yeah. This food is amazing."

The women fussed, trying to push credit on the other person.

His mother wagged a spoon at her. "You must not be used to real food wherever you're from."

"Jersey," mumbled Riley.

"I hear the pizza is good there," said his father.

"My mother liked to cook, but she made stuff like salmon and capers, and things with French names."

A brief discussion between Riley and the women about cooking crossed paths with Kieran and his father going back and forth about the football game unfolding on the screen in the living room. Riley lost herself in a moment of feeling 'normal' for a while, the sense of being an outsider watching someone else's family faded.

She got up to help collect plates, but Kieran's mother waved her off. "Nonsense, child. You're a guest."

"Wanna play a video game or something?" asked Kieran. "My room's upstairs. PC's a bit different than Xbox though."

I wonder if Amber is online. As rude as it felt to want to talk to her friend while at Kieran's house, she *had* to at least say hello. Riley grabbed her coat and followed Kieran down a narrow hallway. In order to get to his bedroom, they had to climb a fold-down ladder to a converted attic with a claustrophobic angled ceiling. Planets made of Styrofoam balls orbited in a mobile at the center, space-themed posters hung on the walls, though they looked more NASA and less *Star Wars*. A black-framed bed held a dark blue mattress against the far corner, with enough space between the foot end and the wall for a computer desk and a chair. Stacks of CD and DVD cases burdened the cheap particleboard furniture into a perpetual rightward lean.

"Wow, guess you were serious about the engineering stuff." She spun around, staring at the decoration. "You wanna like be an astronaut or something?"

"No, I'd rather work on the ground designing and building the spaceships." Kieran walked past her to the computer desk. "That would be a dream. Mom wants me to be a park ranger or something... stand between civilization and nature."

"I dunno. That could be cool too." She threw her jacket on his bed and sat next to it. Her eyes shot to three shiny plastic squares that spilled out of the pocket.

Condom packets.

Kieran had his back to her at the moment, reaching for the power button on the computer. Riley let out a scream and jumped across her coat, hiding the mortifying objects with her chest.

"What?" Kieran whirled around. "Are you okay?"

Red-faced and on the verge of crying, she waved her arm at a bookshelf past the ladder, nestled in the vee of the roof. "M-mouse."

Kieran laughed. "You don't look like the type of girl to scream over mice."

She gathered the sheets to her chest, begging fate not to let him see what Dad did to her.

"Okay, okay..." He tromped over. "There's no mice in this place. I bet you saw a shadow."

As soon as he went by, she gathered the packets and stuffed them in the inside pocket, which had a zipper. She rolled to sit up, clutching the bundle of raspberry cloth in her lap. No doubt, her face was almost the same color.

I am going to kill him. Oh, My God! Dad!

Kieran studied the area around the shelf for a moment, moving some boxes out of the way. "Nope. No mice." He approached, looking confused. "You okay? You look nervous as hell. If you're not comfortable being here… I'm… I—"

"I trust you." She couldn't look at him. "It's not… I mean, I've never been in a boy's room before, but I'm not like, afraid of you or anything."

He crossed by and sat in the computer chair. "I'm glad to hear that, but you look like you're ready to scream and run if I twitch wrong."

She shoved the jacket to her side—away from him—and took a few deep breaths. That explained the serious 'are you sure this is what you want' Dad gave her. "Uh, it's not you."

Kieran tossed a wireless controller on the bed. "Wanna do something co-op or versus mode?" He pointed at a stack of game boxes.

"Thought you were a 'mouse guy.'" Riley tried to relax and not think about what would've happened if he'd been looking when she dropped her coat.

"For shooters, yeah. Everything else, controller all the way."

"Can we pop into *Call of Duty*? I wanna say hi to a friend." She flicked a fingernail at the controller.

"Your friend using an Xbox?" He raised an eyebrow. "No cross platform. Different sandbox."

"Oh." Riley frowned at the rug for a moment before looking up. "What's that one?" She pointed at a DVD case; on the cover, a sad-faced teen girl stood behind a man with a rifle in the midst of a destroyed city.

He tilted his head, as if appraising her level of skittishness. She couldn't help but mirror his little grin.

"It's a post-apocalypse game with zombies… *The Last Outpost*. We can multiplayer the story mode if you want. It's intense, but I don't think you're in the mood for jump-out-of-your-seat scary. How 'bout a fighting game?"

"Oh. Whatever you want." She scooted to the foot of the bed with the controller in hand. "I'll go easy on you."

KEEPING SECRETS

R iley got out of the Trans Am at two minutes to ten, and rushed through a thigh-deep dust cloud peeling away from the tires. Kieran's eighty mile an hour trip down NM 51 rattled her less than the trip into town that afternoon. He trotted after her to the small porch. She whirled, handled about two point one seconds of eye contact, and found herself staring at his stomach as he walked over. Rigid, nervous, and probably blushing like hell.

"Hey," said Kieran. "Don't I get a goodbye?"

Kiss?

"Uhh, sorry. I'm"—*pissed off at my dad*—"trying to get inside before I'm late." She froze, both excited and petrified at the thought of him trying to touch her. "Thanks for dinner… hanging out was kinda fun."

He grinned. "Yeah. Next time I won't be so easy on you."

A thud inside the door made her turn scarlet. *No Dad! He's talking about the game.* "You weren't going easy. You were getting your ass kicked. I saw you getting a little pissed off. Wasn't like at pool where you were trying to let me win." Riley grinned.

Kieran scratched his head. "Yeah, so… Maybe we could co-op *The Last Outpost* next time? I'd rather be with you than against you."

Riley's brain took 'against you' the same way Dad's probably did. Red lights and sirens went off in her head as awkwardness reached alarm levels. He seemed to feel the tension making her body rigid and took a step back.

"You should go in. It's getting late. See you Thursday?"

"Yeah." She bit her lip and kept standing there.

He winked, whispering, "He's watching us."

Riley looked down at her sneakers. "Yeah."

"See you soon?"

"Okay." She ducked inside before she had to look at him again.

Dad was on the couch. He never sat on the couch, not once since she'd been there. Always, he'd been at his desk. Riley nudged the door closed behind her back. The sound of Kieran's car starting made her twitch. Still, the AM radio and some woman on CNN debated in his bedroom.

"Oh, there you are." Dad smiled over his shoulder at her, as casual as if he'd not noticed them outside.

Riley waited for the sound of Kieran driving away to grow silent, and stomped over.

"How was your date?"

She stuffed her hand in her jacket, rummaged, and threw the condoms at him. "I'm not a whore!"

He looked down at them, showing little reaction. "I just wanted you to be prepared."

"Dad! How could you?" She balled her hands into fists. "You might as well have called me a megaslut in front of him."

"I don't understand why you're so upset. It's just a precaution."

"We're not fucking!" she screamed. For a moment she stood, breathing hard and trying not to hit him. "I haven't even kissed a boy yet, Dad. I'm not a tramp. You think I'm easy? What the hell is wrong with you? It's like you're missing that filter that normal people have between their brain and doing stupid, embarrassing shit to the people they supposedly love."

"Riley." He reached, but she ducked away from his hand. "You're that age; he's that age... things can happen. I'm not saying that's what you want, but in the heat of the moment..."

"I don't *believe* you!" She backed up. "You don't even know what it feels like!" She burst into tears and ran to her room, slamming the door before diving face-first into her pillow.

FLANNEL PAJAMA PANTS TICKLED THE TOPS OF HER FEET AS RILEY SHIFTED her weight from side to side by the kitchen counter the next morning. She used the last of the eggs, stretching them enough for two omelets by stirring in some potatoes and cheese. While she whisked the mess in hopes of creating something suitable to cook, Dad emerged from his room and went to set up the coffee maker.

"Still mad at me?"

"Yep." She didn't look up from the eggs.

"I'm sorry. I don't understand."

"*That's* why I'm mad at you." She tightened her grip on the bowl so it didn't go flying.

"I did not mean to imply you were specifically going there to have sex with the boy, but I know how boys that age are. You're at a vulnerable stage where you're half little girl and half grown up, and you've also been through hell."

Her whisking slowed.

"I'm not saying he *is* the type of boy to do so, but someone that knew your situation could exploit it and take advantage of you."

She stopped beating the eggs. "They fell out onto his bed. He almost saw them. Do you have any idea how it would look if he found out I went to his house with a pocketful of condoms?" Riley pushed the eggs aside to keep tears from falling into them. "I'd never be able to show my face in this state."

He flicked the switch on the coffee maker, which set to burbling. "That does make sense."

"I promise I won't do anything with him. Mom already gave me the talk. If I get pregnant, there goes school and any hope for a decent job. Besides, it's not like boys even notice me anyway."

He put a hand on her shoulder. "I'm sorry."

She squirmed around and hugged him. "I'm still mad at you, but okay."

"I trust you, Riley." He let go and took a seat at the table.

Let's see how he likes awkward. "Thanks. I'll bring him here when we decide to have sex the first time. I'll feel safer with you in the next room."

"There you go, sounding practical like your mother again." He slurped coffee.

A twinge of nausea churned in her belly. *Unreal.*

"However, I doubt you are being serious. You'll probably find a nice, secluded spot. The first time your mother and I—"

"Dad." She slammed a pan down on the stove. "TMI."

"… University had this tree …"

"Lalalalalalalala." Riley stuck her fingers in her ears. "Not listening to parents-having-sex stories."

She refused to look at him on her way to the stove with the bowl of egg-potato-cheese slop.

———

RILEY CROSSED HER ANKLES, HEELS ON THE COFFEE TABLE AND BUTT ON THE couch. She stared at the flaking polish on her toenails, now convinced it would chip or fall off before the nails grew out. Old nail polish seemed all of a sudden like a crummy thing to use as a shrine to remember Mom. Even if she had applied it before Mom passed away, she could come up with something better as a memorial. She heaved a sigh, and stared at the book in her lap. Whatever the Air Force was doing took an enormous crap on the satellite signal. Every channel she tried came in as blurry lines of rainbow distortion mixed with white bands. Dad rushed back to the military radio to poke Colonel Bering about it as soon as she'd asked.

"What's that?" asked Dad, passing behind her.

"The Good Earth," muttered Riley.

"Oh. Yeah, I had to read that in high school too." He stopped. "You know I haven't made contact with the school in town yet…"

"Yeah, it's from the one I would've gone to in Jersey. I'm only reading it because Mom would've wanted me to."

"You must be bored." He chuckled. "TV still down?"

"Yeah."

She stared at black smudges on the paper, barely aware they were even words, much less grasping what they meant. Dad drifted off to his room and got to typing on the computer. Late morning rolled into afternoon. Riley made it about fourteen pages in before she headed to the kitchen to assemble sandwiches for lunch. She plated one and brought it in to him. He worked the keyboard so fast, he had to be smashing gibberish rather than forming coherent lines of program code.

"Hungry?" She offered him a ham and cheese on wheat.

His eyes lit up like she'd brought filet and lobster tail. "Best daughter in the world."

My life is over; at least Dad has a kitchen slave. She looked down. "When is the internet coming?"

Dad held up a finger while chewing for a moment. "Should be next Wednesday."

"Why's it taking so long? There can't be that many people out here trying to get to the web."

He shrugged. "Probably just to be annoying. Maybe they had to order the antenna custom."

"That's not gonna mess with your, uhm… thing?" She pointed at the green radio box.

"Nope." He ate another bite. "Wow, this is good."

"It's ham and cheese, Dad. El Mundane-o."

"Different frequencies. They couldn't possibly interfere."

"'Kay." She trudged back to the sofa, picking at her sandwich while making a heroic effort to progress through the book. *This is stupid. Why can't they just let us read stuff we like instead of a Chinese soap opera?*

Riley shifted to lie sideways on the couch with her head on the arm. Minutes later, she was on her belly, propped up on her elbows. Twenty minutes after that, her back was on the floor with her legs hooked over the cushion, book hovering above her head.

A knock at the door preceded a heavy thud from Dad's room. He rushed out with a 1911 pistol concealed by his right thigh.

"Jesus, Dad. Calm down." She sat up, tucking a napkin in the book to mark her place.

He crept to the window, peering under the curtain. A thin sliver of daylight drew a line down his face over one eye.

"Oh. It's that boy again." He relaxed.

"Put the gun away." She darted to the door, opening it and stepping outside onto warm, coarse stone. "Hey."

Kieran's white tee shirt and blue jeans had a new companion today: a denim jacket. Merely looking at it made her want to sweat. "Still wanna go to the movie theater?"

"Oh crap, it's Thursday."

"It's cool if you can't."

She pushed the door open. "I forgot what day it was. Dad?"

"Yes?" Came from the bedroom.

"Can I go to the movies with Kieran?" *If you say something awkward again, I will scream.*

"Is it important?"

She crept to the doorway by his room. "Why?"

He had the radio headset on again, a little paleness in his cheeks. "No reason. I'm worried. I'd like you to stay close to home for the next few days."

The disappointment at being denied surprised her. Her hangdog expression said more than a begging whine could have hoped for.

"Fine. However"—Dad held up a finger—"you're to be home before dinner. If anything weird happens, I want you home right away." He stood, raising his voice. "Kieran?"

Riley sidestepped to allow him to stand in Dad's doorway.

"Yes, sir?"

"I understand Riley wants to go to the movies with you."

"The movie theater, yeah."

She squinted at him, confused by the strange clarification.

"I want her home by six."

Kieran nodded. "No problem."

"Also." Dad leaned back in his chair. "If anything out of the ordinary happens. Anything at all, I want you to bring her home right away. Don't let the police or anything else get in your way."

"Whoa. Dad..."

"Are you sure it's okay Mr. McCullough? It's just the movie theater, it's not that important."

Dad looked at Riley. "She needs to spend time with some people her own age. It's"—he glanced at the SINCGARS—"probably just an old man being too cautious."

Riley fidgeted with her jean shorts, hoping they weren't *too* short for Dad. She braced for him making an awkward remark, but he said nothing. Once that fear passed, she smiled. "Thanks, Dad. I'll be home on time."

He tossed her an old digital watch.

"What's that for?"

"So you know what time it is. People used to wear them before everyone had a cell phone."

"I know what a watch is, Dad. Geez." Riley attempted to put it on, but even at the smallest loop, it fell off. *Into the pocket it goes.*

She led the way to Kieran's car and hopped in before he'd made it halfway across the front yard, yelping at the touch of hot black leather on her bare legs. Kieran laughed and took off his jacket for her to use as a seat cover. Riley smiled, pushing herself up so he could slip it under her.

"Your old man seemed a bit weirder than usual today. He off his meds?"

Riley rolled her eyes. "He's not *on* meds. He's..." *They'll try to get information out of you.* "Had a lot of work stuff lately. They want him to finish this software thing by the end of the week. He's fried from working fourteen hours a day."

"Oh. Yeah, my dad gets crazy too when they keep Tommy's open long for special events."

He drove the dirt road a lot faster than Riley would've dared in a pickup truck. She held on for dear life, even though the car took it well.

"Who's Tommy?"

Kieran slowed for the turn onto NM 51. "The dude he bought the place from. Never bothered to change the sign. At first, there wasn't the spare money for it, but then they made a running joke out of it. Whenever someone asks where Tommy is, they say he'll be back in an hour."

She laughed.

The Trans Am devoured the open highway between the dirt road and Las Cerezas; he slowed to twenty-five in town and followed along the curving dirt path that led out toward the trailer park. Riley leaned up to her window to peer out at about three dozen house trailers. Most were white, some pink, and a few adobe brown. Old people sat in lounge chairs. A grandmother stood watch over a pair of naked toddlers running in circles around a kiddie pool squealing with glee. At the center of the park, a large tree held a barefoot girl on a swing; she looked perhaps ten, and had her attention absorbed by an e-reader.

Riley blinked at the piece of technology. Las Cerezas was a mole on the ass of nowheresville, a trailer park here seemed like it should still have donkey powered carts and pump wells. *Hmm, maybe this place isn't as primitive as it looks.*

She faced ahead as Kieran accelerated. A few minutes later, the road curved north, and she gawked at an enormous outdoor movie screen marred with holes and streaks of rust. Before it lay a parking lot full of metal poles, each about as high as a car window, arranged in a grid pattern. Ten rusting cars that hadn't driven in decades clustered in a spot near the center, but closer to the back. He pulled up alongside a still working but battered jade-green El Camino.

Lyle, Camila, Luis, and three other boys she'd not yet seen sat around on the rust buckets guzzling beer. One of the new boys had a guitar out and fiddled with a chord progression, cringing at the last note as if it bothered him even though it sounded fine to Riley.

The cloud of smoke surrounding Luis explained the mellow look in his eye.

"Oh. That's why you said 'movie theater' instead of 'movies.' Geez, this looks like the set of Mad Max."

"Yeah. Welcome to La Cerveza, where there's nothing to do but drink." He leaned right, looking at her with a whimsical grin. "Whenever you want to go home, let me know. If this ain't your uh… 'scene,' you don't have to stay."

"It's alright." She climbed out, grunting to push the massive door closed behind her.

The sound of it slamming drew all eyes to her. Fortunately, only the three new people gave her anything more than a passing glance.

"That's Black Chakra," whispered Kieran. "Luis's band. They're all from T or C."

"Oh." Riley swiped her hands at her stomach, trying to stuff them in the pockets of a sweatshirt she wasn't wearing. She grumbled. Her jean shorts were too tight to use the pockets for hands, so she let her arms dangle… feeling awkward and gangly as they approached. Camila offered a friendly wave, and trotted over with an unopened beer.

Doctor Farhi's voice spoke in her mind. *Alcohol and stress. Hereditary factors.* Dad answered, *S'pose you shouldn't work for a bank.* "You got water?" Riley smirked. *I don't wanna wind up like Mom.*

"Look at the good girl," said Lyle. "No one cares out here if you're underage. Even the cops know it's boring."

Riley shot him a sour look. "It's not that. I'm like, allergic to alcohol. It could kill me." *Where did that come from?*

Camila winced. "Oh, that blows. Sorry. Uh, Ly, did we bring anything else?"

"I got some Jack in the truck… some Bacardi too."

"Oh, you." Camila rambled at him in Spanish.

"It's okay," said Riley.

She hadn't been particularly thirsty until she thought about having nothing to drink in the middle of the desert. *Already lied about it, gotta run with it.*

"I got it," said a Chinese-looking kid with midnight black hair and six rings through his lower lip. "I was gonna go for snacks anyway."

He nodded to her as he passed on his way to the El Camino. The look seemed friendly, if not a little patronizing.

"So who's the jailbait?" The voice emanated from a white boy with a scarlet streak of hair over his head that resembled a dead ferret, tail dangling in front of his left eye.

"Suck it, Wayne," said Kieran. "She just moved in."

"People don't move *in* to Cerezas, man. Everyone's trying to get the hell out." Wayne puffed at the hair over his eye. "Only people who come here don't wanna be found. What's she hidin' from?"

"Nothing." Riley didn't feel comfortable sitting on rusting cars with short shorts on, so she wound up cross-legged on the dirt. "Just trying to find the most boring city on the planet for a summer project."

The kid with the guitar tweaked the last note of the chord, seemed to like it, and played it twice. He let silence linger for a few seconds and went into a delicate intro, singing with a melodic, soulful voice.

"The world, I call avarice. My soul it tries to own.
This path I see, enlightenment. I know I walk alone.
Free your mind and body both, from tethers to the greed.
Realize that nothingness is your only need."

The light acoustic intro gave way to a distorted shredding of strings that sounded reminiscent of '*Ride the Lightning*' era Metallica, and he growled:

"Attachments.... Meaning less.
Free your soul.
Attachments... Mean-ing-less.
Free your sooooul.
Cast aside... Ma-ter-i-al.
Ties that bind."

Luis played air-bass while making music-ish noise with his mouth. The guitarist repeated the chords again without words and let it trail off to silence.

"Wicked," yelled Camila.

"New song?" asked Kieran.

The El Camino kicked up a spray of dirt, speeding around in a donut before zooming down the road.

"Yeah." The kid with the guitar seemed lost in some manner of meditative state.

He could've been a football player, as big as he was. Both sides of his neck had black tribal tattoos covering them, and the back of his right hand had one that looked like a Chinese character. Riley tilted her head. It resembled a number '30' with a swoosh and a dot over it.

"What's that mean?" she whispered.

"It's the symbol for '*Om*'," said the guitarist. He finally opened his eyes. "I'm Jaime."

Despite his size, he seemed like the least threatening of everyone here. She accepted the handshake. "Riley."

"I still think Jaime is a girl's name," said Lyle. After a dawning look of enlightenment, he laughed. "And Riley's a boy's name. You two should hook up."

"The Air Force will be lucky to have such a deep-thinking mind," said Jaime. "Assuming you don't draw teddy bears and smiley faces in the dots on the ASVAB sheet."

"Right here." Lyle grabbed his crotch.

Jaime plucked the strings, playing the same riff again. "Hey, that's Camila's. She'll stab me if I go anywhere near it."

"Damn right." Camila grabbed Lyle's crotch. "This belongs to me."

Riley looked away.

Kieran reclined on the ground next to her. A few half-started conversations about music came and went. Camila and Lyle drifted off behind a crumbling Chevy van for predictable reasons. Jaime became re-absorbed in working out the chord progression of his new project. Wayne leaned on the car by Jaime, banging on the hood to add drums. Luis seemed to have fallen asleep with a smoldering joint precarious between his fingers.

Riley gave up trying to keep her flip-flops on and extended her legs straight, propping herself up on her elbows. The wind whistled through the old projection surface, tinged green and streaked with dark red smears around the mangled parts. "What made those holes?"

Kieran got a mischievous look. "Depends on who you ask. Some people think aliens did it."

"What, like the little grey dudes?"

"Yeah." He shook his head with a light eye roll. "Most people think it was the military, a bomb went stray from the test range over the hills."

"That's like a hundred miles east or something," said Luis.

Wayne raised his arm to the east. "Yah, man... but planes. They like, go fast."

Riley squinted at the screen; patches of exposed metal glinted bright in the midday sun. "A bomb would've knocked the whole thing over."

"Cluster bomblets wouldn't," said Lyle.

"Probably idiots using it for target practice," said Kieran. "Or kids throwing big rocks. No one really knows."

The holes looked too large to be the result of bullets, too small for bombs, and no two were the same size. She leaned back resting her weight on her palms and staring straight up. "So, what's the school like?"

"I dunno," said Kieran. "Like every other small town high school, I guess." He squinted into a light wind that teased his hair. "Probably not as exciting as what you're used to. Not as many people. Bet they're friendlier here than Jersey. Dad said everyone there's always in a bad mood. Always like, in a hurry and stuff. Mom says everyone east has lost touch with nature."

She leaned against his arm. "Your mom like a hippie or something?"

"My grandmother was a shaman."

Riley let her weight settle into Kieran and watched a pair of clouds drifting by overhead, two wads of cotton dropped in a swimming pool. Wind flapped her hair around her face. "That's cool."

"If you're interested in nature stuff, there's a couple of hiking trails around Elephant Butte."

She fell flat on her back, giggling. "I'm not sure I wanna walk near an elephant's butt."

"Now I know you're from out of state," said Jaime. "No one makes that joke but out-of-towners."

"And little kids," added Luis.

She sat up, tucked her feet under her, and pulled her hair out of her eyes. "So, do you wanna go to school for aerospace or save the animals?"

Kieran straightened, narrow eyes aimed at the horizon.

He looks so... majestic. She blinked. *He's not Mexican... he's an Indian.*

"Mother says when the time is right, I'll make my choice. It will come to me."

"You can ask the peyote," said Luis. "I know a guy."

"You know, I believe my mother wouldn't have any issues with that." Kieran chuckled. "Dad might object... cops too."

"What's peyote?" Riley frowned, trying to tease out a familiar-sounding name from the rest of not-so-popular culture. *I think that DARE cop said something about it.*

"It's a cactus," said Kieran. "With hallucinogenic properties."

"Cops won't touch you." Luis held up a finger. "Protected religious freedom and crap."

"Oh." *Drugs.* Riley shivered. "So, you're an Indian?" She blushed. "Sorry, I mean Native American?"

Kieran didn't seem offended. "Mom is Apache. Dad's originally from Guadalajara."

"Cool. I've never..." *Seen one before? Geez, stick both feet in your mouth.* "Uhm... Sorry."

"Eh, I'm not that traditional." He put an arm around her.

Riley expected every muscle in her back to lock at his touch, but the awkwardness faded at his smile. She leaned against him.

"Sure he is," said Luis. "A week from now, he'll be out at midnight dancing naked around a bonfire."

Riley blushed.

Kieran side-armed a clod of dirt at him with his free hand. The boys laughed, but Riley couldn't look at either of them. Her imagination gave her the image of a fire dance, and wouldn't take it back. The crunch of the El Camino's return distracted her. The lip-ring guy jumped out with a big plastic cooler atop which balanced two red-and-white-striped paper boxes. Riley bit back a whine of protest as Kieran stood and pulled her upright to join everyone wandering over.

Lip Ring Kid set the cooler down on the hood of an ancient car.

"Easy, that's a '62 Catalina," said Kieran.

"It's a piece of shit," said Luis. "Even your medicine couldn't bring it back to life."

After Wayne grabbed the two boxes of hot wings, Lip Ring opened the cooler and handed Riley a bottle of water from a six-pack. She grabbed a wing, unprepared for the level of spice painted on it. The first bottle of water vanished in a chug, the second she sipped. Camila and Lyle emerged from behind the old van, adjusting their clothes back into place. Luis held his hands up over his head, slow clapping.

Being among these people felt less awkward now than the first time at Tommy's, though thinking about what had gone on out of sight a few yards away lent an undertone of discomfort. Riley sat against the front end of the Catalina, careful to only let cloth touch metal. The boys made a Frisbee out of a hubcap for a while; Lyle and Luis hit the Corona hard enough to lose the ability to speak. Whenever Luis got a hold of the hubcap, someone had a long walk.

Jaime and Wayne existed in a world apart from everyone, taken by the muse and working out the rhythm for the new song.

She sipped water, content to watch the boys horse around. Sudden motion on the ground attracted her attention downward. Seconds away from her toes, a pale scorpion ambled over the dirt. Riley screamed and leapt up onto the hood. Her shrieking continued until the creature had vanished under the old hulk, and Kieran had run to her side.

"It's just a scorpion," he said. "They're usually not aggressive unless you step on them."

She whined at the flip-flops she'd left on the ground thirty yards away by where they'd been sitting. "Will you get my shoes?"

"Those won't help much," said Luis. "You step on them and the tail will still come up and over." He poked her in the foot with a chicken bone. "You got boots?"

"Sneakers." She frowned.

Kieran patted her knee. "It shouldn't be too much of a problem... just watch where you step and be careful around dark places."

"I don't wanna be near it." She reached up.

Kieran hooked an arm under her legs and carried her a few steps away from the old car. She stared at his face; her heart pounded. As embarrassing as it was to be 'the helpless girl,' having his strong arms cradle her sent electric tingles down to her toes. She held on, wishing the short distance to where they sat would take all night to get there. Her body tensed as if about to step into molten magma when he moved to set her down.

"Scorpions... Great, now I'm going to be staring at dirt all the time."

Kieran sat on the ground and held his arm out, offering a spot. "If you had held completely still, it probably would have walked right by. You might not have ever seen it."

"That doesn't make me feel better." She slid in under his arm, sitting with her legs tucked to one side.

He started off by talking about scorpions, but wound up telling her about his meeting with a jaguar when he was ten. Riley couldn't quite imagine Kieran as terrified as he explained himself to be, and tried to ignore her suspicion this was another Robbie Zimmer situation. Kieran seemed happy to be with her. Oddly enough, she didn't get the sense he wanted to lure her into some embarrassing set up. Also surprising, not one of these kids had yet said a word about her figure—or lack of one. An hour later, she'd mostly forgotten about a scorpion coming within inches of her foot.

"Ready," yelled Luis.

Riley glanced over, where all four members of Black Chakra, plus Lyle, had lined up with their backs turned.

"Aim," yelled Luis.

Five zippers opened.

"Oh, my..." Riley hid her face against Kieran's arm. "Are they?"

"Fire," yelled Luis.

"Yeah. Come to think of it… that's not a bad idea." Kieran got up with a grunt, and went over to join the firing line.

Three bottles of water had also created an issue for her, but she was not about to join the guys. Camila noticed her urgent look and walked over. Riley twisted around and spotted a crumbling building by the entrance. The front face had the appearance of a concession stand, though a sign of a stick figure in a dress adorned a door on the far right side. She set off for it, but the other girl caught her by the arm.

"Oh, no. You don't want to go in there."

Riley glanced at the boys. "I'm not just going to…"

"No one has cleaned that bathroom since 1971. I don't even want to think about what's growing in the toilet."

"But… but…" Riley whined.

Camila smiled. "Now you know why I'm wearing a skirt."

"I can't believe you and Lyle—"

"Hah." Camila laughed. "We were just making out. He'd never do *that* in public."

"I've never… you know…"

"Pissed outside? That just means you've never been to a real party." Camila took her hand and pulled her upright. "There's a little ravine over there for cover. I'll go with you."

Riley shrank in on herself. "I don't want you to watch either."

"I'll stand guard, and then you can do the same for me."

"Okay."

Riley followed her to where a cut in the ground deepened to a ledge running around the right side of the old drive-in theater. Innumerable bottles, cans, and cigarette butts accumulated at the bottom, as well as some rusted car parts. Terrified of finding more creepy-crawlies, Riley took her sweet time going down the hill until she could no longer see any of the people up top. Desert stretched off in three directions, open for miles. The boys horsing around above and behind still sounded way too close.

Maybe I'll just hold it. She cringed, bouncing on the balls of her feet. Off in the distance, several tiny specks appeared in the sky, emitting a heavy, thudding drone. They were far away, but had the look of something military—and drove right toward Las Cerezas.

Or not.

RILEY FLAILED, WAVING HER ARMS IN AN EFFORT NOT TO LOSE HER BALANCE while climbing a steep embankment in flip-flops. She snagged a handful of rough roots, and pulled herself up enough to see Camila with her back turned. At the sound of her grunting, the other girl whirled around.

Camila grasped her hand to help her up the last of the ridge. "You okay? I was about to come down after you with a search party."

"Uh… yeah. Fine." Riley swatted dirt and green leafy crumbles off her legs.

"Okay, my turn."

Riley rotated away while Camila descended. *Shooting guns, peeing in the wild, almost getting bit by a scorpion. What's happening to you, Riley McCullough?*

"Hey, Riley, check this out," yelled Camila.

"Gross. No thanks."

"No, not that. Look."

Against her better instincts, she did. A cloud of dust out in the sands trailed behind what appeared to be a military convoy. She watched the vehicles approach, until they turned onto the dirt road leading past the front of the old drive-in, heading toward Las Cerezas. Five semis covered in fluttering camouflage tarps, surrounded by Humvees with machine guns, crept in a single file. Soldiers manning the guns glowered as if annoyed she dared look in their direction. Through a gap in one tarp, she made out what appeared to be large, green missiles with angular contours and little wings.

The thudding of helicopters going overhead a second time made her shiver.

Camila climbed the hill, tugging at her gypsy skirt until it sat right. "Wow. Looks like they're on their way to Holloman. Never saw a caravan like that before."

That counts as weird.

Riley lost one flip-flop as she sprinted over to Kieran, and grabbed him. "I need to go."

"You're trembling." He let her cling. "Relax, it's only the Air Force."

"Whoa," said Lyle. "They kinda look like AGM-129s… but those were supposed to all be decommissioned in 2012."

"What's that?" Riley dug her fingers into Kieran's shirt.

"Nuclear cruise missiles." Lyle shielded his eyes for a moment, and shook his head. "Nah. They're probably some kinda UAV we haven't seen yet. 'Course, maybe some idiot from Texas forgot a storage unit. Oops, sir, found some more old nukes."

"Weird," said Luis.

"Fuck you, Lyle." Wayne raised a middle finger.

"He's from Texas," whispered Kieran.

"Yeah." Jaime took a long swig from his Corona. "I've never seen them ride like that in the middle of the day. Must be important. Especially with an aerial escort."

Dad's pallid face leapt to mind, followed by the overflight of bombers days ago. She glanced up at Kieran. "Please take me home."

Kieran looked disappointed by her decision, but offered no protest. She ran over to her errant flip-flop, grabbed it, and carried them with her to his car. Her mind raced, drawing connections between the Korea thing on the news, Dad talking about the Ukraine, bombers, now nuclear missiles transported out in the open.

No, no, no. This is bad. Dad's gonna shit his pants.

"Hey..." Kieran said, as soothing as he could get his voice to sound. "You're acting like you've seen a ghost. What's wrong?"

"I'm scared." She dropped her flip-flops and stepped on them.

"Obviously." He looked her in the eye. "What of?"

"World War Three," she muttered, reaching out to take his hand.

Kieran held in a chuckle. "You've been watching too many movies. It's not going to get to that point. No one is crazy enough to hit 'the button.' The idiots want to control the world, not melt it. If someone does something, they'll all do something, and then there'll be nothing left. Even the craziest dictators know that."

Okay, that makes sense. She stood up on tiptoe and kissed him.

Kieran seemed surprised. "Random. Not that I mind... I could stare into those deep green eyes of yours forever."

She blushed, grinned, and looked down. "I couldn't do that at the house; Dad will shoot you. He's got a problem with *them*."

Kieran glared. "Native Americans?"

"No." She held on to his shirt. "Oh, God, no. He's not a racist. I mean the people in town. He thinks everyone in Las Cerezas hates him."

"He's so reclusive. Anti-social behavior gets people suspicious. I hear people at the restaurant talk. They say he's up to something."

Riley leaned up as if to kiss him again, whispering. "I shouldn't say this, but he works for the government." *Shit. That's exactly what Dad's afraid of.* "Uh, he—"

Kieran silenced her with a kiss. A bit different from the childish peck she'd opened with. She moved with him as he twisted and pressed her back against the car. Riley closed her eyes and followed his lead, not wanting the moment to end. *This* was her first kiss.

Robbie Zimmer can go to hell.

She lowered her weight off her toes, gazing up at him with a giddy half-grin.

"He probably has good reason to keep his secrets. I don't need to know."

Wow. He didn't paw me at all. "Yeah," she whispered.

"S'pose we should get you home."

Riley forced her fingers into the tight pocket of her jean shorts, adding a little shimmy to help slip the watch out. Sun glinted off the display as she tilted it over to check the time: 4:49. She stuffed it most of the way back in before threading her arms up around his head, grasping her wrist behind his neck. He set his hands on her hips. Riley's heart skipped about, getting into a boxing match with the butterflies in her stomach.

"I got a couple minutes."

WATCHING

An uneasy feeling sat like a stone in Riley's stomach, agitated by the deep, throaty rumble of the Trans Am engine vibrating the seat. She kept her eyes pointed down as they passed through Las Cerezas, twirling a strand of loose denim between her fingers.

Farther east, a cloud of dust whorled across the desert. With the intimacy of the once-in-a-lifetime moment of her first real kiss gone, she couldn't help but dwell on the convoy full of missiles.

"You okay?" Kieran reached over.

She took his hand and clung. "Yeah. It's nothing."

His touch doused her fear under a wash of warmth that spread over her face and chest. She tried to think of what to say; talking about something would stop her from worrying about what the military was doing or what Dad might be dealing with. Before anything came to mind, she caught sight of the speedometer at fifty on the nose. He didn't seem to be in much of a hurry.

"Maybe this town doesn't suck all that much."

"Oh?"

You're here. Her brain kicked in before the words slipped out—too sappy. "I guess I could get used to it. Jersey was so loud and busy." *And didn't have you.*

He pulled up to the house and stopped. "Oh hey, I got you something."

He reached behind her seat and came back holding a plastic bag, which he handed to her.

"Mrr?" She peeked in at a DVD case with an Xbox version of *The Last Outpost.* "Oh, that was expensive."

"It wasn't that bad." He winked. "It's like three years old now. Like I said, the story mode is much cooler. We could co-op between platforms."

"As soon as we get internet, yeah. Thanks." She crawled up as if to kiss him again, but thought better of it. "Uh… Dad's in the window."

She slid back to her seat and opened the door, using one foot and both arms to push the massive thing open. Kieran followed her to the porch. Again, she came close to kissing him, but Dad continued to hover.

"You wanna hit T or C maybe Saturday? Little more to do there than out here."

She grinned. "Okay. Um… does this mean I'm like, your girlfriend now?"

He shot an appraising glance at the sky. "Do you want to be?"

Riley bit her lower lip, looked down, felt all sorts of weird, and giggled. "Maybe."

"I'm glad you're here."

Mom… She looked into his eyes. "I'm… uh… I—"

"I know. You're not glad to be here. That's not what I meant."

"I'm glad I met you."

"Me too."

Before they could kiss, Dad pulled the house door open. Riley sensed him about to say something mortifying and cut him off.

"He was just leaving, Dad."

"Mr. McCullough." Kieran nodded at him. "I'll stop by… Saturday?"

Dad offered only a blank stare.

"Okay then." Kieran winked at Riley. "Maybe I'll see you then."

"Bye." She waved.

She didn't move until his car was an indiscernible speck in the distance. Dad waited a few steps inside the house, startling her with his 'looming titan' routine.

"Dad?"

"Put your arms out, legs apart." He held up a device similar to what security guards waved over people at airports.

"Uh, Dad?"

"Just do it."

She stood as if frozen in mid jumping jack while he ran the wand up and down her arms, over her fingers, and around her body.

"Okay, you're clean."

"What's that? A 'did my daughter just have sex' detector?"

"No, I'm checking for electromagnetic signals."

"Like a bug?" *Just a little melodramatic.* She let her arms fall against her sides. "Dad, I saw something strange."

"A clown on a unicycle juggling flaming piglets?"

"I said I saw something strange, not dropped acid." She wandered to her room. "An army convoy with trucks went through town."

Riley leaned into the doorway of her room to toss the Xbox game on the bed, intending to get started on supper before doing anything else. When she turned to walk back, Dad was inches away.

She screamed.

He caught her before she fell. "What? You okay?"

"You scared the crap out of me."

"Sorry. What did you see?"

"Uh, five big trucks with camo stuff on them and Humvees. Looked like they were loaded up with missiles. Lyle said they weren't supposed to have them anymore, like 'decommissioned' or something a couple years ago. Then he said they might have been UAVs."

Dad went pale again, and wandered to the living room where he paced an erratic figure eight. His lips moved as though he spoke, but he lent no voice to his breath. Riley stood motionless. All the worry she'd felt at the strange sight came back in triplicate. Dad stopped pacing two minutes later, blinked, and looked at her as if he'd forgotten whatever had been on his mind.

He smiled. "You seem… happier than you've been since you got here."

That was… messed up. "I think I have a boyfriend." She kicked her flip-flops into her bedroom and walked to the kitchen. "I'm gonna try to make tacos tonight."

Dad chuckled. He headed for his room, but paused by the fridge. "I suppose you'll have to get used to that food now."

"He's not Mexican, Dad. He's Native American." She thought about his father. "Well, half."

"I know. It's pretty obvious when you look at him."

Riley skimmed over the directions on the back of the box of taco seasoning. "Yeah, I guess I was thinking about stuff. Can we get a phone?"

"They won't run a wire out here."

"What about getting my cellular turned back on?" She grabbed cans of refried beans and a frozen packet of chicken. "I so need to tell Amber about Kieran."

Dad ducked into his room. "I don't trust cell phones. *They* can watch you through them."

"Which 'they' are you talking about? The people in the town, the government, or the KGB?"

"Little of column A..." His chair creaked. "Oh, and they're the FSB now."

"Seriously?"

"Well, I doubt the townies care. Anyone with the knowhow can tap a phone and watch or listen to everything going on around it. I handle too much sensitive intel for that. Why do you think I live out here in the middle of nowhere?"

Pain in the ass. "I can't call her from Kieran's house... that would be too awkward."

"Why would that be awkward?"

"Because!" *Geez, he is so clueless.* "I can't talk about a boy with him right behind me. When is the Internet coming? I suppose I can wait and chat her."

"Wednesday, remember? Six days." Dad lowered his voice. "Copy, sir. Go ahead."

Oh, that's not too bad. "Okay. Dinner'll be ready in like, forty minutes."

FIRE ON THE MOUNTAINS

Dad went straight to the radio after supper. Despite not having Internet access to get any help from, the tacos came out okay—if a pale shade of what she'd had at Tommy's. Of course, Dad couldn't stop going on and on about how amazing they were. She smiled as she packed the dishwasher with plates, forks, and pans. He seemed in a much better mood after eating, maybe he would let her go see Kieran again in the morning. The setting sun made the little window over the sink look more like an oil painting than a view to the outside, and cast the kitchen in a warm shade of orange. Riley wiped down the counter, tossed the cloth into the sink, and went to her room.

The DVD waited where she'd left it. She scored the plastic open with a fingernail, snagged the disc, and popped *The Last Outpost* into her Xbox. She started playing at 7:18 p.m., after an annoyingly long installation finished. The plot centered on a man and his daughter who managed to survive a nuclear apocalypse, and then reemerged in a world full of irradiated zombies. She chose to play the girl, a sixteen-year-old whose non-fatal exposure to a virus had given her some kind of special powers. The 'Dad' was all guns and long range; the girl seemed more like an 'agile melee' character.

She started with a pair of standard combat knives and a basic crossbow with eight bolts. After an hour and change of creeping through the sewers of a nameless city, she found a crowbar, which the game portrayed as a two-handed weapon. Apparently, the character Lisa was strong enough to knock the shambling enemies twenty meters away on a single hit. Eventually, Riley stopped rolling her eyes at the superpowered heroine, and got into the storyline.

Most of the game revolved around their trying to survive endless hordes of mindless zombies, insane thugs, wild animals, and the harsh environment while making their way to Eden 3, a supposed oasis where civilization had reestablished itself. Lisa also wanted to find and rescue her mother, who had been abducted by one of the wild gangs populating the wasteland. When dialogue revealed Lisa's mother disappeared when she was fourteen, Riley had to pause the game to gather herself. About forty minutes after eleven, she got up, went to the bathroom, had a cup of water, and trudged back to her bedroom.

Around midnight. That's when Mom died.

Riley slipped out of her jean shorts, ditched her bra, and put on a knee-length tee shirt. Now comfortable, she stretched out on the floor with a pillow under her chest and grabbed the controller.

The digital teen wanted so desperately to see her mother again, Riley wound up crying right along with her as she begged and begged her dad to risk going after her. Predictably, the father gave in and the two set off on their journey.

Father and daughter split up at several points, giving Riley the sense the girl played as a stealth character while Dad was more of a run and gun type. *This is like Thief and Call of Duty had a baby.* Enough action sequences permeated the somber storyline to let her keep going. Dread built up in her heart that they'd find Mom dead. So far, the game had been that bleak. The Earth, post-apocalypse, looked like a horrible place. Whenever a zombie lunged out of the dense grass around an old warehouse, Riley screamed louder than Lisa. Twice, she died because she fumbled the controller.

I shouldn't be playing this in a damn dark room.

Sneaking around behind a camp of gangers whitened her knuckles on the controller. A thug in a leather vest and sunglasses spotted her, but a quick sprint to a hiding spot under a semi-truck trailer lost him. She stayed still for three full minutes while ten virtual wild men walked in circles around the truck, unable to find her despite being less than two feet away in the game world. All the while, they joked and taunted about what they'd do to such a sweet young girl. Eventually, the crowd thinned, and Lisa pounced on the only man to remain, killing him from behind and dragging him to the ground as easy as pie.

After clearing the warehouse, a cutscene played where the characters interrogated a dying gang member. Lisa convinced her dad not to execute him, but the thug pulled out a hidden pistol as the two turned their backs to leave, and shot the father. He crumpled to the floor as another combat session began with the 'boss ganger.' After she killed him for the second time, more cutscene set up the next mission: Lisa had to escort her wounded father back to their safe house for medical supplies before he died. (She assumed someone playing as the father would be escorting a shot Lisa.)

I wonder how the game would handle co-op here. Not fun to have your character disabled. They probably add an NPC.

In her haste to beat the timed mission, she stepped on an unseen land mine in a field full of stacked concrete sewer pipes, killing them both and sending her back to the 'load last save point' screen.

The clock at the bottom of the screen read 1:42 am.

"Damn, it's late." She shut down the game and crawled from the floor to the bed.

RILEY FOUND HERSELF SITTING UP IN BED, UNSURE WHY SHE WAS CONSCIOUS or why her heart raced. She looked around as if in a dream, wide awake and exhausted at the same time. Something crashed at the other end of the house.

She opened her mouth to yell, "Dad," but her voice vanished under a tremendous explosion outside that lit the eastern sky over the mountains bright orange and shook the house. Seconds later, it faded to black. Had a previous bomb knocked her awake?

Dad scrambled in the door. A third explosion occurred seconds before bright light flooded the room. A horrible scratching roar seemed to pass right over the house.

"Daddy!" Riley screamed.

He grabbed her wrist with one hand and the camouflage backpack he'd planted in her room with the other. She looked around, disoriented as he hauled her down the hall to the kitchen.

"Put that on."

Riley caught the 'go bag' and started sniveling from the look in Dad's eye as she slipped it on her back. She shrieked as another detonation thundered right overhead, shaking the house and knocking a few cups off the shelf.

Dad snatched his AR15 and an ammo can, flinging the rifle over his shoulder before grabbing Riley's wrist again. He shoved the patio door open and sprinted into the desert. Riley stumbled along, trying not to fall, cringing and ducking each time something went *boom*.

Chaos surrounded her on all sides. Scintillating white light spread over the sky, eerily like the flash they always show in those nuclear disaster movies. Riley whimpered and looked away, crying out whenever her bare feet found a rock or a bit of scrub.

After what felt like forever, Dad halted in a crouch by a mound of dirt. He stuck his hand into it, lifting a wooden frame similar to a huge cargo pallet disguised as ordinary ground with sheets of burlap, dirt, and bushes. Beneath it, a vertical cinderblock-walled shaft led underground, six feet on each side.

"Go, go," yelled Dad.

Riley jumped as another explosion pounded the earth. She hesitated at the edge. Dad grabbed the backpack and lifted her on to the metal ladder. Sniveling, she scurried down some thirty feet over metal rungs that felt like ice bars. She moved like a robot until her toes found frigid concrete. A *clank* rang from overhead as Dad shut the hatch.

She backed away from the ladder, pressing herself against a grey-painted metal door. Dad dropped down so fast it seemed as though he somehow slid along the ladder rather than climbed it. He rushed over and gave her a head-to-toe glance.

"You okay? Did you get hit by any shrapnel?"

Riley stood numb. Another blast outside made her jump, but she didn't make a sound. When she didn't react in another ten seconds, he lifted her shirt up to her armpits and spun her around.

"I don't see blood. Does anything hurt?"

She shook her head.

Dad let her shirt fall, pulled the inner door open, and nudged her inside. She stumbled to the northwest corner of an underground chamber, about eight feet wide and twelve long, stretching to her right. Against the opposite wall sat a shelf with several pairs of boots, stacks of folded military fatigues, canteens, boxes of stuff, rope, and some tools.

At the far end of the room, a Frisbee-sized showerhead hung on a naked pipe, reminding her of chemistry class and the emergency wash.

She cringed as a resounding *boom* rumbled the ground, knocking dust off the ceiling. The southeast corner had a heavy, armored door that looked like a cross between bank vault and submarine hatch, complete with a wheel at its center above a standard-looking keyhole.

"We're going to be fine, Riley. You have to stay calm." Dad ran to the thick door and spun the wheel. After it locked with a clank, he grunted and hauled the door open. "In."

She stared.

"Riley!"

She jumped and blinked.

Dad grabbed her by the backpack and pushed her into a chamber larger than the last, twenty by thirty feet at least. To her left in the near corner, an exact copy of his radio set occupied a wooden table. A single bed, more of a cot, lay beyond it at the center of the left wall, past which sat an exposed toilet. The opposite corner had a smaller door, made of white plastic. A wide bookshelf rested against the wall at the end, between the toilet and door, and a mini-kitchen stood at the middle of the right side wall.

Two thick, wooden poles as big around as a telephone post supported the ceiling in the middle. The nearer of the two had a whirring aluminum pipe affixed to it, tipped with ventilation slats and a couple of blue fluttering streamers. A square folding table took up the center of the room, atop a faded blue oval throw rug. One metal chair by it wore a thick layer of dust. The southwest corner to Riley's immediate right was home to a four-foot tall safe.

The air smelled damp and musty, the concrete floor felt clammy with a hint of wetness.

She spun in place, twitching each time an explosion sounded overhead. Silt fell in waves off the ceiling with every concussion, raining grit on her hair. Dad dropped his backpack on the floor by the radio table, pulled the heavy door closed, and spun the wheel. After flipping a locking bar in place, he finally seemed to calm down. He glanced around for a few seconds before grabbing a faucet-like knob protruding from a copper pipe and spinning it clockwise until it stopped.

"This is like those dungeons creepers build to hide their kidnap victims." As the adrenaline of running through explosions wore off, she felt less and less comfortable being outside wearing only an oversized tee and panties. "I don't like it here."

"Creeper dungeon? What kind of movies did your mother let you watch?" Dad looked over from the radio, eyebrow up.

"Uh… that was the news, not the movies." She shivered. "It's freezing in here."

He didn't look over. "There're pants in your bag."

She became aware of the weight of shoulder straps, once more realizing a heavy pack perched on her back. Another detonation thundered the ground. Something in a cabinet by the mini-kitchen station fell over. The image of the military convoy, the missiles, and the bombers in the sky looped on the movie screen of her mind.

"Dad, what's happening?" She shrugged out of the backpack and ran to him. "Dad…"

"I don't know yet." He fiddled with the radio. "I'm trying to find out."

Riley screamed and ducked into a squat at a particularly loud blast, which caused the lights to falter for a second. She jumped on the bed and curled up in a ball, huddled at the pillow end, which was closest to Dad. The scratchy green wool Army blanket wasn't much, but she felt better clinging to it.

"This is Black Sheep. Colonel Bering, copy?"

Boom. More dust fell from above.

With a whimper, Riley drew her knees to her chin and shivered. Her mind raced. North Korea on the news, the nuclear missiles driving by, the terror-stricken look in Dad's eyes that morning. What had the radio told him? Did Russia do something? She thought back to dad on the phone in Mom's house, talking about the death of some guy with a Russian sounding name.

Boom.

She pulled the blanket up over her face and cowered. Not long after another explosion, a droplet of water hit her on the head. She looked up at copper piping along the ceiling. One went to the back of the toilet, with a branch off headed to the mini-sink along the south wall.

"Colonel Bering, copy. This is Black Sheep. What is your status? Over."

Boom.

That time, Riley didn't twitch. She ducked deeper under the blanket; only her eyes faced the world.

"Damn. Comms must be out." Dad fiddled with a dial. "Black Sheep to Colonel Bering, come back?"

Riley sniffled, shivering from fear as much as cold. Worry in Dad's voice piled onto her already anxious mind, until a faint red glow winked on from a box mounted to the wall by the armored door. She perked up enough to get a better look.

The light emanated from behind a transparent plastic front. It wouldn't have frightened her as much as it did, if not for the radiation symbol painted in black upon the clear part.

"Dad?"

He shifted in the chair so he could look at her.

She pointed. "What's that red light mean?"

As soon as he saw it, a tear ran out of the corner of her father's eye. "No…"

THE WORLD IS GONE

Riley stopped sobbing maybe an hour later. Rumbles continued pounding overhead, though no dust fell on her anymore. Fetal, on her side, she stared across the bunker under the folding table at the micro-kitchen. Scenes from *The Last Outpost* flooded her mind, changed to fit the real world. What happened to Amber? Was the East Coast hit too? How many died? Did Las Cerezas still exist?

Kieran.

Riley jumped out of bed and ran to the door. She tried the wheel, but it refused to budge, even with her grunting and bracing a foot on the freezing door.

"Riley!" Dad ran over and grabbed her arms. "What are you doing?"

"Kieran's still out there!" She wailed. "We have to go get them."

He pulled her away from the glowing red box. "No, Riley. I'm sorry… we can't go outside. There's lethal radiation up there."

"But…" She struggled to reach for the wheel. "We have to *try!*"

He collected her in a bear hug, pinning her arms. "I'm sorry, honey. There's nothing we could've done." He shot a wary look at the red light. "We're lucky we got in here when we did… a matter of minutes."

They said the same thing about Mom. She pictured Tommy's melting away to smoke in the heat of a nuclear inferno. Her legs gave out and she wound up hanging in his grip. He carried her to the bed, sat on the edge, and held her like a four-year-old who'd had a nightmare.

"He can't be dead. I just told him I'd be his girlfriend. No." She bawled.

Dad held on until her loud, wracking sobs faded to soft whimpers. He eased her off his lap and pulled the blanket over her shoulders before heading to the bookshelf. Riley lay motionless. He returned holding a white bottle with a mushroom cloud on the label and handed her a pill.

"I don't want it."

He pressed it into her palm. "You should take this. It's iodide. It will protect you from radiation uptake and damage to your thyroid."

She opened her hand and looked at the innocuous white pill, which could've been an aspirin.

Dad returned with a plastic cup of water.

"Aren't you going to take one?"

"I'm over forty so it's not that important. Besides, that'll mean more for you."

She sniveled. "Please don't leave Kieran and his family out there."

A distant rumble shuddered the ceiling.

"We're still under attack. That red light means there's lethal levels of radiation within a hundred yards of the way out. Holloman or Area 51 must have taken a direct hit. If we go outside, we're going to die. Slow, painful, horrible deaths."

She gulped down the pill and lapsed into another round of sobbing. Dad squeezed her close, crying a little himself.

"What happened, Daddy?"

"I'm not sure. Probably North Korea, but it could've been Russia. Hell, maybe even a foreign agent compromised India and launched something at random. Past couple of months, the world's been like a room full of angry cats. Step on one tail, you have a huge crap storm. You saw those missiles… command had to have been expecting something. I don't think we went down without a fight." He grumbled. "Hell, for all I know, maybe we shot first."

"Does that mean the world is gone?"

"I hope not, Sweetie… I really hope not."

RILEY CURLED UP ON THE BED, STARING AT THE FAR WALL. THE detonations stopped, but the red glow continued. Dad had, over at least an hour, failed to receive any word from Colonel Bering or anyone else on the radio. All Riley could think about was Amber, Kieran, and Mom.

For a brief moment, she felt ashamed of herself for being grateful that no one would be able to live in her old house.

"Riley?"

"Mmm."

"I need you to do me a favor. I can't leave the radio yet. Would you go into the crawlspace and check the water? I turned the main on when we walked in, but I wanna be sure."

"Okay." She didn't move.

Dad gave her two minutes. "Soon please."

She pushed off the cot and sat up. "Where's the crawlspace?"

He pointed at the white door. "There's a lever with two settings. Up is takin' from the well, down draws from the storage tanks underneath us. To the right of the lever is a little red light. If it's on, set the lever to internal. If it's off, you can leave it on well."

She wandered to the door. "What's the red light for?"

"Radiation check. The well's covered, so it should be safe from fallout. However, ground seep might contaminate it. Depends on how severe the radiation is. The dirt should filter most of it."

"Okay."

The cold concrete floor numbed her toes by the time she reached the white plastic door. It opened with little effort, revealing a long, narrow room with metal shelving on both sides. Countless cans of SpaghettiOs as well as hundreds of brown packages lined the shelves. A square hatch plate on the floor waited at the end of the shelf on the left. She stumbled over to it robotically, squatted, and pulled it up. It had no ladder, but the floor at the bottom was only about four feet down.

Riley ignored the frigid metal on her butt as she sat and slipped through, lowering her toes into loose, damp dirt. She remembered the scorpion, yelped, and pulled herself up. Fortunately, a box on the shelves had a few flashlights which worked, and she peered at her own footprints.

No scorpions in sight.

She dropped down again and crouched. Two massive plastic tanks flanked a control box on the left side. The right had what appeared to be a battery cluster covered in winking lights. *Seems really stupid to put water and batteries so close.* She crawled up between the tanks, noting the switch was up and the red light was off.

Not wanting to linger in the filthy space any longer than necessary, she scurried back to the opening and pulled herself up, sat on the edge with her legs dangling, and swatted dirt from her shins and feet.

"Colonel," said Dad in the other room. "Good to hear your voice. How bad is it?"

Riley lowered the crawlspace hatch, careful not to let it clank, and crept back to the main room. Dad swiveled around in the radio chair as the door behind her creaked closed. He looked paler than Mom did in the hospital.

She shivered, unable to bring herself to ask.

Dad looked down. "Riley… It's all gone."

A hundred images of Mom, Amber smiling, her old home, and Kieran flashed in her mind. She swallowed the saliva in the back of her throat and covered her mouth with both hands, trembling as she crept across the bunker. When she got close, he grasped her hips and looked her straight in the eye.

"We're still alive, Squirrel."

All she could do was stare at him. The next detonation overhead caused a faint twitch.

He brushed her hair away from her face; she stood numb, barely noticing his patting and squeezing. His lips moved, but she didn't hear him. Dad reached up and patted her cheek. Sound seemed to start back up again, as if she'd surfaced from being underwater.

"… eetie, come on."

"Huh?" She blinked. "The world can't be over. No one's stupid enough to—"

Boom. A low rumble shook the walls.

"I'm sorry, Riley." A hand on the back of her head pulled her face to his chest. "I'm so very sorry."

THE DAY AFTER

Day Two.

Dreamless sleep faded to still silence. Riley stretched, wondering why her bed felt strange. The coarse wool blanket against her arms shocked her eyes open. She gawked at the plain concrete above her. *Not a dream.* Her lip quivered. Dad snored in the radio chair, headset still on. She covered her mouth and wept for everyone she'd just met in this horrible little town. It was too much to believe that Kieran, his mom, dad, aunt, and all his friends were gone. She thought of little Jesse and that adorable childlike face, and felt sick to her stomach.

Maybe some of them survived, hiding in their basements?

Radiation was a slow killer.

She shifted at a painful presence in her bladder. Dad snored again. She glanced from him to the open toilet and back. *Oh, no way. Screw it; he's asleep.* Riley slipped off the cot, cringing as her bare feet froze on contact with the floor. Once the initial shock wore off, she crept over to a standard house toilet. It appeared clean, as though it had never been used. She turned around and sat on it, noticing she could see right over the bed to her father. It took her a moment to get up the nerve to pull her panties down, and she used her oversized shirt to hide as much of herself as she could.

Letting go while in plain sight of her father, even while he was asleep, was another matter entirely.

He snored again.

Stay sleeping. Stay sleeping.

Dad yawned and stretched.

"Don't turn around!" she screamed.

"Huh?"

"Dad! Please." She couldn't bring herself to say why.

He started to look back, but whipped away as soon as he noticed where she was. "Sorry. I never expected to have company if the need arose to use this shelter."

This is so, so, so much worse than going outside. She distracted herself with memories of how when Amber's younger brother was five, he had zero regard for privacy and would walk in and use the bathroom no matter who was in there. It didn't help. She tried to rush the issue, but had little luck. After an arduous fifteen minutes, she felt better, but sat there for a while more.

"I'm gonna get up now. Don't turn around."

"I promise." He held up a Boy Scout hand gesture.

She waited another minute, staring at his back. Eventually, she reached down and pulled her panties back in place under the shirt and stood. *Oh, God... he's gonna use the toilet too.* She flushed.

"You decent?"

"Yes."

Dad went to the storage room and returned with two brown packages. He set one on the table for her and dragged his radio chair over.

"What's that?" She lowered herself onto the metal seat, teeth chattering.

"MRE. Military ration. Open it; there's pouches and stuff inside. We eat one of these in the morning and one at night. Of course, that's a high-energy output schedule. We should probably have one of these in the morning and some canned pasta at night unless we're doing heavy work. If we're just lying around all day, we should have only one."

Riley aimed a forlorn stare at the brown block for a few minutes before opening it, finding it packed with smaller pouches. Writing identified the contents: an entrée (chicken breast), pretzels, peanut butter, a flat packet bearing the scary title 'beverage base powder orange,' crackers, plastic utensils, and one marked 'flameless ration heater.'

She took the entrée pouch, peeled the end open and sucked on it like an infant with a bottle, holding it in both hands. Dad glanced at her with sad eyes, and brushed a hand over her head. Riley jostled with the contact, but otherwise didn't react.

This didn't happen. This couldn't have happened. Everyone's dead? No, I'm dreaming. I spent all night playing a post-apoc video game. That's why I'm dreaming this. I know I'm dreaming, so I'm supposed to wake up now, right?

After nothing about her situation changed a minute later, reality crushed in on her. Riley chewed on the plastic, squeezing the goop inside up like toothpaste.

Dad shredded through his MRE, stuffed all the garbage back into the original brown pouch, and went back to the radio. Riley continued sucking on the packet for a while after it was empty. Eventually, she let it fall to the wayside and took the crackers. She pulled her legs up, heels on the chair, clutched the saltines to her face, and nibbled tiny bites while staring into space. Kieran's smiling face lingered in her memory; over and over, his voice repeated, "No one is crazy enough to hit 'the button.'" *How had the almost-best day of my life become the second worst?*

"Copy, sir. Thank you. Sorry about Lillian." Dad let out a long sigh.

He spun his chair around. At the sight of her, he covered his mouth and shed two tears. Dad moved to her side, squeezed her shoulder, and ran his hand over her head. She continued gazing at nothing, wanting to react to his touch, but unable to find the ability to move.

When she ran out of cracker, she left her hands together at her chin. Dad scooped her out of the chair and carried her to the cot, sitting with her sideways in his lap. Some time later, she went from squirrel pose to one arm limp in her lap and the other clutching his shirt.

"What did Bering say?" she whispered.

"He's in Cheyenne, safe in NORAD. His wife didn't make it. DC is ash. The United States has suffered a full-scale nuclear strike from multiple hostile nations. We fired back, but there's not a lot of intel right now about how bad things are."

"If Kieran's dead, shoot me."

He shook her, hard. "Riley McCullough. Don't you dare say anything like that again." Tears ran down his face. "I won't lose you too."

She sniffled.

"As much as it hurt you to lose that boy, ten times that is what it would do to me to lose you. You understand?" He shook her again, softer.

"Yeah. I can't believe he's dead too. Mom... Why is God mad at me?"

He kissed her on the cheek. "If he exists, I think he's mad at humanity in general."

"Do you think Mr. Hensley survived?" She laid her head on his shoulder.

Dad grumbled. "I hope not, but that would be the way fate works, wouldn't it?"

"Yeah." She reached up and grasped his shirt by the collar. "I don't want to die."

He kissed the top of her head. "You're not going to die. Nothing can get us down here."

Glint flashed at the edge of her vision, drawing her attention to water droplets gathering on the copper pipe. She tracked one as it fell, and looked up from where it landed to the armored door. The zombies from *The Last Outpost* couldn't batter through that.

"Dad, are there gonna be zombies?"

He chuckled. "Zombies only exist in two places."

Riley lifted her head to look at his face. "Where?"

"Voting booths and church pews."

She sighed, letting her head thud into his chest. "That's not funny."

"No, it's sad." He ran a hand up and down her back, reminding her of Mina.

"Can zombies break in here?"

"Riley, there's no such thing as zombies."

She stared over her shoulder at the door, waiting for the mindless thumping to start. Perhaps an hour later, she nodded off, but snapped her head back up.

"Okay, you need to rest." Dad stood with her in his arms, turned around, and lowered her onto the cot before covering her with the blanket. "Get some sleep. I'm going to try to find out what's going on. I'll sleep once you're up."

Riley shifted around as he returned to the radio, pulling the blanket up to her eyes and staring at the door. The red light in the sensor box flared and faded in a slow, repeating cycle, making her think of a heartbeat.

I can't sleep when there's zombies outside.

BETTER OFF

Day Three.

At some point during the zombie-free night, Dad joined her on the cot. She lay there for some time, clinging like a terrified little girl who'd had a nightmare and run to her parents' bed. With a couple hours of sleep in her brain, the idea of zombies made her feel silly. *Dad must think I've cracked. Zombies... really.* She pulled her fingers across her eyes, displacing crumbs, and climbed over him to get out of bed. After using the toilet, she snagged a granola bar from the storage closet and spent the next hour pacing in circles around the bunker, drifting through periods of boredom, sorrow, and disbelief.

She stopped, gazing up at the ceiling. *The red light is still on, but it's been quiet.*

Riley trudged over to the bookshelf and knelt, shuffling sideways while examining titles. Two copies of *Nuclear War Survival Skills* sat at the top left. Next to them were several operator manuals for US Military weapons as well as land mines, and about six different medical studies regarding radiation poisoning. She kept scooting right. *Anarchist's Cookbook, Teflon Bullets, Basic Electrical Engineering, Ricin: Silent Killer, A Culture of Conspiracy, The CIA Exposed, They're Watching.* Riley shuffled faster. The middle part of the shelf had normal sounding titles, even if they looked old. *Moby Dick, The Iliad, Don Quixote, The Odyssey,* and a host of other books she figured only people ordered by teachers to read would bother touching. The third shelf had a few books by Dan Brown and perhaps everything Tom Clancy ever wrote, plus a copy of Sun Tzu's *The Art of War*, as well as A Bible, Koran (translated), and an English version of the Talmud.

Sheesh, Dad. A little light reading?

Dad groaned as he got up and went to the radio. She plucked *Da Vinci Code* off the shelf and trudged to the cot around the 'go bag' she still hadn't moved from the spot where she dropped it two days ago. Modesty didn't seem very important anymore. Nothing did. Besides, Dad hardly looked at her. He spent most of his time absorbed by the radio.

He walked past the bed. "Shitting."

She scooted around to put her back to him and tried to ignore the horrible sounds. The smell wasn't as easy to disregard. Riley wadded her shirt over her face, coughed, and tried to read with watery eyes.

"Oh, don't give me that. It's not all roses and butterflies when you use it."

She flipped a page, not acknowledging his comment.

Dad returned to the radio, trailing a more intense blast of awful. She coughed again. "Turn up the fan."

"It's going through an NBC filter. It can only push so much air." He jumped into his chair and donned the headset. "This is Chris McCullough out of New Mexico, attempting to reach any survivors. Anyone hearing this, please, copy."

He repeated the radio spam every ten minutes for the next two hours while she read.

Dad sucked in a quick breath. "Yes, sir."

Riley perked up.

"I understand. Yes, she's fine, thank you for asking. Depressed, but I don't blame her. First her mother, now… yeah. That's good, sir. No contact from assets. Will do, sir. Six months? More than likely. I'm stocked for five years, but I wasn't expecting a teenage daughter in here… She'll probably shower our water gone in two." He chuckled.

Dad leaned back and stretched.

"What'd he say?" Riley set the book down, using the blanket for a bookmark. She crawled on all fours to the end by the radio. "Dad?"

"The president made it to safety. He's out of reach. Our country will go on in some form. No word from Europe, but early signs say it's probably been melted back to the Middle Ages. DC is on fire. We're still not sure who started it."

She sat back on her heels. "What happens in six months?"

"Colonel Bering said they should have enough resources to send a Blackhawk out to our location then and give us a ride to wherever they wind up reestablishing civilization. Not all that bad, sweetie."

She flopped on her side, no longer interested in the book. What did that matter anymore? What did anything matter?

The lights went out; the vent fan sputtered and fell silent.

"Crap," said Dad. "Well, there goes the infrastructure. National power grid always was a rickety hodgepodge."

"I thought you had solar panels?"

"I do." Dad grumbled. "You'd think out here in the middle of the desert they'd work great, but the damn things crap out on me all the time. Good for a backup, but I haven't worked the kinks out enough to wean off municipal power. We've been running on city juice."

She tried to figure out where the ceiling was, peering into the infinite black. "How long is it gonna stay dark? Are we gonna run out of air?"

"Until we flip the switch. Would you mind going to the crawlspace again?"

"I don't like it down there."

"You're a lot smaller and more flexible than I am, but I don't want to force you."

Riley lay silent for a few minutes until a chair squeaked. "It's okay. I'll go."

She crawled off the cot, fumbling around in the dark until she bumped the table. Her hand followed the edge to the post. She guessed at a quarter turn left and walked forward until her groping found the bookshelf. From there, she hand-to-handed her way right until her fingers brushed the storeroom door, reached inside to the shelf, and repeated the process until she grabbed the post at the end. A few passes of her foot swiping back and forth found the flashlight she'd left on the floor by the hatch, and she stooped to grab for it.

Light made her squint, but her eyes adjusted fast. She pulled up the hatch and dropped down onto the chilly dirt floor and musty air of the crawlspace. The battery cluster still winked and flashed with little green lights. It had its own control box with a similar up-down switch as the water, though she got nervous getting close to it.

"Dad," she yelled. "Will this thing shock me?"

"Don't touch metal," he shouted.

"It's all metal." *Gee, Dad. Thanks.*

She reached out, grasped the handle, and tugged it down. Something inside the box made a loud *click*, and an amber light came on. At the same instant, a shaft of light appeared where the hatch was.

"You got it," yelled Dad.

Riley duck-walked back to the opening and stood in the hole with the floor at the level of her collarbones. "There's a yellow light on the thing."

Dad muttered. "The solar panels must be covered in fallout from the blast. That light means we're not getting much power from the panel array and running on battery more than anything. We'll have to hope for a windy day to clear them off."

"What time is it? Maybe it's getting dark out?"

"Ten after noon. We might be having a nuclear winter scenario too."

Riley planted her hands on the floor and hauled herself out of the hole. She kept the flashlight with her and moped back to the cot. The lights were on, but weaker than before. "Nuclear winter sounds bad. Are we gonna run outta heat?"

"If enough sediment got blasted into the atmosphere, it will block out the sun. That in turn may cause a die-off of plant life, which could lead to the atmosphere becoming unbreathable as we run out of oxygen."

Riley dropped the flashlight.

"Bering didn't say anything about that though." Dad tweaked another dial on the radio set. "That, he would've mentioned. Don't get too worked up about it."

She picked up the light and tossed it on the bed before moving to stand next to him. Dad fiddled with the buttons on the bit that looked like a calculator and turned a few more knobs. Riley looked up at the ceiling, terrified to imagine what sort of hell existed thirty-odd feet over her head.

"Dad? Slap me," she droned.

"What?" Dad looked up, stunned.

"Not too hard; just give me a slap enough to hurt. I wanna wake up."

He slipped an arm around her and pulled her into his lap. Riley flopped like a doll, letting gravity take her body wherever it wanted. Dad rocked her for a moment, then bounced his knee, seeming confused at how to deal with her current state. When last he'd been around, she'd been little. He repeated his broadcast for survivors a few more times. She shifted, clutching a fistful of his shirt close enough to her face to make sucking her thumb seem like a good idea. The soft sound of his beating heart and the warmth of his chest were all that kept her from a complete spaz-out.

Time lost meaning. After a while, she'd gone from a limp body draped over him to a shivering girl curled up in his lap the way she used to do when she was six. Each time Dad repeated the broadcast, she came a little closer to crying, but couldn't find the energy. She set her feet together on his right thigh; he clasped a warm hand over them.

"You're cold as ice, hon. Where are your socks?"

"Dad?" Was that faint, pathetic whisper hers?

"I love you, Riley."

"Mom's better off, isn't she?"

"Depends on if you believe in that whole afterlife thing."

"Even if there isn't." She flexed her toes up and examined the flaking polish. "She's better off gone than alive in whatever's out there now."

"Probably."

"You knew this was going to happen, didn't you?" Her eyes had no focus, her voice no energy. "That's why you raced to get me. Why did you wait so long?"

"Lily didn't want to live out here." Dad twisted a switch on the radio. "She liked her technology and Starbucks too much."

"She might be alive if she was here. It's so boring, she wouldn't be stressed out."

"I'd have had to kidnap her." His gaze became distant, and his voice quieted.

"You were gonna leave me there?"

Dad gnawed at his finger for a few seconds. "I knew it would happen, but not this fast. I... figured you'd be at least eighteen before..." He sighed. "Your mother made her choice."

"She's dead." Riley let her head tilt forward until it touched her knees. "Amber's dead. Kieran's dead. Cora at Hernandez Grocery is dead. Sergeant Rodriguez is dead. Camila and Lyle and Wayne and Jaime and little Jesse... They're all dead."

Riley shut her eyes.

"I'm sorry, Squirrel."

"They're all dead." Her voice came out barely audible.

Her father whispered soothing, meaningless things into her hair. None of it reached her brain as anything more than the presence of sound. The Internet had never shown up; she hadn't gotten a chance to talk to Amber—now she never would. No tears came at the realization, but the hollow space in her chest grew. She tried to remember what her friend looked like. Random images of their last few minutes together in the Perkins parking lot felt like years ago.

"Dad," she croaked in a hoarse whisper.

"I'm here." He pulled her tight for a second and kissed the top of her head.

Riley gathered her hands together at her chin. "Did Amber suffer? Were they scared?"

"For an event like this, the government wouldn't bother warning anyone. All it would do would create panic and add a short period of terror and misery before the nukes hit."

She trembled, imagining Amber and her parents stuck in traffic, trying to flee population centers. Fights in the street, men grabbing anything female they can get their hands on. Amber's imaginary scream made her cringe.

"I don't think Jersey got hit directly. It's possible they're not dead. I don't know."

"Huh?" Riley lifted her head to make eye contact. "Jersey wasn't hit?"

Dad smiled. "The missiles didn't have any change for the tolls."

Riley gaped at him for a second before tears slipped out with a giggle. "You're an asshole."

He chuckled. "I'll try to find out as much as I can when the colonel is back on comm. Chances are, NYC was a primary target, which puts Jersey in a heavy fallout zone. The most likely scenario is that they weren't incinerated by the initial blast, but are experiencing high doses of radiation, chaos, panic—"

"Stop!" yelled Riley. "Please… just stop."

"Uh…" Dad winced. "Sorry. I wasn't thinking. Uh…" He scratched his head. "Look, I don't wanna lie to you, but—"

"You don't know." Riley took a deep breath and let it out in a long, shuddering exhale. "Hiding from looters in their basement is better than evaporated. Thanks for trying to give me a little hope."

Dad patted her shoulder. They sat for a few minutes without saying a word before he put on the headset and resumed broadcasting his call for survivors every fifteen minutes. Riley huddled against him, lulled to sleep by the sound of his voice reverberating in his chest.

23

SIX DAYS UNDER

Day Six.

With the lights off, the eerie red glow emanating from the box on the wall made the bunker seem like it belonged in Hell. Riley curled up at her dad's side, sharing the cot. He snored, but she didn't mind, as it lulled her into a fitful sleep punctuated by horrible images of Kieran disintegrating in a wave of nuclear fire or Amber being chased down an alley by the pervs from *The Last Outpost.* Riley dreamed of climbing the ladder to a smoking wasteland and stumbling around in the scorch mark that used to be Dad's house. Beyond the charred husk of her Sentra, Mom appeared as an angel to bring her back home. She started running toward her, arms outstretched, but the old man from the funeral burst through the white light and tore Mom's wings off, screaming that she didn't deserve them.

Riley shot upright, her face wet, equal parts devastated and furious.

Dad shook coffee grinds out of a metal tin into a glass beaker by the mini-kitchen. The hot plate smoldered and gave off the stink of burning silicon. *Dream.* She covered her face with her hands for a moment to take a few breaths. *Mom deserved her wings.* With a sour face, she wandered to the toilet, indifferent to Dad being up and about. He added water from an electric kettle, replacing the stink of silicon smoke with the fragrance of coffee. Dad kept his eyes down until the sound of a flush broke the silence.

She got up and went to the shelf, picking at stuff on the bottom row where Dad had stashed a number of articles of clothing. Most of it looked military in design, and all of it was for an adult man. The plain ochre boxers would fall right off her, the tank tops as well. Forget the fatigue pants. Fatigue jackets on the other hand might work, though they'd be more like a long-sleeved dress.

"You should change, hon. You've been wearing the same shirt for a week."

When I put this shirt on, Kieran was alive.

Riley looked up at him with a 'so what, who cares' expression. "None of this stuff will fit."

"Look in your bag." He smiled. "Coffee?"

"Yeah."

He handed her a metal mess kit cup half filled with harsh black coffee, and joined her at the folding table for another breakfast of MREs. Again, she cradled the food in two hands. He dropped another iodide pill by the cup. Riley stuck it in her mouth like an automaton and reached for the coffee.

"We'll be okay, Squirrel." Dad ran his hand over her head as if stroking a cat.

She shrank inward, exacerbating the similarity of her posture to the animal from whence her nickname originated. After the entrée pouch crinkled empty, she looked up at him. "I'm scared."

"I am too." He pointed up. "There's enough dirt between us and the outside world to stop any radiation from getting in. The whole place has a faraday cage around it, so nothing bad can touch us."

Riley reached a trembling hand for the pretzels. "'Kay."

Dad caught her wrist. "Your hand is shaking."

"I'm scared," she whispered.

At her squirrel routine with the pretzels, Dad put an arm around her and held on. "You're worrying me, kiddo. You haven't eaten like that since you were seven."

She mumbled through nibbles on the pretzel. "I'm scared."

He patted and squeezed for a few minutes as she snacked, before crouching by his backpack. Riley watched water drip from the overhead copper pipe running to the mini-sink, trying to track each droplet as it plummeted. *What if we're the last two people left in the world? What's it going to be like outside if we ever get out of here?* She thought of the thugs from the game. *Is someone gonna try to kill Dad to kidnap me?* She pulled her feet up onto the chair and wrapped her arms around her legs as another fat droplet fell.

Clonk.

The Beretta, plus Dad's hand, landed on the table in front of her. "It's fully loaded with one in the chamber. Safe is on. Keep this with you at all times."

She stared into nowhere. "Okay."

He leaned around to put his face in front of hers. "Riley? Come on, hon. You're still alive. I'm still alive. Don't give up on me, please."

She let a half-eaten pretzel tumble out of her hand and clamped on to him, trembling. She relaxed after a long while of him rocking her and running a hand over her hair. He startled and glanced at the radio all of a sudden as if he'd heard something. After giving her a kiss on top of the head, he ran to the chair and fumbled with the headset. Riley glanced over her shoulder at the radio table. *I didn't hear anything. Did the bombs hurt my ears?*

"This is Black Sheep, proceed, Colonel."

Riley sucked down the last of her coffee and stared at the camo backpack. While Dad muttered a series of noises and short 'yes's' and 'no's,' she dragged it over to the cot and opened it.

Six pairs of panties, six sets of socks, two full canteens, four MREs, two pairs of black fatigue pants in her size, four plain white shirts, and a pair of small combat boots. She stuck her foot, dirty and bare, into the boot, testing the size. A little big, but workable. She pulled it off and dropped it.

"So, close to a worst-case scenario then." Dad grumbled for a moment. "No, there's been no contact from any of my assets since we went underground. I understand, sir. Six months is very doable. We'll see you then."

"Sounds bad," said Riley.

"Major strikes have hit all US population centers. Manhattan, Trenton, that whole area you lived is..." Dad choked up.

The hollow in her heart grew out to touch her ribs. Numbness colored the world grey.

"I wouldn't have even known what hit me." She went to the bookshelf and picked *The Hunt for Red October.* Apparently, Dad *did* have every Tom

Clancy book ever written—in chronological order. "Right? Just flash, gone."

He forced a choked reply. "Yeah."

"Well, then I'm glad I'm with you." She snagged the Beretta on her way to the cot and dropped it next to her while taking up her usual cross-legged position.

"It might've been kinder," Dad muttered. "Colonel Bering says society has collapsed. He's not sure if there will be a rebuilding. The generals are at each other's throats trying to figure out who's to blame. Can you believe they're fingering the Democrats for this? Even after the end of the world, it's all fucking politics."

"You want me to die now?" Riley looked over, not feeling much of anything at the idea.

"No. No. Never. I just mean… The world out there now. It's not a great place to be a pretty, young girl. Some guy sees you and…"

She shivered. *That was just a video game. Even murderers hate kid-touchers.* "Everyone can't all be rapey lunatics."

"No, you're right. Everyone can't be… but all it takes is one."

Kieran… Riley daydreamed about finding him dancing around a bonfire in full Native regalia. *He's an Apache; he can survive.* She opened the book. *Stop lying to yourself. You're never going to see him again.* She slid the book up to her knees to keep the tears off it.

At the end of chapter four, she looked over. "Dad? If Bering isn't coming for us, how long do we have to stay underground?"

"Until it's safe."

She glared at the box on the wall. "What do you think it's like out there?"

He moved from the radio chair to sit on the cot. She leaned against him.

"Hard to say, really. There's so many variables. It depends on the quantity and yield of the devices used, as well as where they landed. Radiation and post-detonation fires are usually worse than the initial blast, over time. Some areas will have been wiped out, and others will fade slowly as radiation poisoning takes ten times the lives the primary release did. If enough matter was ejected into the atmosphere, it might be a dark nuclear winter out there with no sunlight, no crops, and pockets of survivors without food."

She shuddered. "Sorry I asked."

"Of course, since there's so little out here, we might find it better than we think. I doubt our enemies would waste a full-scale weapon on empty desert... unless they believed all those stories about aliens at Roswell. Really, it's anyone's guess until we look."

"Okay." She scooted her feet back and forth under the blanket to warm them. "So how long until we look?"

"Most survival guides advise at least two weeks or so after there's no detectable radiation." He gestured at the wall by the armored door. "About fourteen days after that red light goes off."

"Oh." Riley leveled her glare at the radiation monitor, trying to turn it off by sheer force of will.

The light flickered, but remained on. Riley sighed and frowned at the book. A few chapters later, her stomach growled. She set the book down, using the blanket to mark her place, and trudged to the storeroom, where she stood between shelves and shelves of MREs and canned pasta, broken up by a small collection of canned veggies and several boxes of store-brand granola bars. *Five years' worth of food.* She reached under her shirt to scratch at her belly. *Dad said we should only eat twice a day.*

"Since you're in there." Dad not-quite-yelling from the radio table made her jump. "Check the water light?"

Riley looked down at her dirty feet, flexed her toes, and sighed. "Why didn't you put the light upstairs?" She plodded over to the hatch.

"I meant to... wasn't expecting the world to blow itself up so soon. Thought I had time."

She lowered herself into the crawlspace and scampered around the nearest water tank to the gap between them. Crawling around in the dirt was getting her filthy, but who cared anymore? Much to her relief, the radiation warning light remained off. Her eyebrows came together. She crawled back to the entrance and climbed out, swatting dirt off her hands and legs before closing the hatch and heading for the main room.

Dad muttered at the mic, repeating his usual survivor mantra. Riley paused by the vibrating support column, standing in the warm downdraft of air while staring at the radiation light on the wall. *That doesn't make sense.*

"Dad?" She crept over to the wall by the door, stopping when her toes hit a thin puddle. "The light is off downstairs. Why is this one on?"

"Sorry." He took the headphones off and smiled at her. "What?"

She pointed at the dull red glow behind the plastic window. "The well light's off. If there's radiation, wouldn't it be on too?"

"The well's sensor is on the intake pipe at the bottom of the well. That detector is wired to sensor posts arranged around the hatch on the surface. It's picking up fallout, which didn't get into the well... remember, I have a covered well."

"But if it's radiation, wouldn't it go through the cover?" She backed away from the slimy spot of floor, wiping her left foot dry on the concrete.

"Fallout is irradiated dust and soil, sucked into the air by the detonation and deposited over a wide area. It's fine particles. The well is sealed, but there's a layer of it on the ground over our heads."

She trudged to the cot, eyes downcast. "Fallout lasts for years, doesn't it? We're gonna be in here a while."

He grumbled. "Yeah, probably."

Riley put her hand on the Beretta. Dad's voice replayed in her head. *Could you kill a man to protect yourself?* She bit her lip, wondering how terrified she'd have to be to point that thing at a human being. Her hand trembled, not liking the answer her brain came up with.

"Dad?" she whispered.

"Yeah?" He didn't turn around.

"Please don't die."

He looked back at her. "It's not on my to-do list, hon."

24

PERCUSSIVE MAINTENANCE

Day Eight.

A persistent smell saturated the air in the bunker, which Riley could only think of as 'sweat sock.' She stared over the top of *The Cardinal of the Kremlin* at her toes, and past them at Dad. He'd gone into a robotic recitation of the same transmission every fifteen minutes for the past two days. Between each two-hour period of survivor spam, he'd try to raise people with military sounding callsigns like 'Foxtrot-Two-Two' or 'Baker-Four-Nine.' None of them answered.

Her new world seemed on the low end of tolerable until Dad broke his rhythm, lowering his forehead to rest on his hand. Riley shivered, sniffling at the sight of her father looking so tired. He seemed about ready to give up on the world. She hunkered down, trying to focus on the story in her lap. Five minutes later, his voice startled her.

"Attention anyone who may be receiving this message. My name is Chris McCullough, and I am at a place of safety. If anyone is receiving this message, we are located approximately twenty miles due east of Truth or Consequences, New Mexico."

She dipped her gaze back to the page, and squirmed. "Dad, I've got an itch."

"Scratch it." He sat straighter. "Unless you mean like you want to touch yourself... which is perfectly natural."

"Eww, Dad, really?" She rolled her eyes. "No, I mean like an *itch* itch. It kinda hurts."

"Where?"

Her silence answered.

"Well, you have been wearing the same underwear for eight days."

"Open the door. I wanna use the shower in the hall."

He shook his head. "Not shielded out there."

"What kind of idiot puts the shower outside the vault door?"

"The kind of idiot that doesn't want to waste drinking water. Use the sink. That's not a cleaning shower, Squirrel. It's meant for coming in from the outside and getting rid of fallout particles."

"The sink?" Blood rushed to her cheeks. "Are you nuts?"

"No. Wet a washcloth and hit the critical points. They call it a field shower."

"Critical points…"

"Face, pits, crotch, and crack… hopefully in that order."

Riley looked at the page; the words became meaningless squiggles for a second. She wasn't sure what bothered her more: that Dad suggested she wash herself in the bunker with him there, or that she didn't die of embarrassment when she gave it serious consideration.

"Will you put like a bag over your head or something?"

Dad swiveled around in his chair, raising both eyebrows. "You could also go into the storeroom and close the door."

Duh.

Riley dropped the book and leaned down to grab clean undies from the backpack. She bounced to her feet and snagged a cloth from the peg on the wall over the sink.

Dad pointed at the stack of five white pails behind the toilet. "Grab a bucket, take some water with you."

Riley pulled the top one out, ran some water in it from the sink, and carried it to the storeroom. She wedged the door closed, peeled off her fetid clothes, and proceeded to run a bar of plain soap and the freezing washcloth around 'the critical points.'

After a bit of bouncing around and hand waving to air dry, she pulled the clean set of undies on and covered her breasts with her arms, regretting her hasty search for cleanliness. *I am an idiot. I forgot a shirt.* She contemplated putting the one she'd been wearing back on, but one whiff of it made her gag. She cracked the door an inch, and peeked.

Dad had his back turned, still broadcasting for survivors.

"Dad, I forgot a clean shirt. Don't look."

"Okay." He leaned back in the chair, eyes closed. "You know right after we got married, your mother used to walk around topless—"

"Dad!" she yelled.

He chuckled.

Riley scurried to the backpack and grabbed one of the white shirts. It wasn't as long as the other one, and left her underwear exposed. She stared at herself, not caring if Dad saw her panties. Apathy faded after a moment, and she pulled on a set of the black fatigue pants. They were baggy enough to be comfortable, and a little long in the leg. Unless she jumped up and down in place, they'd stay on without a belt.

"Safe."

Dad glanced back with a wink. "You almost look human again."

"My hair stinks." She paced around, feeling cooped up. Sitting on the bed was getting old, fast. After a few circles, she got up to a jog. Nylon ties at the bottom of the pants whipped about as she picked up speed. After ten laps, she stopped and ran in place for a minute before she dropped and did five pushups.

"Now what's gotten into you?" Dad raised an eyebrow.

"I'm sick of sitting around doing nothing. The world's gone to crap. I should be like training and stuff. Lisa did pull ups and stuff every morning."

"Not too bad an idea." He paused. "Who's Lisa?"

"Character from a game."

Riley did sit-ups until her gut ached. She'd spent so much time playing *Call of Duty*, now she was going to be living it. She thought about *The Last Outpost*, and wondered if she could talk Dad into heading east in search of Amber. *No. She's dead. He said the whole East Coast got vaporized.*

Discontentment at being locked up underground boiled over after another ten minutes. She stomped over to the radiation detector, her mortal enemy, and glared at it. The red light bulb inside the housing fluctuated in intensity, as if it got power from a hamster on a treadmill gaining and losing speed. This time she didn't care about stepping in a puddle.

"I hate this thing."

Dad looked over. "That thing saved our lives. I might've gone outside by now if we didn't know it was fatal."

She let off an exasperated noise halfway between growl and sigh, and bashed her fist down on top of it, hitting a patch of water.

The red light went out.

"Dad?"

"Hmm?"

"Dad!" She bounced on her toes.

"What?" He looked over.

"It's out." She shifted to raise her arm, showing him the bottom of her fist. "And it's wet."

He scrambled out of the chair and stumbled over. The copper fitting coming in from the well passed right over it; a fat droplet formed at the bottom of one of the silvery solder marks. All along the left side of the alarm housing, trails of water streaked through caked dust.

"You shouldn't have hit it. Now we won't know when it's safe."

Riley scrunched up her face, about to bawl like a five-year-old being yelled at. Her onrush of tears stalled on the way to her eyes. She balled her fists. "No. I didn't hit it that hard. It's wet. Maybe it shorted?"

"I doubt it. Might be a shift in the wind pushing the fallout around. Let's keep an eye on it for a few days. If it stays out…"

"Do you have a manual for this thing?" She took a step toward the bookcase.

"Printout, bottom shelf, far right."

Riley squatted, sifting among a bunch of stacks of copier paper held together by black metal clips. Eventually, she found one with a drawing of a familiar looking alarm box and a logo for a doomsday prepper website. "You bought plans for a radiation detection system on the Internet?"

"Yep. They're all over the place."

She flipped through it, lost by all the algebra and schematics. The drawings didn't seem impressive. "Are you sure it works?"

"Yes, I tested it with some Uranium."

Riley blinked at him. "Where the crap did you get Uranium?"

"EBay."

"Really?"

"Yep. I mean, it was weak… but enough to test with." He put the headset on. "Colonel Bering, this is Black Sheep, come back."

Riley cast a dubious look at the plans and stuffed the home-printed manual back on the shelf. "If water got into that thing, could it make it light up?"

"The odds of that are incredibly remote… but, I suppose technically possible." He jumped as if startled. "Yes, sir. Thank you. The perimeter rad sensor is now indicating a clear condition. About ten minutes. Riley hit it, and it went out. No, I don't think so. She's not that strong."

Riley stuck her tongue out at the back of his head.

"Possible water infiltration to the housing. Yes. Will do." He took the headset off. "If it stays out for 24 hours, I'll take the handset and check the outer room."

"Okay." The idea of getting out of here was as appealing as it was frightening. What if everyone topside had gone 'rapey' and insane? "Dad, do you think there's God?"

"Your mother was an atheist."

"I know. Are you?"

"I don't have an opinion. There's a lot that humanity hasn't been able to figure out. It wouldn't surprise me if there was a God, or if God was really an advanced alien species laughing their intergalactic testicles off at the mess we've just made of our planet. There's a lot of evidence among ancient civilizations... Aztecs, Mayans, the Nazca lines, even the Egyptians. Some of them had knowledge of astronomy and astrophysics that we're just beginning to comprehend today."

Riley stepped on the nylon tie dangling from her pant leg, cinching it tight around her ankle and almost tripping herself as she crossed the bunker. "So you think aliens came to the Earth two thousand years ago?"

He made faces at the wall. "No. I don't think so. If there were aliens capable of reaching Earth, they'd have been back already."

"So you *do* believe there are aliens?" She sat on the edge of the cot and loosened the tie.

"If you think about how many individual planets exist in the universe, by pure mathematical odds alone, there *has* to be at least one other planet where life occurred, probably more like millions. It's a mathematical certainty that there is something out there, but given the vast distances... and who knows what kind of tech level they have. Everyone always assumes aliens are super advanced. What if we were the head of the pack?"

"Not anymore." Riley frowned.

"That's an idea." Dad laughed. "Maybe the advanced aliens that visited us 2000 years ago blew themselves up just like we did, and that's why they never came back."

Riley fidgeted with the nylon strap, tracing it back and forth over her foot. "Do you think Mom's dead because she was an atheist?"

"Not for a second." Dad's face reddened. "I should've punched that old bastard right in his old nose."

"Doctor Farhi thinks it was—"

"Stress, yeah. Chances are it was a Russian operator with a tight-beam focused microwave weapon capable of inflicting deep-tissue damage from far enough away for her not to notice."

Riley blinked.

"Or," said Dad with a blasé shrug, "maybe it was just alcohol and the stress of her job."

She glared. "You don't sound very upset she died."

"I am, inside. What good does it do to fall apart?" He ran his fingers over the radio unit. "Now, I've gotta stay strong for you."

"This isn't fair."

Dad tapped his fingers on the radio table, a rhythmic thrumming that grew louder over the next minute. "I tried. I really tried, Riley. I tried so hard to protect you two by leaving. I'm so sorry. This is all my fault."

Though he sounded tired and bored rather than sad, Riley sensed anguish in him. She crawled to kneel on the pillow end of the cot and hugged him from behind. As soon as she touched him, he gave in to soft sobs.

"You didn't do this, Dad. Crazy politicians did."

"I tried. I knew you'd be better off without me." He shook his head in an endless back and forth. "I couldn't protect you."

She kissed him above the left ear, and whispered. "You did."

"No, Riley… this is all my fault. You're stuck down here because of me." He looked at the door. "What are we doing?"

Riley squeezed him as hard as she could. "Stop, Dad. You're scaring me."

Dad quieted, resting his hand on her arms where they crossed under his chin. She shivered. If Dad hadn't taken her in, she'd have been vaporized. Yeah, it sorta was his fault she was stuck underground, but it was better than the alternative. Riley rested her chin on his shoulder, gazing at the flickering lights on the radio. Soon, he resumed calling for survivors.

No one answered; only a faint hiss came from the headphones.

25

BREAKING THE SEAL

Day Nine.

Beretta parts littered the square folding table in the center of the bunker. Sixteen hollow point 9mm bullets formed a miniature stockade fence around the empty magazine. Riley sat with one heel on the chair, reaching around her leg to work a toothbrush through the crevices of the upper slide. The first time she'd tried to disassemble the pistol, the spring shot across the room and skittered under the bookshelf. It took her over an hour and some creativity with a rigid copper wire to retrieve it.

Every minute or two, her heart would threaten to stop as she got the urge to check the radiation detector by the door, fearing it would be on again. The sight of it still dark let her breathe again. After an hour of cleaning the pistol, she gave up and dropped the brush.

This is as clean as I'm going to get it.

She stuck the spring over the barrel, slipped it into the slide, and grabbed the pistol grip. After a bit of grunting and squirming, she squeezed it together and flicked the lever to keep the spring from flinging it to pieces again. With a triumphant smile, she set the gun down and grabbed the magazine. Bullet by bullet, she snapped them in, leaving one on the table. Riley checked to ensure the safety was on, locked the slide back, and put the stray round in the chamber. She held her breath, aimed at the storeroom in case it went off, and let the slide rack. For a few seconds, she didn't move, not fully confident holding the weapon.

"Dad?" She picked up the full magazine.

"Hmm?"

"The light's still off." She slid the mag into the handle and clapped it tight. "Think it's safe to check outside?"

"I'm not sure." He pulled the headset off and made his way to the detector.

Riley set the Beretta down, pointed away from her, and lowered her foot to the floor. Dad leaned left and right around the box like a bee looking for the perfect place upon a flower to land; she bit her lip. *Maybe this is a bad idea. What if everything outside is poison?*

Clonk, clonk. Dad gave the alarm two light taps with a hammer to the side. *Clack.* One to the top right corner.

She jumped.

"There's condensation inside the glass," said Dad.

"Does that mean water got in?" She felt neither hope nor dread.

"Yep." He glanced down. "All this water on the floor, the damn thing's been dripping probably since we walked in the door."

More than a week's worth of beard had left a frizzy, wanton explosion of brown hair on Dad's face. It lent an erratic, wild quality to the look of mission in his eyes. He hunted down a screwdriver from the tools section of the bookshelf and took the clear plastic face off. He huffed and puffed at it, waved his hand, and used the postcard-sized panel to fan it harder.

"It's definitely wet in there."

Riley pulled her left foot up onto the chair, hooking an arm around her shin and gazing at the faded remains of polish on her toes. Such a trivial little gift from Mom had made her so happy. Now, who had time to care about nail polish?

The world was still alive when I painted them.

Mom was dead. Amber was dead. Kieran was dead. A good chance existed that everyone she'd ever not hated was dead. Her house was probably gone. Her old school had likely become a pile of toothpicks and ash. Scene after scene of her old neighborhood played a slideshow in her head.

All those people.

"Dad?"

"Yeo?" He whirled with an attempt at mixing 'yeah' and 'yo.'

She kept quiet a moment. "What's the point?"

"Of?"

She looked up at him, expressionless. "Surviving? If the whole world is dead, why bother?"

He slid the plastic rectangle into the detector box and walked over, pulling her head against his chest. "We don't know it's all gone yet."

"Colonel Bering said it was."

Dad's hand on her cheek, rough and warm, held her against his body with gentle reassurance. "A lot of people are dead, yes. That doesn't mean every human on the face of the planet is gone. Look at us. Two people in the middle of nowhere managed to make it. There'll be more. Pockets of civilization have survived. No one nuked the third world. Maybe we could make our way west and find a boat… go to the Caribbean or Hawaii or something."

Riley glanced at the detector box, brushing her hands down her thighs in a nervous, repetitive gesture. "How long does fallout last?"

"There's a lot of variables."

"Do you think it blew away already?"

"Maybe it rained." He patted her on the cheek and crossed the room to the shelf, where he set to rummaging. "The initial blast might have scattered enough debris around the outside area to set the detector off, and maybe the water kept it showing an alarm condition after the background radiation faded to survivable levels."

"I don't want you to die." She jumped up.

"Good," he said without looking back. "I don't want to die either. A-ha!"

Dad held up a device that resembled a yellow lunchbox with a handle, and a length of wire connected to a short, metal pipe. On second thought, it looked like a gizmo from *Ghostbusters.* She crept up behind him as he fumbled with fixing wires to a huge squarish battery with spiral contacts, leaning up on tiptoe to get a better look. After a moment, the device came to life, emitting a series of quiet ticking sounds.

She let her weight down on her heels. "Whazzat?"

"Geiger counter."

Riley pursed her lips and blinked at it. *Yeah, normal people have those lying around.* She crossed her arms and gazed up at the roof with a lump rising in her throat. *Normal people are dead now.* A sudden inspiration took her, and she trotted to the storeroom and draped herself headfirst through the hole, dangling upside down.

The amber light by the batteries had gone out. The solar panels must be working.

She grunted, dizzy from the blood rushing to her head and pulled herself up. When she jogged back to the bunker, Dad was in the midst of exploring it from corner to corner, waving the pipe around in front of him. The ticking gained and fell in frequency, but the device's reaction didn't sound alarming to her untrained ears. He lingered at the thick door for ten minutes, moving the sensor around the seam.

"Dad, the solar panels are on." She pointed at the storeroom. "Light went out."

"Hmm. I'll be damned." He snapped the detector wand into a socket on the housing and flicked a switch. The device stopped ticking. "Nothing above background standard. Maybe we got lucky."

She swallowed a mouthful of saliva. "Uh…"

Dad patted himself down, checking pockets, paced back and forth for a moment, and whirled to face her. "Wait in the storeroom."

"Huh?"

"I'm going to open the door and check the outer chamber." He grabbed at her shoulders, urging her in the direction of back door. "Wait in there."

"Is this gonna help?" She kicked the flimsy, white plastic.

"Not much, but it gives you more distance from the opening."

When he spun around, she grabbed his arm. "Don't."

"I thought you couldn't stand it down here?" He paused.

She wrapped her arms around him. "It's better than being dead."

"I promise you, if it shows even three times a normal background reading, I'll stop."

Riley backed into the storeroom again, crouching against the shelf. Dad grabbed the Geiger counter and approached the armored front door. He made another pass around it with the sensor before lifting the lock and swinging it down to free the wheel.

She whined. "Don't let the nuke in."

"We're good." Dad set the Geiger counter on the floor between his boots and grabbed the wheel, let out a weak grunt, and shoved. The metal ring spun up to a blur, drawing bars out of the top and bottom. Dad took a knee and held the wand up to the gap as he pushed the door outward. Still, the ticking sounds remained calm and slow.

Riley leaned her weight forward onto her hands, whining at him as he crept into the outer room. "Dad…"

"Stay there," he said.

Geiger counter held high, he slipped out of sight.

Riley crawled two feet into the room, reaching at the door. "Dad, no. You said two weeks after the light went out; it's only been a day."

"Hmm. Interesting." His voice echoed in the other room.

No! She leapt up and ran to the doorway. Dad was halfway up the ladder, holding the wand over his head.

"Dad."

"Get inside."

The harsh command shocked her to a halt. She crept backwards, taking tiny steps, until she bumped against the support post. Vibration from the ventilation fan ran through it, rattling her teeth. She covered her face with her hands, trembling.

Minutes later, Dad swept in, pulling the thick door closed behind him. He walked past her, paying no attention to her shaking. "Well, my face didn't melt off."

"Dad!" She looked back and forth between him and the door three times, and ran over to him.

He dragged his backpack to the table, put it on a chair, and checked the contents. "I'm going to do a wider sweep outside. No rads by the hatch."

"No." She whimpered, putting a hand on his back. "No."

"You are without a doubt a teenaged girl." He chuckled. "Beg like hell for something and as soon as you get it, you don't want it anymore."

"But, Dad." She pulled and pawed at him. "We don't know what's up there."

"Correct." He zoomed off to the storeroom, yelling once he'd gone out of sight. "Exactly why I need to recon. I couldn't find any radiation at all topside. I'm going to do a wider sweep, check the house, the truck… maybe we can expand our range." He put a gentle hand on each cheek, cradling her head. "You don't want to spend the rest of your life down here, do you?"

"No." Riley swooned on her legs and stumbled back until she fell seated on the cot. *The Last Outpost* replayed in her mind. Broken fences, scorched farm equipment, crazed farmers with glowing red eyes and scythes—a father and daughter trying to survive the apocalypse.

This is a dream. I played that stupid game, and it got in my head.

She slapped herself across the face. "Wake up."

Blinking spots danced across her vision.

"Riley Dawn McCullough, wake up!" She hit herself again, seeing stars.

"Riley?" Dad poked his head out of the storeroom. "What on Earth?"

"Up, up, up, up!" She slapped herself in time with each word, falling over sideways into a sobbing ball.

She wasn't waking up. The bunker remained.

Warmth circled her eyes, a part of her wanting to give in and wail like a little girl, but all she managed to do was send a vacant stare across the room. Her cheek tingled. Dad rushed over, touching a fingertip to the spot, proving it tender.

"Oh, Riley… You've gotta hold it together." He scooped her up and hugged her tight. "I wish this was a dream. I do. I wish the bombs never dropped. I wish your mother wasn't killed. I wish I never left."

"Don't leave. You won't come back." She gripped his arm with both hands. "I don't wanna be an orphan."

"Two days ago, you were ready to kick down the door and go outside."

"So?" She pouted. "Doesn't mean I'm right."

"Look… we can't stay underground forever. This is a great shelter, but the less we need to consume our resources, the longer we'll be healthy. I owe it to you to check outside. I swear on my life that if anything looks dangerous, I'll come right back."

"Nooooo," she whisper-whined.

"Do you trust me?" He ran a hand over her head.

"Yeah." She sniffled.

"Okay. I'll just check the immediate area. Any whiff of radiation, and I'll rush back. I should've gotten a reading of some kind in the shaft, but I didn't. That's the only reason I'm going to risk this."

She didn't like it, but if she objected, she'd make a liar out of herself for saying she trusted him. Clinging tight and whimpering didn't count as lying. He held her for a few minutes more and gestured at the mini-stove.

"About time for lunch. I'll wait till after."

"SpaghettiOs," said Riley. "Can we have SpaghettiOs?"

"Okay."

Slumped on the bed, Riley couldn't take her eyes off him as he went to the storeroom to get cans and heated them on the hot plate. A short while later, he carried two steaming bowls to the table, and put one next to the Beretta.

She moved to her usual seat while he pulled the chair from the radio table over. Spoon after spoon of canned pasta went into her mouth; Riley barely bothered to chew before swallowing. In the game, the father and daughter survived countless times because they weren't alone. The programmers took great pains to set up situations where teamwork was mandatory. Fortunately, in the single-player mode, the AI was competent.

Video games don't exist anymore. All the programmers are gone.

She put a hand on the Beretta. "I wanna go with you."

"Nope."

"Dad. I don't wanna be alone."

"Nope." He fanned his lunch to cool it off a little. "Not risking anything happening to you."

"Please?"

"I need you to do something important while I'm gone. Someone's gotta stay on the radio."

She pouted. "But..."

"If Colonel Bering decides to pick the few hours I'm wandering around out there to ask if we still need a ride to civilization, I don't want to miss it."

"Awright."

"Not to mention if there are any other survivors, you should keep broadcasting."

Riley couldn't help but feel like she'd never see him again. After he finished his bowl, he packed four MREs in the backpack with four thirty-round magazines for the AR15. She idled the spoon around the half-inch of orange goop at the bottom of her bowl as he sat on the cot to put on socks and boots. Dad shrugged the backpack over his shoulders and went to the gun safe in the southwest corner.

"05-18-02," said Dad. "In case you need to get in here."

"My birthday," she muttered.

"Maybe someday you'll believe I never stopped loving you... or your mother."

If you love me, you won't go outside. "I do. It's just a bad combination."

"You don't like your birthday?"

"Mr. West in computer class said family birthdays and pet names are the first things hackers try."

"Well... if some deranged wastelander manages to A, find this bunker, B, survive to get into it, and C, figure out what my daughter's birthday is... they can have the guns."

Dad hefted the AR15, inspected it, and loaded a fifth magazine. Riley didn't even jump when the bolt slammed forward. He slung it over his shoulder, picked up the Geiger counter, and walked up to the table. When he looked down at her, his face held no emotion.

"Riley—"

"Don't."

He raised an eyebrow.

"If you say 'I love you' or 'goodbye,' it's gonna feel like you're not gonna come back."

Dad stood still for a few seconds with the same blank face. "See you in a few hours."

"That's better."

She gazed down at her pale feet peeking out from under the crumpled, black pant legs, not looking up as the dull tromp of his boots on the concrete floor grew faint. The *thud* of the armored door closing made her twitch. At the scraping, metallic sound of the wheel turning, she cried silent tears.

Goodbye, Dad.

After she could no longer hear him climbing the ladder, she plodded to the radio chair. Unlike the one at the table, it had cloth cushions, which held Dad's scent. She curled up and put the headset on, which flooded her ears with a soft hiss.

"Attention survivors. My name is Riley McCullough. If anyone can hear me, you're not alone. I'm transmitting from New Mexico, near the town of Las Cerezas. Attention any survivors."

She traced a finger back and forth over the front of the olive drab radio. Overall, it had the profile of a stereo rack component. At the center, a numeric pad resembled a calculator with a few extra buttons: 'freq,' 'erf ofst,' 'time,' and 'batt call.' The tiny LCD screen above the keypad was blank. She recognized an empty coaxial cable port at the top left corner next to the word 'ant.' Below it, sat a circular blue socket with five bronze studs in a star arrangement labeled RXMT. Two similar ports on the right bore the labels AUD/FILL and AUD/DATA. The rest of the space was full of seven knobs surrounded by incomprehensible white lettering. Terrified to touch anything but the transmit button Dad showed her, she pressed it again.

"Attention anyone who survived the bombs. Any survivors, please respond."

Riley shifted in the seat so she could see the front door. Her stare roamed around the bunker, the bunker in which she was now alone. She gasped with panic and flung the headset off. Squealing, she ran to the table and grabbed the Beretta in a two-handed grip, clutching it to her chest as though it were her most prized possession. Once her breathing calmed, she crept back to the chair. After putting the headset on again, she curled up facing the other direction—at the door—and kept the pistol aimed between her knees.

Every fifteen minutes, she spoke into the radio. Riley clung to the pistol, and the hope that if she obeyed her father's instructions, he'd come home safe.

DEADLY FORCE

Day Eleven.

Consciousness swept over Riley's mind. Her eyes fluttered open, and she found herself still in Dad's chair. The Beretta dangled in her right hand, at the precipice of clattering to the floor. She gasped and tightened her grip around it, sitting upright at the realization she'd fallen asleep on radio watch.

"Dad?" She looked around. "Dad?"

Silence.

After a few minutes, she stood and stretched away the discomfort of sleeping in a fetal position. Her brain tried to get terrified and pissed off at the same time, winding up nowhere. She held the gun in both hands, pointed at the ceiling, barrel close to her cheek, and crossed the room. At the storage area door, she paused like every cop she'd ever seen on TV and whipped around to aim at the empty space.

I'm alone.

Worry faded to sadness. The wall clock showed the time at 10:42 a.m., Sunday, 07/24/16. *Dad's been gone all night. He was only supposed to be a few hours.* She slouched. *I knew it.* Riley felt too sad to cry, and too sick to eat. She plucked at the waist of the fatigue pants until they fell around her ankles and availed herself of the toilet. For a long time after she no longer needed to sit on the bowl, she remained, occasionally pointing the gun at the door. There was no point in getting up. There was no point to doing anything. Why bother spamming the radio? *I'm the only one left on the planet. If anyone else survived, they probably speak Russian or Chinese or Korean or subhuman wasteland babble and won't answer me anyway.* There was no one else left.

There had been one other, but he was stupid.

Apathy and hope went after each other like a pair of angry tomcats. Her stomach growled; she pulled her pants up and trudged to the storeroom to snag a granola bar. Somehow, the Beretta had become a subconscious accessory that followed her everywhere. It seemed so unreal to think that she'd ever been terrified of a handgun. She stopped at the mini-sink and stuffed the gun in the waistband of the fatigues.

When I put these on, Dad was still alive.

Riley doled out a portion of coffee in the French press and put only enough water in the electric kettle for one mug. Beretta in hand, she peeled the blanket away from the cot and curled up on the radio chair with it. The same faint hiss came out of the headphones.

"Good signal, but no one transmitting," her father had said. As long as she heard the hiss, everything was working.

"Attention survivors," she droned. "This is Riley. I'm in a safe place near Las Cerezas, New Mexico. If anyone's still alive, please reply."

The burbling of water got her moving a short while later. With a warm mug of black coffee cradled to her chest, she huddled on the chair with her feet tucked under her, listening to the emptiness of white noise. As her father had done, she squeezed the button every fifteen minutes and recited her lines.

When the clock read 13:18, she gave up on repeating some variation of an 'I'm a little girl alone and defenseless, come attack me' spiel and cracked open an MRE. *Dad would want me to eat.*

She sucked down a glass of water, and sipped a second. After cleaning out the food packets, she wedged them all into the outer casing and put that in the garbage bag. Pacing. Back and forth, arm swinging around with the gun in her hand. Her mind raced for anything to do. She picked up *The Cardinal of the Kremlin* and resumed her place, but forgot what had been going on altogether and gave up after six pages. She didn't care enough to start from the beginning again. Another glass of water. More pacing.

Riley orbited the bunker countless times. Eventually, she flopped on the folding chair and draped herself over the flimsy table. The somewhat-padded vinyl surface had absorbed a lot of gun oil and cleaner. Scattered parts and tools gathered in piles where they'd been pushed out of the way of meals. Daydreams of Mom's funeral played in her head, and at some point, the body in the casket became Dad. She daydreamed about having the Beretta with her that day, and shooting the old man for being so mean. In the world humanity had rebirthed, a person could avenge an insult like that with a gun and no one would care.

Her arm stretched out over the top, and she plucked a brush out of the cluster. It resembled a toothbrush, but its olive drab plastic and black bristles said it had been made for weapons detail, not the inside of anyone's mouth.

Her mind presented her with reasons Dad was late: got lost because he hid the bunker too well, fell in a ravine and had a broken leg, bandits got him, walked into a rad zone and melted, giant scorpions ate him.

Jesus, Riley, you're getting silly.

She froze, staring at the brush for a few seconds before clawing at the heap of tools. Rods that Dad screwed together to clean the barrel of the AR15 jangled to the middle of the table. Riley grabbed two of them, hands shaking, and screwed them together forming a longer strut. A few patches of duct tape pinned another single section crossways. After squeezing it in place, she taped the toothbrush to the impromptu crucifix as a stand-in Jesus.

"I know Mom didn't believe in you..." She set it on the table, staring at it. "I'm not sure I do, but I'll try anything to get Dad back."

Silence.

"Please?"

Twenty minutes later—and no Dad magically appearing—she slipped off the chair, sinking to her knees and sobbing. She sprawled on the floor, not motivated enough to move. At least an hour went by as she kept asking no one in particular why Mom had to die, why Dad had to go away (probably die), and what the world did to deserve burning. The Beretta, heavy against her belly, offered a way out. She looked down at it and frowned, casting a sidelong, guilty glance at the toothbrush crucifix.

"I'm being ridiculous." She got up and walked to the radio chair, nylon ties thwapping at her feet. "Dad would want me to keep trying to live."

She set the Beretta on the table and rubbed where it had dug into her skin, curled up, and put on the headset. One hour blurred to the next as she droned at the mic over and over. Her eyelids got heavy and she snuggled to the side and let them close. When she looked up, the clock read 20:04.

"Dad's not coming back." She hugged her knees to her chest. "Why did he have to be stupid?" *It's my fault. I shouldn't have bitched at him for being stuck down here. If I didn't break the alarm, we'd be together.*

Her face contorted in preparation for soul-wracking sobs, but she froze with only two tears racing each other down her cheeks. "What if he's hurt and can't get back?"

She flew out of the chair and stomped over to the bed, pulling on socks from her 'go bag' followed by the combat boots. They were stiff, but he guessed the size well enough. Her heart pounded in her head as she laced them tight. She had to go out there. Dad was counting on her, just like the game. *He went alone, that's what went wrong.* In the gun cabinet, she found two extra magazines for the Beretta, and loaded them before stashing both in her left thigh pocket.

Two circuits around the room failed to give her any more ideas about what to bring. As soon as she put her hands on the wheel to open the big door, the word 'light' echoed in her brain. Once she had a flashlight clipped to the lip of her left hip pocket, she grasped the wheel and pulled with all her strength.

It creaked. *Dad made this look so easy.* Grunting and panting helped, and eventually she twisted it enough to retract the bars. Riley flung all her weight against it, boots sliding on the floor as she heaved. Inch by inch, it moved forward without a sound. Seeing the outer room brought back the fear of radiation, and he had the Geiger... but it's not as if more bombs dropped.

It was clean when he left; radiation doesn't just pop up out of nowhere, right?

Cautious steps brought her halfway to the ladder before she whirled around to push the door closed. She did not close it all the way, nor did she turn the wheel.

I might need to get inside fast.

At the base of the ladder, she pulled the waistband of her pants away from her belly and nestled the Beretta in to free her hands for the climb. The thirty some odd feet of ladder felt like miles as she hauled herself up one rung at a time. Huddled at the top, she listened to silence. No light leaked in past the burlap-covered hatch. Dad had closed it on his way out, presumably so the disguised opening would protect her from marauders and looters.

I'm coming, Dad. Don't be dead.

A tentative hand pushed against the raw wood; the pallet lifted, allowing a cool desert breeze in. The air smelled crisp and fresh, making the bunker feel stagnant already. She peered over the rim of the shaft at a dark blue sky, luminous with the last moments of twilight.

It shouldn't be dark at twenty 'o clock. Holy crap, the Earth is like off its axis or something.

She swallowed her fear and pushed, finding it a little tricky to climb out while supporting the hatch. Riley slithered through the space, belly crawling out into the desert sand. When the pallet clattered to the ground behind her, it looked like an innocuous lump of dirt. Two flat-topped boulders, about as big as large dogs, flanked it at ten paces to either side.

That's how you marked it, Dad.

Without daylight, she couldn't see the house. The night of the nuclear strike had been a blur. For all she knew, they had run for hours... but it had likely been much less. Two slow spins gave her a rough idea of which way east was, and she remembered Dad going straight out the patio door. The back of the house faced north, so that meant she had to go south to get to the house.

Fearful of attracting unwanted attention, Riley didn't bother pulling out the flashlight to look for tracks. If Dad went anywhere, he'd probably have gone to the house. Maybe she'd gotten herself too wound up over it and he'd found the house habitable and simply fallen asleep in his own bed.

No. He wouldn't have forgotten me. Something bad happened.

Determined, she marched on.

A few minutes of walking led her to the edge of a ravine deeper than she remembered seeing before. *No, this isn't the way.* She backed up and followed the edge for a little while until deciding she was getting herself even more lost. *Crap. Crap. Crap.* She trotted in a direct line away from the ravine, one hand on the gun, the other on the flashlight. A steady breeze from her left side felt good enough to get her to stop and enjoy fresh air. When she took a deep breath, the scent of cooking meat filled her nostrils. She caught herself drooling before her brain ascribed meaning to the smell: beef.

Flickering yellow-orange light caught her eye. A fire. She slowed to a silent creep, and moved in that direction. The wavering glow cast long shadows from the far side of a hulking vehicle similar to a stranded RV or a trailer. In the dark, she could make out only the overall shape, but not the color or condition of the walls and windows.

Maybe Dad fell and hurt his leg? Is that his campfire?

She advanced. Hope became dread at the sound of unfamiliar voices murmuring. At least two figures moved around near the fire, on the other side of the trailer. Her mouth watered. It wasn't Dad, but that smelled *soooo* good. She thought back to playing *The Last Outcast* and used her virtual training at stealth to stay in the shadows. Riley had a lot of practice evading 'vision cones' of AI-controlled baddies, and hoped it was at least somewhat close to reality as she edged up to the near side of the dead vehicle. The creak of flimsy aluminum on the roof scraped in the wind overhead, startling her to a halt. For a second, she debated if she should run away or if these people might be able to help her find Dad.

"Bored," said a man on the other side. "Think we'll catch anything?"

Riley froze.

"Word is they were seen 'round here." A few deep gulps broke the silence. "Ahhh, that's good shit. Leas' you got lucky findin' that meat."

"Indeed, Bird, indeed."

She crouched. *Raiders or bandits... Who names their kid 'Bird?'*

"Only thing'd make this night better is some tight pussy," said the wheezy man.

"I hear that," said Bird. "You shouldn't have got rid of yer last one."

"Bah. Bitch was crazy. I had to do it."

Her eyes widened. *Oh, shit. If they see me, I'm so raped.* Her hand slapped on the Beretta; she yanked it out of her waistband and flicked the safety off. *I gotta get out of here.* An empty aluminum can crunched under her first step back.

She tensed her legs to run, but at the sound of boots skiffing closer in the dirt, she ducked under the vehicle.

"Huh," muttered the near man. "Who's there?"

"Think that's one of 'em?" asked the other one.

I don't wanna think about what they'd do to a young, pretty girl out here, said Dad's voice in her mind.

A set of blue jeans and black boots approached. "Didn't see no lights."

Riley crammed herself against the axle, trying to melt into the dark.

The more distant guy took a step closer. "Me neither."

"You hear that?" asked the near voice.

Oh, no. Trembling hands lowered the Beretta to aim at the shins three feet away from her. When Lisa hid beneath the semi trailer, Riley had been scared for her. Being in the situation for real set her heart racing, her palms sweating, and her entire body trembling. Images of dirty, hairy men coming after her with leashes, ropes, and chains flashed in her mind. No way would that happen to her. *The world's over. This gun is the only law left. They wouldn't hesitate to hurt me.*

"Hear what?" The more distant man stood with a grunt. Shadows moved around the fire.

"Somethin's movin' under the trailer."

Just like the game. Lisa can do it. I can do it. She moved her index finger from the side to the trigger. *It's not a person; it's a rapey monster... Just a silhouette, a target.* The trembling wouldn't stop.

The figure took a knee and grunted.

Shaking hands made aiming difficult, even at such short range. She brought the Beretta up, waiting to see his eyes. Tears streaked down her face and the memory of SpaghettiOs welled up in the back of her throat. *Please go away. Please don't make me do this.*

Dense, curly beard crept into view followed by a bit of chin, then nose. He grunted, beer gut making it cumbersome for him to peer too far down.

Her finger took up the slack on the trigger, another smidge of pressure and it would go off. One human hair's width of travel, and she'd kill a man.

"Lonnie, grab the rifle," said the near voice. "Probably a coyote after the meat. Eesh. Whatever'tis smells funny."

"Yah," said the near voice.

Bang.

The crack of a gunshot rang out in the distance. Riley's jaw hung open; her body seized. She had to look back and forth from the pistol to the man to believe the noise hadn't come from her weapon. How her finger hadn't clenched when she jumped... Three more shots followed; men shouted, but they were too far away to make out words—or maybe they weren't even men anymore.

"Zat you?" asked the near voice.

"Nawp," said Lonnie. "Someone' havin' fun a bit west. I see muzzle flare."

The man close to the trailer grunted and stood. Riley aimed down at the dirt, taking her finger off the trigger and hyperventilating. *Oh, God. Oh, God.*

Safety on.

Both men jogged around the fire to the side of their camp farthest from her. There was nothing between her and a stack of already-cooked meat soaked in dark sauce. She crawled forward, all attention focused on a little folding stool with a plate on top of it. Fifteen paces past the campfire, a barrel-chested man and a skinny man attempted to look into the distance.

"What ya figure that was?"

The skinny one shrugged.

Overwhelmed by the siren call of cooked beef, Riley darted out of cover and snagged the biggest piece she could get her hand on. Two imposing shadow-figures whirled around, gawking at her. She didn't think about the Beretta in her hand, focused completely on the wonderful fragrance as she gave them a wild-eyed face and jammed the food into her mouth with a snarl.

"Hey!" yelled one.

She grabbed another piece and sprinted away from them.

"Shit, get her!" yelled Bird.

"What the hell was that?" yelled Lonnie.

The clomping of boots behind her added fire to her step. She ran hard, able to see enough by way of moonlight to avoid tripping over rocks or slipping into ruts. Two out-of-shape, rapist biker-bandits wouldn't catch a too-skinny fourteen-year-old who'd been 'training' to survive for the past four days. Nope. She was good. If she could outrun the overweight girls who kept stuffing her in lockers, she could outrun these two. A wild thought brought a manic smile, her grade school tormentors—still in New Jersey—were, in all likelihood, dead.

Rocks, bushes, and a cactus or two shot by. Drool and sauce ran over her chin and down her neck. Even after she could no longer hear them, she kept going until her legs couldn't take any more. She gasped for breath around the barbecued meat in her teeth, feeling light-headed as her run faded to a staggering lope. After a quick look back at empty darkness, she headed for a shallow ravine and huddled against the side, well below view. The Beretta went into her right thigh pocket to free her hand, and she took the first rib out of her mouth and licked her lips. As awesome as it was, she savaged it with little regard for taste, snarling and gnawing until she had bare bone in her grasp. She threw it aside and took the second piece in both hands, nibbling and licking at it slow enough to taste. It occurred to her she must look like a carnivorous rodent, which made her think of Dad calling her 'Squirrel.' Adrenaline gone, she shivered with fear, guilt, and sadness, crying while she gnawed on her purloined feast.

I almost shot a guy.

After almost two weeks of MREs and SpaghettiOs, the taste drew eager whimpers despite the tears flowing full bore from both eyes. For a short while, she forgot about everything but the awesomeness in her hands.

When no meat remained, she licked sauce and dirt from her fingers and scraped her teeth over the bone. The weight of the Beretta in her pants reminded her that not every meal would be free. Eventually, she would have to kill something—or someone.

She leaned back against the soft earth, closing her eyes as the wind played with her hair. *I love your green eyes.* Kieran's voice whispered from the ether. The image of him backing away from Dad's cold stare warped her face into a grimace of sorrow. Riley put a hand over her mouth to stifle the crying. Hot tears slid down her cheeks, onto her neck. Those men could be close. *I gotta hide. They're gonna get the rest of their gang and come hunting. They saw me. They know I'm a girl.*

Fear and fatigue got her to stay still for a short while. As long as it remained silent, she let herself enjoy the freedom of open sky. She sniffed the bone, wondering what kind of meat it had been. It tasted like beef, but...

She grabbed her gut. *I... no. That was not human.*

It tasted too good to throw up. *Definitely beef. Maybe dog?*

A distant shout startled her, though it came from too far away to make out words. With the Beretta pointed down and to the right, Riley climbed the far side of the ravine and looked around. Stillness blanketed the flat ground in all directions, with no sign of a campfire anymore. That meant she had covered enough ground and would probably be too much work for them to find. Dad's words haunted her. A girl like her had to be too tempting a prize to let go without a chase. The face of the delivery driver who'd brought the car appeared in her memory, leering, grinning. In her imagination, his hands tore at her clothes. She knew her mind made him scarier than he had been, but she nonetheless squirmed and tightened her grip on the pistol.

After three deep breaths to summon the energy to move, she climbed out of the ravine. Again, everything looked the same no matter which way she faced. She wandered for a little while until moonlight glinted off a distant rock; a rush of hope filled her. Riley ran to it, but it was too round and tall, not the marker Dad set up. Another boulder some distance away also proved wrong.

For what felt like hours, she roamed from rock to rock, chasing shadows and ducking into ruts whenever she heard any sound. The longer she walked, the more she regretted disobeying Dad. She could still be safe, if lonely, in the bunker. Worst-case scenario, she could find a ravine and wait for the sun to come up. Her heart leapt at the sight of another boulder, but when she skidded to a halt next to it, she realized she'd seen it before. It had a familiar gouge down the side.

I'd be able to see home in the daytime. I'm going in circles.

She froze. Her lip quivered.

I didn't call it 'Dad's house.'

Riley pivoted left, opposite to the way she'd walked past that rock before, and stomped forward.

"Mom, I know you didn't believe in ghosts, or spirits, or God, or angels or whatever... but just in case you were wrong, if you're there... help."

Four paces from another large stone, the ground moved. Riley fumbled with her flashlight, spotting it on a snake at the same instant it rattled. Much to her surprise, she neither screamed nor dropped the flashlight. She pointed the gun at it, not that the reptile recognized the threat. The rattler curled up, shaking its tail. Riley backed off.

"Crap."

"Over there," said a man. "Might be her." Definitely not Dad, and definitely too close for comfort.

"Eep," she whispered, and cut the flashlight.

A brief sprint took her to the opening of another ravine. She slid like a runner going into third base and skidded below ground level, out of sight. Riley got her feet under her again, crouching low enough to keep from being spotted as she crept forward. Flashlight beams teased at the area behind her. The trench lasted for thirty or so yards, making for a long crawl. At the far end, she poked up to look around, shivering and trying with all her effort not to breathe hard enough that she made noise. The overall shape of the terrain here seemed familiar; not enough to know where she was, but it felt like she'd been here before. Riley let her gut lead and walked, curving to the right a little and straight at a pair of wonderful, flat boulders.

The mound of dirt between them was no mound of dirt at all.

"We know you're there," yelled a man's voice. "No one's gonna hurt you. Drop the gun and come out."

She hauled the pallet up and scooted under it onto the ladder, taking care to lower it so as not to let it slam and make noise. Four rungs down, the crunch of people walking around outside got louder. Riley hurried along, pulling the Beretta when she reached the bottom. With the gun aimed straight up, she backed to the armored door. Her breathing seemed thunderous. Her fingertip teased at the trigger. If anyone opened that hatch, they'd regret it.

I will not be kidnapped.

Her heart pounded against her ribs. People went back and forth, accompanied by low murmurs. *Men hunting me.* She squeezed the Beretta; the gun in her hands reassured her trembles away. All the advantage was hers. They had one six-foot hole to go through, and she had sixteen bullets.

Eventually, the activity outside faded to silence. Her arms ached from holding the gun aloft so long. She stashed it in her pants and pulled the massive door open, scooted inside, and dragged it closed behind her.

The *thud* made her cringe. "If they heard that, so what… they can't get in."

Safe inside the bunker, she spun the wheel, pulled the lock down, and took three steps backwards before turning around.

No Dad.

Exhaustion and depression ganged up on her. Riley trudged across the room, kicked off her boots, slipped out of the fatigues, and fell face first on the cot with the Beretta under her pillow. A little burp brought the taste of barbecue back to her mouth. She licked her teeth clean of a few strands of stringy meat. Adrenaline kept her trembling, and sleep at arm's length. Riley closed her eyes and tried not to think about how close she'd come to killing someone.

"This was supposed to be the best summer…" She sniveled, wanting to hide in her bedroom in New Jersey and never come out.

Dad needs me.

Tomorrow, when the sun was up, she would try again.

IS THERE ANYBODY OUT THERE

Day Thirteen.

D reams of being a super-powered teen cutting down zombie bikers in a post-apocalyptic city faded to the bland Army-green blanket upon which Riley's face pressed. Sleeping in a tee shirt, panties, and socks would've been comfortable had she been *under* it instead of on top of it. Teeth chattering, she rolled over and bundled up on her side.

The bunker was still short one occupant.

It took a shade under fifteen minutes for urgency to overpower her disinterest in a cold room, and she scurried to the toilet before racing back to get her pants. She eyed the cot, but shook her head.

No, I can't give up.

She made coffee, after which she picked at an 'omelet' MRE while slurping a brew she thought strong enough to disintegrate teeth. All the while she ate, she looked at the cross she'd made, frowning at it. Plastic Toothbrush Jesus hadn't helped.

Mom was right.

Her gaze fell to her lap. *What if God's just slow? I shouldn't piss him off. Grow up, Riley; there's no God. If there was, he wouldn't have let the world kill itself.* She smirked at the door. "Wonder if that old man survived? He's probably running around the ashes handing out bibles."

She giggled

After collecting the trash back into the MRE pouch, she poured the rest of the coffee—Dad's half—into her mug and went to the radio. She reclined, feet at the edge of the cushion, sock-clad toes curled over the edge and coffee clutched to her chest to warm her fingers.

"Attention world. This is Riley McCullough. If there's anyone alive out there, I want you to know you're not alone." *Like me.* "Colonel Bering? Are you there? Is there anyone out there?"

Slurp.

She stared at the clock. Exactly ten minutes later, she tried again.

"This is Riley again. If anyone's out there, please reply. I sound like a little girl but I'm not... and I have guns. Lots of guns with hollow point bullets. No bandits please. I'm looking for survivors."

When the coffee ran dry, she held on to the Beretta. *This is pretty dumb. Nothing could get through that door.*

"Hi World, Riley again. How goes it? We've both had a pretty shitty summer so far, but, if there's anybody out there, please say something."

The same faint hissing continued.

Twenty minutes of silence.

"So, here I am in New Mexico after the world killed itself. I was supposed to be enjoying the best summer ever with my friend Amber, who's probably also dead now. We used to play *Call of Duty* all the time. It's not really so much fun to be living the game. My mom was Lily. She died a few weeks ago when the FSB pointed a microwave gun at her head. At least, that's what Dad thinks. I don't know if he's joking or serious. I hated it here at first... I mean it was lame enough even before the world ended. I met a boy and he liked—"

She let off the transmit button, choked up. Riley refused to let herself cry anymore. Her silent stare failed to elicit any reaction from the radio. She gasped and sucked her grief in, though her eyes grew watery.

"He liked me. His name was Kieran. The whole town had something against my dad, but now they know he was right. They made fun of him for being prepared, but he saw what was coming. There's gotta be more people out there like him with bunkers and protection and radios and stuff. Please say something."

Hiss.

She pulled the headset off and dropped it on the table. "This is a waste of time. I guess I'll just stay here until there's no food left and then hope I don't get killed." Sigh. "No, that's stupid. It's light out now. I gotta go find him."

Slam.

A reverberating crack of wood echoed outside in the front chamber. Riley started to scream, but bit down on her left forearm to muffle it. All the bandits would need to hear was a terrified girl and they'd pound the door down with their... Riley shivered and grabbed the Beretta.

She ran to the south wall, hiding behind the mini-kitchen station with the gun pointed over it at the door. Metal clanking grew louder. The sound was unmistakable—boots on a ladder. The rhythm was wrong, zombie like.

Her thumb flicked the safety off.

Thump.

Something hit the door.

Thump, thump.

"Zombies can't beat through a vault door," she whispered.

Thump, thump. The wheel rattled.

"Go away," she whispered.

Silence.

She didn't move; when her legs started to shake, she went from squatting to kneeling, but kept aiming over the sink at the door.

Small bits of metal jangled outside. She gasped. To her horror, the locking lever moved. She wanted to run over and grab it as it opened, but couldn't summon the courage to abandon her cover. When the wheel rotated, she squeezed all the blood out of her fingers against the Beretta's handle.

The wheel stopped with a *clank.* Her finger tensed on the trigger.

Bloody fingers slipped around the edge of the door. Riley raised her aim point, estimating where the head would be on an adult man.

"Go away," she yelled. "One more inch, and I'll shoot."

"Squirrel..." wheezed a faint voice.

Her body went limp.

"Squirrel?" The door slid open a few inches farther.

"Dad?" She dropped the gun in the steel sink and leapt to her feet.

Dad staggered in, left hand pressed to his side, right groping at the air.

"Daddy!" Riley ran to him, bawling.

Her impact almost took him off his feet. He groaned. She held on and sobbed against his chest for several minutes.

"Sorry. I had to lose a couple of bandits. They were looting the house."
He grunted. "Help me to the cot."

"Dad?" She leaned back as he staggered into the bunker.

The front of her shirt had turned red from blood. Riley screamed. Dad
shrugged off his backpack, let the AR15 clatter to the ground nearby, and
fell onto the cot with an agonized grunt. She hadn't noticed until then
how pale his face looked, or how weary he seemed.

"I thought—"

"Not yet." He reached up to brush her cheek with dry, scratchy fingers.
"I'm not dead yet. One of the bandits winged me. Nothing serious, but it
hurts like a bastard. Grab the first aid box."

She ran to the bookshelf, snagged a white plastic thing about the size
of a lunchbox and ran back to him. Her hands shook too much to open it.
Dad peeled his camo shirt off, revealing a darkened olive-drab tank top
with a hole in it about halfway between armpit and hip, an inch or two in
from his left side.

"Missed the vitals," he wheezed. "I think it went all the way through."

Blood welled out of the hole each time he moved. She pawed and
clung, finding an exit wound on his back too. Riley made fists, took two
deep breaths, and ripped open the first aid kit.

"You're bleeding."

His expression didn't change from neutral. "That happens when a
person gets shot. Help me get this shirt off."

She did most of the work, leaving him to sit there and make zombie
noises as the fabric separated from the wound.

He squeezed her forearm. "Tweezers. Get the fibers out of the hole."

Joy at having her father alive overpowered any squeamishness. One by
one, she plucked threads of shirt and fatigue jacket out of the holes in
front and back.

"Wipe it down. Wash it with alcohol, then put a gauze on it with tape."

She tilted her head forward, eyebrows raised. "Won't that hurt?"

"Oh, yes. I believe it will." He made a weak gesture at her backpack. "I
got you some tampons. They're in your pack."

"Dad! Now is not the—"

"Give me one to bite on."

"Oh."

She rummaged her 'go bag' until she found a pink box in one of the
side zipper pouches. He'd gotten cheap ones, but who cared about that
anymore. After gathering isopropyl, gauze, and two washcloths, she set

about the task of cleaning him up as best she could. Dad's fingers crushed around her shoulder when she dabbed the area with alcohol. He screamed past the cotton between his teeth. It hurt her to hurt him, but the wound had to be cleaned or he'd get something nasty and die anyway.

"Pack some cotton into the hole. In a few hours, you'll need to change the dressing with fresh stuff."

Blood swelled up and out as she pushed cotton into his back and taped a patch of gauze in place over it. He stretched out on the cot with a long, wheezing groan, and she repeated the process for the entry wound.

"Lucky thing all they could scavenge was ball ammo. I'd be in bad shape if they had hollow points."

Riley knelt beside the cot, holding his right hand in both of hers. "What happened?"

"I made my way back toward the house. Geiger was clean. Figured I'd go inside and check on stuff, but there were a couple of looters by the door. As soon as they saw me, they went for their weapons. Son of a bitch was fast. I didn't even have a chance to get a shot off."

She squeezed his hand.

"I didn't want to lead them to you, so I took a long circle. Found a hiding spot and dug in." He gazed up at the ceiling, groaning.

Riley grimaced at the blood all over her shirt and hands. *He's lost so much blood... He's not gonna be okay.* She brushed hair off his forehead and plucked bits of scrub bush out of his beard. It would take another nuke going off—in the bunker—to get her to let go of his arm.

"Mother flying windless."

"Huh?" Riley blinked.

Dad chuckled. "Side burn. Snowy brain."

"Dad, what is wrong with you?" She put an arm across his chest and held on.

He rolled his head to the side; the mirth in his face faded to serious. "Moon aliens walk dark."

"Stop it!" Riley wanted to shake him, but hesitated because of the wound. "Dad..."

His eyes seemed to go in and out of focus. "Squirrel?"

"Yes, I'm here. It's Squirrel." She kissed him on the forehead. "I'm here. I love you, Dad."

"Bandits, outside." He raised his right arm, pointing up. "Danger. Acorns hiding."

She clutched his arm to her chest, the back of his hand against her cheek. "Dad, stop talking like that. You're freaking me out. You're all I've got left. Don't die. You can call me Squirrel all you want if you promise to stay alive."

"Okay." The glazed look in his eyes faded two seconds before he closed them. He gurgled a few belabored breaths. "I won't die then."

Dad drifted in and out of sleep over the next hour. At the sight of crust at the corners of his mouth, she got up and brought him water, feeding it to him a sip at a time. He continued muttering incomprehensible phrases. Each time he babbled, she shivered. The man on the cot seemed nothing like Dad. It felt as if someone else had jumped inside his skin. She hovered at his side, clinging to his arm.

Two hours after Dad returned, she warmed a can of SpaghettiOs and spoon-fed him. He seemed to recognize the smell right away, and offered a grateful smile. *Wow, he really does like them.*

"I'm sorry, Squirrel. I tried to protect you when I left. I never meant to hurt you."

She held up the spoon again. "Dad, this isn't your fault. W-we'll survive. Just like you said."

I'm not gonna lose him too.

The process of giving him the entire bowl of SpaghettiOs proved a laborious task. Once he'd finished eating, she knelt on the floor, half draped on the cot. Nothing mattered but Dad. She wouldn't make the same mistake she'd made with Mom.

"Tell me what to do, Dad." She clutched his limp hand to her cheek. "I'm right here."

A smile almost formed on his blue lips.

UNRAVELING

Day Fourteen.

Feeding Dad wasn't so bad. Treating and dressing a wound was worse, but not intolerable. Repurposing a saucepan to a bedpan, and cleaning Dad up after the fact was even worse than Armageddon. Riley scrunched her face and looked away as she emptied it into the toilet and flushed. About ready to vomit, she rinsed the 'pot-that-shall-never-again-touch-food' and set it on the floor.

Her legs protested moving. Sleeping on her knees next to him had left everything sore and her neck stiff. She collected some fresh gauze and a clean washcloth.

Blood had soaked through the bandages into the cot and left her shirt gory enough to suggest she'd taken a bullet herself. Dried crimson trails stained her bare legs all the way down to the shins. She coaxed him to roll onto his side so she could get to his back. Dad barely moaned when she plucked the cotton balls out of the bullet hole. Thick, scabrous chunks flaked away as she wrenched tweezers back and forth to dislodge a dark wad. Hours ago when she'd done that, he'd screamed.

"Dad?"

He moaned again.

"Dad. Dad. Wake up." She put a hand on his shoulder and shook.

"Mmm. Squirrel, what time is it?"

"Uh... Eight after eleven."

He didn't respond.

"Dad!" she slapped his shoulder.

"Ouch. Let me sleep."

Riley taped clean gauze over the wound on his back and eased him flat. He waved his finger about, murmuring, as she peeled away the dressing on his front and replaced it with a new one. He had about the same reaction to it as he had the other—almost none.

"Do you want coffee?"

Dad laughed. "Ground water brown. Glowing accountant clicking."

"Stop that!" Riley screamed, clenching her hand into a fist around the old bandage. "You're seriously freaking me out."

His eyes fluttered closed as his arms fell limp at his sides. Subvocal muttering continued. Riley ran to the radio.

"Hello, anyone. This is Riley. I'm in a bunker near Las Cerezas. My dad's been shot by bandits. Is there anyone out there? We need help. Please. He... I think he's dying."

Hiss.

She waited a minute and repeated the message. When that got no reply, she darted to the bookshelf and fumbled over the titles in search of anything helpful. One first aid book had little information in the way of gunshot wounds, and seemed written by someone who had a serious fascination with CPR and frostbite. The second looked like it came from 1962.

"Dad?"

He didn't move. Dread gripped her.

The book went flying as she leapt up and ran to him. He opened his eyes when she grabbed his wrist.

"Hi Squirrel. Coffee ready yet?"

She held on to his arm, kissed his knuckle, and sniffled. "I'll make it now."

At the sink, she twisted the plastic tap to let water trickle into the electric kettle. She fixated on the bubbles forming around the stream. *Dad's dying. He won't admit it.* She turned off the faucet. *I can't let him die.* Careful not to make a sound, she set the e-kettle down without turning it on and tiptoed over to where she'd left her pants. After slipping into the fatigues, she sat on the floor by her boots, pulled them on, and tied the laces.

Dad muttered something about Colonel Bering.

"He hasn't answered," said Riley. "Dad. I'm going to find help."

"Don't go out there." He sounded hazy and out of it, but coherent. "Danger."

"You're dying. I gotta do something. If I just sit here and hide, I'm going to lose you too. You're not gonna be okay, Dad. You're bleeding too much." She tucked the Beretta into her waistband. "I'm not going to lose both my parents in the same summer."

Dad flapped his arm in a feeble attempt to grab her.

"Hang on, Dad. Don't give up."

"No," he wheezed. "Too dange…"

When Riley went to turn the wheel to unbar the door, it occurred to her that neither of them had closed it when Dad returned. For hours, she'd slept with nothing between her and the wasteland but a disguised trapdoor. She didn't have time to panic over that now, and rushed through the outer room to the ladder. Blood-caked hands made grabbing the rungs difficult; she clambered to the top and shoved the pallet up to reveal clear, blue sky marked by three distinct cottony clouds. Warm, dry air lifted her hair off her face, clean and crisp without the taste of a confined space.

"Wow… no red blobs in the sky. No nuclear winter."

That gave her hope. Somewhere, someone might be able to help Dad. He said the house was still standing. Her best chance would probably be at T or C… maybe Albuquerque. Hospitals are huge and made out of concrete. Maybe there were some people left. She'd go to the house, get the truck and go hunting doctors.

She set the pallet down and fiddled with the burlap to make it look like dirt again. In the clear light of almost-noon, home stood out like a sore thumb to the south. It looked like he'd built his bunker about two hundred yards away… so close… *how the hell did I get lost the other night?*

Boosted by worry, she trotted straight at it. A few minutes later, she rounded the corner to the front and headed for the pickup truck. A layer of dust had settled over everything. *Crap. Keys.* She spun on her heel to face the front door, where a small white paper fluttered in the breeze. From where she stood, she could make out a PNM logo above the word "notice."

What the heck is that?

She got three steps closer before the crunch of a shoe coming around the far corner of the building her made her freeze. Her first thought was the men she'd stolen the ribs from had found her. They'd probably taken over the house. They had to be the guys who shot Dad. She swallowed hard and darted to the right at a full sprint.

"Police, stop where you are!" shouted a man.

P-police? Riley skidded to a halt. "What?"

"Riley?" asked a familiar voice.

She turned around.

Sergeant Rodriguez, in uniform plus bulletproof vest, stood about fifteen yards away with a younger white man next to him, also in uniform. Both had their hands on their weapons. A surge of hope burst from her chest. She grinned, wide-eyed.

"Sergeant Rodriguez!" she yelled, and ran toward them.

As soon as they got a good look at her, the cops pulled their Glocks and aimed at her.

"Gun!" shouted the younger man.

Terror locked every muscle. Riley screamed and halted.

"On the ground, now!" roared the white guy. "Get down."

She shivered, unable to move. *What did I do? I'm a kid! They're gonna shoot me.* She glanced down at herself, the bloody shirt, the gun in her pants. The younger cop glared. Sergeant Rodriguez, who also had his weapon out, held up one hand at his partner. Her arms locked, refusing to obey.

"P-please don't kill me," she mewled.

Rodriguez lowered his voice to a more soothing tone. "Riley. Listen to me. Do not move."

"I… can't." After a two-second pause, she whined.

"Kneel down and put your hands behind your head."

She gritted her teeth and let her legs go, falling to her knees, shaking.

"Very slow now, lie flat on your belly."

Riley worked her way down. A few seconds after her cheek touched dirt, the cops crept over. Having pistols aimed at her head at such close range terrified her into uncontrollable trembles. One of them gathered her arms behind her back while the other pulled the gun out of her pants. Handcuffs clicked around her wrists. Fingers slid up and down her body, patting and invading pockets. The young cop took the two extra magazines from her left thigh pocket.

"Jesus, Marty, this kid was ready for war."

Sergeant Rodriguez grasped her by the bicep and pulled her up so she sat on the ground with one cop on either side of her. She stared at him, wanting to scream, cry, throw up, and wet herself all at once.

"Sergeant Rodriguez! You're alive!" Her face flooded with hope. "Please help!"

"Yeah, kid," said the other cop. "You surprised? Guess your old man isn't as bad ass as you think."

Daddy. "Huh?"

Sergeant Rodriguez looked over the Beretta. "It's full. She hasn't fired it."

"Or she reloaded," muttered the other guy.

"One in the pipe and a full mag... doubtful." Rodriguez looked down at her. "Whose blood is that?"

"My Dad's. He's been shot by bandits. You gotta help him! He's dying." She fidgeted at the cuffs, which seemed to grow tighter.

"Bandits?" asked the other cop.

She sobbed. "Bandits shot him when he went out to check for radiation. It's my fault. I shouldn't have hit the radiation detector. It stopped glowing, so he thought it was safe."

"Riley," said Sergeant Rodriguez. "Slow down, take a breath, and tell me what happened."

She sniffled, wiping her running nose on her knee after she couldn't reach her hand up high enough. "Nuclear war. DC's gone. The world's gone." She sniffled. "I can't believe you're alive. It's so good to see you. I-I thought everyone was dead. Please, you gotta hurry, Dad's dying!"

The young cop whistled and twirled his finger by the side of his head.

"Knock it off, Lawson." Rodriguez looked back to her. "Why are you carrying a loaded gun?"

"I don't wanna get raped. Society's gone. People would grab me."

Sergeant Rodriguez squatted and looked her in the eye. "Riley, listen to me. Nothing's happened. The world is just fine."

"What?" Trembles returned.

"Kieran called us a few days ago because he was worried. No one has seen you or your dad for two weeks. He drove out here a couple times and the place was abandoned. He asked us to check on you."

"Kieran?" She gaped at him for a moment. "Kieran's alive?"

"Why wouldn't he be?" asked Sergeant Rodriguez.

Riley doubled over, sobbing. "Because the world war happened. I saw the missiles. The sky was on fire. Colonel Bering said the Russians and the Koreans shot at us."

He squeezed her shoulder. "Riley. Look at me. What's more likely?

That the world went up in nuclear flames or your father has some issues with reality?"

She sat up and sniffled. "W-what?"

Sergeant Rodriguez pulled the radio mic on his left shoulder closer to his mouth. "Hey, Carlos, come back?"

"Go ahead, Rod," crackled a voice out of something on his belt.

"Did Armageddon happen?"

The radio was silent for a few seconds. "Bullshit, the Mets aren't going to the series."

Riley stared at him, so overwhelmed she couldn't speak, cry, or scream. Her mind replayed the night she almost shot a man for food. If this was true—if the world was still really there, she'd almost murdered some guy. All her body was willing to do was shake. After a moment, she lurched sideways and threw up bile and coffee. Officer Rodriguez supported her enough so she didn't fall face-first into it, and patted her on the back. She wrung her arms around, trying to get her hands free to wipe a tickling tendril of slime dangling from her nose.

"You know where your dad is, you tell us, or you're looking at accessory to attempted murder of a peace officer," said Lawson.

She swiveled her head to look in his direction, but all she saw as a blur of tears as she coughed up more brown slime. "What?"

"Will you take it down a notch, Hank? Can't you see this kid is traumatized?"

Lawson shook his head. "She's just as batshit nuts as her dad."

"Riley," said Sergeant Rodriguez. "Your father pointed a weapon at Officer Roma the other night. We were out here to do a wellness check on the two of you."

"He's dying," whimpered Riley. "You gotta help him. Please, I'll show you where he is. Please, don't kill him. He said he saw looters."

Officer Lawson made a cuckoo whistle.

"Please. He's in our bunker. We thought the war..." She sniveled and cried for another few seconds. She strained against the handcuffs, desperate to wrap her arms around him and hold on to someone. "Is the world really still here?"

"Yes, Riley," said Sergeant Rodriguez.

"Kieran's still alive?"

He nodded. "As far as I know."

"Amber?"

"I'm not sure who that is."

Riley's heart thumped. Worry for Dad, terror about how much trouble she was in, and too much relief to quantify slapped her brain into mush. "My friend from Jersey."

Sergeant Rodriguez looked her in the eye. "The East Coast is still intact. There was no nuclear war, Riley."

"But the sky exploded."

"The Air Force was conducting night bombing exercises. We had no specifics, but they gave us a heads up in case the locals called it in." Lawson chuckled. "Every time they do something in the dark, people go UFO crazy."

"The infrastructure collapsed. We lost power," she whispered.

Sergeant Rodriguez glanced at the house. "PNM cut your power. Your father hasn't paid the bill in six months. While we were looking for you, we checked up on him. He'd been doing some software work via a temp agency in T or C, but they haven't seen him since May."

"No apocalypse?" Another wave of nausea came on. "I didn't shoot anyone. It's Dad's blood. He's hurt bad." The cuffs clattered as she tried to hug him again; she wound up leaning against his leg.

"Where is he?" asked Sergeant Rodriguez.

"That way," she pointed with her nose. "Please hurry! I'll show you; the bunker's hidden."

Sergeant Rodriguez hooked an arm under hers and lifted her to her feet, keeping a grip on her bicep. "Okay, let's go."

Lawson's distrustful stare made her shy away and shrink in on herself. She sniveled as Rodriguez walked her along, allowing her to steer but not move too fast. With the sun out, the path back to the bunker seemed obvious, though wind had eroded the footprints they'd left during their midnight escape. Riley cast a longing glance at the house to her left; a month ago, she had all summer to hang with Amber, goofing off and not having to worry about anything.

She let her head hang. *What happened? Mom's dead. Dad's dying, and I'm going to jail.*

TRUST UNEARTHED

Riley stopped to cough up traces of vomit every few yards. The pinching steel around her wrists terrified her. Never in her life had she so much as gotten detention at school. Somehow, she'd skipped over petty teen things like getting picked up for shoplifting or speeding and jumped straight to felony arrest for a firearm offense. Sergeant Rodriguez kept a hand on her arm, not tight enough to hurt, but enough to make her feel like a prisoner rather than a guide. Still shaking, she walked toward the two identifying rocks two hundred some odd yards away.

"A-am I being arrested?" she whispered.

Officer Lawson glared.

Sergeant Rodriguez shook his head. "Not yet. The cuffs are for our protection as well as yours. We don't know what kind of mental state you're in, or what you may or may not have done. We don't want to have to shoot a kid." Three paces later, he spoke again. "Did you do anything you should be arrested for?"

"I stole some meat from a couple of guys... I thought they were bandits." She stared at her boots for a moment, and looked up at him. "They weren't bandits, were they?"

"Nope. Lonnie and Freebird... camped out hoping to get some photos of aliens or UFOs. We ran into them while hunting for your dad. Said they saw a scrawny kid running around with a gun. Figured it might be you, but I wasn't expecting you to be armed. We've been out here hunting for the two of you for three days."

"Sorry. I'll pay them back for the ribs. I thought the world was over. I didn't recognize them… It was dark. I played this stupid game, and all I could think about was bandits who wanted to kidnap me."

Officer Lawson laughed. "Freebird's part of that biker group that helps abused kids. He's a damn teddy bear."

"The other guy said he needed to get a new girl 'cause he had to get rid of his last one," muttered Riley. "I thought he killed her."

"Lonnie got divorced a few months ago," said Rodriguez.

"Oh." Riley stopped. "It's here." She pointed the toe of her boot at the fake dirt mound. "Under that."

Officer Lawson circled it. "What kind of traps you got on this thing?"

"Nothing." She cowered, but looked up at Rodriguez. "I'll open it if it you take the handcuffs off for a minute. It's safe."

"No way, kid. Not till we secure the area." Lawson looked at Rodriguez. "Want me to stash her in the car and get backup out here?"

"No!" wailed Riley. "He's gonna die if you wait. He's bleeding real bad. Please…"

"What's under there?" asked Rodriguez.

"There's a ladder down to a tiny room with a door. Another small room with a shower and an armored door to the main bunker. Dad's in a bed on the left side."

"How many weapons?" asked Lawson.

"His AR15 is on the floor by the bed. There's a Remington 700 and three handguns in a safe, but it's locked."

Lawson scowled. "We should call in SWAT from Albuquerque. This is over our pay grade. Going in there is a death trap. He might have IEDs too."

"No," muttered Riley.

Rodriguez let go of her arm and lifted the pallet. Both cops peered down the shaft. Riley shifted around, trying to squeeze her hands free.

"Madre de Dios," muttered Rodriguez.

"Let me go down first," whined Riley, bouncing. "He won't shoot me. Even i-if… he's—" She stared at the ground. *Crazy.* "Please, hurry. He's dying."

"Riley?" asked Sergeant Rodriguez.

"If he's messed up in the head, he'll still think you're bandits. He'll freak the hell out, and I don't wanna think about what he could do. He won't hurt me. I'll calm him down so you can go in and help him."

"I'll put her in the car," said Lawson.

She yelled when he grabbed her arm. "Please, no. No! You're gonna kill him!"

"Hang on, Hank." Sergeant Rodriguez leaned close, staring into her eyes. "Tell me you won't do anything that I will regret."

"I swear I won't! I'd rather have Dad in jail than dead. Please, let me help."

"You can't be serious," said Lawson. "At best, she becomes a hostage we let him have… at worst, she grabs a gun, and we have to shoot her. You can't let a child go into a situation like this. I don't know about you, Marty, but I don't want a dead kid on my conscience. This stinks to shit and back."

"Please…" she whined. "I swear I'm not gonna do anything bad. There's no time. He's gonna die."

Sergeant Rodriguez studied her face for a moment before glancing at the ladder. He put a hand on her shoulder, tapping a finger for a few seconds.

"This is contrary to policy, and probably reckless on my part, but I'm going to trust you. You need to stay calm. Don't make any quick movements, and do *not* let me think you are reaching for a weapon of any kind. If we tell you to do something, you do it."

Riley nodded.

"Marty, this… no," said Lawson.

Sergeant Rodriguez pushed her shoulder so her back faced him. She trembled until he grabbed the chain and unlocked the cuffs.

"We don't have a better option." Rodriguez tucked the cuffs back into their holder on his belt. "If we let him die down there, we're not doing our job right."

Riley turned around and hugged him, making Lawson pull his gun again.

"Thank you."

Lawson relaxed. "Watch that shit. I thought you were reaching for his weapon."

"I'm going to go down to the bottom of the ladder first," said Rodriguez. "You follow me. Lawson, last." He pointed at her. "Don't run, don't make any sudden moves."

"Yes, sir." Riley held her hands up.

She shied away from Lawson as Rodriguez went over the side and down. Fearful the other cop would shoot her if she twitched, she crept to the edge and waited until Rodriguez reached the ground. With slow, telegraphed motions, she oriented herself over the ladder and climbed down. The sergeant put a hand on her back when she reached the bottom, and guided her by the shoulder to the armored door.

"Okay," he whispered. "If this gets out of control, you hit the floor and stay down. Do not move." He shook his head. "I'm putting my career on the hook for this, kid. Don't make me regret it."

Riley traced an X over her chest. She edged to the door as Lawson made his way down the ladder. Rodriguez held her back until the other officer was ready behind him. He reached over her head and pulled the door open.

"Dad?" Riley crept in. "It's me. I'm okay."

He lay on the cot, seeming asleep. Hoarse, labored breathing emanated from his mouth. She tiptoed over. Rodriguez peered around the doorway behind his Glock. She held her hands up in a show of 'I'm not doing anything bad' and glanced down. The sergeant's gaze followed hers to where the assault rifle lay on the ground. Riley kept her hands in the air and nudged the weapon with her boot, pushing it away from the bed toward the door. Rodriguez tensed, but kept his Glock low.

When the weapon was out of Dad's easy reach, she moved to the cot and sat on the side. "Dad?"

"Hmm?" His eyes peeled open. "Squirrel."

She cried. "Yes. It's me. Dad... You have to listen to me."

"I'm dying. I know. I'm sorry, Riley. I tried. You have to survive."

"No, Dad. You're not gonna die." She grabbed his hands and held on tight. "There wasn't a war. The world isn't gone."

"What?"

"It's in your head, Dad." She cried harder. "You almost shot a cop."

"Colonel Bering..."

Riley shook her head. "I don't know why he said that. There's no war."

Lawson moved closer.

Dad gasped when he caught sight of the two cops. He tried to sit up, but Riley threw her weight over him. He grunted from the pain, the only reason she overpowered him.

"No, Dad. Stop. The police are here to help you. You need to go to the hospital." She wrestled to control his hands. "They're not dead. No one is dead."

Officer Lawson seized Dad's arms and held him down. Rodriguez holstered his weapon and pulled Riley off, guiding her back a few steps while Lawson contained her panicking father. Riley couldn't watch, and buried her face against the cop's shirt.

"Daddy! Please let them help you," shouted Riley.

After a brief struggle, Dad wheezed and abandoned the will to fight.

"He's lost a lot of blood," said Lawson, for the first time sounding not like an asshole. He eyed the bandages. "I'll stay with him. Looks like the bullet might've nicked the spleen."

"Nicked?" asked Rodriguez.

Lawson looked at Riley with guilt in his eyes. "If it hit full on, he wouldn't... uh... Yeah."

"Dispatch, this is Rod, I need an ambulance out to the McCullough place, ASAP."

Dead air.

"Shit, the radios aren't working down here," said Rodriguez.

"Use Dad's." Riley pointed at the SINCGARS.

Lawson, standing at the head of the cot, looked at it. "You mean the one with no antenna connected?"

"What?" Riley blinked. If not for Sergeant Rodriguez holding her, she'd have fallen to her knees. "N-no antenna? What?"

"The ANT plug is empty, there's no way this thing would've gotten a signal this far underground without a lead to an exterior antenna." He looked it over. "This is military. How the hell did he even get one of these?"

Riley gawked at the wall as if she'd been slapped. "Dad said there's a faraday cage around the whole bunker. That would... stop radio, wouldn't it?"

"Yep," said Lawson, reaching for the first aid kit. "I'll stay with him."

"Rod..." wheezed Dad. "You survived." He faded in and out, half smiling. "No rads up to the house. We got lucky."

Her lip quivered at the sight of Dad, still thinking the world had ended. Riley had her doubts too, but the cops immaculate uniforms didn't look the least bit dirty, and neither man acted in any way that felt wrong.

"Come on." Rodriguez tugged Riley to the door. "You shouldn't be in here. Lawson used to be a corpsman in the Army, your dad's gonna be okay."

She climbed the ladder, emerging from the heavy, stagnant dimness to clear air and bright sunlight. Fear, nerves, and vomiting left her feeling as though someone had punched her in the stomach. Sergeant Rodriguez came up a few seconds later. Riley turned her back and put her hands behind her, shivering. She expected cuffs again, but he took hold of her arm and led her back to the house.

"Dispatch, this is Rod. I need an ambulance out to the McCullough place. One adult male, gunshot wound. Lost a lot of blood." He paused. "Guys, we found him. Suspect neutralized, stand down. Bring it in."

A series of responses came in rapid succession, mostly 'roger' or 'copy.'

He brought her to the rear door of a police car bearing markings for Truth or Consequences PD. Again, she put her hands behind her and waited, but he guided her into the opening by the door.

She glanced at the seat and the metal grating between the front and back. Afraid to spook him, she leaned against him with slow movements. Her heart ached, her throat tightened, and her eyes refused to stop leaking. For a moment, she couldn't find the ability to speak, and stared at him. Whatever look was on her face had an effect, as Rodriguez seemed close to tears himself.

"It's really not all gone?"

He took a long breath. "No, Riley... For better or worse, the world is still going on."

Approaching sirens invaded the silence, devouring the wispy noise of the wind.

"Thank you for not killing my dad. I'm sorry for what he did."

"Not your fault, girl." He sighed. "I need to ask you to wait in the car. I'll leave it running so there's AC."

She sank back and sat, pulling her legs in. He shut the door, which she knew wouldn't open if she tried it. Her hands clutched bony knees through the thin, black fatigues. She almost shot a man; she probably deserved to go to jail too. Riley didn't much notice the car start, but jumped when he closed the driver's door. She stared at faint red marks on her naked wrists, wondering how long Sergeant Rodriguez's leniency would last.

Wailing sirens cut out as an EMT van and another police car rumbled up. Rodriguez jogged over and stepped onto the running board of the ambulance, pointing in the direction of the bunker. She sniffled, pressing her forehead to the window to watch the flashing lights and dust cloud drift away.

When the ambulance stopped in the distance, three men and a woman got out and readied a bright orange coffin-shaped thing with straps and handles. The sight of the medics lent weight to Sergeant Rodriguez's claim the world had not ended. This looked too organized to seem like a small pack of survivors. One by one, they disappeared into the shaft, taking the strange device with them.

Please stay alive, Dad.

A few minutes later, Lawson emerged, followed by a woman in an EMT uniform. Next came her dad, strapped to the orange shell, which another cop below pushed up and out of the shaft. They righted him and carried him to the waiting ambulance. She wanted to run to him, and battled with the handle, even though she knew the police car wouldn't open. Riley pounded on the glass until the ambulance doors closed, and sagged limp. Her stomach churned, wanting to throw up again, but there was nothing left inside her to come out.

Sergeant Rodriguez and Officer Lawson made for the car she sat in, while another six or seven cops descended into the bunker. Two went to the house. Rodriguez got in the driver's seat, Lawson next to him.

"You okay, kid?" asked Lawson.

"I don't know," she wheezed.

Sergeant Rodriguez tried to look reassuring, but the steel mesh between them reinforced the feeling of being in a cage. "Everything's going to be fine, Riley. It's over. We're going to take you to the hospital for a routine exam, alright?"

"'Kay." She glanced left at the dust trailing the ambulance racing off to a city that still existed.

The car rolled forward and made a slow turn around the house. Locked in the back seat of a police cruiser, she stared at the building, wanting nothing more than to run inside and dive into her own bed. Rodriguez straightened out on a path to the dirt road leading to NM 51. Riley jostled in the seat, numb as her home slipped away from her for the second time in less than two months.

"It's over," she whispered, shrinking in on herself. "It's over."

LUCID

S ergeant Rodriguez guided Riley by a hand on the back down the halls of Sierra Vista Hospital in Truth or Consequences. Her flip-flops popped in a limp serenade that mirrored her mood. A small purse bounced off her left leg. Riley wasn't sure if Sergeant Rodriguez broke policy again by bringing her home to clean up and change, but she was grateful for fresh clothes, real soap, and real breakfast—even if it did come from the cafeteria at the police station. For days, all anyone would say about her dad was that he was 'improving.'

An unlocked cell at the tiny, local police station had served as her bedroom for the past three nights. Aside from two trips to T or C to visit a shrink and a child advocate, she hadn't been anywhere but there and an interrogation room. Sleep had been little more than periods of blackout while staring at the walls. At any moment, she dreaded she'd look up to find the cell locked.

He pulled her to a stop at the side of the hallway. "Riley, your dad's been taking medication for about three days now. He may seem different than the man you remember."

She fidgeted, grasping the front of her flip-flops with her toes. "Yeah. The advocate said he was schizophrenic."

"That's right." Sergeant Rodriguez nodded. "The man he was hearing on the radio isn't real."

"Yeah. I kinda figured that out when Lawson said it had no antenna." *I'm a moron. I could've stopped all of this.* She glanced away from the handcuffs on his belt, dreading the moment he'd use them. "Paranoia and hallucinations."

"I'm sorry, Riley. You've been through so much." Sergeant Rodriguez held his breath, offering a concerned expression for a few seconds. "You should know he's probably looking at a few years in a facility—a hospital, not jail."

Her lips quivered. *Don't cry.* She swallowed. *I'm gonna be an orphan.* "'Kay. That's good, right?"

"For him, yes." He nudged her forward again. "We'll be right outside the room if anything gets out of hand."

"I trust him." She crept down the corridor staring at her feet, trying to radiate the impression she wouldn't try to run away. No trace of polish remained.

A few minutes later, a gentle squeeze and twist of fingers brought her to a halt by a door where a young Hispanic officer sat reading a book. His nametag said Roma. *That's the guy who shot Dad.* He looked in his early twenties with short, black hair and a boyish face. It surprised her she didn't hate him on sight. Perhaps because his fast reflexes prevented Dad from being responsible for murder. Of all the ways the situation could have gone: cop dead, Dad dead, both dead, things had turned out pretty good. It was bad enough what happened, but at least no one died.

If he'd killed one, they'd have shot him for sure.

A device on a post by the bed beeped in a steady pulse. Seeing Dad laying there with all the tubes and stuff plugged into him was scarier than sleeping in a cell at the Las Cerezas precinct, even if they had left it open. A twenty-four hour presence at the front desk was all the lock they needed to keep her there.

Not like I have anywhere to run.

Riley looked up at Sergeant Rodriguez. He offered an encouraging nod and patted her on the shoulder. She edged into the room and moved around to the right side of the bed, trying not to look at the handcuff linking her father's left wrist to the frame.

"Dad?" she croaked.

His eyes opened. The beeping picked up a little speed. "Squirrel."

"Daddy." She broke down, hugging the arm that reached up to touch her.

"Looks like I'm gonna make it." The hand brushing her cheek slipped around behind her neck and squeezed. "I'm so glad to see you. Those shorts are too short."

"You're smiling." She giggled despite tears. "I've never seen you smile like that."

"I'm on meds." A hint of shame lurked behind the fog in his eyes. "I... The... I've lied to you."

"I don't care." She sat on the edge of the bed. "You're alive."

"You kept asking me why I left, and I've never told you the truth."

Her throat tightened.

"I figured out I had some head issues." He fidgeted the blanket between his fingers. "It would only get worse, and I couldn't admit it to anyone but Lily. I didn't want you two to suffer watching me decline. I fled like a coward." His eyes watered, and it took him a moment to find his voice again. "I thought I was sparing you."

"Dad..." She rubbed a hand up and down his arm. "Why didn't you get help? You keep saying you loved us, why did you go away? Why didn't you at least *try?*"

"I... didn't trust the doctors. I thought they wanted to control my thoughts. I didn't want you to see me like that." He stared at the ceiling lights, lost for a moment. "I didn't think I was that bad. Once I got out to the desert, everything seemed fine. I guess I fell into a routine."

"So you're okay with meds?"

"More or less." He let his fingers slip off her shoulder and down her arm until he could hold her hand. "How are you doing? I... I'm so sorry for making you think everyone was dead. I wasn't trying to—"

"I know, Dad. They told me you couldn't help it. You thought it was real. I'm a dumbass. I should've doubted more, but I kept seeing stuff... Korea on the news, those missiles... the bombs were scary as hell."

Dad let out a wheezy laugh. "The cops told me it was just an exercise. The 'nuclear flash' we saw was flares to light up the bomb range." He almost giggled. "That explains why we didn't evaporate. Guess I can't really outrun a nuke. How are you holding up?"

I'm going to jail. I've spent the past four days sick to my stomach. "Okay." She traced lines on the bedding with one finger. "They haven't let me see Kieran yet. I had to meet a detective and a psychologist. He thinks I'll be okay. Said I was strong and resilient."

"You are, Squirrel. Just like your mom."

She moped. "He also said they won't let me live with you since you're nuts."

He cringed. "Yeah... Doesn't matter anyway now. I'm going to wind up 'involuntarily hospitalized' for a while. Not exactly sure how long." A dazed grin settled on his face. "They're still trying to figure out if I'm competent."

"Dad..." She shivered. "I don't wanna go 'into the system' when I get outta jail."

"Jail?" He cocked an eyebrow. "What would you go to jail for?"

"Carrying a loaded gun, stealing meat, 'brandishing' a pistol at those two bikers. I didn't... it was just in my hand."

"Look, Squirrel." He squeezed her hand as the semi-coherent fog in his eyes flashed to clarity. "You blame me for everything. I don't care. Tell them it was my fault. I made you carry it. Besides, it was my property... you were home. Castle doctrine."

"No, Dad." She sniffled. "I don't wanna lie."

"They're just looking for conviction stats." A familiar old gleam shone in his eye. "Kids in jail are dollar signs. The companies that run the facilities pay off the judges to throw kids behind bars for made up crap. You go in innocent and come out a mess that the mental health people squeeze money out of for the rest of your life. They'll twist anything you say around and use it against you even if it's nothing. Don't say a word to them without a lawyer."

Riley trembled. "O-Officer Rodriguez is nice."

"That's what they want you to think so you open up and give them enough to hang yourself."

She grabbed him by the shoulders. "Dad? The paranoia is back."

"You watch the news often enough; you tell me. Besides..." He grinned, letting his head fall against the pillow. "You survived the apocalypse. You can survive anything."

Riley wanted to laugh, but all she could do was flash a weak smile. "Yeah..." After a moment of silence, she bit her lip. "Dad?"

"Hmm?"

"Wanna watch a movie?" She took out a DVD case out of her purse.

"Is that..."

"Ratatouille." She sniffled. "I hated this movie so much because it was the last one we watched together before you disappeared."

He cried, grabbing her with a tight one-armed hug, while mumbling, "Sorry," repeatedly into her chest.

"Don't. It's done." She sat up, sniffling. "So?" She shook the case. "Movie?"

"I'd love to."

Riley fed the disc to the small hospital-provided combo TV/DVD unit, kicked off her flops, and climbed up to lay beside him. Twenty minutes or so in, she plucked the half-eaten blueberry muffin from his tray and held it to her face in both hands.

"You used to do that whenever we watched movies." He stroked her hair.

She leaned into his hand. "You used to do that every time we watched movies, too."

Sergeant Rodriguez poked his head in, glanced from them to the screen, and backed out without a word.

Riley didn't think about losing her father again; she'd gotten him back, even if he was a fragmented mess. He was still her father, her *alive* father.

"If you were nuts, how'd you work?" She mumbled.

Dad pulled her a little tighter. "I had a nice little savings before I left. Your mom helped here and there with the occasional donation. Real estate is so much cheaper out here."

"They said all Mom had was your email. How'd she send you money? Why didn't she tell you to come home and get help?"

"PayPal." Dad swung his head around in a grandiose roll of the eyes. "Oh, she did sometimes. Not too hard though. Maybe she was afraid of what I'd do. I had a couple of scary moments." Guilt washed over his face. "About a month before I left, your mother came home late from night school. I didn't even recognize who she was. I'm amazed we didn't wake you up." He hesitated, lip quivering. "Neither of us wanted to hurt you."

"You wouldn't have hurt Mom..." She bit her lip.

"I..." He shook his head. "Not if I knew what I was doing no... that's why I had to go. I didn't trust myself after that. If anything would've happened..."

She poked him in the side. "You should've gone to a doctor... gotten help."

"It all made sense to me at the time. I'm sorry, Riley. If I could take it back, I would."

Riley picked at her shirt. "How'd you live out here?"

"There *is* a Ted... I did programming for him on and off. Bits of game code, network drivers, couple of custom inventory management packages. Pay isn't as good as back east, but to New Mexico, it's decent...

I had a bunch of money saved up before I came out too." A look of alarm spread over his face. "Damn, I need to pay the power bill."

"Bit late for that." She nibbled on the muffin. "Mom knew you were nuts? She didn't put that in her, uh, will."

"She kept threatening to come out here and drag me back to Jersey. I don't think she was expecting things to happen when they did." Dad kissed the side of her head. "Your hair smells nice."

A shadow moving by the door made her shiver and imagine handcuffs closing around her wrists as soon as she walked out of the room. She snuggled against him, no longer able to speak under the combined sense of Mom's death, Dad going away, and her own imminent incarceration. All she wanted was to go home to her bed and hide under the covers. She'd gladly eat SpaghettiOs every day if it would put things back the way they were. Savoring every last moment with Dad would have to suffice. She cuddled with him as a cartoon mouse cavorted on the screen. Before too long, she giggled like a six-year-old watching a movie with her father. For a little less than two hours, they might as well have been on their living room couch, father and daughter laughing at a silly movie.

Once the credits rolled, Sergeant Rodriguez stepped in and gave her a meaningful look.

"I gotta go." She started crying again.

"It's not goodbye," said Dad. "It's see you later."

She slipped off the bed, clinging to his hand until Sergeant Rodriguez cleared his throat. Riley tried not to feel sick to her stomach as she moped over to him. She clasped her hands in front of herself and stared down— at bare feet.

"Oops. Forgot my shoes." Riley took her time walking back to retrieve her flip-flops.

"Don't forget your disc," said Dad. "I expect you to bring it next time you visit."

She sniffled the whole time she ejected and re-boxed it. After snapping the case closed, she walked over and wrapped her arms around him. "See you later, Dad."

He waved. "I love you, Riley."

Riley hesitated at the doorjamb, until the weight of the cop's presence pulled her out of the room. Sergeant Rodriguez walked at her side through the hospital, down the elevator, and out past the lobby to the parking lot. She was grateful he'd spared her the embarrassment of being hauled around in handcuffs, but dreaded the moment they were out of the public eye. Were cops always this nice to kids looking at felony charges? How far could his charity go?

Probably all the way to the police car.

"Riley!" yelled a voice she'd never thought she'd hear again.

Kieran.

He came running over and grabbed her, lifting her off her feet in a breath-stealing hug. Riley lost the ability to speak for several minutes, sobbing tears of joy. She held on, legs wrapped around him, clinging for dear life.

"They told me what happened. Did you really ask about me?"

"Yes," she wailed. "Sorry. I can't stop crying."

"I drove out to pick you up Saturday, but the house was empty. Both cars were still there, so I walked around, but…"

"Sorry."

"Hey, don't blame yourself."

She sniffled. "I'm so stupid."

He gave her a firm squeeze and set her back on her feet. "You're not stupid. It was a… oh, what do they call it? A perfect storm of coincidence."

The shrink said I'm still desperate for a father figure. Riley frowned at his shoes. "I'm gullible. I believed him."

"Anyone in your situation would've done the same. I'm so glad to see you're okay. Everyone… uh, never mind."

"What?" She furrowed her eyebrows, tears stopped.

"Uhm…" Kieran fidgeted and scratched his head. "People in town, they kinda thought the old guy'd finally snapped and killed you or something."

"Oh, my God." She gasped. "He's not that kind of nuts. I thought *you* were dead."

Riley shivered in place for another six seconds, and kissed him. His eyes shot wide; he stood there like an innocent bystander as Sergeant Rodriguez cleared his throat twice.

"Sorry." Riley lowered her weight back onto her heels, leaving her hands clasped around his neck. "You're really alive. You're really here."

"I know you, uh… got some stuff to deal with, but call me." He handed her a folded piece of yellow paper. "Call me as soon as you can, don't care what time."

She took the paper and held it to her chest. "Okay."

Cold, foreboding dread seeped into her limbs as she faced toward the waiting police car. She paused at the door, waiting for the cuffs, but

Rodriguez put a hand on her head and guided her into the seat. She almost suppressed the flinch when the door closed.

Guess they're gonna be friendly till I get sentenced. She peered up at Kieran through the window as the door closed, trying not to cry again. The wider he smiled, the more her heart ached with fear.

Sergeant Rodriguez is being nice and not doing it in front of him.

OUT OF THE ASHES

R iley scuffed her feet back and forth, making a continuous *ka-whoosh-snap* with her flip-flops on the linoleum tiles. Fear was better than ten cups of coffee. Another sleepless night curled up in an open jail cell hadn't done much for her nerves. Her fingers dug into an unremarkable brown bench in the hallway of some scary government type building in the heart of T or C. A few people walked back and forth, all in suits and looking lawyer-y. She kept her gaze down, ashamed. Every time a police officer appeared from a side hallway or walked by, she flinched, wondering which one of them would come for her with chains.

Riley, the good girl, is gonna go to jail. Mom would be devastated.

Sergeant Rodriguez had vanished through the office door two feet to her left over a half an hour ago. Only soft murmuring had come back out since. He'd asked her to wait here, by some miracle not tethering her to the bench. Of course, where would she go? If she ran, they'd only add 'attempted escape' to the charges… Besides, she had nowhere to run to.

They'd find me at Kieran's.

She mulled back and forth over the four-hour meeting she'd had with some woman—Detective Contreras—that morning. Against Dad's suggestion, she'd explained everything that happened as best as she could remember. She glossed over how close she'd come to shooting the biker, saying she was afraid he'd rape her if he got his hands on her. The detective, and the psychiatrist sitting in on the interview, appeared to agree her father had primed her into a suggestible mental state. They seemed to like it when she said she'd been terrified at the thought of shooting anyone.

I wonder how many years I'll get for stealing barbecue ribs. Was running at a cop with a gun in my pants a crime? The color drained out of her face. *Thank God I wasn't carrying it in my hand; holy shit, I was a bloody mess. They'd have shot me.* Breakfast did a backflip in her stomach. *Going to jail is getting off light.* She let her head thud against the cinderblocks behind her, wondering if 'kid jail' was anything like the jail they show in movies. The desire to be in her own bedroom, her own sanctuary, away from all the craziness was so strong it hurt.

The doorknob twisted. She shot upright in the seat.

Sergeant Rodriguez exited the office with a manila folder under one arm. He looked down at her for a moment before walking past to sit on the bench at her side.

"Am I going to jail now?"

"Where did you get that from?" He chuckled. "No, Riley. The DA is not going to file any charges against you. You didn't really do anything illegal. Freebird and Lonnie were more worried about you than you think. Everyone's looking at you like a victim in this case."

She covered her mouth with her hands and shook. No words came to mind.

"Your father is going to be held for observation. Looks like the judge will find him not responsible by reason of mental disease or defect. He'll be hospitalized for some time, I can't say how long, but he won't go to prison."

She smiled and let her arms fall in her lap. "I guess I can't stay home, huh?"

"Nope. Not at fourteen."

Riley shrank in on herself. "Guess I go to a shelter again?"

"Probably." He leaned back. "Usually."

Fear danced in her belly. Memories of horrible stories about sadistic foster parents from the news left her shaking.

"You seem like a nice girl. Not sure why the universe decided to let you have both barrels."

She sniffled. "I dunno."

Sergeant Rodriguez pulled the manila folder out from under his arm and laid it across his lap. "I had a feeling something wasn't quite right when I saw you at the store. I couldn't put my finger on it, but you had that air around you like something was wrong."

"On the ride to New Mexico, some waitresses thought Dad was abducting me. They said I looked 'forlorn.'"

"That's a good word for it." Sergeant Rodriguez chuckled. "You still kind of do."

"I guess I knew something wasn't right." She wiped her eyes and tucked a strand of hair behind her hear. "When Dad sat near me at Mom's funeral, my first instinct was to get away. He seemed scary."

"It's not your fault, Riley. You're a kid." He took a breath. "Speaking of which, you need a place to stay, and you don't seem too happy about the idea of going into the system. I've already talked it over with my wife, Elisa. We've got a spare room. If you're open to the idea, we'd love to have you."

She gasped. A minute ago, she'd expected him to slap her in cuffs and drag her off to jail; now he was offering to take her in. Never in her life had she imagined a cop could be so... nice. Mute, she covered her mouth.

"There's one small issue."

Her heart fluttered.

"Do you think you can put up with an extremely loud nine-year-old boy? My son Daniel is a handful and then some."

"What?" She gulped. "You're serious?"

"I convinced the advocate that after everything you've been through, 'the system' is probably not the best thing for you. A kid in your situation has a high chance of winding up on the wrong end of the law years down the line. You need some stability after the year you've had."

She stared at nothing.

"Not to mention, they'd probably send you to Albuquerque or Las Cruces, which would complicate visiting your father. So much has gone wrong for you, I couldn't turn my back."

"I thought you were gonna lock me up." She took deep breaths.

"I still might, if you don't behave yourself." He winked.

A hesitant smile formed on Riley's face, followed by a grin and a nervous laugh. "Uhm..."

"Take your time; it's a lot to think about."

"I... You'd really let me live with you? That's so... much." *I need to tell Amber I'm still alive.* Riley reached out to him. "Do I at least get my one phone call?"

He clasped her hand. "Of course, this is America."

She grinned. "Okay." The handshake became a hug. "Thank you, Sergeant Rodriguez."

"You're welcome. That does seem a bit too formal now. If you're under my roof, you can call me…" He rubbed his chin. "Hmm. Marty doesn't seem proper. I wouldn't feel right asking you to use 'Dad', 'hey you' won't work either."

"Mr. Rodriguez?"

"I guess that'll do for now." He stood. "Let's go, I'll introduce you to the family. Tonight you can couch surf. Tomorrow maybe I'll grab a van and we can pick up your things."

She got up and followed him outside, walking on autopilot to the back door. He went around the trunk to the other side and smirked at her over the bar lights.

"Stop looking like you're in trouble." He waved her forward. "Get in up front."

Riley pulled the door open and gazed out at the desert. What was supposed to have been the best summer in her life had turned into the weirdest. Her horrible rollercoaster ride of grief, terror, loneliness, and panic came to the most bizarre end she never could've imagined. She sent a weak smile over the roof at Sergeant Rodriguez, and climbed in.

A pang of sadness at the loss of Mom lifted at the thought her father would be okay, and Kieran still wanted to be with her even after the whole town knew her father was nuts. It wouldn't be the awesomeness she'd spent the entire year looking forward to, but the remaining weeks of summer didn't look so bleak anymore.

"Dad would flip if he knew I was living with a cop."

Sergeant Rodriguez chuckled. "He knows. I asked him before I spoke to the advocate. Having his blessing on the whole thing made it a lot easier."

She gaped at him, speechless.

"He's a different person entirely when he's on his meds." He pulled out into traffic, craning his neck at the rear view mirror. "Your dad thought it would be a good idea too. That whole stable environment thing. We're both a little worried about you after all you've been through."

Riley leaned back in the seat, gazing at the blue sky. Buildings of Truth or Consequences slipped past on both sides. It wasn't much to look at, but the idea of living in Las Cerezas seemed nice. She wondered if she'd ever come to think of the Rodriguez house as 'home' the way she'd acclimated to Dad's place. Probably not, but it might eventually feel 'safe.'

"You can talk to me about anything you like… or you can stay quiet."

Amber is going to go crazy. That's going to be a three-hour phone call. She went over in her head what to tell her friend first.

After a few minutes, he glanced at her with a concerned expression. "I can't tell if you're relaxed or about to throw up again. Are you okay?"

Riley leaned her head back. "I haven't been sleeping. Can I answer in the morning?"

His moustache curled as he smiled. "Alright."

THE NECROPOLIS

Warm patches of sunlight glimmered among the folds of a clear plastic shower curtain decorated with blue and brown diamonds. Two small bowls of seashell soaps on the toilet tank filled the upstairs bathroom with the scent of lavender and pine. Riley perched atop the closed seat, one heel up, toes splayed. She leaned forward, knee to chest. Blue felt pajamas specked with white dots would've been too warm in Dad's house at this hour, but this place had AC. She held a bottle in her left hand, arm curled about her shin, and took care to work a tiny brush over her toenails. The sight of the glittery blue polish made her think of Mom, but all the images she recalled were happy. A wistful smile formed. Somehow, some way, Mom was watching over her still. *Of all the thousand and one ways things could have happened...* She hugged her leg, knowing Mom was with her under the RV, making sure she didn't shoot.

Riley swapped feet and spread a layer of deep blue polish on the big toenail of her right foot.

Her mind leapt to meeting Lonnie and Freebird two days after moving into her new room. She *had* to apologize. Though she'd walked in rigid and trembling, the guys were nothing like what their exterior would imply. *Would I have yelled at him to go away before I fired?* She closed her eyes and felt warm inside. *Yeah... probably—as long as he didn't try to grab me.*

A knock at the door, rapid and light. "I need to pee." Daniel Rodriguez waited all of two seconds before opening the door and peeking. "Please."

"Gimme a minute."

He bounced in place. "There's a boy here lookin' for you."

Crap. "What time is it?"

The kid shrugged, and walked in.

Riley, nail polish in one hand, brush in the other, shuffled like a broken tin man over thick beige carpet down the hall to the second door on the right. In her new bedroom, she flopped on the floor and finished the last two toenails.

"Riley?" yelled Elisa Rodriguez. "Kieran is downstairs."

Her throat tightened at the realization Mom would never get to announce a boy. She exhaled, thinking happy thoughts of the time they had. Sergeant Rodriguez's wife was an okay stand-in. Riley stick-walked to the door and poked her head out and to the right, at the stairway.

"Couple minutes, Mrs. Rodriguez."

She turned a hair dryer on her toes for a moment, trying to speed up the polish setting. *Dammit, I'll just be careful.* After changing into a gossamer white babydoll top and jean shorts, she frowned at her socks. *Not dry yet. Screw it.* She grabbed her purse and darted out the door to the carpeted steps.

Kieran stood on a panel of false wood grain tiles by the front door, next to a pile of shoes. Elisa had a thing about shoes in the house: ¡prohibido! Anyone unwilling to remove them had to remain on the four-by-four foot square at the door.

He had his thumbs hooked in the pockets of his jeans, red and white flannel shirt open halfway down his chest showing off his plain white tank top. As soon as he looked up, his face brightened. Riley almost fell twice trying to run down the steps, and stumbled into him on accident on purpose.

A large grin spread over his face as he caught her. "You look great."

"I always dress like this."

"No." He seemed to consider kissing her right there, but Elisa wandered in from the kitchen. "I mean, you look happy."

So many emotions crashed together, she couldn't answer right away. She opened her mouth, but Elisa cut her off.

"So, where will you be going?" She shot Kieran the 'cop eyebrow raise.'

"One of our friends is in a band. They're playing at the Necropolis."

Kieran handed Mrs. Rodriguez a small card. "I wrote the club's address on the back."

"Black Chakra?" Elisa blinked. "That doesn't sound very warm and fuzzy." She chuckled and shook her head. "Okay. What time will you be back?"

Riley pulled her flip-flops away from the pile of shoes with her toe, and stepped into them.

"The concert ends at ten. I'll have her back as fast as the speed limit allows."

Elisa patted him on the shoulder. "I'd rather have you back a little later and alive. I see that car you've got."

Kieran held his hands up. "No way would I do anything stupid with Riley in the car. She's too important."

She narrowed her eyes at him, warmth rushing into her cheeks.

"Oh, before you go." Elisa hurried off to the kitchen.

Riley leaned against him, whispering, "Important huh? Is that why you drove ninety?"

"Straight line, wide open, daytime." He squeezed her hands. "We can go slow if you want."

Her eyelids heavy, she leaned up to kiss him. The sound of Elisa's approach didn't matter. Kieran returned a polite kiss. Riley grinned at his awkward attempt to be 'proper' in front of Mrs. Rodriguez.

"Riley." Elisa held out a white iPhone 4. "Marty added your phone to our plan. It'll stay there as long as you're responsible with it."

"I thought I lost it!" Riley clutched the slab of tech to her chest. "Thank you."

"Well. You've got a police officer looking out for you now, so…"

Riley glanced at the phone. "He wants to know where I am at all times." *Ugh. Electronic leash.* A silent sigh escaped her mouth. *It's better than no one caring about me.* She tucked the phone in her purse after making sure the battery meter showed a charge.

Elisa smiled. "You two be safe… and have a good time."

"Thank you, Mrs. Rodriguez." Kieran smiled at her and opened the door for Riley.

The blue Trans-Am sat in the driveway behind Mom's Sentra and Elisa's little black Ford Escape. Riley looked around at the street. It felt strange having neighbors again. Aside from the abject lack of grass, this patch of Las Cerezas seemed like it could've been lifted from suburban New Jersey.

She scooted between the nose of his car and the rear bumper of Mom's, and slipped into the passenger seat. The car roared to life and settled to an exhilarating purr. As Kieran backed out and pulled away, she shot a text to Amber to update her on the new cell phone info.

"I'm surprised Sergeant Rodriguez is letting you go to the concert." Kieran reached over and held her hand.

"Me too." She dropped the phone back in her purse. "Guess he trusts you. Or maybe I need to do normal things."

"So, what's it like living with a cop?" He paused at a stop sign, glanced in both directions, and took a left turn.

"I dunno. They're nice. Danny's being a brat though. I feel like the new cat in the house, and the old one's pissed off."

"Ahh, he'll get over it. How's your dad doing?"

Riley stared to the right at houses drifting by. "He took a plea or something. Mental hospital instead of jail. He signed it."

"Well that's good, I guess."

She clutched his hand and looked up at him. "I feel so lost. Mom died right in front of me. My dad's away. I don't know if I can handle something else going wrong."

He made fleeting attempts at eye contact while pulling onto the highway. "It's normally pretty damn boring here."

"Yeah." She gazed into her lap, mesmerized by the stretched shadows of denim fray on her thighs. "I feel like such an idiot for believing him. I kept seeing things that didn't make sense, but he always had an explanation."

"Don't. Anyone in your situation would've probably been the same." He grinned. "You saved his life."

"I s'pose." She shifted in the seat to lean against him. "Mr. Rodriguez wants me to go see a counselor for a bit, just to make sure I'm not like 'mentally scarred' or something."

"Are you?"

"I dunno." She sighed. A little worry that refusing would throw her back into the legal system sped her heart up. "I guess I'll go. Mom always used to say it was silly how half the world is in therapy."

He put an arm around her shoulders. "I got the feeling you weren't too comfortable around Lyle and Luis… if you wanna bag early and do something else just let me know."

"'Kay. Maybe I didn't give them much of a chance. I was still pretty upset at being dragged across the damn country when I met them. Luis did kind of creep me out. I didn't like the way he looked at me."

Kieran shook his head. "He gets that a lot. He's usually baked as hell. He wasn't trying to imagine you naked; he was trying to figure out what planet you came from. It's just the way his face is shaped."

Riley laughed.

"Oh, how's your friend back east?"

She picked a sleep crumb from the corner of her eye. "I was up all night talking over Xbox. I hadn't said a word to her since I left. When I told her about everything that happened, I could almost hear her screaming from Jersey without the headphones. She's trying to talk her parents into letting her fly out here for a week or two."

"That's cool."

Riley frowned. "I doubt they'll go for it. They already took her to Mexico this year, and her dad would never let her go that far away from home alone. Maybe next summer they'll take a family trip."

He nodded.

Twenty minutes later, they rolled into the city.

Kieran slowed for traffic, looking at her once they stopped at a light. "Ever been to T or C before?"

"Yeah… visiting Dad in the hospital and stuff. Before that, we only passed through it once when I first got here." She squinted at the brightness outside. "Wait, maybe we got gas here."

"I guess it's okay. Retirees. Spas. Hiking. Couple museums. Still wanna get outta here though." He winked.

She managed to finally smile for the first time in a while, though the butterflies in her stomach wouldn't stop fighting. Going somewhere with a boy, and she didn't at all expect a cruel joke waiting for her at their destination.

Kieran drove to the lot of an imposing one-story grey adobe building covered with black line paintings of skeletons with musical instruments surrounding a mosh pit. Bones formed the word 'Necropolis' over a set of double doors.

"Wow, this places looks like a *Doom* level." She pulled the handle and used her foot to push the heavy door open.

"It's new." Kieran killed the engine and got out. "The club only opened last month, but it's pulling people from all over. Jaime's been busting his ass to get in the door. If tonight goes well, they're probably going to be opening for Lacuna Coil next month."

Riley gasped. "Seriously?"

Kieran led her to the door. "Yeah. I don't know how the hell this place got a big name like that but, hey."

Air conditioning slithered up Riley's bare legs in the foyer, making her second-guess her choice of attire. A massive man with a shaved head, leather vest, white shirt, and jeans stood by the door with his arms folded. As soon as he saw her, he frowned.

"Lemme guess, you're twenty-one but have a young face."

She swallowed. "Uh, no. I'm fourteen."

The man looked as shocked as if she'd slapped him. "Holy crap. I didn't think there were any honest kids left." He pointed at a skull mounted to small podium. "Need your hand."

Riley grasped the skull. The man rolled a rubber stamp over the back of her hand, tagging her a 'minor' in big, red letters.

Kieran offered a resigned chuckle and held out his arm. "Sixteen."

The bouncer pulled a black curtain aside after stamping him. Kieran ducked in, pulling Riley along by the hand. Skeletons, skulls, and loose bones clung to every possible surface. Far to the right, a bar sat behind a cluster of tables. A stage dominated the central area, already containing Black Chakra's equipment. Their mascot, a skeleton in lotus pose with green flames in its eyes, adorned the drum kit.

They wandered past the seats in the rear and the standing area/mosh pit closer to the stage, heading to another section of tables on the left side where Camila, Lyle, and Luis sat. Riley tensed, expecting to relive the awkwardness of her last meeting with these people. Luis noticed her first, and smiled. He seemed much more sober than before. His still-dazed grin didn't strike her as menacing at all anymore.

Camila's hand bore no stamp, and humor lit her eyes when she noticed Riley's. "Hey, *kiddo.*"

"Hey." Riley sat in the chair Kieran pulled out for her.

"Yo." Lyle looked her over. "Sorry to hear about your old man. Rough. Glad to see you're okay."

"Thanks," mumbled Riley.

"Aww." Camila drifted over to give her a hug. "Sorry if we were like… insensitive about him before. We didn't know he was like, legit crazy."

"Neither did I." Riley felt her back muscles tensing, but relaxed when Kieran sat close enough to keep an arm around her. "I probably shoulda realized."

"Yah." Luis nodded in slow motion. "You guys wanna hang after the show?"

"I gotta go home right after." Riley offered a weak smile. She almost wanted to stay and hang out, but pulling something like that the first time her foster parents trusted her seemed like a bad choice, and she'd had enough of bad choices for a while.

"Hey, it's cool." Luis nodded.

Jaime wandered out from a hidden curtain, a guitar on his back. He approached Luis, but looked at Riley. "Hey, kid. Glad you got away alive."

Riley squinted. "I wasn't kidnapped. Dad thought the world ended. We were hiding. He almost shot a cop."

"Yo…" Luis snapped his head up as if startled. "How come your Dad never lost his shit before when they did an exercise before? He's almost on top of the bomb range."

Camila threw a handful of napkins at him. "Ass. Try to be a little more sensitive."

"It's okay." Riley fidgeted with a plastic straw, spinning it on the table. "I dunno. I guess it was just 'cause everything that was going on. He freaked when I told him about the convoy we saw. Maybe it put 'nukes' in his head or something. It kinda felt like we were scaring the shit out of each other and it kept getting stronger."

"Yah." Luis gestured at the stage. "Like a feedback loop."

Wayne, drumsticks in hand, emerged from the same curtain. "Yo, we gotta half hour before we need to prep."

"Aww, damn." Jaime reached across the table with a fist.

Riley looked confused for a second, then touched her knuckles to his.

Jaime pressed his fist into hers, then lowered his arm. "Difficult way to wind up here, but welcome to New Mexico. There's reasons to everything that happens. The trick is seeing what they are before it's too late."

The Chinese kid with the lip rings appeared on the stage. He waved at the table, pointed at Riley, and gave a thumbs-up before kneeling to fiddle with some of the sound gear.

"Don't mind fortune cookie," said Wayne. "He's sucked up too much nag champa."

"Such aggression." Jaime brought his hands together like a meditating monk. "You must learn to release your anger."

"Uh, okay." *Whatever that is.* Riley draped herself over Kieran's shoulder and smiled at her new friends.

When she looked up at his smile, he leaned in and their lips touched.

Riley gave in to the kiss, holding on as if the two of them were the only people left alive. They gazed into each other's eyes for a moment after. Lyle and Camila took their cue and embraced. A twinge of nerves rattled Riley's arms as she watched them wrestle with their tongues. Kissing Kieran on the lips had been awkward, scary, thrilling, and wonderful... but having his tongue inside her mouth? A wave of light-headedness swept over her. As gross as it sounded on the surface to think about, she found herself looking up at him and considering it.

Kieran caressed her cheek. "I love your smile. It's nice to finally see it." He kissed her again, but she chickened out on the tongue. "You sure you're okay?"

"Yeah, I think so." Riley smiled at him. "I survived the apocalypse, right?"

fin

ACKNOWLEDGMENTS

I'd like to thank Sam Hunt (author of the *Outlaw King* series) for providing an initial concept cover that gave me the inspiration for this book. I had asked him about what he would do for a cover for another one of my novels (Caller 107) and rather than give me an opinion, he sent me an image. While it was amazing, it didn't work out as a cover for that book. I resolved to write something based on it. Many hours of staring at the image eventually produced the story you've just read.

Much gratitude to Lisa Gus for being a huge help editing this book.

Additional thanks to (in alphabetical order):

Tony Baker (author of *Survivors of the Dead*) for his assistance and advice about police related tactics and information.

Joseph Cautilli, Ph.D. LP, LPC, LBS, BCBA-D, BCIS for help with information regarding mental health issues.

Dr. Darin Kennedy (author of the Mussorgsky Riddle) for assistance with medical information.

Ricky Gunawan for the chapter art.

Merethe Najjar for proofreading.

Ann Anderson Noser (author of How to Date Dead Guys) for invaluable critique feedback.

Special thanks (beta reading, feedback, and support) go out to:

Mark Junk
    Denise Kalicki
    Amy Spitzley
    Nerissa Spitzley
    Wilbert Stanton
    Leslie Whitaker
    James Wymore

ABOUT THE AUTHOR

Originally from South Amboy NJ, Matthew has been creating science fiction and fantasy worlds for most of his reasoning life. Since 1996, he has developed the "Divergent Fates" world, in which *Division Zero, Virtual Immortality, The Awakened Series, The Harmony Paradox, and the Daughter of Mars series* take place. Along with being an editor at Curiosity Quills press, he has worked in IT and technical support.

Matthew is an avid gamer, a recovered WoW addict, Gamemaster for two custom RPG systems, and a fan of anime, British humour, and intellectual science fiction that questions the nature of reality, life, and what happens after it.

He is also fond of cats.

Visit me online at:
    Facebook: https://www.facebook.com/MatthewSCoxAuthor
    Amazon: https://www.amazon.com/author/mscox
    Pinterest: https://www.pinterest.com/matthewcox10420/
    Goodreads: https://www.goodreads.com/author/show/7712730.Matthew_S_Cox
    Email: mcox2112@gmail.com

OTHER BOOKS BY MATTHEW S. COX

Divergent Fates Universe Novels

Division Zero series

- Division Zero
- Lex De Mortuis
- Thrall
- Guardian

The Awakened series

- Prophet of the Badlands
- Archon's Queen
- Grey Ronin
- Daughter of Ash
- Zero Rogue
- Angel Descended

Daughter of Mars series

- The Hand of Raziel
- Araphel
- Ghost Black

Virtual Immortality series

- Virtual Immortality
- The Harmony Paradox

Divergent Fates Anthology

(Fiction Novels - Adult)

The Roadhouse Chronicles Series

- One More Run
- The Redeemed
- Dead Man's Number

Samantha Moon Origins series (with J.R. Rain)

- New Moon Rising
- Moon Mourning

Maddy Wimsey series (with J.R. Rain)

- The Devil's Eye
- The Drifting Gloom

Samantha Moon Case Files series (with J.R. Rain)

- Blood Moon
- Dead Moon

Young Adult Novels

- Caller 107
- The Summer the World Ended
- Nine Candles of Deepest Black
- The Eldritch Heart
- The Forest Beyond the Earth
- Out of Sight

Middle Grade Novels

Tales of Widowswood series

- Emma and the Banderwigh
- Emma and the Silk Thieves
- Emma and the Silverbell Faeries
- Emma and the Elixir of Madness
- Emma and the Weeping Spirit

Standalones

- Citadel: The Concordant Sequence
- The Cursed Codex
- The Menagerie of Jenkins Bailey
- Sophie's Light

CPSIA information can be obtained
at www.ICGtesting.com
Printed in the USA
BVHW03s1209200918
528046BV00001B/37/P